Dreaming of the Dance

Daughters of the Duchess, Volume 1

Gemma St. Claire

Published by Frances Brown, 2025.

PLEASE NOTE: The basic story behind "Dreaming of the Dance" was previously published as an historical romance under the title "The Warrior and the Wildflower" under the pseudonym Everley Gregg (Dragonblade Publishing), a title intended for a mature audience.

"Dreaming of the Dance" has been revised to qualify as a "sweet romance."

A Glossary of Medieval Terms

Here are some terms used in this book that the reader may not recognize.

Bailey: The open area between the castle buildings and the outer walls, also called the courtyard.

Battlement: A walkway around the upper edge of the curtain wall used by archers to protect from invasion.

Chemise: A lightweight, loose-fitting undergarment that acts as a slip under a dress (kirtle).

Club Foot: A birth defect where the Achilles' tendon is unnaturally shortened, resulting in a severely twisted ankle. In the Middle Ages, a babe born this way was labeled a...

Creple: A cripple.

Curtain Wall: The outer walls of the castle grounds, very tall and thick, made of stone.

Dais: A raised platform within the Great Hall, where meals were taken. The dais was where the royalty sat, along with honored guests and the Captain of the Guard.

Keep: A fortified tower, either round (like a silo) or square, within the castle's curtain walls. This was the safest place in the castle, where the royalty slept, and was considered the last refuge if the castle were attacked.

Kirtle: An overdress, worn over the chemise (slip). Also called a cotte or cotehardie.

Ostler: The individual responsible for the care and training of the court's horses, and often the dogs and hunting birds (raptors) as well.

Portcullis: A heavy, vertically closing gate protecting the entrance to the castle grounds.

Roundlet: A medieval cap with a padded roll around the rim.

Solar: These was the historical equivalent of a private living room, office, or den.

Author's Notes

Historical romance is traditionally set in England or Scotland. But what was happening on the other side of the English Channel? Was there no romance alive in the provinces of France?

During the Middle Ages, this area was known as the County of Flanders (modern-day France, Belgium, and the Netherlands). The regions lost their independence to Burgundy (the French House of Valois) in 1405. Duke Philip III of Burgundy, also called "Philip the Good," ruled over the Flemish lands during this period, and under his rule, the extravagance and richness of court life reached its pinnacle.

If ever I went back in time to live in the Middle Ages, 15th Century Flanders is where I would want to be.

One of Duke Philip's indulgences, as pegged by the Bishop of Tournai, was his "weakness of the flesh"—in addition to his nine legal offspring, Philip produced at least eighteen illegitimate, i.e. "bastard" children by twenty-four documented mistresses.

At least.

After being widowed twice, Philip married Isabella of Portugal in 1430. Not a shrinking violet by any means, Isabella became an important and influential member of Philip's court, establishing a reputation as an expert negotiator.

Although Philip provided well for his male bastard children, the females have vanished into obscurity. To history, they are essentially forgotten.

Duchess Isabella chose to accept Philip's "weakness of the flesh," endeavoring to right some of the wrongs. In this author's interpretation of her personality, she chose to gather the many "bastard" daughters, and to involve herself in their upbringing.

As an author of romantic fiction and one obsessed with this period of history, I decided to make liberal use of artistic license and bring some of these forgotten daughters back to life.

These are their stories.

Enjoy the Journey!

Gemma

Chapter One

February 1436
        Ghent, Flanders
    Eva

Eva sat huddled in the corner of her family's quarters, on the second floor of the tiny tailor shop just off Market Square. The fire in the hearth threw little heat, sputtering on the damp wood she'd tossed on the grate earlier. Winters in Flanders could be damning, with day after sunless day of miserable cold and constant drizzle. Eva shivered and pulled the homespun blanket closer about her shoulders.

The mending task in her lap bored her, made her angry, even. Was she to spend the rest of her life like this? A lowly seamstress in a tailor shop, with only day after day of joyless monotony stretched out before her. As though the needle heard her thoughts, it stabbed her finger, drawing a drop of bright blood. Quickly, she drew it to her mouth.

"God's bones, be damned ye!"

"Eva! Your language, and around the children," her mother scolded. Then, turning to the small boy and younger girl who were playing with clay horse figurines by the window, she said, "Griet, take Tomas down to the wood pile. Try to find some dry for the fire."

"I'm sorry, Maman," Eva mumbled as her siblings left the room.

"What ails you, Eva? Your mourning has no basis." Marisse crossed her arms and glared at her daughter.

Eva sighed. "The winter has been endless, Maman. I surely will die here, hidden in a tailor shop, mending the trappings of the rich forever."

Marisse's expression softened, and she came near to crouch beside Eva. " 'Tis not a horrid life, Eva. You have a solid roof o'er your head, meals to fill your belly, and a fire to warm ye." She paused, glancing back over her shoulder toward the doorway. "At least, 'tis warm most of the time."

Able to fight it no longer, the anger simmering in Eva's belly bubbled to the surface. " 'Tis not the life I desire, Maman. I am no sinner. I deserve better." She tossed the mending down on the floor and struggled to her feet.

But her crooked ankle gave way, pitching her sideways to grab for her mother's arm. This, she knew, was her true damnation—born a creple, with a crooked foot, Eva was able to walk, but only very carefully. A pronounced limp brought the flaw to light, even hidden beneath her skirts.

Defeated, broken, she sank back into the chair, tears extinguishing the flames of her anger.

Her mother said nothing, only pulled her close and crooned a soft melody. Eva knew why she offered no words of solace.

There were none to be had.

The missive arrived by courier, a messenger on horseback, one clothed in velvet and gilt trappings. Much more elaborately than a common peasant.

Eva sat on her usual perch, a stool in the chilly back corner of the shop. She usually did not pay any mind to the muffled clatter of hooves on cobblestone. This was a common occurrence along this narrow but well-travelled street. It was only when the clopping ceased at the shop's front door that she laid her needlework in her lap and looked up.

Her mother also left her work to meet the messenger inside the door. A cold blast of winter wind followed the man inside to flutter the garments hung along the wall, its cold breath seeping under the worktable. Eva shivered and tucked the folds of her woolen skirt more tightly under her.

A messenger's arrival was not uncommon in the tailor shop. Many times, the bourgeois sent orders this way. If Eva's parents had fashioned garments for the patron before, she already had their measurements recorded, their patterns made. Requests for new garments often arrived by missive, especially in winter.

It was only when Marisse gasped and held a hand to her throat that Eva rose and, her steps uneven, hurried to her side.

"What is it, maman?"

Marisse pointed a finger at the seal holding the rolled parchment closed. Wide eyes studied the face of the courier, a very young man whose smooth, boyish face was flushed from his cold ride.

"This is... a royal seal. Is this from—?"

"Yes, Madame Geretsz. The missive is from the Duke."

Affording a small bow, the messenger turned on his heel and left, the heavy oak door thunking closed behind him. Marisse turned wide eyes on Eva. "Philip has not contacted me in many years," she whispered.

Her mother's words rang of apology. And so, they might.

Marisse had once, for a short time, been a mistress of the Duke, Philip III of Burgundy—one of the Duke's many. Philip the Good. 'Twas how Eva came to be.

It was Duke Philip who had arranged for her mother's betrothal to Andries Geretsz, the Flemish tailor with whom the Duke had done much business. Andries took Marisse in, married her and agreed to care for her bastard child. But he did not grant Eva with his family name.

It was only Eva's siblings, her younger stepbrother and sister, who didn't know the truth of their older sister's lineage. Even now, at five and six years of age, they were too young to yet understand their mother's past. Her siblings were Griet and Tomas Geretsz. Eva was simply Eva of Utrecht, the name of the city where she was born.

With trembling fingers, Marisse slid her thumbnail under the seal, carefully, trying not to crumble the wax circle bearing the seal of the Order of the Golden Fleece. Even now, Eva could sense her mother's reverence. Her own emotions were jumbled.

Did she respect her mother's loyalty to the Duke? Mayhap. But in all good conscience, how could Eva respect what it was that her mother had been to the powerful Burgundian? A mistress. Nothing more. She herself was among Philip's countless bastard children, though not one granted the title. Eva laid no claim to anything from her father's court, even though some of his out-of-wedlock daughters were recognized.

Eva of Utrecht, at just shy of sixteen winters, had accepted her fate. She knew no nobleman, no knight of honor would ever ask for the hand of a child born out of wedlock, especially one swept aside by a powerful Burgundian Duke. Especially one who, born with a club foot only partially corrected by the healers, had been left with an uneven gait. She would remain a seamstress, a tailor's daughter, until some man—a local craftsman, or mayhap even a commoner—grew lonely, pitied her, and took her for a wife.

If ever.

A missive from the Duke himself, however, could signal a change. A glimmer of hope sparked in Eva's chest.

She watched, waiting patiently as Marisse read the words inscribed on the parchment. She was surprised to see her mother's eyes fill with tears. When she finally looked up, Marisse's voice cracked as she said, "Philip is sending for you. You are to attend the May Day Festival at his castle in Coudenburg."

Eva drew in a sharp breath, her heart stilling in her chest. Her shock could not quell the questions rising sharp within her, like shards of broken glass.

"How, Maman? I have no fine dresses to wear to a festival. I can barely walk, let alone dance—"

"Philip orders, in this message, for an exquisite gown to be fashioned for you of the finest silk, at his expense."

In a rare display of affection, Marisse embraced her daughter. Was she happy for her? Or simply relieved she would no longer be burdened with her imperfect daughter for whom she'd have to support until some man took pity on her?

'Twas relief, Eva was quite sure. But worry swirled through her all that day and into the night. She lay in her bed as the winds rattled the windows in her tiny, shared bedchamber above the shop. Her thoughts spun like a leaf in the gale. Why now, after nearly sixteen years of ignoring—or perhaps denying—her existence, had her true father decided to acknowledge her? Did he have plans to provide for her future after all?

Eva dared not even hope. Albeit reluctantly, she had struggled to accept her lot, the daughter of tailors, destined for a commoner's life. Still, she possessed pride. Eva was comely, with a river of golden-blonde hair so long she often sat upon it, and womanly curves developing already beneath her plain chemise and kirtle. She had mastered the craft of plying cloth into exquisite garments, producing stitches so fine they were almost invisible.

Invisible. This had defined Eva's existence since the day she was born. It was how she'd remained to her father, the Duke, since she was nothing more than a love-child—and one with a disfigurement. Even her stepfather preferred to ignore her existence, as she remained a constant reminder to Andries Geretsz of his wife's sins. Philip had arranged the marriage. Andries had accepted Marisse and her infant daughter, but that didn't mean he loved Eva as he did his own children.

Now Philip had summoned Eva to the grand May Day celebration at his luxurious palace in Coudenburg. In truth, she'd never ventured beyond the gates of Ghent. Eva couldn't put a name to the many emotions swirling through her—shock, excitement, anticipation, but also a healthy dose of fear. Eva was not trained in the ways of the court. She did not know what to expect, or how to act.

Eva had heard of these great celebrations. The French duke who reigned over their lands hosted the most extravagant feasts of the day, the May Day Festival among the most joyous. The chatter at the Market Square revealed details of the celebration, with tales of bonfires and bountiful food and drink. Music, and dancing. Therein lie the root of her fear.

Day to day, Eva got along pretty well with her twisted foot. It remained hidden under the hem of her kirtle and, if she took her time when walking, no one was even aware. But dancing? Impossible.

A shroud of shame, one which did not belong to her, had lain like early morning fog over Eva's life as long as she could remember. She despised it. She also resented it.

Eva did not know what Philip had planned for her. An arranged marriage? A spark of excitement stirred. Mayhap her dreams of finding love with a titled knight weren't so impossible after all.

There it was again, rearing its sinful head. *Pride.* One of Eva's biggest flaws, beside and in spite of her physical deformity, was hubris.

More likely, based on her mother's reputation with the Duke, Philip had less honorable plans for his bastard daughter. Would he put her to work as a kitchen maid? A handmaiden to one of the court's nobler ladies? Mayhap he planned to give her away to one of his courtesans as a mistress. Eva's stomach soured and she turned on her side, pulling the rough woolen blanket up over her head. She had over two, long months to wait before her questions would be answered.

At least, in the meantime, she would gain an exquisite gown of the finest silk, a gown befitting one far above her common station. Would she get to choose the fabric, she wondered? Or had her sire designated the specifics in his missive?

As she lie there, her nightshirt and blanket twisting ever tighter around her, her mind churned. Yet despite her fears, one emotion floated to the top of her heart. Hope.

A week later, Marisse took hold of Eva's arm and led her to the workroom at the back of the shop. A large wooden table stood in the center, the place where the cloth was laid out to be measured and cut. There, on the smooth oak surface, lay a bolt of silk. Pale green, woven in a delicate pattern of acanthus leaf swirls, the brocade was the most beautiful fabric Eva had ever seen. Atop it lay coiled yards of ribbon so brilliant, they appeared to be spun of pure gold. Marisse lifted the ribbon, letting her fingers entwine with the loose ends of Eva's long tresses.

"It will go well with your hair," she said. "And the silk matches the color of your eyes. Perfectly."

Her mother's countenance wavered behind Eva's quick tears, and she spoke through a painful knot in her throat.

"I will be away for my name day, Maman."

Marisse rubbed her daughter's arm. "Do not despair, Eva. My hope 'twill be the most wonderful name day you've had in your entire short life."

April, 1436
　Coudenburg Castle, Brussels
　Mathieu

"I have no desire to exhibit the talents of our fine falcons to a crowd of strangers, drunk on the Duke's wine."

Mathieu de Flandre, head ostler and falconer at the Coudenburg castle, spoke with conviction, knowing all the while his own opinions meant little. He served as squire to Simon La Laing, Admiral of Flanders. Mathieu honored his lord, a good man whose roots grew close to his own. They were both men of Flanders, a region under Burgundian rule for the past two decades. Some of the Flemish had made the best of it, like Simon, who had been knighted under Philip's elite Order of the Golden Fleece.

Mathieu, however, had not been afforded the same luxuries, but had accepted his fate, honoring the House of Valois. Although his father had died before he was born, fighting to protect Liège from the Burgundians, history was already written. Mathieu grew up under Burgundy's rule and felt blessed he'd been accepted as a squire to the admiral.

On the road to knighthood, 'twas as far as he intended to go.

"Oh, come now, Mathieu. Don't tell me you wouldn't relish the opportunity to show off your talents—and those of your fine hunting stock—to all of the eligible young women at the May Day Feast. You are past twenty winters, are you not? And still you have not taken a wife."

Simon waited for Mathieu to tighten the girth on his palfrey's saddle before taking the reins and continuing his lecture. "Philip has sent invitations far and wide for this year's festival. I'm sure there will be many ripe flowers—all coming here, on display for your perusal. Ready for picking." He winked as he settled into the saddle. "I shall be gone for several days, Mathieu. I trust you will keep all well in order here at the castle?"

"Of course, my lord. As always."

Mathieu watched Simon ride off, a bolus of resentment settling in his gut. A wife? He turned back toward the stables, shaking his head. He had nothing to offer a bride, as his allegiance lay twisted in the jumbled heap of his own history. How could he take on a wife when his own future remained as obscure as the meadow hidden by the early morning mist?

Mathieu was a man torn. The son of a knight, true, and his pride and ambition had once driven him down the path to warrior. His conscience, however, caused him to question this goal.

Mathieu's father, brave commander of the militia, had fought the good fight at Othée to defend Liège from overthrow by Duke John of Bavaria. But victory was not to be his. Just when he believed the Burgundians had arrived to help them win the battle, he realized the ferocious warriors were there not to help them, but to overthrow their forces. As he lay dying on the battlefield, Mathieu's father knew the child his wife carried would never know the brave warrior who was his sire.

And so, he did not.

As Mathieu matured, he realized his only path to knighthood would place him within the very same army of warriors who had overthrown Liège.

The army who had killed his father. This was not a choice Mathieu cared to pursue.

He had also witnessed these knights in action as they oft passed through his city of birth. These men thrived on savagery, with little regard for the virtues of chivalry. This was not who Mathieu was. Absently, his hand went to his cheek, running his fingers down the length of the scar that marred his face. No matter that the healer had done a fine job of stitching. The puckered, pink line running from his temple to the corner of his mouth remained as a constant, visible reminder, fortifying his decision.

Although he had decided not to pursue his sword and spurs, Mathieu still believed in the code of chivalry. Knighted or not, he vowed to adhere to these virtues.

A wife? No, not even remotely in his plans. But a tryst with a pretty young thing with a low tolerance for the Duke's freely flowing libations? Yes. Oh, yes. That might definitely be worth taking out one of Simon's gyrfalcons, even a peregrine, at the May Day Festival to show off to the ladies.

What Mathieu hadn't figured on was the Duke's directive for him to act as chaperone. When Simon returned after nearly a fortnight, dusk was settling over the manor. The Admiral had reportedly been meeting with some of the Duke's merchants in Bruges. Mathieu barely finished helping the admiral down off his mount and taking the dust-coated reins from him when Simon began without so much as a greeting.

"Philip is sending you on a most important mission, Mathieu. You must take with you a most gentle palfry and travel to Ghent. In the days before the May Day Festival... there is a young woman there you must retrieve. She is to be brought here to Coudenburg."

As he unsaddled his lord's sweaty horse, anger and resentment rose in Mathieu's chest. He was no escort, no lowly courier to be sent on missions such as these. He was a squire, the ostler and falconer here at Coudenburg. And he had many preparations to oversee at the castle for the festival—"

"I know what you're thinking, Mathieu."

He'd never been good at hiding his emotions, no matter how hard he tried. Although he kept his tongue, he snapped the girth leather free and yanked the saddle from the horse's back with a little more force than necessary.

Simon knew Mathieu fairly well. The admiral had become somewhat of a father to him these past years. Sometimes it seemed as though the man could actually read his mind.

A heavy, gloved hand landed on his shoulder. "Mathieu. Do not despair. This mission is no common task, but one the Duke honors you to complete. The lady you must retrieve is a very special one, indeed."

A lady. *Harumph.* Probably just another one of the Duke's mistresses. The ostler grabbed a handful of straw and began rubbing down the sweaty horse's coat. Steam rose from its body in the cool of the early spring evening. Mathieu knew of Philip's escapades, as did all of his Dukedom. Not that the Duke bothered to hide his transgressions. Rumors abounded about the Duke, and although Mathieu realized not all could possibly be true, he highly suspected those regarding his "weakness of the flesh" bore truth. Philip had, in fact, brought a number of ladies to stay with him at Coudenburg, and not all of them had been one of the wives he'd taken over the years.

While Mathieu completed the horse's rubdown—a rougher one than usual, but the palfrey didn't seem to mind—Simon was conducting his walkthrough of the stables, as he always did after an absence. This, too, curdled Mathieu's ire. It was as though Simon didn't trust him to keep things at the castle exactly the way his lord desired. Still, Mathieu knew he was lucky. He had only come into the position of squire by good fortune and the benevolence of the Duke and his admiral. He had not been born into a family of noble blood—at least, not noble in the eyes of the Burgundian court. He had not, as was customary, begun his training as a young boy.

Still, to be doubted? After all this time? To his knowledge, he'd never let the admiral down.

But inspection was apparently not the purpose of the admiral's walk through the stables this evening. La Laing emerged with a thoughtful expression, pulling on his short dark beard, his mouth pursed.

"Germaine, I think, would be the most suitable mount for your charge."

Mathieu, his thoughts simmering inside his own head, blinked and looked up from his work. "Germaine? She is our oldest mare, my lord. Surely, she is in no shape for such a long journey."

"The young lady you will be retrieving, Mathieu, has no experience in the saddle. Besides, she is young and delicate, from what our dear Duchess conveys."

Mathieu blew out a breath and faced his lord. "Ghent is a long day's ride on a strong horse. With Germaine in tow—"

"Your trip will be taken over two days, not one." He removed the roundlet from his head and scrubbed the road's dust from his cropped, black hair. "The Chateau Alst is just over halfway between Ghent and Brussels. Stopping there will make the trip easier on the young lady."

Mathieu finished his grooming, struggling to hold his tongue. Now he would be acting as chaperone for not one day, but two—and entertaining, as well as ensuring the safety of the damsel overnight. Again, as if reading his mind, Simon gripped Mathieu's shoulder.

"As I said, my boy, the Duke would not consider just anyone to take on this mission. The young lady is, I'm guessing, somewhat dear to him—or mayhap to Lady Isabella." Mathieu met his lord's dark eyes, which were twinkling with humor. "She is Philip's daughter. One of his first... by a tailor he kept in Utrecht for a time. When he was much, much younger."

Mathieu blinked and stepped back. "His daughter? A bastard daughter? Isn't the Duchess planning to attend the May Day festival?"

Simon patted his shoulder and looked down, stifling a smirk. "Yes, yes she is. Isabella knows all about Philip's escapades. Their union, as you know, was a tactical arrangement. One based more on alliances than affairs of the heart." Simon turned and strode away toward the castle, his long red robes rippling about his ankles.

Mathieu stood beside the horse, reins in hand, in a state of shock. He was fond of Philip's current wife, and the Duchess Isabella seemed to favor him as well. He had taken the Duchess out multiple times on the hunt, teaching her how to tether and hood her young peregrine falcon properly.

He had also heard that Isabella had taken it upon herself to locate, and gather, the Duke's illegitimate daughters for such festivals. 'Twas not his place to question, yet he could not, for the life of him, understand her reasons. Still, Mathieu did not want to be the one to ride into the manor trailing one of Philip's youthful "mistakes."

Simon hesitated, glancing back over his shoulder. He stopped, turning to face the ostler, hands on his hips.

"Not only does Isabella know about the girl, but she's taken an interest in helping shape the young lady's future. Eva of Utrecht will be staying here at Coudenburg for a time after the festival is over. Mayhap beyond." He paused, casting his gaze to the ground. "I must also tell you, Mathieu. The girl has a... a disablement. A defect from birth. Minor, but she has difficulty walking, especially over uneven ground."

Mathieu closed his eyes and dropped his forehead against the horse's sweaty neck. Not only was he being saddled with an innocent to chaperone on an overnight journey, but a creple as well. After leading the admiral's horse into the barn and tethering him in his stall, Mathieu turned and, scanning the building to ensure he was alone, drew back a balled fist. With all his might, he punched the wooden divider. The palfrey, head already buried in the hay, paid him no mind. This wasn't the first time the horses had witnessed one of his tantrums. But Mathieu knew that in order to maintain his position, he must learn to hide, if not tame, his volatile nature.

'Twas a shame Mathieu shunned the thought of knighthood. Verily, he thought a knight's life may well suit him. He certainly possessed the fire required to bolster a man's courage in riding into battle. Now, however, he could only defuse his explosive outbursts of temper with pain.

Chapter Two

A*pril 1436*
  Ghent
Eva

Another missive arrived from the Burgundian Court in early April. The weather had eased, with the longer, warmer days teasing pale green buds out of bare branches. Eva was outside, working the soil in the tiny plot of land behind the shop where her family grew vegetables.

"Come now, Tomas. Don't play in the dirt or Maman will have my head."

Her younger brother, just past five winters, sat in the freshly turned soil letting it run through his fingers. He was a pudgy cheeked lad with a shock of straight, dark hair just like his father's. He turned brilliant blue eyes on her.

"I am helping, Eva." His smile melted a corner of her heart.

Her sister, Griet, stomped over and yanked the child to his feet, sweeping the dirt from his tiny braies. "You're not helping, Tomas," she scolded. "You are making a great mess of yourself."

Eva sighed as she studied the children. She adored them and, with both her parents busy most of the time running the tailor shop, had taken on the role of their primary caretaker. Not that she minded. She knew, no matter how she dreamed of a family of her own, the dream would probably never come to pass.

Even if she married, bearing babes would be a risky matter. She glanced down at her twisted ankle. 'Twas a trait she might pass on. Eva could not imagine the horror of birthing a babe with deformity such as hers. Mayhap one worse.

But marriage—just the word made her feel faint. A man who honored her, mayhap even loved her, and a household of her very own... these were mere dreams, dangerous dreams of things that could never be. And even if, perchance, the opportunity presented itself, Eva had decided one thing for certain—she would not marry for convenience. She would only marry for love.

Alas, the chances for the man of her dreams discovering her here, in a tiny tailor shop with a needle in her hand, were slim. Even if it did come to pass, the chances of such a man accepting her, with her status and deformity, were close to none.

Still, there was the festival. She had nearly forgotten about her upcoming trip to the May Day celebration at Coudenburg. It seemed as though a fantasy, an impossible dream hovering elusively in her consciousness. But there was proof. Her beautiful green gown had been completed and stored in a trunk now for over a month.

More than a moon had passed, though, and there had been no news. In fear of disappointment, she'd pushed the event to the back of her mind. Besides, every time Eva imagined travelling so far away from home, all alone, to a place she'd never seen and with folk she'd never met, her insides twisted.

Marisse stood at the back door of the shop and beckoned to Eva. She could see the parchment in her mother's trembling hands. Another missive. What news could this one hold? Here it was—the news the Duke had changed his mind. She was surprised Philip had even bothered to send another message at all.

"An escort, with extra palfrey and chaperone, will arrive for you a fortnight hence, Eva, to escort you to Coudenburg." Marisse's voice wavered, and Eva suddenly noticed how much older her maman had grown.

"A palfrey," Eva repeated. "Not a carriage?"

Marisse held her daughter's gaze. " 'Tis not what it says in this missive, daughter."

Another wave of dread washed over her. The distance, Eva knew, between Ghent and Brussels was over a day's ride away. Eva had never been on a horse in her life.

As though her maman read her mind, Marisse said, "Andries will take you to Weers' stable. He will teach you how to ride." She paused, raising one eyebrow. "At least, in the short time remaining, he will show you how to sit a ladies' saddle, so you shall have a chance of staying atop the beast."

Two days later, Eva's stepfather led her by the elbow through the Market Square, toward a side street leading to the stables. Having no mount of his own and often requiring to rent a beast for travel, Andries knew the ostler there well. Stumbling along to keep up with her stepfather over the uneven cobbled street, Eva's heart lodged painfully in her throat.

Her stepfather had little patience for her. Andries accepted Eva, kept her housed and fed, but had no time for her otherwise. He seemed repulsed by her disfigurement. Eva feared that the moment she came of age, Andries would actively pursue a marriage for her, whether one of her choosing or not.

She was surprised he had consented to take her to the stable. But she mused, yes he would. This trip to Coudenburg, she reasoned, was one more step in ridding him of her.

Once, in the summer past, Stefano, the merchant's apprentice, had offered to take her for a ride on his master's tall, black palfrey. Just the memory made Eva shudder. Stefano did not have a ladies' saddle, so Eva would have had to ride the beast astride.

That, she knew, was entirely inappropriate, and therefore out of the question. And Stefano, for all of his dark good looks and smooth talk, raised the hairs on the back of Eva's neck. Why this was so, she did not know.

At the stable yard they were met by Weers, the ostler, a broad, squat man with thick arms and a swarthy complexion. He wore a simple woolen cotehardie over hose, his leather boots wrapped tightly around sturdy ankles. A piece of straw stuck out from one side of his mouth.

He greeted Andries with a curt nod. "Come hither. Your young charge shall receive her first lesson in the stable yard."

Eva stood clinging to her stepfather's arm, partly to keep her balance, and partly due to raw fear. The stable yard was a dirt patch tucked between the buildings, lined by a rail fence at the far end. The space was only slightly bigger than the garden behind the tailor shop. The ball of worry in her belly loosened a bit. She need not worry about the horse running off with her, not if contained within this small area.

Her worries leapt anew, though, when she heard the clip-clop of hooves approaching from within the stable.

Weers was not a tall man, but next to the furry brown beast to which he was tethered, he appeared no bigger than Eva's five-year-old brother. Her eyes widened and she staggered back a step. Andries roughly tightened his hold on her arm.

Andries had no patience for his stepdaughter, no matter what the circumstance.

"This is Tyrion," Weers said, shifting the straw from one side of his mouth to the other. He studied Eva, his gaze sweeping her from head to hem. His expression softened. "I see you are afraid, lass. You're but a wisp of a girl. I know Tyrion must look to you like a giant from the land of dragons. But be assured, milady, he is as gentle as a kitten."

"A very big kitten," Andries said through a chuckle. He turned to look down at her. "Do not worry, Eva. Weers is to be trusted. If he says the palfrey will do you no harm, then it will be as he says."

As if the beast understood their words, Tyrion bobbed his gigantic head up and down, then stomped the ground with a massive hoof.

"Oh, my. Papa, his head is bigger than I am," she murmured. Her whole body was trembling now, and she wished she had relieved herself once more before leaving home. Terror of climbing atop the great beast only added to the embarrassment she knew was imminent: lifting her skirts to reveal her twisted foot.

Weers went on to explain the contraption strapped to Tyrion's back. To her, it looked like a small, padded chair.

"You won't be riding astride like a man, milady. You'll sit here, sideways, with your feet resting on this shelf." He patted a small wooden step laying against the horse's side. It looked like the stool her mother used to reach cloth on the upper shelves in the storeroom.

Andries urged Eva closer to the animal. "Pat Tyrion on the nose so he gets to know the smell of you. Then let's get you aboard," he barked impatiently.

The horse's nose was as soft as the brushed underside of leather. Tyrion lowered his head and peered at her. His eye was as big around as her fist. A sudden calm came over her as she ran her fingers over the horse's warm muzzle. She lifted her chin.

I can do this.

Weers led Tyrion to the mounting block, a chunk of tree trunk standing near the stable door. He offered Eva his hand.

"Come, milady. Step up on the block, then up onto the saddle."

Eva shot her stepfather a wary glance. Climbing stairs were a challenge for her, since her one foot was unable to turn flat. Balancing on the outer edge had become second nature for her at home, with one hand on the railing. But here, out in the open and beside this giant creature—"

Andries did not give her time to think twice. In one swift movement he wrapped an arm about her waist and lifted her until both feet perched on top of the block. Instinctively Eva grappled for something to hold onto, latching one hand on the front edge of the chair-like seat above her. Before she could suck in another breath, she felt a firm hand on her backside, and up she went.

Eva gasped as she settled into the worn, tapestry-covered seat. She was suddenly higher up in the air than she'd ever been—even higher, she was sure, than when she peered out of the windows of their second floor living quarters. Dizziness overcame her and panic rose in her throat like a spoiled meal.

"You're fine, just fine, milady," Weers murmured as he squeezed her leg through her heavy woolen skirt. "Now pick up the reins. Don't worry, I'll be holding on to Tyrion's head for this first ride. You won't need to do the steering until next time."

On their way back from the stables, Eva was so excited she fairly bounced along at her stepfather's side. Gone was her terror, her stomach had settled, and even her gait seemed surer. She chattered to Andries the whole way back to the tailor shop.

"Did you see me, Papa? Waaay up high on that gigaaantic palfrey?"

"You did well, Eva," he mumbled, his voice flat. "And yes, the mount was large. My guess is Tyrion was once a knight's horse, a charger in his younger days. I would wager the mount your escort brings to carry you to Coudenburg will be a sight smaller."

As usual, her stepfather regarded her with little more interest than he would a perfect stranger. Stiffening, Eva straightened her shoulders and went silent, bottling her enthusiasm within.

She was a stepchild, and a crippled one at that. Eva had come to accept her position in this life, masking her low esteem with pride she had no right to own. 'Twas her only means of survival.

When they returned, Marisse was waiting for them in the shop. She was deep in conversation with a very somber-faced Stefano. The apprentice had come to make a cloth delivery from his master, Giovanni Arnolfini. The Italian turned soulful eyes on Eva, taking her hand and bowing.

"Greetings, Stefano." She greeted the merchant's apprentice civilly, but without warmth.

"I hear you have been to the stable," Stefano replied flatly. "I am affronted. I have offered to take you riding in the past."

" 'Tis more urgent now. Did Maman not tell you? I'm going to the May Day festival at Coudenburg castle. I need to learn to balance atop a horse for the journey."

Stefano worried his cloth cap against his chest, his brows knitting together. "Your maman told me. You are going to this festival... alone?" His dark eyes flitted back and forth between Marisse and Andries, both of whom remained silent for a long moment.

Finally, Marisse spoke up. "Eva's father sent a missive, requesting her attendance. An escort will be arriving—"

"That is not only improper, but unsafe," Stefano snapped. "How can you allow such a thing?" His tone escalated from indignant to angry.

How dare he? Eva thought as she squinted at the pompous apprentice. *He has no claims on me.*

Marisse laid a hand on Stefano's shoulder and spoke quietly. "It is her father's will. He is the Duke. We cannot deny his wishes. Besides, I am certain she will be safe and properly cared for."

Stefano fisted his hands at his sides, glaring now at Andries. "You have no say in this, Geretsz?"

Andries lowered his gaze and shook his head. "I have none," he said flatly. "I am not the girl's father."

Eva watched the banter between her parents and Stefano in disbelief. Why should a cloth merchant's apprentice care so much about this invitation?

Stefano's shoulders rose and fell. "So, 'twill be the Duke himself I need to address, when the time comes. Is that right?"

Andries nodded, then turned and disappeared into the back room.

Eva's gaze snapped to her mother. "Time for what?"

Stefano, still tense with anger, bowed stiffly to Marisse before lifting Eva's hand to brush his lips across it. He held her gaze and murmured, "I will visit again, milady, before you take your leave."

Eva's stomach rolled over in her belly.

Mathieu

The Lady Duchess, Philip's third wife, Isabella of Portugal, arrived at Coudenburg Castle almost a moon early. She brought with her wagonloads of provisions for the great banquet, dozens of house staff to cook and clean, as well as a veritable army of the Duke's knights for protection.

Mathieu watched as the cavalrymen filed in past the gatehouse and into the bailey. Led by their Captain, Sir Engel Knape, the men wore minimal protective gear beyond a simple chainmail vest over their woolen tunics. Mathieu studied Knape's broadsword, bobbing in its scabbard at his charger's side, its bronzed pommel bearing the coat of arms of Philip the Good. Yet he wore no insignia on his mail-covered chest.

So. The *good* knight had not yet been indoctrinated into Philip's elite Order. A secret satisfaction slithered into Mathieu's belly.

Mathieu knew Knape's history. The man may have grappled his way up through Philip's ranks to lead his personal escort of knights, but in Mathieu's opinion, there was no way the Captain deserved to wear the emblem of the Golden Fleece. Knape's conduct throughout his thirty-odd winters put him far below the high Christian standards of Philip's distinguished Order.

Why was it only Mathieu who seemed cognizant of the fact? In truth, he knew why. After all, Engel Knape was Captain of the Duke's Royal Guard. Who would dare question the integrity of such a man? Surely not a lowly ostler.

Knape saw him watching, and the Captain's mouth twisted into a sneer. Mathieu swore someday he and Knape would come to terms. The man himself was one reason Mathieu had abandoned his journey toward knighthood. The Captain would rule him if he were knighted. Knowing

Knape as he did, Mathieu wasn't sure if he was a strong enough man to swallow that much of his principles and pride.

Absently, he lifted his hand to run a finger down the puckered scar on his cheek. It had healed well—on the outside. 'Twas hardly noticeable, but one of the reasons he wore his hair long.

On the inside, however, the wound still ran deep. It had changed him—irrevocably.

The ostler no longer believed the title of knighthood signified all of the virtues listed on Duke Philip's Order of the Golden Fleece. They were empty words, broken promises. When a man was dubbed a knight, it gifted him with a sword and golden spurs, along with prestige and power. He'd always believed, like his father, the title raised a knight above that of a common man.

Mathieu also knew now the weapons and the power, in reality, merely granted a man permission to live above the law. Above the code of honor to which knights were supposed to adhere. Twelve years ago, Mathieu decided he didn't want to hide behind a title and weaponry.

He wanted to live the life of a decent, honest, and virtuous man. Mayhap he would find a lady who might appreciate him for these values, marry him, and gift him with children. Living in the shadow of the gallant knights, however, always placed Mathieu at a disadvantage. He may be the admiral's ostler and falconer, but to most his status remained little above that of a peasant.

Mathieu turned his back on the men as his pages scurried to take the men's horses. As Admiral La Laing's squire, he enjoyed his life, caring for the horses, the dogs, and the hunting birds. He worked hard, remained focused on his duties, and did his best to control his temper.

In the meantime, he had plenty to keep him busy in the weeks before the festival. Although preparations inside the walls of the keep were laid upon the servants, everything between its massive doors and the curtain wall fell on Mathieu's shoulders. The mounts must be fit and well groomed, as riding and hunting would be among the activities offered to the guests. The dogs must be well nourished, yet hungry enough to scout out quarry. The falcons must be properly maintained and handled often to ensure their suitability for the hunt.

The horses were still shedding their wooly winter coats, and he spent hours every day scrubbing their bodies. The wooden stable doors and windows were flung wide to air out the stale, foul odor of urine from the animals wintering long hours indoors. His aviary, where the hunting birds were kept, must also be stripped and scrubbed. After a long, dreary winter, the falcons seemed to relish their outdoor perches, preening and sunning themselves while Mathieu worked.

All of this had now to be completed early, as well. Mathieu bristled at the thought he alone had to work ahead of schedule, since he would be departing in less than a fortnight for Ghent. One fine spring morning, he was grumbling to himself about the lot he'd drawn. *Courier. Escort.* 'Twas an insult not only to his position, but to his pride.

He was sweeping down the stable aisle when a servant appeared before him.

"A message from the Duchess, my lord. She wishes to go on the hunt this noon. Her highness asks you to saddle her mare and prepare Cornelijs for the hunt." After delivering his message in quick and nervous words, the servant bowed and scooted out the stable door.

Mathieu brightened. He loved the hunt, and 'twould would be good for the horses, dogs, and falcons as well. It had been a wet, rainy spring, and Mathieu had not had as much opportunity to exercise the animals outside the castle walls as he would have liked. Seeing the sun rising high over the keep already, he set about to groom and saddle his own as well as the Duchess' mounts.

He knew, being the lady requested Cornelijs, they would be hunting pigeons, doves, waterfowl, and grouse. Cornelijs was one of Isabella's most cherished peregrines, whose high speed and amazing accuracy always ensured the party would return with a bevy of fowl. She carried the bird with her whenever she travelled between the various Burgundian castles. Mathieu himself had carefully unloaded Cornelijs' traveling crate when the caravan had arrived.

The Lady Duchess would handle Cornelijs, but which bird should Mathieu take out this noon? His gaze swept over the yard before the aviary where the falcons and hawks stretched their wings in the morning sun. His gaze landed on a smaller, younger bird, speckled brown with a dark-banded tail.

Magda, he thought. He'd been training the young goshawk Simon had brought him from the Netherlands for over two moons. This would be Magda's first real outing. He was anxious to see how the goshawk would fare. He also hoped this would serve to impress the Duchess with his falconry training skills.

His mood suddenly lighter, Mathieu made his way to the stalls to retrieve the palfreys.

Chapter Three

E*va* Eva's escort arrived just after first light on a chilly, dreary spring morning. From upstairs, in the room she shared with her two younger siblings, Eva heard the pounding on the front door of the tailor shop. It was well before the hour of opening. But Marisse had warned Eva to be ready to depart at any time. Her small traveling bag had been packed and ready, tucked into a corner of the workshop downstairs, for several days.

Logistically, she was ready to leave. Emotionally, she was a mess. Her insides felt like a quivering mass of fat sliced from a butchered pig. She braced herself. The time had arrived. Responding to her stepfather's call, Eva bent to place kisses on both of her sleeping siblings' cheeks. Then she smoothed her woolen kirtle, took a deep breath for courage, and made her way down the narrow staircase.

She paused halfway down the stairs to study the scene. The man standing inside the door was younger than she'd expected. In her mind's eye, she'd been imagining her escort would resemble the likes of Weers, the town's ostler. But her escort was far from short and stocky. He was tall and broad-shouldered—very tall, standing a least a head above her stepfather, who was not a small man. Dressed in very practical travelling clothes, a simple cloak over braies, one could mistake him for any other merchant or vendor in the market square.

Except that Eva had never seen such a handsome man in her entire life. His formidable height was enhanced by the ramrod straight carriage of nobility. As he conversed with her stepfather in eloquent Dutch, she could sense a gentleness in the deep timbre of his voice.

Andries turned toward her as she carefully descended the last step. Her knees were so wobbly, she remained, clutching the railing, afraid to cross the open space to the door. Her stepfather pinched the bridge of his nose and turned away. His embarrassment caused Eva's eyes to sting with the threat of tears.

"Mathieu of Liège, this is Eva of Utrecht. We have been expecting you," her maman said.

Eva's mouth had gone dry, and her tongue didn't seem to work either. Blinking rapidly, she suddenly remembered her manners and bobbed a quick curtsy, still clinging to the railing. Her heart fluttered in her chest like a captive bird.

Mathieu of Liège looked like a knight—at least, what Eva's imaginings of an ideal knight should be—only without the armor. Long hair fell over massive shoulders in waves the color of burnished oak. His eyes, dark and warm brown as well, were bracketed with only the tiniest of lines. The man's only flaw she could see was a scar on his right cheek, one that traced a puckered line from his eyebrow to the corner of his mouth.

Although his lips did not curve, his gaze upon her held a smile all on its own.

Eva's breath caught in her throat and for a moment, she feared she would crumple to the floor.

"I am Mathieu of Liège, milady. I have been sent by Philip, Good Duke of Burgundy, to retrieve you." Mathieu offered her a small bow before taking from Andries her small satchel of clothing. "The journey to Coudenburg shall take two days. The Duke has secured us lodgings at the Chateau Alst for this evening. The Lady Duchess has also sent with me her handmaiden, Blanche, to act as chaperone." Her escort patted what she assumed to be a sheathed dagger strapped to his leather belt as he addressed Marisse. "I assure you, madame, your daughter will be safe with me."

Eva's heart leapt. She'd worried so over this journey, she'd never considered the possibility of danger from outlaws. Studying her face, Mathieu continued, his voice gentler.

"These are peaceful times, since Philip's reign. The road between Ghent and Coudenburg is well-travelled. You have no need for worry, milady. Come. We have a long journey ahead." He offered his arm.

Marisse stepped between them. "Mathieu of Liège, I must inform you. My daughter suffers from a... disfigurement. She is not truly creple, but her gait can be slow and unsteady at times."

Eva cringed and dropped her gaze to the floor. She wasn't sure if she was relieved her maman had made excuses for her impairment or was mortally embarrassed by it. Until she heard the warm rumble of her escort's voice.

"I have been apprised," he said with a nod. "Have no worry. I will care for the maiden."

The next few moments passed in a dreamlike haze for Eva. Saying goodbye to her mother, Eva felt as though she should battle tears. She could not. Instead, she felt numb.

'Twas her wall. Eva learned early on in her life to protect the vulnerable, more sensitive parts inside of her heart by constructing a battlement of her own. Like the cold stone of a castle's outer walls, Eva's inner guard came up and encased her. As long as she kept her emotions behind this barrier, she could soldier on.

Outside the shop's door, three mounts awaited. One bore the chaperone, an old woman whose scowl seemed to have worn permanent furrows into her skin.

"Your chaperone shall be handmaiden Blanche," the escort said, waving a hand toward the elder.

The palfrey between her pony and the escort's tall, black mount was shaggy, round, and grey. She cast a soft, dark eye on Eva as she approached.

Strong hands wrapped around Eva's waist, and he lifted her as though she weighed nothing. After helping her settle into the velvet-padded saddle, Mathieu fastened a wide leather strap loosely across Eva's lap.

"We will travel slowly, as I've been told your experience on horseback is scarce. There is no need to hurry. We shall make the Chateau Alst well before nightfall." He patted the spotted gray neck of her mount. "Besides, I believe Germaine would prefer the slower pace. She's seen many winters, and for her, this is a very long distance to travel."

At that moment, cold drops of rain began to pelt Eva's cloak. Mathieu scowled and looked skyward. "We may, of course, want to step up the pace to avoid arriving like drowned rats."

Behind them, the dour looking chaperone, Blanche, mumbled under her breath. Seated aboard a furry, brown pony, the matron's wispy white hair was contained at her nape in a bun, which she now fumbled to cover with her hood.

Eva nodded, still afraid her tongue would not respond if she tried to speak. She simply lifted her own hood and gathered the palfrey's reins in one hand, clinging to the front of the saddle with the other. The leather felt cold and sticky under her fingers.

With a strap tethered to Germaine's headgear wound in one of his gloved hands, Mathieu mounted his horse. Gray overcast skies hung low over their heads as Eva's palfrey plodded patiently behind Mathieu's much taller mount. Trailed by the handmaiden, the three were halfway across the Market Square when Eva spotted the tall, black palfrey emerging from a street on the opposite side.

It was Stefano, she was certain. He had said he would return to see her before her departure, but the escort arrived earlier than expected. Hoping he would not recognize her, Eva pulled her hood down farther over her face and kept her gaze trained to the hindquarters of her escort's horse.

As they wound their way through the cobbled streets of Ghent toward the road south, the rain continued to fall intermittently. Eva wasn't sure if the source of her chattering of teeth was the cold and wet, or from fear that pressed insistently up against the armor encasing her heart.

Mathieu

All the way up from Coudenburg, Mathieu had grumbled under his breath. This was a trip he didn't want to make, a responsibility he didn't want to shoulder. The task was robbing him of time he desperately needed to prepare for the festival. The weather had decided to turn against him as well, and a cold, damp-ridden wind whipped him in the face. They'd left late morning the day before, stopping for only a short respite during the witching hour. There had been no choice—the aged mare, Germaine, simply wasn't up to travelling any faster or any farther that night.

The chaperone, Blanche, had persisted in constant, barely audible grumbling the entire journey. This certainly did not make the trip any more pleasant.

Now, the heavy gray skies commenced leaking their load. Muttering an oath under his breath, Mathieu tugged his hood down over his face and hunched his shoulders against the rain.

The girl behind him, on the struggling palfrey, hadn't said a single word since he'd retrieved her from Ghent. Mathieu couldn't help wondering if, in addition to being creple, she was mute as well. Not that he minded much. His duty was to deliver the girl safely to the castle, not to converse with her.

Strangely though, the minute he'd laid eyes on Eva of Utrecht, that was exactly what he'd wanted to do.

She wasn't very tall, and not slight of frame by any means. Mathieu couldn't help but notice how the lacings on the front of her kirtle strained to contain her lush curves, although her skin remained hidden beneath the chemise underneath. He also hadn't been able to ignore how his hands fit comfortably around a narrow waist when he'd lifted her into the saddle.

Her face was comely, with full cheeks tinged with color, and huge eyes the color of meadow grass. It was her lips that drew his eye most. Full, lush, and ripened-peach pink, he wondered if they were as soft as they looked.

Not the kind of thoughts I should be having about this young woman, this Eva of Utrecht. She is my charge for the next two days, nothing more.

But there *was* more, and Mathieu reminded himself of the fact—Eva of Utrecht was also a daughter of Philip the Good. Off-limits for certain, even if he had any ideas as to a romantic liaison with the girl. There would be plenty of other maidens coming to the castle for May Day should he decide he wanted to get to know better for an evening or two.

Once free from the city walls, the road widened. Mathieu gathered the tether to Germaine's head, so the palfrey plodded along beside rather than behind him. He glanced over at his passenger, but her voluminous hood hid her face.

"Are you well, milady?" he asked. He could see how her knuckles, peeking out from beneath the cloak, were as white as granite stone.

She turned toward him then, her grass-green eyes wide. But all he got for a reply was a curt nod.

"Are you cold? I have an extra blanket in my pack—"

"No, my lord. I am fine," she snapped.

So, she did have a voice, but one that took Mathieu by surprise. Soft, sweet, and lilting, it appealed, even though her tone was curt. She was very young, and he'd expected her to sound like a child. But a deeper huskiness struck him as more mature, womanlier. Like her lushly curved body.

Stop it. Not of your concern. There are plenty of women folk flocking to the castle in less than a fortnight. Keep your wits about you, man.

Mathieu decided, for the rest of the journey, he would refrain from trying to make conversation with Eva of Utrecht.

The noon hour had long passed, and the wind and rain abated, leaving in its wake air that was still, but even colder. Mathieu drew his hood back and shook his cloak to free it from some of the drenching they'd received. Eva and Blanche did the same. After passing through expanses of open meadow for quite some time, they were approaching a copse of pine.

"I need to relieve myself, my lord. There appears to be an opportunity just ahead," the maiden murmured.

Jolting him from inside his own head, Mathieu snapped his gaze to hers. *Fool.* He should have made the offer earlier, when they'd passed through the last wooded area. Why hadn't the old handmaiden spoken up?

"Of course, milady. We need to rest our mounts as well. I have noticed Germaine has been dragging her feet this past hour."

An ostler whose concern for the horses ran deep, Mathieu worried for Germaine. She would never had been his choice for such a long journey. As Simon's squire, however, he dared not defy the admiral's choice.

After tying the horses to a low-slung branch, Mathieu lifted Eva down from the saddle. Noticing her unsteady sway as her feet hit the ground, he did not immediately release her. A tense beat passed before she glared up at him.

"I have no need of assistance, my lord. I can navigate on my own quite well."

He snatched his hands away as though she were on fire, holding them in the air beside his head. "My apologies. Your mother advised—"

"I am perfectly capable of walking unassisted," she retorted. Lifting her skirts, Eva limped carefully through the brush toward a large-barreled oak tree. Blanche followed, muttering low so that Mathieu could not make out the words.

Shrugging, Mathieu dug in his pack for the loaf of bread and wedge of cheese he'd packed for the trip. She wasn't the friendliest maiden, for certain. He would refrain from attempting to assist her henceforth.

When Eva returned, he turned and offered her his skin of mead.

"Did you bring rations, milady? You're welcome to share mine."

She shook her head. "No. Only my clothing. I'm sorry. I should have planned better—"

But she didn't sound sorry. Her tone was almost... annoyed.

" 'Tis my duty to deliver you, and care for your needs on the way. I brought enough to share. Blanche brought her own rations."

The girl studied him through narrowed eyes, her chin tipped up in an expression of undeniable arrogance. Haughty little wench, he thought. I'll be glad when this mission is over.

They sat on a fallen log after Mathieu cast his extra blanket over the soaked bark. He noticed she sat at the very edge of the covering, tucking her skirts around her and keeping her chin down.

She doesn't want me too close. Mayhap she is afraid.

Eva of Utrecht did very much remind Mathieu of a young falcon, freshly caught and cowering at the nearness of a man. He'd gentled many of these birds, gaining their trust. He couldn't help but wonder if he would be able to do the same with this young maiden.

But why should he care?

"I think the worst of the weather has passed," he began, breaking off a chunk of the coarse oaten bread and handing it to her. "If the winds don't pick up, we should travel the rest of the way without much discomfort."

To his surprise, Eva lifted her chin as she took the bread and met his gaze. " 'Tis true, I am not an experienced traveler, my lord. But I am not a delicate flower either. I shall not wilt, rest assured."

Ah, so not such a timid fledgling after all. Mathieu raised an eyebrow.

"I did not mean to offend, milady." He couldn't help the corner of his mouth quirking. He liked a woman with a bit of spark. This one might keep hers well hidden, but it was there, nonetheless. "Cheese? It's quite a nice Edam."

Chapter Four

As the day wore on, Mathieu worried more and more about Eva's mount. The old mare's gait not only slowed with each step, but she appeared listless and unsteady at times. Eva was not a heavy load, nor was the day too warm for easy travel. He breathed a sigh of relief when they finally arrived at the inn, Chateau Alst. It was later than Mathieu had hoped, but thankfully before full darkness fell.

The inn was a plain-fronted brick building packed tightly between others on Duvers Street in the small village of Alst. A sign beside the heavy oak door labelled it, and an open archway beside the entrance led, Mathieu guessed, to the stables. Passing through the short tunnel, they emerged into a dirt enclosure. A young lad dressed in peasant's clothes dashed out to greet them.

"Good evening, my lord. Miladies." The youth dipped his head in greeting. "Are you needing lodging for your mounts this evening? Or just passing through?"

"We'll be staying, lad. If you could, please, offer the mare an extra measure of oats. She is old and the journey has taxed her strength."

The boy glanced back at the livery. "Sorry to say, sir, but we don't have room indoors for all three horses. We're about filled up this evening." He winced, expecting a scolding. "We have an outdoor pen though, over there." He pointed to a fenced cubicle in the corner of the lot. "I'd be happy to bed the two mares down with straw there."

"That would be fine." Mathieu dug a coin out of the satchel hanging from his belt. "Here's something extra for your trouble."

The boy's face beamed as he caught the coin tossed to him. "I'll rub them down very well, sir."

From the stable yard, Mathieu led Eva to the three stone steps at the rear entrance of the inn. There was no handrail, and he hesitated, glancing down at his young charge. After a silent moment, he heard her sigh heavily. Reluctantly, Eva allowed him to tuck her hand into the crook of his elbow.

Mathieu had only visited this establishment once before. The ground level housed a tavern and common room, where now a fire blazed in the blackened stone hearth. The warmth was welcome, as his clothing had not completely dried. As darkness had fallen, the cold crept mercilessly beneath his cloak. He guessed Eva's trembling was due to the same cause.

"I will speak to the innkeeper and get you settled in your room, milady. You may want to change into dry clothing before taking the evening meal."

The keeper directed them to rooms on the second level, though he made no move to accompany them. Mathieu stressed he and the ladies needed separate quarters. The older man, his wrinkles extending beyond his brow and up onto his bald head, scowled.

"There are two rooms remaining, but they are joined by a door. It's all that is left."

Mathieu watched Eva gaze at the narrow staircase along the far wall and felt her stiffen.

"I will escort you, milady."

Eyeing the stair's rail, Eva straightened and glared at him. "There is no need. I can make it on my own."

Mathieu sighed and watched her climb tentatively up the steps, her knuckles white with gripping the wobbly handrail. Blanche, as quiet and ghostly as her name, followed her. Shaking his head, he ordered a pitcher of ale and made his way to a small table in a corner by the fire.

This maiden—young woman, really—was a conundrum. He knew she'd been sheltered, having grown up in a decent enough tailor shop, but 'twas not lavish by any means. Simon had told him little about her except for her heritage and her age. Sixteen winters. Yes, still very young, but on the brink of womanhood. This was probably why her father, the Duke, had decided to bring her out at the May Day festival. Unmarried young women flocked to this festival, which was a celebration of spring and fertility. Mathieu was well aware that many lords, and knights as well, came to the festival in search of a wife.

Not in Mathieu's plans, for certain. Before any such thoughts entered his head, he had much to decide about his life. Although he did dream of a wife and children, 'twas but an idle fantasy. He could not house them in a small room off the back of a stable, nor support them on an ostler's wages.

He took a deep draught from his tankard and leaned back in his chair. His back ached from the long, slow journey in the cold rain. The fire warmed his bones, as did the ale. He'd almost drifted off when Eva appeared before him. She was alone.

Her hair, which had been bound in a fat braid when he first set eyes on her, was now flowing free over her shoulders. It shone in the firelight like polished gold. Her eyes were wide upon him, and he wasn't sure if what he saw there was fear or curiosity. He'd experienced enough of her thorny side to proceed cautiously around her.

"Milady," he said, rising to pull out her chair, "are you more comfortable?"

He noticed she had changed from the dull grey woolen kirtle she'd travelled in to one in a deep forest green. The shade brought out the color of her eyes.

"Yes, my lord." Bobbing a curtsey, she settled into the chair and watched him as he returned to his own. "Blanche has asked for her meal to be sent up to our room."

Mathieu nodded and relayed the message to the innkeeper. Then he motioned toward the empty tankard before her and lifted the pitcher. "Ale?" She nodded.

An uncomfortable silence fell between them until a kitchen maid brought them two trenchers filled with steaming stew. Rabbit, Mathieu thought, catching the scent. He waited until his companion had broken off a crust of the bread and began scooping the stew into her mouth before doing the same. The girl ate as though she hadn't been fed in a fortnight.

It wasn't until she'd wiped the serving board clean with the last bit of bread that she finally looked up and spoke.

"A fine meal. Many thanks, my lord."

To his surprise, for the first time, her full mouth curved into a smile.

Eva of Utrecht was not an extravagant beauty. But there was something about her smile, the way it brought a sparkle to those intensely green eyes. It lit up her entire face and shot warmth straight through his chest.

At a loss for words and struggling with emotions he knew were inappropriate, Mathieu hardly noticed the slamming of the tavern's back door. Moments later, a wide-eyed youth appeared tableside. The stable boy. He was wringing his hands and visibly shaking.

"My lord, your mare. Please come. I don't know what might have happened—"

Mathieu leapt to his feet and followed the lad outside and across the stable yard. Full dark had draped itself over the town, the only light guiding their way from a torch the boy carried. When they arrived at the corner pen where Germaine and Blanche's pony had been secured, the lad lifted his light.

"I thought she was just lying down to rest, m'lord. But then I noticed she hadn't touched her oats."

The stout, furry pony Blanche had been riding still had its muzzle buried in the wooden trough, munching her dinner. She paid them no mind as Mathieu opened the enclosure and knelt next to the prone palfrey. She lay on her side, her muzzle resting on the thick mat of straw beneath her. Her eyes were closed, and she did not open them when Mathieu called her name.

Cautiously, he lowered his head to her chest. No movement, no whooshing of breath, no heartbeat.

Mathieu clenched his teeth and muttered a curse. He'd warned the admiral the mare was too old for such a journey. Being right, however, wasn't nearly as comforting as it would normally have been.

Germaine had died in her sleep.

Eva

Eva was standing just inside the door, wringing her hands, when Mathieu returned.

"What's happened? Is something amiss?" she asked, raising wide eyes to his. He hesitated—a bit too long, Eva thought—before responding.

Mathieu shook his head. "All is well. We must retire now, milady. We have an even longer distance to travel tomorrow than we did today."

This time, Eva allowed her escort to accompany her to her room. It was full dark now, and the flaming wall sconces cast dancing shadows on the steep staircase. Eva swayed on their base.

The steps were too narrow, however, to allow them to be climbed two abreast. Stepping around her, Mathieu reached out his hand. Eva blinked rapidly and hesitated.

This was entirely improper. But the stairs, in the wavering light, appeared to Eva to be moving. Terrified she would lose her balance and stumble, she meekly laid her hand into Mathieu's. It was warm and rough, but firm.

Entirely improper, but also entirely necessary.

A jolt of heat radiated up her arm as his large, strong hand enveloped hers. *What a strange sensation.* She found the simple joining of hands with this handsome stranger deeply exhilarating. Feeling lightheaded and a little woozy, she lifted the hem of her kirtle and climbed slowly after him.

The ale must be strong. The long day of travel and pure exhaustion have weakened me. I'll attribute these odd feelings to that.

Eva waited outside the doorway as Mathieu ducked into her chamber, where Blanche was already buried under a blanket on the far side of the wide pallet. He drew the door connecting the adjoining rooms closed, sliding the latch bolt fast on the women's side. Then he rejoined her in the hall.

"Sleep well, milady. I will retrieve you early, as I wish to make Coudenburg before nightfall."

They stood so close, she could smell him—wet leather, horse, and something musky and male. Yet not at all unpleasant. Her cheeks suddenly felt hot, and her heart hammered faster. Eva studied Mathieu's handsome face in the dim, flickering light. A day's growth of beard shadowed his jaw, adding to his rugged good looks. She wondered again about the scar.

"Rest well, Eva of Utrecht. If you need anything at all during the night, I am but a threshold away. I sleep light and will hear if you call out or pound on the door."

To her surprise, Eva did sleep—like death, on the pallet beside the handmaiden, who had already stripped down to her chemise and lay on her side, snoring softly.

It seemed only moments later. Loud, persistent knocking roused Eva. There was no light leaking in around the window coverings. She yawned and stumbled to the open the door.

"We leave shortly, milady. Please ready yourself." It was then Mathieu's gaze raked her up and down, and his lips quirked. "You slept fully clothed."

Eva felt the heat rise into her cheeks. "I was cold," she stammered.

Taking the satchel of bread and cheese the innkeeper left for them, Mathieu led Eva across the stable yard. Dawn was just now lifting her own sleepy head over the rooftops in brilliant streaks of orange and blue. Eva stopped short to see the peasant boy standing outside the livery holding the reins—of only two mounts.

Mathieu's horse and Blanche's pony.

"I'm afraid Germaine must remain here in Alst. She is not up to making the rest of the journey." Mathieu's tone was abrupt and husky.

Eva shot a glance over toward the small pen where the boy said he would keep the mares. All she could see in the dim light was a heaping mound of straw. Shocked, she sputtered, "Then... what will I ride?"

"You will ride with me, on Chaucer. I'm afraid you'll have to ride astride. Blanche's mount cannot bear two riders. I am sorry for the inconvenience."

Before she had a chance to consider how completely improper and unexpected her situation, Eva found herself atop Mathieu's tall palfrey—straddling his broad back, no less. Instead of having a padded velvet saddle to cling to, Eva found her only way of steadying herself was to wind her fingers into the horse's mane while she leaned back against the chest of her escort.

Totally inappropriate. Yet totally necessary.

They travelled at a much faster pace than the day before. The rolling motion of the horse's faster gait was new to her, and it took some time to adjust her balance. It wasn't long, however, before the rocking of what Mathieu called a "canter," along with the warmth of the horse's back beneath her, soothed her nerves, and she relaxed. Yawning, she snuggled in closer against Mathieu's chest. Although the wool of his cloak was rough on her cheek, Eva soon succumbed to a semi-slumber.

Why she should feel so safe and secure with this stranger, Eva could not say. Probably because she didn't really have any choice in the matter.

Yet as Chaucer's hooves clomped noisily across the wooden planks of the drawbridge leading up the Coudenburg Castle, Eva couldn't help but feel a twinge of sadness. Mathieu had been nothing but kind and respectful during this harrowing journey. Would this be the last time she would see Mathieu? Or did he live here at the castle?

A page came running as Mathieu dropped to the ground. He reached up and lifted her down, catching her elbow as she swayed. She looked up and shot him a grateful glance. Her legs were stiff, both feet tingly and numb, and she was certain her backside would be too tender to sit upon for many days.

"You leave with three mounts, but return with two?" A tall man dressed in a bright red cloak and matching roundlet stepped out from the livery door.

Mathieu shot him a scowl. "I told you Germaine was too feeble for the journey, La Laing. I had no choice but to leave her in Alst." He hesitated, his gaze sliding to Eva and then back to the tall man. He cleared his throat. "The mare was unable to complete the trip, my lord."

The man called La Laing narrowed his eyes at Mathieu, but for just the briefest of moments. He then turned his attention to Eva, extending his hand as he approached her.

"My lady. I am Simon La Laing, Admiral of Flanders. The Duke told me to expect you. Lady Isabella awaits you in the Great Hall as we speak."

Eva stifled a small gasp and covered her mouth with her hand. Lady Isabella of Portugal, Duchess of Burgundy—awaiting to greet *her*? A young lady barely above peasant status, *and* one bearing the brand of bastard daughter of Duchess' husband? Eva's heart commenced an irregular gallop within her chest, and a sheen of sweat instantly covered her body.

"Come," Simon said, offering Eva his arm. "Allow me to present you to the Duchess."

Chapter Five

M*athieu*
Mathieu watched Simon lead Eva toward the doors of the Great Hall. He handed the mount to his page, then swiped his hands down his face. He was weary and hoped his own presence would not be called for at the evening meal. He yearned for a bar of soap and a basin of hot water, a dry towel and a soft bed.

As he turned to head toward his quarters, though, he cast a glance toward the encampment of the Royal Guard. A row of tents lined the far wall of the bailey where a small fire burned. He heard the talk and laughter of the knights, sitting or standing in groups around the fire. A mixture of emotions warred within him.

Jealousy? Mayhap. Mathieu was essentially a loner in his position, caring for the horses and the hunting birds, with little opportunity for camaraderie with men his own age. The knights were members of a brotherhood. Mathieu had no brothers.

In truth, he had no family left at all. His father died before he was born, and his mother died giving life to a sister who never took her first breath. He was, in truth, completely alone in the world.

As he observed the jocular banter between the knights, a simmering loathing rose up within him. Not all knights, he knew well, were noble and virtuous like his own sire had been.

From this distance, in the dark, Mathieu was unable to make out the men's faces. He guessed their Captain was not among them. Engel Knape, he knew, was traditionally granted a room within the keep. He also spent considerable time in the nearby village, in one of the several alehouses.

As Mathieu turned toward his quarters, he noticed a small movement near the doors of the Great Hall. The whoosh of a cloak revealed a flash of firelight off the golden handle of a sword. Quietly, Mathieu crept in that direction.

When he got close enough to recognize the man, ire twisted in Mathieu's gut. It was the Captain himself, spying unseen from the shadows as Eva passed by on La Laing's arm.

You'd better not set your sights on that one, Knape. She's too young, too innocent to fend off the likes of you. If you try anything with her, and the Duke doesn't take your head, I will do it for him.

Eva

Eva held tightly onto Simon's arm as they mounted the steps to the Great Hall. Even though the admiral was intimidating, tall and broad in his bright red cloak and head covering, his voice was surprisingly soft and soothing. Although he made no reference to her irregular gait, he must have known of it, since he walked very slowly and gave her plenty of time to keep pace beside him. Yet he did not say nor do anything to make her feel self-conscious.

Still, Eva trembled inside. She was dusty and disheveled from traveling on horseback for two days. Her hair, which she'd secured in a braid when Mathieu complained of the long strands whipping him in the face, was coming loose and looked very much like a badly frayed length of rope. And although it felt good to again be navigating on her own two feet, she feared that sitting on a hard bench or stool at the banquet table would prove very painful.

Her backside felt like the palfrey had spent the day trodding upon it, not carrying her atop its back.

As they entered the hall, the aroma of roasted meat made Eva's stomach twist in anticipation. But she was nothing if not sheltered, shy beyond measure. She could hear many voices—young voices, mostly female. Pausing inside the doorway, she turned toward La Laing.

"I am in terrible disarray, my lord. Is it possible for me to freshen myself before meeting the Duchess?"

Simon's eyes softened. "Of course. It was planned." He called for one of the young maidens who was laughing and playing just inside. "Alys! Come hither."

Immediately a girl looking to be a year or two older than herself stepped before them. Her mass of curly hair, a striking shade the color of copper, created a fuzzy halo around her delicate features. Pale, rosy skin wore a sprinkling of matching freckles. She curtsied promptly, nodding to La Laing before turning sky-blue eyes on Eva.

"I am Alys of Burgundy. You must be Eva of Utrecht," she said, a huge grin lighting up her face. "The lady Duchess awaits you."

"Can you please show Eva to the young ladies' quarters and assist her? Her journey was long," La Laing asked.

Eva followed the tall, slender girl through an endless maze of rooms and hallways. The keep was gigantic, and her stomach clenched to think how easy it would be for her to become lost in its depths. Several times, the girl named Alys surged far ahead of her, even though she was trying with all her might to keep up. After the third time Alys had to stop and wait for her, she tipped her head and studied Eva.

"I'm sorry, milady. I forgot about your impairment. I will walk more slowly the rest of the way."

Eva's cheeks felt like they were on fire. Although she did not sense any judgment in Alys' words, she still suffered shame. Did everyone at the castle know of her impairment? 'Twas true, she'd dealt with this condition all of her life. By now, surely, she should have become immune to others' pity.

But, Eva realized, there *was* no pity in Alys' voice. Only regret she had not travelled more slowly. Perhaps, Eva thought, she and Alys could become a sort of friends.

Eva had developed few over her short lifetime. Sequestered at home to help in the tailor shop, she'd never had the opportunity for schooling, or to participate in any social activities for children her own age. She was fortunate, she supposed, her mother had taken the time to teach her to read and write in Dutch, her native language, as well as to speak a little French. Many of her station had not this advantage. Drawing a deep breath for courage, she straightened and struggled to walk faster.

The hallways seemed never ending. How big was this castle? Alys led her finally through a doorway into a large open room. Lines of narrow beds stood in two lines down the center. The only light came from a huge hearth at the far end. Alys skipped down the row of beds and turned in between two, fumbling to light a candle on the small table separating them.

"This is my pallet," she said pointing, "and this one will be yours. The Duchess asked if I would help get you settled. I have been with her now three winters." She flashed Eva a proud grin.

Eva looked around her, bewildered. "Wha—what is this place?"

"This is where the sisters sleep, Eva. It's the dortour. You may not know it yet, but you are among family here." Alys curtsied before her again, her eyes sparkling. "Eva of Utrecht, I am Alys of Burgundy. We do not share a name, but we do share something more important. We share the noble blood of Philip, Duke of Burgundy. Here," she added in a whisper, " 'tis not reason for shame." She tugged on Eva's damp sleeve. "You must disrobe, milady, and bathe before your introduction to the Duchess. Hurry, now. The time is late for the evening meal."

Over the next hour, Eva was dropped into a whirlwind. Servants appeared carrying buckets of hot water, armfuls of dried lavender, and sheets of clean, white linen.

Numbly, with little thought to modesty, Eva complied. Two servants helped her disrobe and step into a wooden tub, where the warm, scented water felt heavenly on her sore body. Gentle hands ran bars of soap over her while others sudsed her long tresses. Only her mother had ever bathed Eva before. But like an obedient child, she allowed herself to be washed and dried. In her shocked exhaustion, her muscles went limp, enjoying the unusual pampering.

Alys disappeared for a time, but returned carrying a gown such as one Eva had never seen. Layers of the fine, ivory linen draped over Alys' one arm. In her other hand she carried a pair of very soft looking leather slippers.

Eva sat near to the fire while a servant combed and blotted her wet tresses dry with lengths of clean linen. Moments later, a white chemise slipped over her head, followed by the lovely linen kirtle. When Alys herself bent to slide the slippers over her feet, Eva noticed the two pattens did not look the same.

With surprise, she noticed one slipper bore a length of padding along the outside of the foot.

Completing her task, Alys stood and took Eva by the shoulders.

"You are in a royal court now, milady. Tonight, you must straighten your carriage and walk proudly into the Great Hall. Over the next weeks, we shall

all—me, your other sisters, and the Duchess herself—school you in the ways of a noblewoman."

Eva blinked at the girl in silence. Surely this was all a fantastic dream, and she would awaken soon, on her own straw mattress in the early morning chill of her bedroom in Ghent.

Alys grinned into Eva's wide eyes. "Come. The Duchess awaits."

Mathieu

Mathieu covered his face and groaned after the servant delivered Isabella's command. It seemed he would be expected to join the Duchess and her young charges in the Great Hall for a late evening meal after all. Tempting thoughts of flopping down on his pallet and burying his face in its fur covering evaporated.

His small charge, Kleine Uil, was not pleased either.

Mathieu had rescued the small owl on the way back from one of the hunting expeditions several winters past. Somehow the bird, barely bigger than his hand, had broken a wing. Lady Isabella's falcon had spotted the small creature, hopping about in the tall grasses at the edge of the woods, emitting a loud *kweeo, kwiff, kwiff* call of distress. Fortunately, the Duchess had a soft heart for helpless creatures. She kept her falcon tethered and allowed Mathieu to retrieve the injured owl.

Kleine Uil had been with Mathieu ever since. Its wing never healed properly enough to allow the bird to fly higher than the rafters of the low stable roof. The tiny creature seemed happy to sleep in Mathieu's quarters by day, and prowl the stables at night, earning his keep by ridding it of small rodents.

Kleine did not like it, however, when Mathieu was away for any length of time. He bent and spoke to the owl as one would to a small child.

"I shall return this night, Kleine. You go about your duties, and I will see you when the moon is high."

The owl hopped out of Mathieu's quarters into the stable, ruffling his feathers in annoyance.

After washing quickly in the warm water his page had brought him, Mathieu donned a clean liéne and braies and strapped on his ankle boots. As he turned to leave his quarters, he remembered the sight of Knape at the keep's entrance. Retrieving his belt, he slid his dagger into the sheath on his hip. He did not trust the knight and knew far too much about the man's history to hold even a mustard seed's worth of respect for him.

Mathieu was just a boy when Knape, then merely a Burgundian knight, passed through his home city of Liège. Mathieu's father had been a knight as well—a good and faithful warrior. Although his sire died before Mathieu's birth, his mother told him much about him, and how he'd valued the principles of chivalry. Knape's behavior far from exemplified these virtuous codes.

The problem, of course, was that Knape was aware of how much Mathieu knew. He came to the realization early on that turning his back on the Captain of the Royal Guard might well someday cost him his life.

When he entered the Great Hall, the sound of laughter echoed off the stone walls. He was surprised the Duchess had allowed the young ladies in her care to remain in the hall at such a late hour. Isabella usually kept her charges to a strict, early curfew.

Tonight, he soon recognized, was a special occasion. He had not been aware of how highly anticipated Eva's arrival had been. What was so special about the girl? Not only was she just another of Philip's illegitimate mistakes, but she was also born with an impairment.

Though the hour was late, the hall bustled with activity. A fire burned in the gigantic hearth, and torches lined the walls, filling the usually dim interior with warm, flickering light. Servants scurried in and out carrying platters of meat and fowl, bread and vegetables. Tantalizing aromas filled the air. When one servant carried in a festive jellied dish, a delighted squeal erupted from the younger girls.

Quite the celebration, Mathieu thought. And the Duke himself had not yet arrived from his negotiations in Lille. He was not expected for another several days.

This was not unusual. Unlike many women of the day, the Duchess held a higher ranking than most. Why this was, Mathieu was not certain. He did, however, harbor a great deal of respect for the Portuguese princess.

The Duchess sat at the high table, the dais, flanked by Simon La Laing and, of course, the Captain of the Royal Guard. A finger of wrath snaked its way up Mathieu's spine, but he quickly shook it off. He must keep a clear head and a civil tongue with Knape, especially in front of Isabella.

The long table stretched out at right angles to the dais with benches on either side. A few of the young ladies had already seated themselves, sitting demurely with their hands in their laps. Others still clustered in a small group near the fire, chattering and laughing.

Mathieu made his way to the dais, where his usual seat next to La Laing awaited. He lowered to one knee before the Duchess.

"Ah, so here you are, Mathieu. I know you must be fatigued from your journey. I wish to thank you for achieving your task. Please, come be seated and share some wine," the Duchess said, her smile warm.

Isabella was an attractive woman, with a porcelain complexion and chiseled features. Dressed in her usual red robe of lush tapestry and double-horned, veiled hennin, she looked every bit the part of royalty. Even as her eyes shone with the sharp intellect and iron-core strength he knew her to possess, her smile exuded a softness she made no attempt to hide.

Still, Mathieu could not imagine how she remained so kind to her husband. Although the Duke showered Isabella with gifts and attention when present at court, he was shameless in his infidelity. Philip loved variety in his women as much as the diversity of dishes on his table. At first shocked by this behavior from a man who decreed to belong "to you alone" at the nuptials, it was obvious Isabella had grown to accept her position.

What choice did she have? At nearly thirty-three years old, the Duchess had been offered only one other marriage proposal since her twenty-first winter. That offer had not materialized.

Now, however, the Portuguese princess wielded greater power in the Burgundian court than most women would ever know. Philip may not be virtuous when it came to his marriage vows, but he was definitely wise. He recognized his bride's abilities in negotiations early on.

"Thank you, Lady Isabella. It was my honor to serve." Mathieu rose and took his seat next to La Laing on the dais. He turned to the Duchess, his mouth set in a grim line. "Did Simon tell you about Germaine?"

"He did." Her eyes closed and she nodded. " 'Twas not your fault, Mathieu. The mare was old. Still," her gaze flashed to La Laing, who was busy conversing with the man seated next to him, "Germaine should not have been chosen for the task. I've already spoken with Simon on the matter."

Mathieu had barely settled when Isabella rose to her feet, raised her knife, and tapped it on the edge of her brass goblet. The young girls still standing scurried to their seats, and all eyes turned upon her.

"This evening, we have the pleasure of welcoming another Burgundian flower into our midst." She smiled as all turned to follow her gaze. "Eva of Utrecht, welcome to the Coudenburg court."

Mathieu blinked, failing to believe the young woman standing in the entrance of the hall was the same one he'd retrieved from Ghent. This was not the dusty, disheveled youth he'd watched La Laing usher into the keep an hour earlier. This was an exceptional beauty.

Eva wore a kirtle of the palest ivory, adorned at the neck and hem with elaborate embroidery. A braided belt of gold matched the long, shimmering waves of hair that swirled well beyond her waist. A circlet of tiny yellow and purple flowers ringed her crown.

She did not look like a maiden of sixteen winters, certainly not one reared in a meager tailor shop.

As she made her way to the dais, Mathieu noticed that even her posture had changed. She held herself tall and regally now, her chin tilted high. Shoulders squared and eyes lowered, he barely recognized her. Even the slight imperfection in her gait was hardly noticeable.

When she reached the dais, she bowed her head and curtsied low. Isabella smiled as she laid a jewel-encrusted hand on Eva's shoulder.

"Welcome home, Eva of Utrecht," she murmured. "We are blessed to have found you."

Chapter Six

E*va* For Eva, the next days blended into a dreamlike blur. She was quickly absorbed into a group of other girls, most very close to her own age, who were staying at Coudenburg. Some lived with the Duchess full-time, others just came for the festivals. They all looked so very different, though, it was hard to believe they were related.

But from what Alys told her, all the girls in residence were daughters of Philip III—albeit born out of wedlock. *Heavens*, she thought. *The Duke must have mistresses in every corner of his Dukedom!*

She was learning much about how to behave like a young lady of the court. Although Alys often whispered minor corrections to her manners when at the table or venturing out into the bailey, none was ever delivered unkindly. Eva quickly found herself becoming enamored of Alys in a very sister-like way.

After the first evening meal, Eva did not see the Duchess to interact with her again. She did catch sight of her, though, leaving on horseback with Mathieu and some of the knights, many holding hunting birds on their gloved arms. Even Isabella! Eva was impressed at the independent spirit she sensed in the Duchess. She vowed she would not only ask to learn how to ride a horse without assistance, but how to handle the falcons as well. Perhaps Mathieu could teach her.

Mathieu. She had not the opportunity to speak with him since her arrival. It pained her, as he was, she supposed, the first person she'd had close contact with on her journey from Ghent. A tiny corner of her heart, however, whispered the reason she missed him went deeper.

Why, though? Eva knew, with her low social status and her deformity, she would be lucky to attract any young man's attention—particularly a squire to a nobleman, one most likely destined for knighthood. She found her thoughts drifting back to Ghent, to Stefano.

She knew the cloth merchant's apprentice had an interest in her, despite all of her shortcomings. For that, she reminded herself, she should be eternally grateful. Stefano, although not bound for knighthood, would someday be an independent cloth merchant—a guild member, in a trade that provided a wealthy living. Her parents both favored Stefano highly, and Eva knew—truth be told, *feared*—the Italian would surely be asking for her hand upon her return from the May Day festival.

The thought shook fear into her very core. Eva could not imagine taking Stefano as a husband. Although he was a likeable enough fellow, and handsome as well, Eva felt only faint revulsion when in the apprentice's presence. Even when he kissed her hand upon greeting her, Eva could not help shrinking away from his touch. Surely, sharing a marriage bed with him would be impossible to bear.

Whatever it was that *happened* in a marriage bed. Eva had no idea. Her maman had never spoken of this to her. She assumed when she reached her sixteenth year, these secrets would be revealed. Her name day was now nigh, and she would come of age while she was here at the castle. She would have to resign herself to wait until she returned from Coudenburg to ask her maman for the secrets she had yet to learn about becoming a woman.

In truth, Eva was in no hurry to learn the details. She shuddered to think of what would be expected of her on her wedding night. Hopefully it would not be a concern for a long, long time.

In contrast, Eva had found close contact with Mathieu anything but unpleasant. Indeed, she'd enjoyed having his arms wrapped around her atop his palfrey. His scent, strange and musky and tinged with leather and oil, had stirred something inside her. A sensation that had not been unpleasant at all.

On the fourth day after her arrival, a messenger approached Eva as she sat with the other girls in the kitchen breaking their fast on bread and cheese.

"Milady, the Duchess wishes to see you in her solar when you are finished with your meal."

When he turned away quickly, Eva called after him. "Wait. Where is this place?"

Beside her, Alys laid a hand on her arm. "I will show you the way."

Eva's heart hammered in her chest as Alys guided her to the solar. The door was open, and multicolored light spilled through the tall, stained-glass windows. Lady Isabella sat near them with needlework in her lap. She smiled at the girls and beckoned to them.

"Come, Eva. I trust you have settled in well. It is time for us to become better acquainted."

Seating herself on a tapestry covered chair near the Duchess, Eva's entire body trembled. She wished Alys to remain, but she did not. When the girl's footsteps faded into the distance, Eva took a shaky breath. Isabella kept her eyes on her embroidery for a few, long moments before lifting them to meet hers.

"Eva of Utrecht. You are the daughter of Marisse, is that correct?" she asked, a gentle smile lighting up her features.

Eva nodded. Again, as happened often when she was afraid, her tongue felt as though it had died in her mouth.

"And you are aware, I trust, that Duke Philip is your true sire," she continued.

"Yes, your grace," Eva managed, forcing her voice to form the words. She feared silence might be misconstrued as belligerence. But Isabella regarded her with an expression of pure kindness.

"Do you know the day and year in which you were born?" Isabella asked.

"Aye, your grace. Verily, my maman told me it was the twenty-third day of April, in the Year of Our Lord 1420." She paused and swallowed, her mouth very dry. "I am soon to have seen sixteen winters."

Isabella smiled. "April twenty-third. The feast day of St. George. The day is, in fact, tomorrow. So, on the morrow we shall celebrate your name day."

Eva blinked. She knew her name day would occur during her visit in Coudenburg, but she was surprised Isabella was also aware. It appeared the Duchess knew much about her—even more, perchance, than Eva did herself.

"We would like the day to be special for you, Eva of Utrecht. How would you like to spend your name day?"

The answer popped out of her mouth before her mind had a chance to stop it. "I would like to learn to ride a palfrey, Your Grace. By myself." She paused again, a knot of excitement forming in her chest. "I would like the ostler—is it Mathieu? I would like him to teach me how to ride. Someday, I would love to learn to hold a hunting bird on my arm, as well. Like you."

The Duchess' eyebrows lifted, and a small smile quirked her lips. "Falconry as well," she blurted. "And you wish your teacher to be Mathieu, specifically?"

Eva felt heat rise into her cheeks and she focused on the knotted fingers in her lap. "Yes, Your Grace. Mathieu seems to know much about the horses—I'm guessing the hunting birds as well. He was very patient with me on our journey."

Isabella set her needlework aside and clasped her hands across her middle. "Mathieu is our ostler, so well he might be the best one to teach you of the horses. But you do realize, to truly learn to control and maneuver a horse proficiently, you must ride astride."

Eva looked up to see the Duchess' face alight with a brilliant smile. "Yes, milady. I do not fear this."

The Duchess nodded. "I will ask for suitable riding attire be brought to you. Tomorrow, you shall ride."

Eva could barely believe her ears. Truly, this was like a dream come true. Even though she'd been taught to never question such good fortune, she couldn't hold her curiosity in check.

"But milady, why? Why did you bring me here? All the other girls as well. They are all... daughters of the Duke?" She paused, swallowing.

Isabella's smile was soft, and she sighed. " 'Tis true, many do not understand my motives. I do not make excuses for my husband's actions—he is a man, and he is the Duke. He does as he pleases. But I envy Philip to have been blessed beyond measure with so many children. I have only one who survived." Isabella paused to sip from her cup. She levelled her gaze at Eva over the rim. "Noblemen recognize and support their male children, even those born out of wedlock. Usually, no one is there for the girls." She set down her cup and clasped Eva's hand. "I have decided to be that someone. And so, Eva of Utrecht, I welcome you into my fold of daughters. Henceforth, see yourself not as the Duke's bastard daughter, but as the stepdaughter of the Duchess."

Mathieu

The last thing Mathieu had time for was riding lessons. With the May Day festival only days away, he still had much to do. The Duchess' servants had provided additional help, but there were extra horses to tend to as well—those of the knights who came with her.

And oh, what horses they did bring. Mathieu oft gazed in envy at the destrier belonging to the guard's Captain. A massively built stallion with a coat of purest white, the horse required extra effort to keep spotlessly clean. An irony, surely, for a black-hearted knight to ride a blindingly white charger. Mathieu was instructing his own pages in how to properly groom the beast when Eva appeared in the doorway of the stable.

His breath caught. The girl truly was a vision. Clad in a woolen kirtle of deepest blue, her wide skirt nearly filled the span of the entryway. The morning sun glinted off the golden braid hanging over her shoulder. She smiled when she saw him, her eyes sparkling with excitement.

"The Duchess sends me," she said simply.

Mathieu stood and crossed his arms over his chest. "Lady Isabella sent word. You wish to learn to ride." He set his lips in a line. He wanted the girl to know his feelings on the matter. He simply didn't have time for this.

"I do. Today is my name day. 'Tis my gift from the Duchess."

"Your name day," he repeated. He couldn't help his own smile from extinguishing his annoyance. "Come, then. Let us begin."

Over the next hour Mathieu went over the basics of handling a palfrey, from leading it out of the stables to sweeping the dust from its coat before saddling. He showed Eva how the feet were cleaned, although he knew a lady would never have need to perform this task. The girl watched him, rapt the entire time, interrupting him occasionally with questions.

She was no simpleton, this girl. Eva of Utrecht may know naught of horses, but she certainly was an attentive student.

Mathieu chose Jannis on which to place Eva for her very first lesson. Jannis was not a very tall horse but was broad and sturdy under his glossy brown coat. After fitting the palfrey for riding, he handed Eva the reins and watched her lead the horse around the bailey. Her gait appeared steadier this day, improved from when he first retrieved her from Ghent. She seemed unafraid, chattering softly under her breath to the animal the entire time.

As he helped her climb onto the mounting block, her questions began anew.

"Is Jannis a boy or a girl?"

Of course. A difficult one to answer, right at the start. Mathieu cleared his throat.

"Jannis was a boy, but he is a gelding now."

Eva leaned on Mathieu's shoulder as he helped fit her left, untwisted foot into the stirrup. He could see then the slipper she wore, fashioned with extra padding on the outside edge. *Ah*, he thought. *The Duchess is perceptive. She has made accommodations for the girl's impairment.*

He helped lift her into the saddle, steadying her with his hand at the small of her back. As he went around to secure her other foot, she asked, "What means this? A gelding?"

Mathieu pursed his lips. This was not a subject he wished to explain to a young maiden. He blew out a breath. "It means he has been altered and can no longer breed a mare. He is gentler now and pays more mind to his master than to his instincts."

He looked up to see Eva's eyes and mouth had rounded. She he did not speak again until he had mounted his own palfrey beside her. As they started off toward the gatehouse, her next question was almost a whisper.

"So, Jannis will be very obedient for me?"

Mathieu smiled. "Aye. You have nothing to fear, milady. Jannis will perform whatever you ask of him. He'll give you no trouble."

As on their journey from Ghent, the handmaiden, Blanche, accompanied them on their ride as chaperone this day. The matron, not unexpectedly, didn't seem pleased about her assignment. She rode her usual thick-coated pony, who looked even less enthused than she.

They passed the blacksmith's stall on the way out of the bailey, where Wallis was busy hammering a glowing red rod of steel on his anvil. Mathieu lifted a hand in greeting.

"Wallis, Jannis here will be needing a new set of shoes soon enough. Mayhap on the morrow?"

"The morrow it is," he called to Mathieu.

"Aye sir."

The day was glorious, with a clear, blue sky overhead and a mild breeze ruffling the grasses on the meadow. Mathieu kept his mount close beside Jannis—close enough to reach over and take control of the palfrey should he stumble or falter in any way. Eva was quiet after her initial bout of questions and seemed to be genuinely enjoying her experience. Mathieu glanced over, admiring her profile. She may have been raised simply, but the lady definitely had noble blood running through her veins.

Mathieu felt obliged to fill the silence.

"You seem quite comfortable in the saddle, milady. You never rode until the day I came for you?" he asked.

She tipped her head. "My stepfather took me to the stable and I did ride, but only twice. Shortly before you arrived." She reached down and stroked the horse's neck. "Jannis is not nearly as scary as Tyrion. That beast 'twas monstrous!"

Her candid expression made him smile. "Tell me about your life there, milady. You were a crafter of clothing?"

"Aye. My parents have owned the tailor shop since I was a babe. I learned to wield a needle before a pen to paper." Her voice was small and flat, as though she was ashamed of her upbringing. "But I did learn this as well. How to read, and how to write," she added, a touch of pride lacing her words. "And you? How did you come to be the Duke's squire?"

He sighed, and his next words somber. "I was born in Liège. My father was a knight, killed in battle at Othée. My maman petitioned the court to secure my position." Mathieu paused. "I've been at Coudenburg, under Simon La Laing, for many years."

"Ah. So, you are headed for knighthood, then?"

Mathieu's lips tightened. "I quite enjoy my position as ostler and falconer for the court." He leaned down to stroke his own mount's glossy neck. "In truth, I prefer to spend time with the beasts more than with my own kind."

Immediately, Mathieu wondered why he'd let this slip. He quickly continued, "Horses, hunting dogs and birds, they depend on us and us alone for their safety and welfare. I enjoy fulfilling that role, and well." Abruptly, he changed the subject. "Do you intend to continue in your parents' footsteps?"

Eva shook her head. "I do not wish to cut and sew cloth all of my life. And Marisse and Andries are not both my parents." She shot him a sharp look. "Andries is my stepfather. My true father, as you may already know, is the Duke himself."

"So I am told," Mathieu said, studying her. There had been a change in the girl since she'd arrived at Coudenburg. Isabella was schooling her, and Eva already seemed to have donned a more prestigious air since the day he met her in Ghent.

It was not haughtiness he sensed, however. It was more an elevated level of confidence, one that suited her. In truth, he'd seen inklings of the trait within her even before they'd arrived.

"What is it you want for your future, milady? If it is not too forward of me to ask."

She fiddled with the leather reins as she spoke, her eyes cast skyward. "I have dreams, albeit lofty ones. Only now do I have the courage to voice them. Until the Duke's missive arrived, I believed there was no chance for me to ever rise above my roots."

Mathieu tipped his head, a stab of emotion piercing his heart. Her humility made him feel a little guilty. Here he had the opportunity for knighthood clearly offered to him and he denied the honor. Eva, until the Duke had decided to acknowledge her, had far fewer options open to her than he.

"And what might those dreams be?" he asked softly.

Eva sighed. "I wish to earn the title of lady, and a fine one. I wish to attract the eye of a grand husband. A knight. I wish to live in a fine home." She turned to him, her eyes shining. "I wish to marry for love." Seeming embarrassed by her honesty, she blushed and dipped her chin.

Lofty indeed, Mathieu thought. The girl definitely has royal roots. These described that which Mathieu may never be able to offer to a woman.

At least, not at this point in his life. Is that what he wanted, though? Or did he want to live the rest of his life in a stable?

She recovered quickly. "I sound like a foolish romantic, I know. All of these dreams are just that, my lord. I am but a tailor's daughter, a bastard one at that. One with an ugly, twisted foot."

Mathieu's heart squeezed. Under her fledgling confidence the timorous child still hid. He reached over and placed a hand on her arm. "The Duchess wanted you here for a reason, milady. Perchance there is a better future for you on the horizon than you may know." He sat taller in his saddle and shot her a challenging grin. "Are you ready to progress to a faster gait?"

Chapter Seven

E *va*

Eva had the time of her life. It only took several strides aboard Jannis' smooth canter for her nervous tension to subside, and she began to enjoy the ride. They crossed a broad, rolling meadow all the way to the edge of the woods before slowing the horses to a walk. With the wind in her hair and the scent of wildflowers all around her, Eva had never felt so free. She turned to Mathieu, her face cramping from a smile she could not suppress.

"What a glorious name day you've made for me, my lord. How am I ever to thank you?" She was breathless, and her heart filled to bursting with joy.

Mathieu's only answer was a nod, his lips quirking before he drew up his palfrey near the forest's border. "Would you like to walk in the woods, milady? 'Tis a fine day, and there is a walking path here I think you might enjoy."

A walk. What sounded like a simple task for any normal maiden was not so for Eva. She hesitated, casting her eyes downward.

"Walking is not my strong suit," she murmured.

"Worry not. I shall be right beside you every step of the way."

He dismounted and tied off his horse before helping Eva down. Although her legs were stiff and her bottom still tender, 'twas a glorious feeling... a feeling of being alive. And when Mathieu's strong hands gripped her waist to settle her on her feet, a new sort of feeling simmered within her.

Mathieu waited until she'd gained her balance in the grass, his arm still wrapped around her. She turned to look up at him, reveling in the warmth of his body against hers. He smelled clean, spicy like fresh cut hay and well-oiled leather. Mathieu may be an ostler, but he certainly didn't smell like the beasts he spent his days with.

"Are you steady now, milady?" She felt his words rumble in his chest more than heard them.

She blinked fast and swallowed, not wishing him to pull away. Yet she did not want him to see her as a burden, one requiring constant coddling. She stood taller and squared her shoulders.

"I am fine, my lord."

Mathieu released her but offered his arm. "The path is cleared of brush by the duchy's serfs, milady. But still, there may be roots and such. The footing is uneven." He tucked her hand into his side and cleared his throat. " 'Tis time I came to be sure the serfs are performing their duties anyway."

"I shall remain here, my lord."

Both Eva and Mathieu spun around to see the chaperone, Blanche, still seated aboard her pony. Eva had almost forgotten she'd followed them.

"I care not for a walk this morn. My bones ache," she croaked.

"As you wish, Blanche. As long as the lady does not mind," Mathieu replied with a shrug.

Eva shook her head.

The sudden damp, coolness under the trees was heavenly after their ride. Eva breathed in the tangy pine air and looked about her. A lovely bush covered with white blooms caught her eye.

"What kind of flower are these?" she asked.

" 'Tis hawthorn. These woods are filled with them." He grinned down at her.

"It's like a park," she murmured.

"Someday, 'twill be," Mathieu said, a touch of pride in his words. "This land is used now for hunting. But the Burgundians have already fashioned a fine park and gardens at Germolles. That's where the court spends their winters. The rose gardens there are breathtaking. I'd love to take you to see them sometime."

Eva's heart began its fluttering, as it had many times since her first day with Mathieu. "That would be lovely, my lord. Roses are splendid, indeed. But the wildflowers in the meadows, growing wild and free.... those will always be my favorite." She paused and peered up at him through her lashes. "They live and grow and prosper all on their own, with no help from any human hand."

As I wish to live my life, she thought wistfully, suddenly lurching into him as her crooked foot slipped off an exposed root on the path.

"Are you well, milady?" he asked.

Dare she be so bold? Why not? After all, he's just the ostler. "Yes, but please, sir, call me by my given name, Eva."

Mathieu's chin tipped up in surprise. "Very well," he answered slowly, "but then you must use my given name as well."

They walked in silence for a few minutes, enjoying the hush of the woods. The wind did not reach them here, the only sounds the crunching of pine needles under their feet and an occasional squawk of a bird overhead. Hearing this, Eva asked, "You are also the falconer for the Duke's court, are you not... Mathieu?"

The name felt new on her tongue, sweet and strangely forbidden.

He patted her hand and nodded. "I am. 'Tis one of my passions, you might say. Simon... Admiral La Laing has the young birds brought here from the Netherlands, where they are abundant. My job is to gentle and train them to be useful on the hunt. I tend to the hunting hounds as well."

Eva tipped her head. "I saw the Duchess with a bird when you went out with the knights. The Duchess takes part in the hunt as well?" She couldn't keep the wonder out of her voice.

"She does. That was Cornelijs, the Duchess' fine peregrine. Lady Isabella was the only daughter among brothers in her home court. She learned to ride and hunt with them. She quite enjoys it." He paused, slanting his gaze down toward her. "Do you have siblings?"

"I do," she said. "They are stepsiblings, of course, but I love them as if they are my own. Tomas and Griet. They are five and six winters old." A twinge of homesickness struck her. "I do miss them. Terribly."

"You enjoy children, then? The Duchess gathers many here—girls of all ages—for the festivals. They should keep you plenty occupied during your stay."

"The Duchess is kind and gracious, indeed." Eva sighed. "I shall endeavor to be like Lady Isabella. I should like to learn to handle the falcons and mayhap join in the hunt." Her shoulders rose and fell. "Someday."

Mathieu's laugh startled her. She'd not heard him laugh since the day they met, and the sound warmed her heart. Then she sobered. "Do you think 'tis silly for me to desire these things, Mathieu? That I wish to become a fine and noble lady?"

He stopped walking so abruptly she nearly pitched onto her face. He quickly stepped forward and grasped both of her shoulders, drawing them closer than she'd ever been to a man before. Eva's heart was beating so hard she could barely hear his next words. He was a good head taller than she, and she had to tip her head back to see his face.

"Nay, not a silly goal at all, Eva. You have the trappings of a noblewoman. I recognized it from first we met."

Time stood still as Eva gazed into Mathieu's eyes. They were brown, an oaken color like his wild mane of long hair, but up this close she noticed there were also specks of gold. His skin, bronzed by long hours in the sun, was still smooth, other than the tiny lines at the corners of his eyes and mouth. It was then the breeze blew back one side of his hair, revealing his scar.

Boldly, she reached up and traced the pink line with her finger. "How did this happen?"

He shrank away and turned his head. "An accident. Long ago. I was a boy."

She wondered then how many winters Mathieu had seen. Absently, she also wondered whether or not he was spoken for.

Not that it would mean anything to her. He was the ostler, not a knight or nobleman. If she were to realize her dream of living the life of a fine lady, surely she must seek a man of higher rank.

Shouldn't she?

He then took her by surprise. Pulling her closer, he stroked the back of his roughened hand over her cheek, and a shudder ran through her. All logical thought evaporated as instinctively, she leaned in and lifted her face. His lips, full and sharply defined, drew her gaze. Eva had never been kissed, but felt sure it was about to happen now. She welcomed it.

The snap of a twig behind her shattered the moment. Mathieu's head shot up, but before alarm could tense her further, he placed a finger to his lips and turned her around.

There, a very short distance away, stood a young doe, ghostly spots still evident on its glossy coat. Its eyes like large black pools, the animal stared at them, frozen. An instant later the deer spun away and sprang nimbly over a fallen log. All Eva could see was its white tail bobbing as it disappeared from sight.

"There are many deer here. Good news, for the Lady Duchess does have a taste for venison."

Eva winced. "So, the Duchess hunts these for the table?"

Mathieu shook his head. "We—the Duke and the other men—use the bow for larger game. The Duchess' favorite sport is hunting fowl. Her falcon is quite adept at bringing them down. When you saw us go out last, her grace brought home an impressive brace of birds on her own saddle."

Eva swallowed. The glamor of hunting, she quickly realized, was much more enticing than the reality of killing and carrying home dead beasts for the table. She sniffed. "Perchance you could just teach me how to handle the birds? Mayhap I could help you in their training."

Again, Mathieu's laugh resounded in the silence around them. He turned her to him once again and studied her with mirth in his eyes. "You are a puzzle, Eva of Utrecht. A delightful one, to be sure. And very beautiful as well."

Mathieu

Mathieu had not been alone with a young maiden in a very long time. None of the other girls Isabella brought to court had ever been interested in learning to ride, let alone handle the hunting birds. A few had expressed ardor for the tiny owl he kept in the stables, but in the way a child might be drawn to a plaything.

This girl was no child. Her wisdom and manner depicted a fine mind and courage reminiscent of the Duchess herself. Yet Eva of Utrecht bore no blood ties to the Portuguese Duchess, only to the Duke of Burgundy.

His attraction for her was only natural, he supposed. Mathieu was a young man in his prime. He also spent very much of his time alone. At this moment, however, gazing into the brilliant green eyes of a beautiful young maiden, he felt stirrings he did not particularly welcome. Stirrings he knew were not entirely proper.

Isabella trusted him to act as Eva's chaperone and teacher. He must not betray that trust. He had just firmed this resolve in his mind when she whispered her next words.

"I like you very much, Mathieu of Liège. You have been very kind to me, and patient, even with my affliction, one that surely has made your duties more difficult."

A corner of his heart melted. Lifting her hand, he kept his eyes trained on hers, vigilant for any signs of hesitation. He found none.

Her eyes grew wide as he brushed his lips once over the back of her hand. The skin was petal-smooth and warm, the scent of lavender overpowering the leather from the bridle reins. He felt her shudder, but she never broke the eye contact, a beacon bearing into his very soul. He pressed his lips to her hand again, and she closed her eyes and sighed.

Entirely inappropriate, yet entirely delightful.

Aye, there was something uniquely special about Eva of Utrecht. Mathieu had never reacted to a young woman quite this way. Purely physical attraction, of course. He was no prude and no youngster. But there was something more to the way Eva affected him, reaching into his heart with her eyes and her sincerity. Innocent, yes, but also strong-willed with an edge as sharp as a dagger's blade.

An edge that was rapidly threatening to cut through all the defenses he had wrapped around his emotions. Even knowing the chaperone was only yards away on the edge of the woods, Mathieu had the wild urge to kiss her, deeply and thoroughly, right here and right now. He had a feeling she would not deny him.

Someday I will make her mine.

The thought whispered its message into his brain, from whence he knew not. Flinching in shock, he took a step back. Propriety leaped to the front of his consciousness, overriding his instincts. Destiny? He cleared his throat.

"My apologies, milady. I do not wish to offend. The Duchess has entrusted me with your safety."

"No offense taken, my lord. Your respect for chivalry is quite apparent." Her lush lips quirked at the edges, her next words enticingly soft and sweet. "I feel completely safe with you, Mathieu."

The warmth that rushed his chest surprised him, and he had to draw in a deep breath to regain composure. Time to go, before the moment drew him farther down a path he was forbidden to trod.

"We should get back. 'Tis almost time for the midday meal. You will be missed."

As they passed through the gatehouse and into the bailey, Mathieu caught sight of the other young girls heading back from the kitchen garden. They carried baskets filled with herbs and early blooms from the spring beds. Laughing and chattering amongst themselves, they hardly took notice of he and Eva's return.

Children. The other young ladies Isabella gathered around her were, truly, yet children. It was, he supposed, why she brought them here—to fill the aching holes left by the two children she'd buried. Only the young Charles had survived, and the child had not yet seen three winters. Isabella also had taken it as her duty to educate and refine as many of the Duke's out-of-wedlock children—particularly the daughters—as possible. Many came to the court with little in the way of refinement.

Eva of Utrecht was different. He wondered what it was that made her so. After all, she had just now passed sixteen winters and was raised by common tailors.

Mathieu's page, Rogier, came running to help Eva dismount. He waited as the boy lifted the lady down, wishing it was his own fingers wrapped around her tiny waist. As his boots hit the ground, he turned to see Eva smiling up at him.

"My greatest thanks, Mathieu, for a very enjoyable ride." She stroked the horse's steaming neck. "And to you as well, Jannis. You are a fine paltry. A wonderful name day excursion. I hope to do this again, very soon."

Mathieu itched to reach for her hand, to place another kiss on her soft skin, to breathe in her scent once more. But not here, not in front of all in the bailey. Holding her gaze, he spoke low, trying to inject as much of his feelings as he could into his words. "I, as well, Eva."

"Well, well! The ostler is now a riding instructor, I see. How quaint."

The booming voice from across the yard caused them both to jump. Mathieu's skin prickled as he recognized it. He spun to face Captain Knape, striding toward them.

"Good morning, milady. You're looking most lovely this morning. Did you have a pleasant jaunt with our stable boy?"

Mathieu struggled to ignore the insult and clenched his fists at his sides. He would not lower himself to confront the Captain. Not here. Not in front of Eva. He was surprised when the maiden took a wobbly step toward Knape, dipping a curtsy and bowing her head shyly.

But then, she lifted her gaze to meet Knape's. "I beg pardon, Sir Knape, but Mathieu is the ostler, not a mere stable boy. He was very kind to take time away from his considerable duties to accompany me."

Knape's sly grin made Mathieu's skin pebble. The Captain moved closer to the girl, swaggering to a stop an arm's length away. "Oh, I'm well aware, milady. But 'tis obvious neither the Duke nor the admiral asked for my opinion when making his selection." His dark eyes shot to Mathieu's, spiking yet another wave of ire in the ostler's chest.

Knape then returned his attention to Eva and his expression softened. "I do hope your morning was enjoyable. May I escort you to the Great Hall? I believe the young ladies are gathering for the noon meal." He offered his arm.

Eva flashed Mathieu a pleading look. "Thank you for taking me riding this morn, my lord. I must admit, it has stirred a great hunger in me." She placed a hand across her middle.

He could do naught but close his eyes and nod his consent.

Mathieu watched as Eva crossed the bailey and disappeared into the hall. He was shaking with temper, and his stomach churned with the sour dregs of resentment. He yearned to punch something. Preferably Knape's sneering face, but he knew this was impossible. He could not retreat to the stable to assault the boarded stalls, as was his wont. 'Twas midday, and the place was alive with activity—pages scurrying about, cleaning, forking hay, and grooming the horses. Mathieu groaned in frustration.

Sighing, he headed toward the aviary. Working with the birds always calmed him. These creatures, although wild and brutally aggressive, knew how to temper their impulses.

From them, Mathieu knew, he had much to learn.

Chapter Eight

E*va*

That evening, Eva was disappointed Mathieu did not join them for the meal in the Great Hall. Isabella was also absent from the meal. Alys told her that Philip was expected any day from his business at Lille, and she assumed all were busy making preparations for the Duke's return.

She and the other girls spent the cool evening hours in the garden. A lively discussion about the upcoming May Day festival buzzed around her, and Eva listened in rapt wonder. She had never attended any kind of social event like this one, only Market Day fairs in Ghent with her maman and stepfather.

There, she'd not been a participant. She merely observed the festivities while she worked. Her job had been to run the tailor booth while her parents made the rounds, promoting their business. There was usually music, but no feasting or dance.

Dance. The very word made her heart still. The word was repeated again and again during the girls' chattering. With horror, Eva realized participating in this activity was an integral part of the celebration.

Eva never learned how to dance. Truly, learning to walk unassisted had been difficult enough.

As darkness fell and the girls began trickling off toward their quarters, Alys sat next to Eva on the turf bench lining the garden. She placed a hand on Eva's shoulder.

"I know you must be overwhelmed with all this talk of the festival. But do not fret. May Day is a wondrous event. There is a spectacular bonfire! And music and feasting and dance—" Alys stopped in mid-sentence, glancing down toward Eva's feet. "You do not dance, I venture."

Eva shook her head. "Nay."

"Do not worry. The bassa is a very slow dance, performed in a group."

Eva's evening meal had congealed into a hard ball in her stomach. Even navigating at a normal pace in a straight line consumed all of her concentration to avoid ending up on the ground. The special slippers the Duchess had fashioned for her helped some, but navigating was still a challenge. The very thought of having to learn new ways of moving her feet—without losing her balance *and* in front of everyone else—made her feel ill.

"I will ask Margriet." She patted Eva's shoulder. "We will teach you on the morrow."

At that moment, a figure appeared near the entrance to the garden. A young man, not much older than she, stood twisting his cap in his hands. Eva did not recognize him at first, but knew she'd seen him before. Alys jumped immediately to her feet, smoothing her skirt.

"I promised Rutger a walk around the garden, Eva. Can you find your way back to our chambers without me?" Alys asked, her eyes alight with excitement. The boy's face shone with a strange light as well.

One glance between Alys and this Rutger spoke volumes. Nodding, she said, "Go on, Alys. I will be fine."

Eva sat for a long time on the turf bench, watching as the light faded from the sky. *So, Alys had a suitor*. Thinking back, Eva remembered where she'd seen the young man before. On their way out of the gatehouse, he'd been assisting in the blacksmith's stall. He looked so different now, all cleaned up, his face no longer blackened with soot.

Sighing, she wondered if she would ever draw the attention of a prospective husband. A *suitable* one, she reminded herself. Eva wasn't sure if she was willing to live the life of a blacksmith's wife. 'Twould be no better, she decided, than spending the rest of her days in a tailor shop, wielding needle and thread. Mayhap worse.

As darkness fell, she rubbed her arms to ward off the chill of not only the cooler air, but of being alone in the garden. Climbing to her feet, she began making her way across the bailey toward the keep.

A small sound caused her to stop and turn. There, in the entrance to the stables, a small bird appeared, hopping along the ground and making a high-pitched, screeching noise. The creature sounded distressed. Instinctively, Eva made her way in that direction.

She was startled when Mathieu appeared from the darkened interior. He did not see her at first. His eyes were fixed upon the small bird, whom he was scolding.

"Now Kleine, you know you cannot venture out into the open. You will quickly become a meal for another. Come." He crouched to scoop the tiny bird up in one hand, perching it on his shoulder. "Your quarry is aplenty right here, within these walls."

"Mathieu?"

Startled, the ostler looked up and saw Eva approaching. He seemed not only surprised but perhaps a little embarrassed. One hand went up to steady the bird on his shoulder.

"Eva. Good evening, milady. Have you lost your way to the keep?"

"I have not, but I heard the squeals of the bird."

He smiled and inclined his head, still stroking the animal with his fingers. "Oh, 'tis only Kleine Uil. He's just awoken from a fine days' rest, and brave. I must convince him daily he is unfit to hunt in the fields and forest like his brethren."

Eva tipped her head and stepped closer. "He is ill?"

"Nay. But he suffers an affliction," Mathieu faltered, his gaze flashing to Eva's feet. "His injured wing hinders normal flight. That and his small stature limit him." He paused to cradle the owl in both hands. "He wouldn't last an hour if I did not keep him in the stable."

Unfazed by the awkward moment, Eva reached a tentative finger toward the bird. "What happened to him? May I touch him?"

"Aye. Kleine is quite friendly. He gets lonely, I think, living in the stable without others of his kind."

Ah, Eva thought, I know this feeling. I have been an outcast, an oversight, for most of my life. My mother is ashamed of me for who I am, and my stepfather for... well, everything. Trying to shut out the painful memories, she concentrated on the ostler's tale.

Mathieu went on to explain how he'd found the tiny raptor, and how the Duchess allowed him to take him in. Kleine, in the meantime, closed his huge, round eyes and leaned in as Eva gently stroked his feathers.

"He will never fly?" she asked.

Mathieu shook his head. "The wing did not mend properly. He can make his way to the rafters of the barn to dodge a flailing hoof, but barely. His kind often pursue quarry by hopping about on the ground, though, which he does quite well." He smiled down at the bird. "Kleine Uil earns his keep by keeping our stable free from mice."

Eva's heart squeezed at the affection she heard in Mathieu's voice. He was obviously quite fond of the tiny creature. She met his gaze.

"He has an incapacity not unlike my own. And yet you care for him anyway."

Mathieu shrugged. "As I told you before, I enjoy my time with the animals more than with people, sometimes."

She gazed at him, and her heart softened at his words. He was a gentle man, this ostler. Yet he handled, even trained, huge horses and wild raptors. A conundrum, yet a truly endearing one.

"I so enjoyed our ride today. Mayhap we can repeat the outing soon?" She was standing so close to him, his scent surrounded her. Leather, and soap, and a masculine, musky scent she found quite appealing.

"Of course, milady. But probably not until after the festival. It's coming up quickly. I have much to prepare." He sounded genuinely regretful, and it touched her. But mention of the feast caused her fear to rear its ugly head.

"I know. I am excited, but nervous as well. I hear there is dancing."

The booming of a deep voice from across the bailey caused them both to jump.

"Yes, Eva of Utrecht! Dancing is a huge part of the May Day celebration. I should be most honored to teach you the bassadance."

Captain Knape had snuck up on them again, and Eva flinched. It almost seemed as though he stalked her when she was out in the bailey. She had decided she did not like this man, one who she felt looked at her much as he did the finest meats on the banquet table. She knew her place, however, and that she must respect him.

After all, he was a knight, and not just any knight. He was Captain of the Duke's Royal Guard.

She dipped a curtsy and replied, "Thank you, Captain. But Alys has already arranged for Margriet to teach me."

He grunted, his mouth twisting in annoyance. He turned his attention to Mathieu, shooting a venomous glance at the owl on his shoulder. "I see you still have your damaged plaything. You should really let the poor creature wander the bailey, my boy. My men would love to use him for target practice."

Eva bristled, a hand flying to her mouth. "You will do no such thing! You cannot be so cruel, Captain Knape."

Immediately, Eva knew she'd spoken above her station. The narrowing of Knape's eyes spoke volumes of his disapproval. He glared at her.

"Cruel, perhaps. But that what it takes to sustain a knight in battle. Bravery, courage, and yes, cruelty—these qualities keep a warrior alive on the field," he spat. "Some men do not possess these qualities." He spoke through clenched teeth, his eyes trained on Mathieu the entire time.

Eva knew she should hold her tongue. But 'twas not in her character, mayhap one of the traits she knew was to her failing. Bristling, she straightened to her full height and said, "So, using a defenseless, damaged creature as target practice teaches your men to succeed on the battlefield? I think not, Captain Knape. What of the other virtues of knighthood? Charity, prudence, and valor? What is so valiant about killing a tiny, defenseless owl?"

Anger flared in Knape's eyes, and Eva took a step backward. It wasn't the first time her errant tongue had landed her in trouble. She dropped her gaze to the ground. Immediately, she sputtered, "Begging your pardon, my lord. My opinions have no place here." She glanced at Mathieu, who glared at the Captain with an emotion she found almost frightening. *Hatred.*

Yet he was as helpless as she against the Captain of the Royal Guard.

"Darkness falls, milady," Mathieu said, his voice low. "Allow me to escort you to the castle."

Knape stepped between them, so close, a cloud of yeasty ale enveloped her senses. The man had obviously imbibed his share this evening. "That won't be necessary, stable boy. I will escort the lady to safety."

She knew she was trapped, and she cast Mathieu a desperate look as they made their way across the bailey. Anger, frustration, and disgust filled her. Yet she was not one to be intimidated easily. Lifting her chin, she asked, "Captain

Knape, is not Mathieu of Liège destined for knighthood? Why do you insult him so?"

Knape's dark chuckle echoed in the gloaming. "I've known Mathieu since he was a boy. His mother petitioned for his position as a page for this court, long ago. Fortune shone upon him when the good Admiral La Laing took him on and made him a squire. But that does not mean he has what it takes to earn his spurs and sword." He reached up to tug on his beard. "The boy's heart is too soft, milady. He wouldn't last an hour on the battlefield."

The thought of Mathieu falling prey to an arrow or mace made Eva shudder. She'd always dreamed of falling in love with a knight, since legend told they were the most noble of men. However, knights often went off to battle, never to return. Being a knight's wife would mean a life filled with fear and uncertainty, would it not?

Then there was the question of chivalry. Was it all a lie? A fanciful tapestry of romance woven to deceive the ladies?

Yet if Captain Knape represented the epitome of knights, his brand of chivalry didn't fit Eva's perception.

On one point, she had to agree—she could not imagine Mathieu maddened with the kind of wrath it took to run another man through with a sword. He cared for the horses and the falcons with such tenderness and had shown such kindness to her.

He had admitted as much to her already. The life of a knight was not for him.

Eva sighed. Mathieu was a good friend—her first here at Coudenburg castle. She thought back to the moment in the forest where she'd almost allowed him to kiss her. In that moment, the wild imagining had stirred within her that perhaps Mathieu was her "knight," the one of whom she'd dreamed.

In this moment, she realized it could not be true. Although she hated to admit it, Knape was right. From what she had seen of the ostler's ways, Eva feared Mathieu was too tender-hearted to ever rise to the rigors demanded of a knight. How could one truly fall in love with a man of such little strength?

"So, tell me. Tell me it all! I want to know what I can look forward to when the festival begins day after the morrow."

Eva sat cross-legged on her pallet across from Alys, who was busily weaving a circlet of ivy with lengths of colorful ribbon. Around her feet, the younger sisters were playing with the mound of streamers. Alys had charged them with untangling them. Instead, they were making a game out of snarling them further. Eva smiled as she tousled the auburn curls of one of the younger girls.

How she missed her siblings. Heaving a wistful sigh, she continued her questioning. "Aside from the dancing, I mean," Eva added quietly. "Is that circlet for you? Will you show me how to make one for myself?"

Excitement bubbled through her like water from the spring. The holiday had been celebrated in her hometown of Ghent, but Eva had never been permitted to take part but only observe from the tailor booth on the sidelines.

Alys smiled up at her. "One question at a time!" Her tongue peeked out of her mouth in the corner as she concentrated on twisting the ends of the vine securely with the ribbons. "It starts on the morrow, after sunset," she began, glancing up at Eva. A look of enchanted wonder sparkled in her eyes. "First, at dusk, all the fires in the castle, even in the kitchen, will be extinguished."

"Why?" Eva asked.

"So the sacred bonfire can be lit, outside of the curtain wall. 'Tis purifying, the fire, and represents the power of the sun we hope to yield us a bountiful growing season. The bright flames ward off evil that may curse our people and livestock."

Eva eyes widened. "And then what happens?"

Alys plopped the circlet down in her lap. "Well, there will be food and drink. Servants bring baked treats and sloe wine from the castle kitchen, enough for all, even the villagers. The manservants gather the bones from the evening meal and toss them onto the fire as well. It makes the smoke smell bad," Alys pulled a face and pinched her nostrils closed, "but the foul smoke is supposed to better ward off evil spirits."

Eva tipped her head. "I thought the Duke and Duchess were Christian. This ritual sounds pagan."

Alys bobbed her head. "They are Christian—we all are. But the festival is a tradition dating many winters, to our pagan roots. 'Tis called Beltane."

"Are we allowed to stay up for the bonfire? After dark, outside the castle walls?"

"We are, for a time. 'Tis a very special night. A night for romance, they say." Alys winked at her. "Most of the girls are too young, but for me, and you now too, the night could be one when we find our true love."

Eva's mouth gaped. "True love? I thought the knights vied for their ladies' honor at the jousting? Is there not jousting?"

Alys laughed, shaking her head. "You have heard too many fanciful tales, Eva. There will be jousting, the afternoon that follows. But 'tis not a real joust. 'Tis all in fun. There's no bloodshed. At least, not on purpose."

Eva stared at her fingers, twisting in embarrassment. "I have been kept very sheltered, 'tis true. This will be my first time to participate in the May Day Festival."

Alys leapt off her pallet and crouched before her, leaning in close. "This is my third. Lady Isabella may allow me, this year, to go into the woods with the others in search of the hawthorn." She paused, glancing about to be sure they were alone. "Methinks this may be the year when Rutger asks the Duke for my hand."

"Rutger? The blacksmith's apprentice?"

Alys' eyes shone as she bobbed her head. "Aye. He asked me to wed at Christmastime, but he wanted to save more coin first. So we can live outside the castle walls. He's been working on a small cottage, near to the blacksmith family's abode." She squeezed Eva's hands. "Rutger says now he has enough coin to finish the roof before winter comes."

Eva's head reeled with this new information. Was Alys truly in love? She wondered what that felt like.

"So, you think Rutger is your true love, then?"

Alys' smile shone like the morning sun. "I don't *think* he is. On all that is holy, I'm for certain Rutger is my one and only." Alys grabbed the beribboned circlet from her pallet and twirled in place before holding it out to Eva. "I made this for you, Eva of Utrecht. Mayhap, if you crown your lovely hair on the morrow's eve, and on May Day too, you will find your true love as well."

Eva wondered if she would ever find her true love. How would she know when it happened? She knew what she wanted in a future husband. At least, she *thought* she knew. It certainly wasn't Stefano, the clothier.

Could it be Mathieu? It was true, he made her heart flutter when he was near. His touch caused her skin to burn and her mind to scramble. Is that what love was?

Eva sighed. Reality crashed down around her. She was a commoner, a bastard daughter, and one with a crooked foot. True, she was talented in her craft and could learn to be patient. But would the right man ever come into her life and warm her heart the way Rutger did for Alys?

As she ran her fingers over the ruffled ivy and colorful ribbons in her hands, Eva wished with all her being for the husband of her dreams. Here in Coudenburg, during the May Day Festival, was her very best chance of finding such a man. Surely more likely than sequestered in the back of the tailor shop in Ghent. She must find a way to participate in the festivities.

To dance.

Mayhap this girl Alys spoke of, this Margriet, the kitchen maid, could help her find a way.

Chapter Nine

Mathieu All the next day, servants from the castle as well as people from the village trekked across the meadows surrounding the outer walls, carrying wood for the bonfire. Mathieu had excused a few of his own pages, as well as those of the Duke, to help with the task. A great deal of excitement buzzed in the air, and Mathieu heard more laughter carrying across the keep than he had for a very long time.

For him, it was business as usual. The horses needed tending and grooming, the equipment cleaning and oiling. The hounds should be fed a light meal, keeping them keen for the hunt. For festivals past, both the Duke and Duchess had requested a hunting expedition early on the morning of the holiday, since much fresh game was needed for a bountiful feast.

He pondered the fact that the Duke had not yet arrived from his business in Lille. 'Twas not surprising for Philip, who did everything at his own pace and pleasure.

But finally, the Duke arrived. When he did, the noon sun shone directly overhead, and he was accompanied by a dozen of his most trusted knights. A trumpet heralded his arrival, echoing outside the gatehouse. Mathieu couldn't resist the temptation of rolling his eyes. The Duke did like his pomp and pageantry and always announced his arrival with the blare of the trumpet.

He liked Philip well enough but could not hold a great amount of respect for the man's personal values. How could one admire a noble who kept a mistress in every town, and who spawned children out of wedlock more often than he sneezed? Besides, Mathieu had come to be very fond of Isabella and had a great deal of respect for her. It saddened him to see how Philip took the gracious woman for granted.

They came through the portcullis, dressed in Burgundy's traditional colors, with flags of red, yellow, and blue waving in the breeze. Mathieu heard the tittering of young voices and saw the group of young ladies—Philip's *other* daughters gathered here by Isabella—peeking out from the garden gate. His mouth thinned in disdain.

It wasn't the Duke at whom they gawked. It was the twelve knights surrounding him, all huge men decked out in chain mail, some wearing helmets that glittered in the sun. Their spirited chargers pranced in place with excitement, stirring up a veritable dust cloud in the bailey.

Ladies loved the knights. In reality, Mathieu knew 'twas the fantasy of knighthood they swooned over. He was painfully aware that most of these men couldn't even name the twelve virtues of knighthood, let alone conduct their lives in alignment with them.

Mathieu knew too much about Duke Philip's knights. He'd seen firsthand how the brawny men entertained themselves. His stomach roiled with the memory.

Pages came running for the rest of the party's mounts, but Mathieu himself approached the Duke, dropping to one knee at the head of Philip's enormous grey stallion.

"Your Grace. I am glad you have arrived safely." Rising to his feet, Mathieu took the horse's reins as the Duke dismounted. "Shall I send word to Lady Isabella of your arrival?"

Philip was a tall man, with angular, sharp features and broad shoulders. He cut an impressive figure, dressed in black from head to toe. His eyes were dark and keen as well, reminding Mathieu much of those on his falcons. Philip turned those eyes now on his ostler.

"Mathieu. Good to see you, my boy. Are the preparations for the feast well underway?"

Mathieu stiffened even as he nodded promptly. "Yes, my lord. All is near complete."

My boy. Mathieu resented at how the Duke addressed him. But in truth, Philip had been addressing him this way since he became Simon La Laing's squire—over ten years ago.

Although he'd been a boy then, he was no longer. 'Twas no wonder the Captain of his guard, the pompous Captain Knape, looked down upon him so.

"Good, good. Yes, please send word to Lady Isabella that I've arrived and would like to speak with her in my solar."

Duke Philip

Philip entered his solar to find Isabella seated at the desk beside the castle's steward, a ledger and leaves of parchment spread out before them. The lady was keeping checks and balances on the duchy's wealth. Warmth filled Philip's chest as he considered his Portuguese bride. He'd done well in choosing this fine, intelligent woman. Hardly a pretty plaything, Isabella was so much more. She was not only adept at political relations but was also well-schooled in the numbers.

"My lady grace," he began, crossing the tiled floor with long strides, "so good to see you."

Isabella rose immediately and curtsied before him with a bowed head. "Philip. Welcome home."

He kissed her hand and then barked at her assistant. "Leave us, Guarin."

"Have the kitchen maids bring us refreshments, please," Isabella called after the steward as he left.

As soon as the door latched shut, Isabella motioned toward the chairs flanking the windows. "Please sit, my lord. How were your dealings at Lille?"

Philip relaxed into the velvet upholstery and heaved a sigh, his mouth grim. "We have opened discussions about an alliance with Charles of France regarding Calais. 'Tis not proceeding as smoothly as I had hoped."

"I'm sorry to hear that. Do we remain peaceful allies?" she asked, a thin eyebrow lifting.

"For the time being. Yes, for the time being," Philip avoided her gaze, not wishing to discuss this subject any further. Not now. Not on the eve of the festival. He shifted in his seat. "Our ostler tells me all is about ready for May Day. I look forward to this celebration of spring."

"Mathieu has been exceedingly helpful, my lord. He even went all the way to Ghent to retrieve Eva."

Philip blinked, momentarily confused. Who was this Eva she spoke of?

She tilted her head, her eyes boring into his. "Eva of Utrecht. You do remember Marisse, I trust?"

"Ah, yes." Philip sobered. "Of course. So, the girl has arrived?" He cleared his throat. "Is she comely?"

Isabella sat back in her chair, and Philip noticed her knuckles whiten with her grip on the chair's arms. "Very. Not unlike her mother, I would wager."

Philip's gaze strayed to the window, where he had a clear view of the stables and blacksmith stall. " 'Twas a very long time ago, Isabella. Before I knew the wonder of you." He pinned her with a smile he hoped looked sincere.

"Aye, at least sixteen winters past. Her name day was yesterday. Will you assist me in locating a suitable husband for her? I would hate to see yet another of your daughters end up in a peasant's hovel."

Ignoring the jab, Philip watched Wallis through the tall window, checking the shoes on his destrier. His assistant struggled to steady the monstrous stallion. "I'm assuming Rutger is still intent on wedding Alys?"

Isabella closed her eyes and nodded. "He intends to ask for her hand in the coming days, I am told." She exhaled the slightest of sighs.

"This does not please you, my lady?"

"He is not a noble, sorry to say." Isabella folded her hands in her lap. "But Rutger is a fine young man. He will soon earn his own blacksmith stall, mayhap here at Coudenburg, since Wallis intends to return to Germolles with me in the fall. And Alys loves the boy." She paused, riveting him through hawk-like eyes. "I suppose a union for love trumps one for title."

Her voice was soft and distant, almost as though she spoke to herself more than to Philip. Again, he chose not to rise to her challenge, regarding her in silence. 'Twas easier to deal with an intelligent woman this way. No wonder Philip yearned to spend time with the simpler, peasant wenches. They asked no questions, falling instead in awe at his feet.

Philip liked it much better this way.

She straightened then and lifted her chin. "Yes. I approve of the marriage. I'm quite certain Rutger will be approaching you to ask for her hand before your stay here ends."

A long pause fell between them before Philip asked the question he loathed to raise. "How many new daughters will I meet *this* May Day?" He swallowed, his mouth suddenly dry.

"Only two you've not met before. Beverielle, and of course, Eva. She is the only one old enough to plan a future for, though. Alys will soon be spoken for. With Beverielle, we have a little time."

We. Part of Philip softened to know his wife had taken on this task—of securing stable futures for his bastard daughters. Another part of him wondered why this was so.

But deep down, Philip knew the reason. Isabella was a virtuous woman, with strong Christian morals and a sound sense of justice. She had vowed, from first she'd discovered the considerable extent of his wanderings, to ensure a Burgundian-worthy match for each of his daughters, even if they had been born out of wedlock.

The fate of the boys, she'd left to him, which he minded not at all. They were easy to place, in positions at court, in monasteries, or in strategically selected marriages. The males of the Burgundy line were more easily controlled. With the daughters, Philip cared not even to try. He wasn't sure if he admired Isabella for her intentions or thought her quite mad.

Isabella leaned toward him. "I would like to seek a match for Eva of Utrecht this very summer. She is young, but wise and quite headstrong. It is unfortunate she possesses an infirmity."

"Yes, I remember hearing of it. Is it disfiguring?" Philip scowled. "This must have come from her mother's line. The Burgundians have no such afflictions."

Isabella's mouth flattened. "It is not disfiguring. Under her gowns, it is quite invisible. She walks with only a slight limp."

Philip snorted. "A husband will surely see what's hidden beneath her skirts."

A knock on the door interrupted the rapidly rising tension in the room. Two servants entered carrying trays bearing small cakes, a pitcher of wine, and two goblets. Relief flooded Philip. He stood.

"Come, let us celebrate the arrival of spring." He poured the wine and handed one goblet to his wife, raising his own. "To May Day."

She touched her goblet to his and repeated the toast. "To May Day."

After taking a sip, she continued, her tone flat but surprisingly ominous. "And to finding a suitable match for your newly discovered daughter, Eva of Utrecht." She paused, a terse silence falling between them.

When she continued, her tone had soured, as with vinegar. "Oh, and of our son? Charles? So good of you to ask after him. He is quite well, the energetic young lad. I will ask Jehanne, our nurse, to bring him to your solar after the noon meal."

Chapter Ten

E *va* May Day's Eve dawned cloudy and cool, the threat of rain evident in the deep-hued clouds on the horizon. The air in the girls' chamber felt clammy, as though the rain was hiding in plain sight. As Eva peered out through the window, she frowned.

"How can we have a bonfire if rains come?" she asked aloud, to no one in particular.

" 'Twill not rain," her younger sister, Jutte, joined Eva at the window. "The spirits of spring shan't allow it!" Jutte stamped her slippered foot.

Alys rose from her pallet and joined them, looping an arm around Jutte's narrow shoulders. Hailing from Brussels, Jutte of Brabant was only a winter or so younger than Eva. Yet Jutte seemed so much more a child.

"Rain is not a bad thing, Jutte. We need rain for the flowers, and to yield a good crop at harvest." Alys smoothed a hand down the younger girl's shiny, dark hair. "Do not worry. If the rains smother the bonfire, we shall have a giant blaze in the hearths of the Great Hall."

Alys turned to Eva. "Margriet said to meet her in the kitchen garden after breaking our fast. No one will see us there at such an early hour. We will teach you the bassadance."

Eva nodded but cringed inside. Walking was enough of a challenge. She couldn't imagine how she might maintain her balance to learn dance steps.

The rains did not come, but the dancing lessons did not go well. For one, the grassy footing was soft and did not offer Eva the support she needed to hold her ankle steady. She also felt odd clasping hands with the girl she'd just met. Margriet was a maid who'd been toiling since before dawn in the kitchens. She wore her apron still, covered with flour and spotted with stains. Her hands were reddened and rough, evidence of her endless duties as a kitchen servant.

Yet the girl's face was alight with joy. She was, Eva guessed, only a few winters older than herself. Already, she soon learned, Margriet had married Alain, one of the gatekeeper guards.

"When did you marry?" Eva asked her when they had taken a break to rest on the turf benches.

"Only just last fall." Margriet grinned sheepishly as she laid a hand across her middle. "Already I carry Alain's child."

Eva blinked, embarrassed but curious all the same. "Do you both live here at Coudenburg?"

"Aye. Alain has been gatehouse guard here at the castle for many winters. We have our own quarters off the back of the kitchen. We are fortunate, indeed."

Another young girl, bastard daughter of the Duke, already betrothed, and happily. Eva wasn't sure if this knowledge gave her hope or made her feel all the more an outsider. She carried noble blood in her veins as well. Yet settling for a hovel on the back of the kitchen in which to live... Eva was perplexed at how Margriet could radiate such happiness.

Trying to learn the dance steps was brutal for Eva. Her lack of balance made her so unsteady on her feet, and the attempts to move quickly in following Margriet's lead made her dizzy. It wasn't long at all when her twisted ankle failed her, and she landed in the grass with a thump. Heat rushed her cheeks. All the noble blood in the world hadn't kept her from being born flawed. *A creple.*

Margriet and Alys both rushed to help Eva to her feet. "We are so sorry, milady. Are you well?"

Their images swam as Eva's eyes filled, and she could not answer for the binding in her throat. Nodding, she limped off toward the turfed bench.

" 'Tis no use," she moaned. "I shall not be able to dance on the morrow. I shall content myself with watching you both dance with your true loves."

Margriet tipped her head and studied her sadly. "You are very beautiful, Eva of Utrecht. Surely, you must know that dancing is not the only reason a lady catches her husband's eye." She squeezed Eva's shoulder. "I must return to my duties," she murmured before turning away to toward the kitchens.

Although the morning remained cloaked in a misty fog, rains did not come. By noontime the skies cleared, and bright sunlight warmed the air to steaming. After her failed dance lesson, Eva sought out the Duchess Isabella in her solar. It made her feel better, it seemed, to be in the company of such a grand woman.

"Your stitches are the finest of any I've seen," Isabella exclaimed, examining a kirtle she had asked Eva to repair. "Your maman taught you the craft well."

Eva sighed. "Aye, I can craft with cloth. But 'tis a trade, not a noblewoman's pastime."

Isabella dropped her embroidery in her lap and shot Eva a stern look. "And what do you consider a 'noble woman's pastime?' I am a Duchess, and I love to sew, though my stitches cannot compare to yours."

Shrinking at Isabella's scolding tone, Eva peered up through her lashes. "But you are a Duchess. You have no need to impress anyone with your worth. Your maids and servants craft and mend your wardrobe. Your noble blood speaks for itself."

"I beg your pardon, young lady, but you seem to have a warped perception of what it means to be a noble woman. Or man, for that matter," Isabella huffed. "There are many women *and* men of high status whose values fall far below those considered noble."

Tears blurred Eva's vision, and for a long moment she could not speak. When she finally raised her gaze to Isabella, she realized the woman was still glaring at her in a most disapproving way. Her heart seized.

The very last thing in the world she wanted was to displease this wonderful, caring woman who had allowed her presence here at the castle.

"My sincerest apologies, Your Grace. I did not mean to sound—"

"Haughty? For that is how you sound, Eva. At times you act as though you deserve better than everyone else. What makes you this way? Is your maman conceited as well?"

The words hit Eva's heart like arrows. She began twisting her fingers in her lap, her stomach churning. "Nay, Your Grace. Maman is very humble, indeed." She paused. "But... she is not of noble blood."

The Duchess tipped up her chin and studied Eva through narrowed eyes. "Ah, I see. But you are. You seem excessively aware of the fact. Forget not, young lady, that you may be the Duke's daughter, but a *bastard* one. If not for me, you would not be here at all. Philip probably would not even recognize you as his own."

Eva's eyes rounded as she stared at the Duchess. " 'Twas not the Duke himself who summoned me here?" she asked, her voice small. "The missive was signed—"

Isabella laughed. It was not a happy sound, but one laced with bitterness. "Never. He wrote the letter, with me standing over him right here in my solar, but 'twas me who found you. I was the one to invite you here, Eva of Utrecht. But certainly not to puff up your person with pride."

A hot tear snaked its way down Eva's cheek. "Then... why did you send for me?"

Isabella's shoulders rose and fell on a sigh. Her face relaxed, and she gazed at Eva with softer eyes. "I brought you here because, as the Duke's wife, I feel it is my duty to ensure a stable future for all of his children." She rolled her eyes then. "All of his *many* children."

"A stable future... does that mean marriage to a nobleman?"

Isabella crossed her arms and studied her. "What is it that you want for your future, Eva? Do you want to wed a man for his title? Or because you care for him, in your heart?"

Confusion clouded Eva's mind. She didn't think it was possible to separate the two. "How can one whose blood is noble love a man who is not of her rank?"

"Hmm," Isabella began, her eyebrow rising, "I see you are less mature—and less wise—than I thought. I fear you had been sheltered to excess. Do your parents—your maman and stepfather—do they not know love?"

Eva pondered this a moment. Did love describe what existed between Marisse and Andries?

"I do not think of what my maman and stepfather share as true love. They are partners, in business and in life. But there seems to be no... tenderness. No romance, no... passion." Realizing her audacity, Eva felt her cheeks warm and covered her mouth with her hand. "My apologies, Your Grace. It is just I have a different vision in my head about love."

"A fanciful tale, I am sure. The one touted by the minstrels and bards." The Duchess sighed. "It exists, I am certain. But not all are lucky enough to find that elusive dream."

Isabella's gaze strayed to the window, and a faraway look glazed her eyes. "A lady needs to decide what is more important to her—her status, or her heart. And bear in mind, in choosing either, you may not succeed." She pinned Eva's gaze. "I waited for love, but my father chose my fate—marrying for political connections and status. I had already seen over thirty winters, and love had not found me yet. Mayhap it never would."

Eva stared at her in disbelief. "So 'twas not your choice to marry Philip? Was it not a supreme honor to wed the Duke of Burgundy? The *Grand Duke of the West?*"

She knew her question was rude and assuming, but she had to know. She'd already drawn the Duchess' ire. How much worse could it get?

Isabella just sighed again and motioned Eva to come to her. Kneeling at her feet, Eva found both her hands enclosed warmly within jewel-encrusted fingers.

"Eva, my position is grand and well-respected. My husband treats me well and is good to the many people in his realm. Is that not why they call him Philip the Good?"

The Duchess smoothed a hand down Eva's hair. She was surprised to see a sheen of tears in Isabella's eyes. "I cannot deny—my life is filled with prosperity and comfort, lavish dwellings and wardrobes. Many servants and fine feasts. Yet still, there is loneliness in my heart. I think only love could fill that empty place."

So the Duchess knows not of love? Surely, a woman of her nobility has all that life offers. Except...

"Surely, your child brings love to your heart," Eva said, then faltered. "I know you have lost two children," she murmured. "My heart grieves for you. But you do have a handsome son."

"I thank God every night for Charles. But my only daughters, Eva, are like you. Sisters from other mothers. Flanders' flowers, those whom I have chosen to gather and nurture. To teach."

To teach. The thought had never entered Eva's mind.

"What should I seek to learn from you, Lady Isabella?"

"You should learn the value of love, over everything else." She cupped Eva's cheek in her hand. "Even if you do, you may not find what you seek. Like me, you may have to settle for a life the fates have in store for you. Heed this—do not be in any hurry to bind yourself to a man for status' sake."

Eva thought of Margriet, a lowly kitchen maid married to Alain, a gatekeeper guard. Yet the joy in her expression spoke volumes of the love in her heart. The notion puzzled Eva.

The Duchess continued. "The fates may be kind. Look at Alys. She is, like you, of noble blood. Yet she has been blessed beyond measure to find true love with Rutger, a blacksmith's apprentice." She sighed and closed her eyes. "For finding that kind of true love, I admit, I envy her."

The Duchess' tears spilled over now, even as she smiled sadly. Pulling a lace-edged cloth from the sleeve of her kirtle, she dabbed at her eyes.

"Remember ye this. Status and wealth and power are like strong wine. They are heady and sweet and can blind you to reality. There is one place in your heart, however, they can never fill. Only true love can make you whole."

Chapter Eleven

E*va*
The air in the castle fairly crackled with excitement, the noise in the Great Hall thunderous. The evening meal had been laid, the fare lighter than usual because there would be more feasting around the bonfire. All of this mattered not to Eva. Eating was the last thing on her mind. She'd ridden a crazy wave of emotions today, starting with her embarrassment in the garden, followed by her intense discussion with the Duchess. Her mind buzzed with confused emotions, even as nervous anticipation churned her belly. She wasn't sure if she was looking forward to the next days' events or dreading them.

She also wasn't sure if she believed what Lady Isabella said about true love. Alys may have been happy with Rutger, and Margriet with the gatehouse guard. But somehow, their unions did not exemplify Eva's notion of what true love, life-altering romance was. Surely, if one was patient, it was possible to find true love with a man who literally swept her off her feet with bravery, strength, and chivalry. Was it not?

Was it so wrong to dream for the ultimate in a lifelong partner?

It made Eva wonder if, mayhap, she had some soul-searching to do. Was she seeking an impossible dream? Truly, it would be wondrous to marry a brave and noble knight. But at what cost? And would love come as part of the package?

Then, there was the uncertainty. Knights went off to battle. Some never came home.

Ah, but what dark thoughts. Nay, she must not consider these complications.

Darkness had just begun to fall over the castle when the call rang out for all fires to be extinguished. Servants had ceased stoking the hearths hours before the evening meal, so all had burnt down to mere glowing embers. Eva followed the other girls around the walls of their quarters, snuffing out the candles and torches. Finally, the only light remaining was a fat, tallow candle Alys carried to lead the girls down the halls to the front door of the castle, then through the courtyard. The great doors of the keep's curtain wall were flung wide, and in the distance, Eva saw what looked like a small mountain in the open field ahead.

The night was clear but cool, and Eva wished she had taken Alys' advice to carry a cloak. She now stood with pebbled arms around the "mountain," what was actually a great tower of wood, huddling in close to her sisters to stay warm. Soon men carrying flaming torches set fire to the smaller kindling at the base of the pyre. Within minutes, the dry branches caught, and bright flames licked up the sides toward the sky. When they reached the top, a great cheer went up around her. Warmth filled Eva from the inside out.

The May Day festivities had begun.

Servants flowed out of the bailey bearing trays filled with delightful pastries and tiny meat pies. The bigger men wheeled barrels out on a cart, and long lines formed almost immediately. The villagers brought their own cups made of metal, wood, or clay, and waited patiently for their share of the mead or ale.

Eva glanced around her, wondering if she and the other girls would be offered some of the drink. To her delight, Alys appeared holding two pewter goblets.

"Merry May Day!" she said as she tapped her cup to Eva's.

The mead was sweet but strong, and after only a few sips Eva felt woozy. The footing in the field was uneven and soft, so she was afraid to venture far from the spot where she and her sisters stood. Her balance was compromised even when drink was not to blame.

Rutger appeared shortly after the blaze began. He guided Alys away from the crowd, his arm looped possessively around her waist. When the rest of the girls all scattered, laughing and chattering with other young people from the village, Eva was sorely tempted to flop down in the grass and content herself by simply watching.

Just before she sank to the ground, she felt fingers grip her elbow. Turning, she looked up to see Mathieu.

"Good evening, milady. Are you enjoying our bonfire?"

Eva's breath caught as she studied the tall man beside her. Firelight danced over his chiseled features, reminding Eva once again of how handsome the ostler was. His oaken hair shone in waves over broad shoulders clothed in a crisp, ivory tunic. The leather lacings at his neck were undone, allowing her a peek at peat-brown curls on his chest.

A sudden flutter in her belly made Eva even more unsteady on her feet. She swayed, and Mathieu gripped her arm tighter.

"The footing, or the drink?" he asked, his eyes gleaming. He shot her a broad grin. "No matter. We'll find a grassy spot and settle down to enjoy the show."

He led her far enough away from the crowd so they wouldn't get stepped on, then lowered to the grass, pulling her down beside him. A shudder ran through her. Was it the night air, or being so close to this alluring man, one who smelled clean and spicy?

He felt her shiver and asked, "Shall I fetch you a cloak, Eva?"

She shook her head and snuggled in closer to his side. The warmth of his body through the linen was much more enticing than a rough woolen cloak.

Mathieu peered into her cup and noticed it was empty. "More drink?"

Eva knew she shouldn't. Her dinner had been scant, and the sweet drink was going straight to her head. Before she could answer, he offered her his own goblet.

"Here. Drink, and 'twill warm you from the inside out."

Aye, she thought, that might be true. But mead wasn't the only thing making Eva's cheeks feel warm even as the air around her grew colder.

He's the ostler, she reminded herself, though that persistent voice in her head was growing smaller, weaker.

After the platters of treats were empty, a group of minstrels gathered and filled the air with melody. A dulcimer and flute sent tremulous notes to waft around Eva, bringing with them the magical joy music always did. She smiled and laid her head on Mathieu's shoulder.

Eva laughed as she watched villagers herding their goats and cattle up the hill to pass through the fire's smoke.

"Why do they bring livestock to the bonfire?" she asked.

"To bless them. These people strongly hold to the old customs and beliefs. The smoke from the bonfire is supposed to purify and protect all from evil. Even the animals."

A twitter ran through the crowd when Philip and Isabella appeared, arms linked. They looked the part of royalty, Philip in a bright blue tunic and braies, and Isabella in a flowing kirtle of the same shade. From her double-horned hennin fluttered sheer silk that looked to be made from spun gold. Following them was Admiral La Laing in his usual red cloak with a pearl-studded roundlet on his head. At his side, decked out all in black and topped with chain mail, strode Captain Knape.

Eva dipped her chin shyly when Knape spotted her and flashed her a devilish smile. The Captain may be puffed up with his own importance, she thought, but it was hard to deny what an impressive figure he cut.

The procession made their way through the throng, stopping often to make small talk with the castle folk and villagers. Eva watched them, her mouth agape. She had assumed the nobles would simply watch the festivities from a high window in the keep. Yet here they were, wandering about the field with the rest of the crowd.

They are real people, Eva realized with a jolt. They weren't too proud to mingle among the commoners. Her childish belief in nobles as some kind of godlike beings flickered.

She'd almost forgotten Mathieu was at her side until he shifted, his beard-scruffed cheek brushing against hers. A bolt of heat shot through her. She turned toward him and leaned in until their faces were mere inches apart. His breath was hot and smelled spicy, like the wine.

His gaze skittered over her face, his eyes soft. "I cannot stay late. There's a hunt on the morn," he began. "Philip and Isabella always like to go out on May Day to fatten the table for the feast. So, I won't be joining the others in their search for the hawthorn..."

The hawthorn. Eva remembered Alys mentioning this but knew not what she was talking about. "The hawthorn," she repeated. "Aye... the white flowers we saw on our ride. What significance has this?"

Mathieu's gaze swept her up and down, a slow smile spreading across his face. "My apologies. I forgot. This is your first May Day."

Eva bristled. "And so what of it? I may have been sheltered, but I'm not an ignorant fool. Tell me of this hawthorn and why the young people gather it."

Mathieu's eyes sparkled as he laughed out loud. "Nay, you are no fool, milady. And neither meek nor shy." He paused to drain the last of his wine. "So. The hawthorn has white bark, and white flowers, and blooms right in time for May Day. The wood also burns white-hot—you'll see, if you're still here, when some of the folk throw their branches onto the bonfire." He sobered, searching her eyes. His voice lowered to a sultry growl. "They say the flowering bush represents purity, aye, but also the heat of desire and love."

Eva's eyes widened. "Oh," she said, momentarily at a loss for words.

His breath smelled like honey from the mead, and Eva's eyes drifted over his face, tracing down the pale scar from his eyes to his full lips. They looked so soft, so warm. When he spoke, his deep voice rumbled through her chest.

" 'Tis May Day Eve, milady. May I steal a kiss?"

Her eyes fluttered upward until their gazes locked, and she nodded. In the next moment, Eva's whole body went still, even as a flame erupted within her brighter than the bonfire.

They *were* soft, those lips, edged with the roughness of his beard. The combination was tantalizing. At first, his touch was gentle, a mere brushing of lips over hers. When she sighed, though, it was as though a flood gate opened. Mathieu's mouth slanted over hers, parting her lips with his tongue.

He tasted like honey, too. Eva was surprised at how intimate a mere kiss could be. She leaned in and allowed herself to be enveloped in sensation. A strange fluttering began in her chest and dropped into her belly. Never had she imagined—

Suddenly, the world began to spin around her, and she broke the kiss, gasping. In the heat of the moment, she realized she had forgotten to breathe.

He was smiling at her as his fingers came up to stroke her cheek, his thumb running lightly across her lower lip. "They say the eve of May Day has a sort of magic," he began, studying her face with an intensity that made her heart skip a beat. "I'd have to say, if your kiss is any indication, the magic is not simply a fairy tale."

Eva's blood pulsed in her ears so loud she could hear naught but his words. The roar of the fire, the shouts of the crowd, the music, the bleating of the lambs—'twas all gone. There was only she and Mathieu. Nothing else in the world existed or mattered.

"You seem to be weaving a spell upon me, Eva of Utrecht," he murmured, lowering his mouth to hers once more.

Something deep inside Eva, though, clenched, and she pulled back. *He's just the ostler.* The words echoed in her brain again, like an internal warning. Like an instinct, yet one Eva was not at all sure she wanted to heed. Mayhap, though, he would soon be what she longed for.

She cleared her throat, laying her fingers on his chin. "How long before you begin your training as a knight, Mathieu of Liège?"

It was as though a bucket of cold water had doused the man. Immediately, he drew back, turning to for the mug he'd set on the grass beside him. He turned from her, staring into the bonfire, his posture rigid.

"I believe I told you once before, milady. I do not intend to seek knighthood. I've seen too much." His voice was flat.

Eva didn't understand. *He'd seen too much...* of what? Of battle? Was fear holding Mathieu from pursuing his title? His sword and spurs?

That, she decided quickly, would never do.

Silence fell between them, icy cold, like the night air. No longer did the flames warm her, nor was she close enough to feel his body heat. A shudder racked her shoulders as a strange sadness filled her.

She sighed. "I should like to go in search of some hawthorn."

Mathieu would not meet her gaze. "I'm sorry, Eva. I must return to the stables shortly. I cannot take you to the woods for hawthorn. And heed this—you cannot go unescorted."

Pride rose up like a hissing snake to disguise her disappointment. "I don't believe I asked you to escort me," she shot back. "In fact, I believe I will make it an early evening as well." She struggled to her feet, resentment clenching her gut.

She had no reason to be angry with Mathieu, yet she was—spitting mad. Bu with whom? With herself, for her affliction, and her inability to navigate confidently on her own? Or for inability to douse her childish fantasies?

I waited for love, but it never found me. Isabella's words came back to haunt her. Confusion clouded her thinking and frustrated her. As always, though, Eva bandaged her pain with pride.

When she looked behind her and saw the distance to the gatehouse across the field, her chest tightened. Yes, she wanted to be independent and not in need of any assistance. But she also had not the courage to cross the uneven terrain on her own, in the dark.

Sheepishly, she turned back to Mathieu, noting with another jolt of disappointment that he had not risen to his feet with her. He sat, hugging his knees, staring into the fire, as though she had disappeared. As if nothing had passed between them. As if they had not just shared an intimate kiss. She sniffed. It took every ounce of will she possessed to ask for his help, but she realized with resentment that she had no choice.

"Would you mind escorting me back to the bailey, Mathieu?" she asked.

He looked up at her, his expression impassive. "Of course, milady."

Mathieu

Mathieu passed through the stable to perform his ritual nightly check before returning to his quarters. He'd drank a bit too much mead, he decided, yawning and scratching his chest. Hopefully the morning would not be painful. He had to be awake early, with dogs rallied, horses saddled, and falcons hooded by dawn.

The hunt should have been his only concern, the only thing on his mind. But Satan's cods, he'd let the girl get to him again. Thoughts of Eva filled his head with even stronger medicine than the wine.

She'd felt so soft and willing next to him tonight. Even through her woolen kirtle, he felt her soft curves as she snuggled into his side. Her hair, scented with lavender, tickled his cheek when the breeze lifted the silky strands. And when he claimed those plump, pink lips with his own, his entire world tilted.

Unfortunately, the magic did not last. It was a moment, nothing more.

There was an invisible wall between he and Eva. He sensed it and wondered if it was one she'd constructed specifically against him, or against the world in general. Mathieu knew her affliction embarrassed her. But instead of graciously asking for help, she always lashed out first with prideful arrogance. Was her reaction a defensive move?

Arrogance. The thought crashed down over him like a mace to the head. She'd asked him yet again about his intentions to pursue knighthood. He had told her once before—he was content with his position as ostler and falconer for the court.

Did this Eva of Utrecht—this afflicted, bastard daughter—truly think him beneath her?

Anger rose within him, demanding its usual satiation.

Mathieu halted at the last stall before his quarters and turned into the space, nudging aside the hindquarters of the horse—ironically, Captain Knape's blindingly white destrier. Drawing back his fist, he let fly a punch to the wooden boards beside the steed. The horse jumped, but thankfully did not lash out with a hoof.

From somewhere on the other side of the stable, Kleine Uil screeched.

Chapter Twelve

E*va* She found herself alone in the girl's quarters. All the others, even the very young ones, were still in merriment around the still-blazing bonfire. She watched them from the window, the cool stone of the ledge damp on her palms. As cool, she mused, and likely as hard as the stone in her chest, in the place where her heart used to be.

In the next moment, it seemed, morning was upon her. In the distance, smoke wafted still from the mound of the spent bonfire's embers, a slender trail rising from behind the now-closed doors of the keep. It was barely dawn, the horizon just now glowing with the imminent sunrise. All of the beds in the girls' quarters were now occupied, yet none of her sisters were yet awake—the older girls had stayed out late gathering hawthorn. The younger ones always slept until summoned to break their fast.

Eva watched as a pack of brown and white spotted hounds emerged from a pen beside the stables. Mathieu herded them, fondling their floppy ears and laughing when they jostled for his attention. A spark of warmth stirred in her chest as she watched the ostler interact with the animals.

A kind heart, she thought. *Any man who cares so for the humble beasts must possess a tender heart.*

Several of the knights meandered from their camp toward the stable carrying bows and quivers of arrows, long swords sheathed on hips. There was no tenderness exuded by these men, who ignored the dogs, even as the creatures approached to sniff at their legs. One man even kicked out at one of them, causing the dog to yelp and slink away. He ignored the glare Mathieu shot him.

Another voice rose whispered in her mind: *A kind heart remains soft. A true knight's heart is hard and strong.*

As she watched Mathieu lead out the horses, Eva was suddenly gripped by an overwhelming urge to join them. She knew Isabella would be going. Would she be denied? Chances were good she would, but she had to try.

Quickly donning the riding outfit Isabella had given her, she slipped out of the girls' quarters and made her way through the halls of the keep as quickly as her faltering steps allowed. By the time she reached the front entrance, the doors were flung wide. On the stone steps stood Philip and Lady Isabella, the Duchess' hand tucked into the Duke's side.

She'd arrived just in time.

"Lady Duchess," she called as she made her way to the doorway, "may I join you on the hunt?"

Isabella turned, scanning Eva from head to toe. Then she smiled. "You are up early, Eva of Utrecht. And ready to ride, I see. Your confidence is inspiring. Are you sure you are up to the rigors of a rousing excursion?"

Eva clutched the door frame and swayed slightly, catching her breath. She wasn't used to walking quickly, and her hurried trip had her winded. Forcing a smile, she bobbed her head. "Aye, your grace. I would love to go."

When Isabella informed Mathieu an additional mount would be needed, he shot a glance at Eva and then back to the Duchess. His lips flattened. "I will saddle Jannis," he grumbled.

Her heart deflated. Had her haughtiness last night so hardened him toward her already? Well, so be it.

Shortly, they were mounted and passing through the gatehouse. Knape and another huge knight led the party, with Philip and Isabella next in line. The Duchess carried a hooded falcon on her leather-bound arm, as did Mathieu, riding behind Philip. Eva rode beside the ostler, watching in fascination as the birds calmly balanced on their human perches. At least a half-dozen knights brought up the rear.

A fine day was dawning, the sun casting rainbows through a mist rising over the grassy meadow. The breeze cooled Eva's cheeks. She felt much more secure in the saddle than she had when Mathieu first took her out. She glanced over at him several times, but he ignored her. He had not spoken a word to her since her arrival in the bailey this morning.

Her heart felt raw in her chest. Despite her pride, she'd grown fond of Mathieu, and wished their friendship not to end. His kiss had stirred something within her she could not deny, no matter how hard she tried. Mayhap it should never have happened.

They had ridden a short time when Knape drew up his charger and turned to the Duke. "We will accompany you and some of the other men into the forest, Your Grace. The ostler said there are many deer in this copse."

Philip nodded his consent, then turned to his wife. "Milady, Gaspard and Mathieu will take you to the lower meadow to hunt the fowl." He saluted her with two fingers to his brow before spurring his horse ahead to the woods with the other men. With some hand gestures and a whistle from Mathieu, the pack of hounds divided into two groups. One remained with them, and the others galloped ahead of the knights toward the forest.

Isabella held her horse back until Eva rode up beside her. "Philip and the other knights hunt big game with the bow and arrow," she explained. "Mathieu and I will allow our falcons, Cornelijs and Magda, to take down our quarry for us." She smiled at Eva.

"The birds capture the prey?" she asked, her eyes wide.

"The falcons capture them and bring them to earth, then the dogs will lead us to where they've fallen," Isabella replied. The Duchess rode off ahead beside Mathieu. The other knight, one to whom Eva had not been introduced, reined in beside her.

He was a young man with a smooth, unlined face and unruly dark hair swirling almost to his shoulders. Clad in a woolen tunic and leather braies, he cut a fine figure aboard a muscular grey destrier. When she caught his eye, he nodded and said, "Mornin', milady. I do not believe we've met."

The knight—she knew him to be so because of his shiny spurs and the broadsword bobbing at his side—held her gaze with piercing, sky-blue eyes. A quiver of appreciation rippled through her as she studied his handsome features.

"We have not. I am Eva of Utrecht," she said, adding quickly, "a daughter of Philip the Good."

There was no need to include the word *bastard*, was there?

The knight's lips curved into a warm smile. "I am Gaspard of Lille. I have recently joined the Duke's personal guard."

"You do not hunt?" she asked, noticing he carried neither bow nor falcon.

"I do," Gaspard replied, tipping his head, "but today, Captain Knape asked if I would serve as your escort on the hunt."

So. The Captain was looking out for her welfare, even from afar. Eva's wary opinion of Knape softened.

Up ahead, Isabella and Mathieu had drawn up their mounts and were fiddling with the leather hoods on their falcons. Soon the birds' heads were free, their black eyes scanning their surroundings with sharp jerks of their heads. The hounds, noses in the air, suddenly began baying and took off toward a dip in the meadow. Almost silently, the falcons spread their wings and lifted off, leather tethers trailing beneath them.

"They've scented something," Gaspard said, pointing. "Grouse, or pheasant, perhaps."

In the next moments, the dogs nearly disappeared. All that was visible were the white whips of their tails above the waving tall grass. Moments later, with a thunderous whoosh of wings and feathers, a bevy of fowl burst from their cover to scatter, panicked, into the air. One of the two falcons who'd been circling high overhead went into a dive.

Eva watched in awe as the falcon, the smaller of the two, slammed into one of the fleeing birds in midair. Together, the creatures fluttered to the ground, hidden from view. The second capture followed almost immediately, the larger falcon taking its prey down mere yards from the first.

"Come," Gaspard waved Eva on, "Let us draw closer."

They rode up behind Mathieu and Isabella, who had followed the tracking hounds. The dogs had frozen, statue-like, with their noses and tails rigid as arrows. Mathieu halted and dismounted, moving toward the area where the dogs were pointing.

The grasses were so high, Eva could not see the falcons on the ground, where they apparently were pinning their prey. Mathieu crouched low, clutching something in the fist of his leather glove. In a moment, he stood and headed back toward Isabella, a bird on his arm. He gently transferred the falcon from his glove to hers.

Eva saw then what was clutched in his glove. 'Twas a bloody bit of meat, which the falcon was aggressively tearing at with its curved beak.

Gaspard explained. "The hunting birds bring down the prey, then give them up to their handler, the falconer—that would be Mathieu. He in return feeds them fresh meat as a reward."

Sitting astride Jannis, her jaw slack with amazement, Eva watched as Mathieu repeated the process with his own falcon. He returned to his horse with the raptor perched on one arm, and two dead birds swinging from the other.

"They are... grouse?" she asked of the knight beside her.

"Yes. Two fine, fat birds for this evening's table. A promising start to the hunt," Gaspard replied.

The hunt went on, and it seemed the quarry in this part of the meadow was plentiful. The dogs never travelled very far before another burst of feathers exploded into the air. Eva watched the process again and again, impressed with the skill with which Mathieu handled the falcons.

The birds and the dogs obeyed him without hesitation, watching him as though he were a god. He approached his duty with smooth confidence and an air of pride, which Eva found exciting. She'd almost forgotten the knight beside her when he broke into her thoughts.

"Is this your first time at Coudenburg?" he asked.

"Aye. I hail from Ghent." She paused, not wanting to reveal too much about her birthplace and childhood up until now. Up until the missive arrived from the Duke—or, as she now knew, from the Duchess.

"I was born in Paris," the knight continued. "They tell me I'm related in some way to the King of France. Not that it matters much." He snorted and glanced at Eva, his mouth twisting into a smirk. "I'm a bastard son of one of the court's courtesans, you see. I suppose I was lucky to have gained my apprenticeship to knighthood."

Eva's eyebrows shot up. "My lord... it seems we are kindred souls." Her laughter burst from her, taking with it all the tension she felt inside. "I'm the same. I am, in truth, Philip's daughter, but not in the eyes of the Church."

Gaspard's grin lit up his face. "We have something in common, Eva of Utrecht. I'm so happy Captain Knape asked me to escort you this morning." He reached over and wrapped his fingers around her wrist.

Eva's cheeks warmed. A knight, and a good-looking one at that. A Frenchman, but that was of no consequence. The clothier who pursued her in Ghent, Stefano, was from Italy, and her family had encouraged the union openly.

Yet there was no tingle in her belly when she looked into the brilliant blue eyes of her escort. No bolt of lightning slithered up her arm, as did when Mathieu touched her. Gaspard was handsome, pleasant, and titled, but Eva felt no real desire to get to know him further.

He did, however, fit her fantasized ideal for a husband.

This must be what Lady Isabella was talking about... the difference between marrying for title and marrying for love. Could she love Gaspard? Mayhap. But the spark was not instantaneous.

Surely not the same spark she felt with Mathieu.

It was her true father, Philip, however, who would make the decision for her marriage anyway. A flurry of warring emotions filled her chest. She returned the handsome knight's smile.

"I am glad you have accompanied me as well."

Several hours passed, and the sun was high overhead when Isabella called to the ostler.

"We have enough now, Mathieu. A good start for the May Day feast."

Eva counted the birds. Between the feathered bundles hanging from Mathieu's and Isabella's horses, there was total of twelve grouse. Not nearly enough to feed the entire castle as well as villagers, she thought. That's when she heard the distant baying of the other group of hounds from somewhere within the forested edge of the meadow.

She heard the shouts of men too and, wincing, wondered whether the pretty young doe she'd seen just days ago had met her end. Her group made their way slowly in that direction, to where the men had tied off their horses before entering the woods on foot. By the time they arrived, the hooting of boisterous male voices filled the air.

Two knights emerged from the trees with a stout branch stretched between their broad shoulders. From it, bound by its feet, swung a sizeable deer—but not the doe Eva had seen. This was a buck, budding branches of his velvet-covered horns brushing the ground as they carried him.

Knape emerged shortly behind them but passed by his monstrous ghost-like stallion. He snagged instead the leads of the sturdy pack horses the group had brought along. He and the enormous knight who'd ridden beside him re-entered the woods.

Isabella turned to Mathieu with a broad smile. "We will feast on venison this day—and mayhap boar—as well."

Mathieu

For Mathieu, the hunt signified the epitome of his duties. Training the falcons to do their jobs well, handling the dogs, and keeping the horses fit and obedient were his life's goals. He loved taking Lady Duchess out on a hunt. The thrill of watching his hounds and raptors performing their purpose usually filled him with incredible satisfaction and pride.

Today, however, he had been distracted. He had not wanted to take Eva along this morning, though he knew better than to question the word of Isabella. And when he discovered that the young, new knight from Philip's personal guard had been assigned as her escort, his blood bubbled in his veins.

He had met him, this Gaspard of Lille, at Germolles the winter prior. Then merely a squire, the handsome young man had lofty aspirations and the right connections as well. He was some relation of King Louis of France—a bastard son of a noble's courtesan, he'd learned.

So already, Gaspard and Eva had something in common. Plus, he'd earned his spurs and sword. Philip knighted him at the Christmastime festival past.

Mathieu tried to ignore the lighthearted conversation he heard between Eva and Gaspard throughout the morning's ride. They were close in age as well—the knight had just seen his twenty-first winter. When Eva's laughter rang out time and again, he couldn't deny the prickles to his pride.

He had no right, nor cause, to feel jealousy. But he did anyway.

Mathieu had held the girl, kissed her lush mouth, just hours ago. But because he wasn't a knight, just an ostler, he'd never win the lady's heart. In truth, he wasn't sure if the pinching in his chest was truly jealousy or simply regret for not being the kind of man Eva's heart seemed set upon.

Not that it should affect him, nor could it change his mind about his life's path. Mathieu knew in his heart he had chosen the right vocation. No mere lady's opinion would change his decision.

Then why did her rejection injure him so?

The hunting party made their way back to the castle slowly, two stags and a young boar strapped to the pack horses. As they entered the bailey, a great cheer went up. The castle folk came running to examine the hunt's prizes.

The May Day feast would be fine indeed.

Mathieu watched through narrowed eyes as Eva rode in, side by side with Gaspard. The two were in lively conversation, and Eva's voice tinkled in a lighthearted way Mathieu had not heard from her before. His stomach twisted as he dismounted and sent pages scurrying for the Duke's and Duchess' horses.

He did not, however, move toward Eva to assist her dismount. Gaspard was her escort this day. Let him do the honors.

Since her twisted foot was on the off side of the horse, she had little trouble swinging her leg over Jannis' back. It was only when Gaspard grasped her waist and lowered her to the ground that her secret was revealed.

Playing the role of a knightly gentleman, the Frenchman released her quickly and stepped back the moment Eva's feet touched the ground. No lingering fingers for this noble knight. He turned away from her and began loosening the girth on his own saddle.

Without the support Mathieu normally provided, Eva pitched sideways. Mathieu's heart seized at the sight. Grabbing frantically for the saddle to keep herself upright, her flailing spooked even the sleepy Jannis. The horse grunted and lurched away from her. Her fingers slipped free from their grip on the leather strap. Almost in slow motion, Eva crumpled to the ground.

Despite himself, Mathieu was beside her in three long strides. Gaspard had by then spun around and realized what happened.

But not why.

"Milady, I'm so sorry. Are you alright?" He glared into Mathieu's face. "What kind of ill-mannered beast do you put under such a gentle maid?"

Mathieu ignored him, lowering himself to a crouch beside Eva. She lay on her side, her face lowered so he could not see her eyes. She did not appear injured, but he felt the shame radiate off her in waves. Some of the other knights, realizing there was a lady on the ground, clustered around them.

Silently, Mathieu held out his hand. When she lifted her gaze to his, tears streaked trails in the dust on her cheeks. But she did not accept his offer of assistance. On her other side, Gaspard had dropped to his knees in the dirt, grasping her arm in his gloved hand.

Eva's gaze flashed from Mathieu to Gaspard and back again. Without a word, she pushed herself to a sitting position. Slowly, she inched up the hem of her kirtle to reveal her booted feet. Her right ankle, twisted at an unnatural angle inward, appeared to an unknowing eye to be broken.

Gaspard gasped. "Don't move, milady. You've injured yourself. We will get a litter to carry you inside." He glanced up at the knights gathered around them. "Send for a healer!" he called.

Eva winced, her face crumpling in misery. She raised her hand. "No, Sir Knight. I am not injured. I simply lost my balance."

"But your ankle, milady—"

Mathieu stood and took a step back. It was not his place to explain the lady's affliction, though he sorely wished there was some way he could minimize her embarrassment in this moment.

Even if there was, he knew Eva well enough, even in the short time since they'd met. He wagered she'd simply lash out in anger, as she had at him more than once. 'Twas her way of coping.

He stood by and wondered—would she lash out at this handsome knight in the same way?

Chapter Thirteen

E*va*
   "She is not injured."

The authoritative voice of Lady Isabella rose above the murmurs of those gaping at the scene. Eva looked up to see the Duchess, the Duke at her side, emerge through the parting crowd.

"The lady suffers an affliction," she said, more quietly. "An imperfection from birth." Isabella came forward and lifted her own skirts, crouching to offer the girl her hand. As Eva clambered to her feet, the Duchess raised her chin high and continued.

" 'Tis but a minor flaw, not unlike those we all possess. Some flaws, like Eva's, are in plain sight." The Duchess paused, her gaze scanning those around her, alighting only briefly on the Duke. "Others' shortcomings may not be visible to the eye. Eva's physical affliction changes not what lies in her heart—purity, honesty, and honor."

Eva winced at the Duchess' words. *Was* she pure of heart and honorable? The way she'd been cavorting around with her nose in the air since her arrival at the castle now appalled even her. Obviously, Lady Isabella had more faith in Eva than she did in herself. Her gaze shifted from the Duchess' face to that of Gaspard.

The knight stood, hands clasped, staring at the ground. He was avoiding her gaze. If she could see his face, what would she see there? Scorn? Disregard? Or rejection, pure and simple?

She searched the crowd for Mathieu, but the ostler was nowhere to be seen.

Gaspard

Gaspard made his way toward the encampment of the Royal Guard at the far end of the bailey. He had not dared say a word, or even cast a glance, at the young Eva after the Duchess herself stood up for the young woman's honor. To be sure, he'd been quite taken with the girl on their ride out of the castle. At least, in a physical sense.

He'd been shocked to discover her affliction, 'twas true. Astride a horse, one could not tell. Not that it mattered to him, one way or the other.

No lady, afflicted or not, could change the course he'd set for himself as a young boy. Gaspard was not looking for a wife. He was a warrior and had sworn his oath on that to Duke Philip not five moon cycles past. Peace reigned for now, but relations were unstable with France. Although French by birth, the young knight was no fool and so had sided with the Burgundian Duke. Fighting would come soon enough, and Gaspard looked forward to it.

Still, he was a man, one with needs nature bestowed upon him. Eva had seemed the perfect candidate for a romantic liaison—albeit a very temporary one—during this May Day festival. When he came here with Philip, he had hoped to enjoy the holiday, then ride off days later with nary a glance back. 'Twas still what he intended to do.

Now that he knew more about Lady Eva, and the esteem with which Isabella held her, he hesitated to consider a tryst with her anyway. He might be wiser to seek company elsewhere. There were plenty of young maidens here for the festival. Coudenburg's vast staff alone offered many possibilities.

When he arrived at the camp, the knights—unlike nearly every other body in and around the castle—were lounging, enjoying a morning free from responsibilities. Two of the men moved chess pieces about a board set atop a barrel in their midst. Others stood in a group, exchanging stories and laughing. Still others were sparring with blunted swords, cheered on by a small group of onlookers.

Gaspard spotted Knape, leaning on a tapped barrel standing on a cart in one corner. He was surprised the Captain had returned from the hunt so quickly. He headed in that direction, hoping Knape could provide an empty mug for him.

"How did you enjoy the hunt, Gaspard? I'm sorry you did not get to accompany us into the forest for the real challenge. But I thought you might enjoy meeting the newest flower come to Coudenburg," Knape winked at the young knight, "for this celebration of fertility." The Captain waggled his dark eyebrows.

Gaspard took the cup Knape offered him and filled it with ale. "I did enjoy the morning, indeed. The lady is quite... unique."

Knape's laughter echoed off the stone walls around them. "She is indeed. Eva may be a daughter of the Duke, but for more than one reason, I should think you might consider her fair game, my good knight." The Captain took a long draw from his own mug, wiping the foam off his mustache with the back of his hand. " 'Tis true, Lady Isabella appears to favor the girl. But with her status, and her disfigurement, the good Lord knows Philip shall not worry himself much for her future. 'Twere not for our difference in age, I would target the young woman myself," he added in a low growl.

"Since when has that stopped you?" One of the knights engaged in the chess game glanced up at Knape with a sneering grin. "I've seen you target maidens many moons younger than this Eva—"

"Silence!" Knape barked, stabbing the man with a venomous glare. "Not under the eye of his Grace. We are all," the Captain swept an arm across his group of men, "the guests of the Duke and Duchess this May Day. As your Captain, my standards for behavior must be elevated. My own desires must be kept in check."

"What of the rest of us, Captain?" asked the other chess player, disappointment twisting his features. "I'd hoped to volley with a plump servant girl or two during our stay."

Knape drained his mug and crossed his arms. "As I said, the Duke is in residence, and I am your Captain. I have standards to uphold." He met Gaspard's eye. "As for the rest of you, we all know Philip understands what fuel is needed to keep his Royal Guard virile and strong."

The Captain's maniacal laughter rang out, soon to be joined by every other knight in the encampment.

When the laughter faded, Gaspard took a sip from his mug and studied Knape as he strode away. He had heard things about the Captain of the Royal Guard—not all of them good. Gaspard counted his blessings as having been chosen to join the smaller guard that travelled with Philip, while Knape's crew stayed close to the Duchess.

His knighthood was new. He knew he had much to learn about his station. In order to rise in the ranks, Captain Knape should be his mentor—whether he approved of the man's personal morals or not.

Eva

After returning to the girls' quarters to change out of her riding clothes, Eva wandered through the keep, her heart numb. She felt invisible—a good thing. For everyone else, this morning's incident was long forgotten amidst the clamoring preparations for the feast and dancing yet to come this day. It was easy to lose herself amid the scurrying maids and servants, unseen or unnoticed.

But what kept stabbing Eva's heart, even piercing the numb shield she'd fastened around it, was guilt. She had been cold to the ostler, drilling him yet again last eve about his intentions for knighthood. How dare she? Mathieu was a man she considered among her few friends here at the castle. The Duchess' words echoed in her head.

Haughty? That is how you sound, Eva. You speak and act as though you are better than everyone else. What makes you this way? Is your mamam conceited as well?

The thought of Marisse brought a lump to form in her throat. Of all the people in Eva's small world, Marisse was the humblest, most gracious woman she knew. She wished in that moment she had been born—or could learn to be—more like her.

Eva wandered out of the keep toward the stables. She owed Mathieu an apology, that much she knew. Whether or not he would even allow her to speak it, she knew not. Still, she had to try.

But Mathieu was not in the stable, nor in the kennel where the tired hunting dogs lay sprawled in the shade. Progressing slowly, using the gates and building walls to steady her steps, Eva made her way toward the aviary.

She heard his rumbling voice even before she saw him. Mathieu was in the small sunning yard in front of the building where falcons and hawks sat tethered to raised perches. He was crouched beside one of the smaller creatures, murmuring softly to the bird.

"… a fine hunt. Fine indeed. Lady Isabella was very proud of you. I am as well."

"Mathieu?"

The ostler's head jerked around, startling the falcon, who flapped its wings in agitation before again settling. Mathieu stood, his expression inscrutable.

"Were you injured this morn, Eva? I saw you take a fall." His tone flat, he displayed no emotion at all.

Heat rushed to Eva's cheeks. "Nay. Not on the outside, anyway. 'Twas my pride injured by the mishap more than my backside." She shook her head, staring at the ground. "I have been such a fool."

She heard not his footsteps approaching on the soft grass, but knew he'd drawn near when the scent of oil and leather engulfed her senses. Then her hand, resting on the top of a fence post, was covered by his. Warmth shot up her arm, spreading through her chest like wildfire.

"Not a fool, milady. A bit of a sassy wench, mayhap. But never a fool."

His words, though harsh, were delivered with a softness that surprised Eva. She met his gaze.

"I owe you an apology, Mathieu of Liège. You have been nothing but kind and gracious to me since the day we met. In return, I've been nothing but rude and ungrateful."

His gold-specked brown eyes shone, even as his mouth quirked at one end. "Strike me down with a feather, milady. 'Twere words I wagered never to hear from your lips."

Eva squinted in the bright sunlight, studying his face. He had tied his oaken hair back in a thong this warm day, revealing a sharply cut jawline visible even beneath his days' growth of beard. His tanned skin creased at the corners of his eyes and across his brow, marking him some winters older than the young knight she'd ridden out with this morn. His scar, while plainly visible, only added character to his handsome face. And those lips… lips she knew were as soft as they were demanding. She wondered again at how he'd acquired the scar he bore.

Gaspard's face was smooth and unlined. The knight—even though he'd been dubbed so—had eyes and a manner bespoken of youth and inexperience. A knight's world, Eva knew, was one where experience could well make the difference between life and death.

Mathieu's face was one of a man, not a boy. Eva suddenly realized 'twas his maturity that made him so much more appealing. At least, in one way.

"Shall I show you the aviary? We have many fine hunting birds here." His smile warmed her.

"Aye, I would love that."

Mathieu leapt over the low fence and offered his arm. With her hand snugged into his side, a warm feeling of safety and security washed over her.

He led her around the yard to a line of low coops where the birds were kept. Many were empty, and the pages were busily cleaning these and lining the boxes with fresh straw.

"How many birds are kept here?" she asked.

Mathieu chuckled. "Simon... Admiral La Laing likes his raptors as much as his horses. We'd own dozens more if we had room to keep them. Right now, six reside here year-round at Coudenburg. When Lady Isabella brings Cornelijs, they number seven."

She blinked up at him. "Do you reside at the castle year-round?"

He shook his head. "When the Duchess leaves in the fall for Germolles, I accompany her. Lady Isabella likes for me to spend the winter months teaching the apprentices there the finer points of training the war horses, as well as the hunting birds."

Eva tipped her head. "What happens after their apprenticeship ends?"

"They foster at the Chateau de Germolles for a few winters before vying for their spurs and swords." He turned toward her, taking her shoulders in his hands. "For most, the position of ostler is but a steppingstone to knighthood."

"But not for you," she stated quietly.

He turned away, staring off down the narrow alleyway separating the roosting boxes. "Nay. I have found my calling here, training and caring for the creatures so vital to the success of those knights." He grinned at her. "In truth, I am the knight behind the scenes. I'll bet you did not know a horse must be trained to face battle. At first, they are quite skittish and shy from a lance or a longbow. They are smart creatures, but very timid by nature."

"And you train them?"

"I do. Not with real weapons, but with lances and spears made of soft wood, and a device called a quintain. If you wish, I shall show you one day, after the festival."

"I should like that, very much," she said, warmth spilling into a warm smile she could not suppress. "I should also love to learn about the birds... the falcons. How you train them to hunt."

Mathies stood taller, lifting his chin as he gazed down at her. "Would you like to hold one of them right now?"

Eva eyes widened, but she bobbed her head.

Ducking into a small room at the end of the row of cages, Mathieu returned holding a leather gauntlet and a small pouch.

"Come. I am trying to teach Magda to be more flexible in her behavior. She is our newest bird from the Netherlands."

He led her to the yard where the falcons were all enjoying the warm sunshine. Eva believed it might have been one they had taken on the hunt that morn. The creature stood on a low pedestal, a leather thong tethering its leg. Mathieu turned to Eva.

"Stretch out your arm," he said, holding up the gauntlet.

The leather glove was so large, it slid all the way to Eva's shoulder. She laughed.

"Whatever is the purpose of this contraption?" she asked.

Mathieu hitched an eyebrow and held up a finger. "Be forewarned, milady. The talons on these birds can rip your skin to the bone without any effort at all. Without their meaning to do you any harm."

From his belt, he pulled a smaller leather glove and pulled it on. Then he untied the tether and gently bumped the bird's chest with his fingers. She willingly stepped onto his gloved hand.

"Here, now." He held his arm out toward Eva. "Reach up and bump her on the chest, very gently. Just as I did."

Cautiously, Eva obeyed. The bird hesitated only a moment before stepping onto her wrist. A thrill swelled her chest to near bursting.

"What a magnificent creature!" she whispered.

Mathieu fumbled a chunk of raw meat out of the pouch he'd tied to his waist and tucked it between the bulky fingers of Eva's glove. "Hold this tightly. Let her pick at it and shred it in her beak."

In amazement, Eva watched as this undeniably wild creature sat tamely on her arm, feeding from her fist. She turned awed eyes to Mathieu, who smiled down at her.

"You are a brave lady, indeed, Eva of Utrecht. Not many young maidens would possess the courage to hold a hunting bird."

After the bird was returned to her perch and the gloves to their storage room, Mathieu stood before her, studying her. They stood tucked into a shady spot between the aviary and the kennels, and for the moment, the air stilled with magical silence.

He moved closer, so close his scent enveloped her. She lifted her face to his, an almost instinctive reaction. Her heart began its crazy gallop inside her chest, and her skin flushed hot.

"Thank you, Mathieu. I should like to learn more about handling the birds," she whispered.

"As you wish. I shall love to teach you." Mathieu's fingers lifted to sweep her long hair back off her shoulder. "You are very lovely, milady. You are not yet spoken for in your hometown of Ghent?"

"Nay. I had hoped, when I came here to the castle..."

He silenced her with his mouth over hers. Again, as last evening, everything around her disappeared. There was nothing but sensation enveloping her, quickening her heart, warming her belly, spreading goosebumps on her skin. Mathieu's fingers combed into her hair to splay across the back of her head, holding her closer still. Eva's body melted into him as her defenses disappeared.

Never had she felt this way. She knew 'twas lust she was feeling, a physical desire that oft had nothing to do with the heart. But here, she felt, there was more.

He was a gentle man, but so strong and wise. He had taken the time to humor her curiosity about the falcons and trusted her with one of the Duke's prized birds. Mathieu was much more, she was realizing, than simply a "stable boy," as Captain Knape insisted on calling him.

And their embrace now, with her wrapped securely in his arms, his lips exploring her own, and his scent intoxicating her, was pure enchantment.

When he finally drew back, Mathieu cupped her face in his warm, rough hands. "I was wrong. 'Twas not only the magic of May Day eve. 'Tis you, Eva of Utrecht, who holds the power to weave a spell over me."

A pang of guilt swept over her. Here she had been thinking herself above him. Now she wondered if, truly, she was deserving of earning the heart of a man such as this at all.

She slid her gaze away, suddenly shy and unsteady. "I am but the bastard daughter of a man who would well ignore my existence, if not for the Duchess."

He gripped her chin lightly, forcing her to face him. "Then I shall fall at the Duchess' feet to thank her for finding you, and for bringing you here."

"I am imperfect, my lord. Born disfigured. I am a creple." Her throat felt thick.

"And I am but a lowly ostler, scarred and bearing no title, no lands. 'Tis does not change my ability to make a good life for one I grow to love."

Stunned by the intensity of his words, his gaze, Eva stumbled back. He steadied her with a hand on her arm.

A page wandered into view, carrying an armful of straw. Mathieu straightened and stepped away. He cleared his throat. "How did your dance lessons go? Shall I put in my request now for a bassadance after the feast? Or will I have to wait in line behind one of the knights—or more than one?" One of his dark eyebrows rose.

Eva huffed out a bitter laugh. "Nay, no waiting in line for this lady. The dancing lessons did not go well. Not well at all." She lifted her gaze to his, where his handsome image suddenly swam in her tears. "I cannot dance, Mathieu. I can barely walk without assistance."

"Nonsense," he barked, startling her. "You can dance, and you will. I will make it my personal mission to ensure it happens." He lifted her chin with two fingers, then wiped away her tear with his thumb. "Promise me. A bassadance, after the feast." His words were a soft rumble.

A voice in Eva's head screamed *No!* Just another opportunity to make a fool of herself. Another situation when a stumble or fall would make her infirmity the center of attention. She couldn't bear it to happen yet again.

Was it courage? Or blind hope? She knew not what caused her to gaze up into Mathieu's pleading eyes and whisper, "Aye."

Chapter Fourteen

Eva *va*
The girls' quarters were bustling with activity when Eva returned. Her younger sisters were huddled in one corner, digging through a chest filled with cloth. Bright lengths of fabric were tugged out, examined, and either claimed or tossed to the tiled floor. Their squeals and laughter tugged at her heartstrings.

Children. She did so love them. Her siblings had become her beacon, lighting up the dreariness of her life. A pang of homesickness stabbed her heart. She missed her young brother and sister back in Ghent, a raw ache in her chest. Yet the thought of having her own someday frightened her to death.

How could she ever hope to find a man who would not only overlook her disfigurement, but be willing to risk fathering flawed children? Or who would be satisfied with a life without heirs?

On Alys' and Eva's pallets, elegant kirtles were neatly laid out. Beside them lay the colorful circlets made of flowers Alys had made, with their long ribbon streamers. There were also new slippers.

Eva approached and fingered the rich satin of her new kirtle. It was pale green like the spring leaves, trimmed with white ribbon shot through with golden thread. The chemise to be worn beneath it was pure white, made of the finest silk. Eva glanced over to see that Alys' new gown was much like her own, except it was sky blue.

Alys' eyes were blue, and Eva's green. The Duchess had thought out their May Day trappings carefully, Eva thought. In wonder, she lifted the matching slippers.

Again, as before, her new slippers were specially made, bearing a wedge of firm padding on the outside edge of the right foot. In addition, on this pair, a thick sole of leather lined the bottom. They looked much sturdier than the first ones she'd received.

I may be able to dance in these slippers, Eva thought, her heart leaping in her chest. Even walking would be easier and safer in this new design.

She owed so much to the Duchess. Clutching the slippers to her chest, Eva raised her eyes toward the heavens and whispered a prayer of thanks. Like embers revived by fresh kindling, her hopes and dreams for the future once again burst into flames, hot and exciting.

Mathieu

An hour or so after the nooning meal, trumpets resounded across the bailey and echoing from outside the gatehouse toward the village. This was Mathieu's cue to ready the horses. The jousting course, or lists, had already been set up, with colorful flags and banners dotting the field beyond the outer walls. Two tall poles defined the starting positions. Already, a crowd had gathered to watch the matches and cheer on their favorite knights.

The contestants awaited their armored and decorated mounts. Mathieu had spent the last hours dressing their six destriers in full regalia, complete with protective chest plates and head gear. The joust would be a mock fight—no true lances or spears, but only brittle wooden facsimiles. Still, there was always the danger of injury, if inadvertent. A wooden spear, if it hit the knight or horse anywhere his armor or mail did not cover, could cause trauma.

Mathieu, followed by his oldest and most experienced page, Rogier, led the first two destriers out. Frenzied with excitement, the horses chomped at their bits and flicked nervous foam everywhere. These horses were bred for this, whether it be a mock joust or heading into true battle. They were all stallions, and Mathieu had himself been responsible for training three of the six mounts.

He personally knew not most of the knights fighting, only Gaspard, who had attended the hunt that morn. Being the youngest, the Frenchman would be up first against an opponent of equal experience. The games proceeded thus: riders clashed in high-speed gallops down the lists and were allowed only three lances each. Once all of their lances had broken, or they had been knocked off their horses or injured, the winner would progress to the next round.

The crowd was roaring at a fever pitch when the first two knights emerged onto the field. Mathieu handed off the first knight's destrier, then turned to catch Gaspard's horse, a tall yet massively built stud with a coat of dappled silver. The steed was so agitated he was swinging the page around like a ball on a tether. As soon as Mathieu took hold of the reins, the beast quieted, snorting and prancing in place as Gaspard approached.

"Thank you, my lord," the French knight said, bowing toward the man who, he knew, had trained his charger last year at Coudenburg and later at Germolles.

Ladies lined the perimeter of the lists, waving and calling to their favorite knights. Many waved fragments of cloth in the air, scraps of embroidery or veil. These tokens were offered by the maidens as gifts for luck, as well as symbolizing promise of a possible future liaison—a kiss for the winner, and a dance after the feast.

For some, mayhap more.

When Mathieu turned and saw Eva on the edge of the crowd, his heart sank. She stood among a group of young maidens, their hair flowing free save for the flowered circlets ringing their crowns—marking them as single and available. They were all, as well, waving scraps of silk or veil in the air.

Including Eva.

Gaspard mounted his horse and then, ignoring all the other maidens, approached her. His face shield was raised, and Mathieu saw the gleam of his smile as he snatched the cloth from Eva's hand and tied it around his lance.

She had offered the favour, and the French knight had accepted it.

A sudden wave of nausea washed over Mathieu, and he swiped a hand down his sweat-soaked face. This action should mean nothing to him—'twas all part of the game, he knew—and Eva probably just wanted to join in the tradition. Yet suddenly he wished it were he, and not Gaspard, aboard the fine destrier he'd spent countless hours gentling, training, and fitting.

Before, it had always been enough for Mathieu to know that it was he who played a large part in the winning or losing of these matches. A well-trained, brave and steady mount could carry even an inferior marksman to victory—if the rider was sufficiently skilled with the lance. Today, his stakes in the game had suddenly become much more personal. Participation somehow seemed more important.

The raised platform, the dais from which the nobility watched the match, was erected under a tent at the midpoint of the lists. Here sat Duke Philip, the Lady Duchess, Simon La Laing, and Captain Knape. Mathieu could not help the flame of anger erupting inside him when he heard shouting coming from the dais. As Gaspard plucked the favour from Eva's hand, Captain Knape stood, shaking his fist in the air and bellowing his support.

What the Captain had to gain from encouraging the French knight's attention to Eva, Mathieu had no idea. He knew little about Gaspard except that he was young and ambitious, warrior-wise. As far as Mathieu knew, and from the little he'd spoken with the knight, he wasn't in the market for a wife.

Then again, a permanent relationship was the furthest thing from Captain Knape's mind. Even at his advanced age of thirty-odd winters, he had never settled down. It seemed Knape lived for the moment and the glory—the savagery of battle, and the many pleasures life offered. He was, in Mathieu's mind, typical of most knights, whose egos ruled their actions. He was convinced that many, including the Captain, had lost sight of the difference between right and wrong.

The trumpets blared again precisely at two o'clock, announcing the commencement of the jousts. Gaspard positioned his horse at one end of the lists, having difficulty containing his rowdy mount. The other knight, whose name Mathieu did not know, took his position at the opposite end. This warrior was from a neighboring castle, a guest to the games. With both contestants in position, one of the stewards stood mid-list and held a flag bearing the Burgundian shield up high. When the flag dropped with a mighty whoosh, the horses bolted.

Even aboard the highly charged destrier, Gaspard did an admirable job on his first pass with the lance. He struck the opponent's breastplate straight on, nearly dislodging the man from his horse. His lance, however, split from the impact. When he reached the far end, his squire quickly provided him a fresh weapon.

A mighty cheer went up from the crowd for the French knight, obviously their favorite. Mathieu glanced over at Eva, who was clapping and waving at Gaspard, the warrior whom she had pledged her favour. *Her* warrior. The very notion made the ostler sick to his stomach.

Luck seemed to favor Gaspard this day. The next pass did not fare well for the opposing knight again, as Gaspard's lance struck him on the side of his helmet, knocking it askew. The knight wavered, obviously disoriented for the moment, and a hush fell over the crowd. A blow to the head, although not intended to cause real injury, could well cause serious injury.

Head wounds, whether in play fighting or true battle were, of course, the most difficult to treat. They often proved fatal.

The knight recovered, however and, righting his helmet, retrieved a fresh lance from his own steward. He made a brave attempt to skewer Gaspard in the shoulder during the third round. His weapon merely glanced off the French knight's armor, while Gaspard's lance hit its mark dead on. Striking the breastplate full force in the very center, the man was literally catapulted off his horse, landing flat on his back in the dirt.

Round One of the tournament was over, with the French knight as victor.

The noise from the crowd was deafening, as was the stomping on the boards of the raised dais under the nobles. The Burgundian knights were winning. Although Mathieu would normally have been basking in the glory of his own success—the bravery and skill of the steeds played a huge role in this event—he could feel no joy.

A deep, burning grief, fueled by jealousy, Mathieu turned away from the crowd, as he knew what was coming next. It was customary for the victorious knight to "claim" his lady with a kiss. Anguish burned in his chest as he made his way back to the stables to retrieve the mount for the next round. He cursed his own weakness at allowing his emotions to overtake his common sense. What he felt for Eva had been, of late, quickly transforming from simple lustful desire to something more. For a short while, he'd thought mayhap the unthinkable had happened—he'd found a maid he could settle down with and raise a family. But reality had risen up and belted him across the face with a gauntlet—a knight's gauntlet.

Up against the likes of a handsome, titled warrior, an ostler didn't stand a chance.

Eva

Struggling to maintain her balance, standing in a crush of young woman on the edge of the course, Eva realized she had gotten caught up in the revelry. Now, she had no idea how to extricate herself. It was Alys who'd convinced her to bring along a strip of silk to the joust, slipping it into the sleeve of her kirtle as she'd helped her sister get dressed.

"You must, Eva. I cannot," she had claimed. "My betrothed—or soon to be, with the Duke's permission—is not a knight. He cannot participate in the games. None of the other girls are old enough to offer a knight their token. You must represent us! Gaspard is handsome and kind—you said so yourself. 'Twill mean naught in reality. 'Tis all just a game."

Eva did, truly, feel like a princess, waving her token in the air and calling to Gaspard. These were the tales the bards told, complete with all the excitement and romanticism she'd dreamed of. When Gaspard took her favour and tied it onto his lance, her sisters all huddled around her, cheering. For the moment, she was their champion.

Yet as the jousting came to an end, with Gaspard as the victor after going up against three formidable opponents, Eva feared what be coming next. Alys nudged her as the French knight approached on his sweaty and steaming destrier, whose snorting and stamping scared Eva half to death. She staggered backward, managing to recover only with the help of Alys' proffered arm.

Removing his helmet, Gaspard smiled down at her with a mischievous gleam in his eye. He handed his helmet off to his squire, then dismounted. He stepped closer, so close she could feel the heat radiating off his gleaming armor. The Frenchman slid off his gauntlet and dropped it to the ground, riveting her with a predatory gaze. Without hesitation—or permission—he cupped the back of her head, pulling her to him roughly.

The lady's knight was due his victory kiss.

His mouth was hard, and he smelled of sweat and sour wine. The hair of his scant mustache scalded her skin as he worked his mouth over hers, plunging his tongue insistently against her lips. She resisted, but Eva soon realized there would be no denying him. Revved by his success and high on his achievement, Gaspard was not the gentle, friendly knight she'd chatted and laughed with on the hunt. He was a powerful, male warrior rightfully claiming his prize.

When he finally forced her lips to part, Eva fought the urge to gag into his mouth. He was holding her too tightly against the unforgiving surface of his armor. His kiss was too rough, too invasive. His scent and the taste of him disgusted her, and her stomach roiled in her belly. Instinct took hold as she tried with all of her might to push him away, palms flat against his hot metal breastplate. Just when she thought she might faint, she heard a shrill whistle coming from the nobles' tent.

Breaking the kiss, Gaspard grinned, a low chuckle erupting in his throat. He turned toward the dais and held up one thumb of his other, still-gauntleted hand toward his wildly cheering fan, Captain Knape. As he did, his other hand slid out from under Eva's hair and down her back. Reaching her bottom, Gaspard squeezed her buttock so hard, pain shot through her. Pain... and revulsion.

Eva promptly vomited her noon meal all over the knight's booted feet.

Chapter Fifteen

Mathieu

Mathieu emerged from his quarters, rubbing sleep from his face. Kleine Uil perched on his shoulder, wide awake and anxiously searching the stable with huge, round eyes. Daylight was fading fast, and the ostler had awoken with as ravenous an appetite as his tiny, feathered friend.

The afternoon's events flashed back into his mind with sickening intensity. After delivering the destrier to the competing knight of the last round, Mathieu had quit the games. He'd instructed Rogier to retrieve the mounts once the joust was done. He already knew how this would play out, and he wanted no part in it. Gaspard, he knew, would likely be the victor.

In more ways than one.

The aroma of roasted meats filled his senses as he made his way toward the keep, but Mathieu's appetite had vanished. Although he'd skipped the noonday meal and taken a nap instead, his stomach felt sour. He hoped the nausea passed quickly, as he knew tonight's feast would be a spread fit for any king.

Philip the Good hadn't earned his name by chance. The Duke was famous for his generosity when it came to his people, those who swore fealty to him and his court. This would mark the third May Day Festival that Mathieu had spent at Coudenburg, ever since Admiral La Laing had taken up residence at the castle. Before that, he'd attended many feasts at both Coudenburg and Germolles—Yule, Candlemas, Mabon, Samhain—the list was endless once one included celebrations of handfastings and higher nobles' name days.

Truly, Duke Philip was always up for a feast. And what a feast he hosted.

Admiral La Laing met Mathieu just inside the doors to the Great Hall, which were flung wide.

"Are you hungry, my boy?" La Laing asked, clapping Mathieu on the shoulder. "After your most successful hunt this morn, we shall all feast heartily. I hear the falcons performed flawlessly. And your horses! Gaspard is but a fledgling, but his mount carried him to an impressive win. I do believe you played a big part in his victory today."

So, it had turned out the way Mathieu had predicted. No surprise, he thought. He wondered if the knight gave as much credit to his mount's training as La Laing did.

Before Mathieu's ire could rise he caught sight of Eva, seated between Alys and Beverielle just below Isabella. His heart clutched. The girl was a sight to behold.

Like a beacon, she stood out in the crowded room. She was telling an animated tale to the younger girl on her right—probably of the joust. With the face of an angel, she caused Mathieu's heart to thud heavily in his chest. The voluminous sleeves of her sumptuous green gown fluttered when she gestured with her hands. With full, pink cheeks and sparkling eyes, her flowered circlet ringed her golden hair like a halo.

This girl's halo, he wagered, would tip askew more often than not. Eva possessed the pride of a peacock and had not yet learned how to tame her tongue. Mathieu smiled sadly. She had spirit, much like a young, unbroken filly.

Yet 'twas one of the traits he loved about Eva of Utrecht. Too bad she'd already set her sights upon another. He wondered if the Frenchman would, as he did, appreciate her spunk—or if the knight would extinguish it, as abruptly as the flame from a tallow candle. 'Twas usually the way with a warrior's woman. Their maids were quickly taught to temper their behavior and hold their tongues, like a horse whose spirit had been broken.

Many tables ran the entire length of the long room, and the hanging wooden chandeliers above them burned with so many candles, the effect was nearly blinding. At the far end, the dais rose above all else. Philip and Isabella were already seated, with an empty seat waiting for La Laing to the left of the Duke, and one for Captain Knape beside Isabella.

An extra seat had been added on this night, right beside the Captain. The victor of the jousting sat at the high table. Mathieu bristled to see the beaming face of Gaspard of Lille. He noticed with curiosity that Eva, *the knight's lady*, had not been placed up on the dais alongside him, as was the usual custom.

Had this been his choice, or hers?

Minstrels played a melodic tune from a far corner, setting the mood to light and joyous. At each table, a stuffed swan served as centerpiece, the smaller grouse they'd downed this morn lining the remainder of their length. There were so many platters of dried fruits and small meat pies, there was barely enough room for trenchers at each seating. Servants scurried in and out of the kitchen with yet more bowls and platters. The stronger male servants carried huge pitchers of mead or ale and went from table to table, filling cups.

Mathieu followed La Laing though the hall, breaking away only when they neared the dais. La Laing stopped and turned, pointing to an empty seat just below where he would be sitting.

"I'd like you here, Mathieu. There are some horses I'm looking to buy. I would value your opinion."

Mathieu nodded and took the seat La Laing had chosen for him. Glancing up, he realized he was directly across the hall from Eva. She sat on Isabella's side of the room, just below the seat of Captain Knape. The ostler bristled as he watched the way the Captain's eyes raked over the young woman. She was oblivious, chatting and laughing with her sisters as she popped dried apricots into her mouth.

Her lush, full mouth. Mathieu licked his lips, remembering how the girl's kiss had tasted. It wasn't just honey from the mead. It was the flavor of the young woman herself, her scent, and her warmth that sprang forth in his memory. Whenever he touched her, 'twas like a lightning bolt up his arm. And her kiss, the sweet sighs she made as he'd held her this morn, the way she peered into his eyes as though she meant to speak to his very soul...

He must stop this perilous line of thinking. Better not to dwell upon his growing feelings for a lady he could not have, especially after seeing how Knape appeared to be playing matchmaker for her with his new, young knight. At the joust, Eva made her choice obvious.

Not that Mathieu should have been surprised. She'd made it painfully clear what standards she'd set for her future husband. Gaspard fit the bill perfectly.

If the young knight favored her. Mathieu sighed as he took his seat and lifted a mug of ale to his lips. Even if Gaspard shunned the lady, there would surely be others—of equal status—who would not.

Mathieu had just finished his first course—a rich mushroom and barley pottage spiced with pepper and cloves—when he heard La Laing call his name from the dais above him.

"Are you familiar with the horse breeder, Pierre Barrau?" the admiral called over the din.

Mathieu stood and leaned on the elevated dais so he could hear La Laing better. "I have not, my lord. Where are his stables?"

La Laing wiped his mouth with the linen beside his trencher. "North of Rouen, near Le Havre. It's a four-day ride, three if you ride hard. He's got a new crop of young colts I'd like to see. We could use some fresh blood in our stables."

That's certainly true, Mathieu thought. Germaine had to have been at least twenty-five winters old when she dropped dead on his trip back from Ghent, and Jannis wasn't far behind. Mathieu loved training the horses as well as the hunting birds. For the past three years, however, the only young, strong stock in his stable were La Laing's destrier and the knights' chargers.

Of course.

"Are you up for a ride this coming week?" La Laing pressed.

Mathieu shrugged, struggling to hide his excitement at the thought of new, young horses to train.

"As you wish, Admiral. 'Twould be my honor."

Eva

Eva had never seen such an elaborate—nor plentiful—banquet in all of her life. After nibbling on the dried fruit platter nearest her, her belly was near to full even before the pottage arrived.

Alys, sitting beside her, leaned to whisper into her ear. "Are you feeling better now, milady?" The older girl's freckled skin puckered across her brow.

"Aye. 'Twas just the excitement, and the heat this afternoon. Still, the shame my illness brought upon me." She winced and laid a hand across her middle. "For now, I think I should not have eaten so many apricots."

"Nay, you should not. After the pottage comes the meats—swan, grouse, venison, and wild boar with roasted vegetables." Alys grinned before sipping from her bowl of steaming soup. "And then come the sweets and tarts."

Eva raised her eyebrows and moaned. " 'Tis fortunate this kirtle fits loosely."

"Don't worry, sister." From her other side, Beverielle laid a hand on her arm. "You will need all of your energy for the dancing later."

The dancing. Eva's heart stilled. Although she'd found the new slippers Isabella had fashioned for her made walking much easier, she wasn't so sure about dancing. The painful memory of hitting the grass in the garden during her "lesson" rose to the top of her mind. She glanced around the room, searching for Mathieu.

"You can dance, milady, and you will. I will make it my personal mission to ensure it happens."

Mathieu's words echoed in her memory, and she wondered if he would, in fact, make good on his promise.

Her eyes found him standing beneath the dais, deep in conversation with Admiral La Laing. He looked dashing tonight, dressed in a crisp, ivory tunic belted with braided leather. His hair was loose, falling well past his shoulders in shiny waves. Laughing at something La Laing said, he combed back the long strands from his face with one hand.

Again, feelings Eva did not quite understand stirred in her belly. This was not her sickness returning. She was physically attracted to the ostler, she knew. But 'twas more than that, she feared. Although he was not a mighty warrior, there was something quietly appealing about the man that spoke to her heart. His love for the animals. His caring nature. His patience.

Her gaze drifted to the dais, where Gaspard was speaking animatedly with Knape. He had bathed, his hair wet, molding to his head in a dark mass. He was still unshaven, though, and just the sight of his sparse, pathetic excuse for a mustache turned her stomach. She recalled how it scalded her skin when he'd kissed her.

She slid her eyes back to Mathieu.

One very handsome man, indeed. And of the two, there was no doubt which man sparked a fire in her belly—mayhap in her heart as well. No matter what his station.

Would Mathieu really come through on his pledge to dance with her this eve?

Gaspard had not said one word to her since the embarrassing end to his victory embrace. Her sisters had all come running to her aid and hurried her away to clean her up, rest, and recover. Surely, whatever interest the young knight had for her was quelled after that disaster.

She could only hope.

By the time the sweets and tarts were laid upon the tables, Eva thought her belly would surely burst. The food was magnificent—decadent, far richer and more extravagant than anything she'd ever dined upon. Although she only sipped a little mead with her meal, she felt drunk from overindulgence.

She was gazing off, sleepy and distracted, when suddenly everyone stood. A great bustling commenced, with servants moving all the tables to the sides of the Great Hall. Others appeared with rakes to clear away the rushes covering the floors. The tiled floor was now bare—perfect for dancing. The minstrels in the corner were joined by other musicians, including a harpist, another with a fiddle, and two men carrying a hammer dulcimer.

The more lively, festive music for the evening was about to begin. Again, a flutter of nerves overcame Eva as she huddled with her sisters in a corner of the hall. The other girls were highly agitated, squealing with excitement. Eva watched as Philip and Isabella rose and descended the dais, the Duke holding his lady's hand high.

They would be the first to dance, she realized. Only after the nobles claimed the dance floor would others be allowed to join in.

The minstrels began playing a lilting melody that made Eva's heart sing. She'd often watched, from her stall in the Market Square, the dancing during festivals in Ghent. The activity always struck her as an expression of freedom, of joy. Of course, even if she'd been able to join the others, she knew she could not.

Isabella, in a long, flowing kirtle of purple brocade, wore an expression of unbridled happiness as she stepped down onto the floor. Ermine edged her elegant gown, with wide, pointed sleeves that hung nearly to the floor.

The Duchess wore a single-horned hennin this eve, one extravagantly embroidered and bejeweled. A short, sheer veil flowed from the headpiece.

Philip, also in royal purple, smiled at his wife as they bowed toward each other before the dance. Then they began, bobbing and stepping in time to the music, hands joined, down the length of the Great Hall. When they neared the end, they parted, each spinning away to reverse direction and dance gracefully, separately, to where they'd begun.

Three times the noble couple made their way down the length of the room before bowing to each other, then toward the crowd. Immediately, couples joined them, following the Duke and Duchess to dance in like fashion.

Eva sighed. The dance did not look nearly as difficult as she'd feared, especially the part where the lady held her partner's hand. The solo jaunt back, however, worried her.

She shrank back into the group of her sisters, trying as she might to become invisible. She'd not seen Mathieu since the feast began, when he seemed deep in conversation with a noble who was seated up on the dais. Mayhap he'd forgotten all about his vow to dance with her tonight. And although improbable, the thought of Gaspard asking her to dance sent the meal in her belly roiling.

After the initial round, the minstrels kicked up the tempo of their song. Couples began a much livelier dance, with hops and raised knees that made Eva's stomach clench. Nay, this was a move she was not capable of performing—at least not without incident. Eyeing the doorway just behind where she stood, Eva considered slipping away. Surely returning to her quarters was a safer choice than risking the embarrassment of being asked to dance—and failing.

She didn't get the chance.

As she turned to flee, a firm hand on her elbow halted her. Her breath ceased. She looked up to see Mathieu beside her, one eyebrow raised.

"Leaving so soon, milady? I thought you promised me a bassadance." His eyes sparkled bright in the flickering light from the wall torches, and his voice was a low rumble.

Eva swallowed. "I... I did, my lord. But the bassa is a slow dance, one I might be able to perform. The music the minstrels play now is very fast—"

"Their next song will be a bassa. I personally requested it." Mathieu's smile crinkled his eyes at the corners. "I made you a promise, milady, and I shall keep it."

Warmth shot through Eva, from her toes to the top of her head. *He had requested it.* A slow dance, so he could dance with her.

Mathieu had spoken the truth. Within moments, the tempo of the music returned to its leisurely pace. Many of the dancers, disappointed the faster music had ceased, wandered off the floor to refill their mugs or goblets.

Mathieu took her hand and bowed toward her. "Milady? Let us dance."

As they neared the edge of the dance floor, Eva's heart seized to realize that not only some of the dancers had left, but *all* of them had. She and Mathieu were the only ones left on the floor.

Panicked, she shot a glance up at the dais, where Isabella watched. With a soft smile and nod of her head, Eva knew she had little choice. There was no backing out now.

With his grip firm on her hand, he led her to the center of the room, where the many-candled fixtures flickered overhead. Mathieu bowed toward her again, then stepped back, his eyes never leaving hers. His right hand clasped her left, his other hand tucked behind his back.

Eva's breath caught as he raised their clasped hands high. He tipped his head as if to say, *follow me.*

Then, Mathieu began the steps of the bassa.

Chapter Sixteen

Eva's heart felt lodged in her throat, making breathing a bit of a challenge. At first, her galloping heart, the clamor of voices around her, and the flickering candlelight made her head spin, further threatening her delicate balance. She concentrated on the warmth and firmness of Mathieu's fingers around her own and his riveting gaze to steady her.

When he nodded with such complete confidence, her fluttering heart calmed. In that moment, Eva knew this: even if she herself lacked the courage to perform this night, Mathieu possessed enough for both of them.

They moved forward, one measured step at a time. At first, she focused intently on moving her feet, not only in the right rhythm, but in a way to keep from wobbling on her twisted, weak ankle. It didn't take long for her confidence to soar. After the first few steps, the music wrapped itself around her heart, as did the expression with which Mathieu watched her. Eva let go, and allowed the magic of the moment buoy her.

As she passed them, Eva could hear her sisters, watching from the edge of the room, whispering excitedly to one another. But when she and Mathieu reached the end of the Great Hall and it came time for her to break away from him and turn to go on alone, all of their youthful voices fell into a hush. It was as if they were all, as was Eva, holding their breath.

She shot a worried glance in Mathieu's direction, who was still watching her intently. He nodded his head briefly before the moment of truth arrived. Their hands parted. As her fingers slipped free, the chill radiated up her entire arm.

Eva was glad her long skirts hid her feet from view. She was sure she was not performing the steps correctly but merely moving forward the best she could with one crooked foot. It added a certain sway to her movement. The gentle waving of her arms may have looked deliberate, part of the dance, but they served only to keep her body upright. With a sideways glance to keep up with Mathieu, she proceeded back down the floor toward the dais.

Joy wrapped itself around her heart, a lightness and freedom she'd never experienced.

She'd almost made it when her ankle, fatigued from holding it so stiffly, wobbled.

Mathieu's hand was there, wrapping itself warmly around her clammy fingers. With his support, she quickly regained her balance. His reaction was seamless. Gracefully, he led her in a circle around him until they were at the very place where the dance began. Then, bowing first toward her and then to the audience, they proceeded. Mathieu's eyes shone upon her with so much pride, quick tears sprang to her own.

Eva was shocked to hear soft clapping coming not only from her group of sisters, but from up on the dais. She turned to see Isabella standing, Philip at her side. They were applauding her seemingly small, yet personally monumental, accomplishment.

Captain Knape, along with Gaspard, remained seated.

Alys and Rutger then joined them on the dance floor, following behind as they made their way down the room again. Several other couples followed suit. It wasn't until they'd made this second pass down the entire length of the Great Hall and back that the bubble of magic surrounding Eva burst.

Mathieu paused as they made their turn near the dais, he stopped. His head jerked around, and Eva spied Gaspard behind him. The young knight was tapping on the ostler's shoulder, asking silent permission to take over the dance.

A wave of panic clutched Eva's chest. Mathieu's flattened lips and furrowed brow frightened her even more. Was the young knight challenging the ostler, here, in front of the entire court? And what was his purpose? To establish his superior rank? Or to test Eva's true abilities?

Mathieu

Mathieu could barely contain his fury at Gaspard's interference.

'Twas true, the victor of the joust traditionally danced with *his lady*. But the simple act of accepting her token did not, by any means, entitle the knight to Eva exclusively. And the Frenchman was fully aware of Eva's condition—he'd been there this morning when she'd lifted her skirts for all to see her affliction. He had to realize how frightening, and challenging, it was for the girl to even attempt a dance.

Apparently, the Frenchman did not care.

Eva had fared well with Mathieu by her side, but surely the knight had seen her waver without his hand to support her. Did he mean to shame her? Or was he simply declaring his superiority over Mathieu—a lowly ostler—in public?

A glance back at the dais told the tale. Captain Knape was on his feet, although swaying somewhat, his face flushed from overabundance of drink. He was clapping, motioning wildly toward the young knight, cheering him on. The image brought a memory to flash back into Mathieu's mind that sent rage pulsing through him. Rage, and horror, and sickness.

This scene happened once before, at a time when the ostler, then just a stable hand in Liège, was himself a witness. 'Twas not just a simple dance he'd observed. Being alone, and only fifteen winters old at the time, there had been nothing he could do to stop the horror.

He'd tried to forget that night, yet the memory tormented his dreams time and again, even now.

'Twas the reason Mathieu, although supported by La Laing and urged by the Duke himself, refused to accept his sword and spurs. If knighthood turned men into the animals he'd watched that night in his stepfather's tavern, Mathieu would sooner die than to be dubbed a knight.

Mathieu stiffened, knowing he had no choice but to turn the lady over to Gaspard. He flashed a glance at Eva, whose eyes were as round and wild as those of Kleine Uil. Even though it was one of the hardest things he'd ever done, Mathieu allowed Eva's fingers to slide free from his own and stepped back, bowing stiffly to the young knight who took his place.

Gaspard did not smile as he took Eva's hand, his expression hooded. Mathieu wondered then if 'twas not his idea to dance with the lady at all, but a command pressed upon him. By Knape, his Captain. The more he considered the notion, the more Mathieu felt certain of it.

He crossed his arms and watched as the music resumed, and the line of dancers made their way down the floor. A bolus of anguish welled up within him, worrying over Eva. Shaking with frustration, he could not watch this unfold. He had to get out of the hall. Mathieu slid into the deep crowd of onlookers without a glance back. Reaching a side door to the keep's hallway, he made his escape unnoticed.

When he burst through the doors into the bailey, a blast of cool air fairly sizzled against the sweat coating his skin. He was glad he was alone in the darkness, until he realized he was not. A small fire burned over near the knights' encampment, and several men stood around it, their voices low. Mathieu lengthened his stride, heading directly for the stables, hoping to escape their notice.

He was not quick enough. One of the men called to him, though not by name.

"Hark thee! Ostler! Is the feast winding down so soon?"

Mathieu continued walking, not even hesitating in his step. "Nay. 'Tis done for me, though," he called. "Goedenacht, Sir knight." He hoped by bidding the man goodnight in Dutch, the man would back off. He knew most of the Duke's knights spoke little of his native tongue.

His strategy failed.

"Een moment, alstublieft." The knight answered him in perfect Dutch, asking him to wait. The monstrously large man wearing chain mail over his tunic and leather braies came stomping across the bailey toward him in heavy boots. Mathieu tensed and stopped to face the man.

He recognized him as another who'd accompanied them on the hunt this morn—as well as one who'd competed in the joust. His destrier was one of the handsomest of the knight's mounts, a tall strawberry roan with a chest as wide as a drawbridge. Studying the massive man, Mathieu's brow lifted.

How could this giant warrior have gone down under Gaspard's lance in the final round?

"Ostler... Mathieu, is it not?" The knight stopped an arm's distance away and held out his hand. "I'm Ròidh Keegan. A Scottish import to the Duke's Royal Guard."

"Scotland, eh? Yet you speak perfect Dutch." The ostler extended his hand. "Mathieu of Liège. What is it I can do for you, Sir Keegan?" he asked.

"Admiral La Laing tells of your expertise with the horses. My charger, Dirck, seemed a little off in his step when I returned from the games. I was wondering if you might take a look."

Mathieu clenched his teeth. He did not trust this knight. In truth, any knight. Was this some kind of ploy to humiliate him?

"The horses' foot care belongs to the blacksmith, Sir knight. 'Tis not my specialty."

Keegan shook his head. "Nay, I've already had the blacksmith take a look. He says 'tis naught wrong with the hoof nor the shoe."

The man motioned toward the stables. "I can bring Dirck out for you to see, my lord. I would be much obliged if you would give me your opinion."

Reluctantly, Mathieu fell into step beside the giant warrior. He looked to be not much older than himself—mayhap younger. He did not possess the grizzled hardness of eye and manner Mathieu had come to expect of Knape's men. He accompanied Keegan into the stable and followed him to the stall of his charger, the majestic roan stallion.

"Your mount is magnificent, Sir Keegan. I was honored to ready him for you this afternoon."

"I thank ye for that." Keegan's lips flattened and he shook his head. "A fiasco, those games, were they not?"

The ostler knew to temper his words wisely. "I will admit, I was surprised to see the French knight take you down in the last go."

The big knight snorted. "You, me, God, and the devil as well." A hearty laugh burst from him. Then he turned toward Mathieu and fisted huge hands on his hips. He lowered his voice, his gaze darting the area to be sure they were alone. " 'Twas Knape's doing. The Frenchman is a fledgling. Earned his spurs not even a year past. I was told Gaspard would win the joust, deserved or not, or 'twould be my head on the pike."

Ah. Now it all came clear. Mathieu couldn't imagine how Gaspard had gotten as far as he did in the joust, let alone win the thing. His ruffled pride somewhat settled, he motioned for the knight to bring out his horse.

Sure enough, as Keegan went to back the beast out of its stall, Mathieu spotted the uneven gait immediately. He narrowed his eyes, watching closely as the knight led the stallion out into the bailey. Mathieu grabbed a torch from the entryway.

"Trot him back and forth for me, Sir Keegan."

The knight did as the ostler asked, running beside the horse for twenty paces or so. When he returned, his mouth was set in a grim line.

"He seems worse this eve, by far," the knight grumbled. "What do you think is the cause?"

Mathieu laid the torch on the ground and squatted close to the horse's left rear leg. The animal favored it, allowing only the tip of its hoof to touch the ground. Positioning himself clear should the horse lash out, the ostler ran his hands gently up the leg from the hoof to the hindquarter. When he neared the top, the charger tensed and hopped away.

Mathieu rose and swept the dust from his hands. He pointed to a spot below the flank. "I believe it's in the joint here, above the hock, Sir Keegan. He might have stumbled on a root or caught his hoof in a hole. The length of the lists weren't exactly level, by any means."

Keegan perched his hands on his hips and stared at the horse's leg. "How bad is it, this injury?"

Mathieu shook his head. "There's no swelling. If it's just a strain to the joint, should come right with a poultice for a day or two." He scratched the back of his head, his mouth grim. "If the tendon is torn..."

"God's bones, that's all I need. I really like this charger. I've had him since I was dubbed two years ago. We've become a team, Dirck and me." He patted the horse's muscular neck.

"I'll do what I can, Sir Keegan. I'll pack the joint in wet mud tonight, and we'll see how he looks in the morn. I'm leaving in the coming days with Admiral La Laing for Le Havre. We're going to be looking at some new stock." Mathieu paused, studying the knight. "You might approach the Admiral, Sir Keegan, and ask if you can come along. Mayhap there'll be another charger you can look at... in case Dirck's leg doesn't come right soon enough."

Eva

At Gaspard's side, the trip of the bassa down the length of the Great Hall was the longest of Eva's life. She tensed all over when the knight took her hand, his grip not nearly as firm and reassuring as Mathieu's had been. His hand, as well as his demeanor, was as cold as a winter's night. He avoided looking at her, keeping his eyes trained straight ahead. It was as though he didn't even want to be dancing with her.

Truth be told, after she'd spilled her guts on his boots just hours earlier, she couldn't blame him.

The room held too many people, and the tallow candles overhead as well as the flaming torches on the walls permeated the air with smoky heat. Her cheeks felt flushed, and a trickle of sweat snaked its way down between her breasts. She prayed to God she would not succumb to any more embarrassing displays by her body—displays revealing the truth about how she truly felt about the French knight.

Struggling to keep her breathing even, Eva made her way to the end of the hall. With every faltering step, she knew what was coming—the turn, and her solo trip back toward the dais. Sure enough, when Gaspard's fingers slid free from her own, her ankle wobbled. The distance back to the dais was too far off. She knew she'd never make it. Halting with her feet apart and arms held wide to keep her balance, Eva called to her partner to gain his attention.

"My lord."

She curtsied in what she hoped was an acceptable way to signal the end of their dance. He studied her with only a raised eyebrow, then shrugged. She limped back over to the sidelines, and Alys hurried forward to grip her elbow. Eva was overcome with embarrassment, mortified by her inability to perform even this, such a simple act, unassisted. Here, in view of all, including *her knight*.

Soon after, the minstrels again kicked up the pace of the dance, and the floor flooded with gaiety. Eva's fun, however, was over. The older of the girls, first Alys, then Beverielle, drifted off onto the dance floor on the hand of a partner. Shrinking back, Eva spied once again the doorway leading to her escape.

Searching the crowd, she could not see Mathieu anywhere.

To her relief, one of Isabella's handmaidens approached the girls and motioned for them to follow her. It was time for the younger maids to leave the hall, before the drinking and rowdiness got out of hand. Trailing behind her sisters, Eva followed.

The air, even in the outer passageways, felt smoky and close. Between the exertion of the dance and pure nerves, Eva was having a hard time breathing anyway. Spying the side door leading out into the bailey, she slipped away from the group and stepped outside.

The cool night was heavenly, filling her lungs and cooling her sweat-dampened skin. She carefully picked her way down the stone steps. A clear sky shone with twinkling stars, and a full moon cast the bailey in an eerily glowing light.

A stroll through the gardens, she thought, would be lovely tonight. Mayhap the peace and solitude would act as a balm to her wounded pride.

But alas, Eva was unable to take a walk alone. Not only would she risk a fall, but the flickering campfire and boisterous male laughter from the far end of the bailey reminded her what other dangers might befall her. When she heard a familiar voice, her head whipped around toward the stables.

It was Mathieu, speaking in Dutch with a giant of a man at the head of a massive charger. Eva recognized the knight as the one who'd ridden out with Knape this morn. Had it truly been earlier this day? To Eva, a lifetime seemed to have whizzed by since sunrise.

I should thank him. The words echoed in her head like a command from the heavens. She owed Mathieu much for this night's accomplishment—her first dance. The moment would stand out in her memory for the rest of time as one of the most important of her life.

She did not want to interrupt his conversation with the knight, however, so she waited. Mathieu finished wrapping what looked like muddy linens around the horse's leg and finally stood, returning the horse to the stable. Both men reappeared and shook hands before the great knight headed back toward the encampment. Even traveling as fast as her feet would safely carry her, she could not keep up. Mathieu had already disappeared inside the stable by the time she reached the entrance.

"Mathieu?" she called into the darkness. The torches had been extinguished, and the door at the far end of the stalls leading to the ostler's quarters was closed. Dare she be so bold as to knock on his door? Surely he hadn't fallen asleep so quickly.

The scent of fresh hay and warm horseflesh welcomed her. She could hear the horses munching their supper and the occasional stomping of a restless hoof. The stable was a peaceful place, she thought. 'Twas no wonder Mathieu had chosen this vocation.

She had only taken a few steps into the gloaming before she spotted the tiny owl hopping in the hay toward her. His eyes shone, catching the light of the moon filtering in from outside. She crouched low and smiled.

"Hello, little owl. Are you having a fine hunt this eve?"

Gwooihk.

The bird chirped happily, flapping his wings and jumping up and down. A rustling in the corner caught his attention, and he turned and hopped off in that direction.

"Happy hunting," she whispered as she rose to her feet.

A moment later, Eva gasped when a strong hand clamped around her upper arm. A scream rose to her throat but never made its way out. The rough leather of the gauntlet was so large it covered her mouth and even her nose, so she had trouble drawing breath.

Kweeo... kwiff-kwiff-kwiff!

The last sound Eva heard was the terrified screech of Kleine Uil before her world went black.

Chapter Seventeen

Mathieu

Mathieu washed up quickly and was drying his face on a linen towel before hitting his pallet. It had been a very long day begun many hours ago. Even the brief nap hadn't bolstered his energy enough to withstand any more of the crowd and the clamor inside the Great Hall.

Truth be told, he simply couldn't stand by and watch Gaspard—*the knight*—displace him from Eva's side on the dance floor. 'Twas a symbolic as well as actual insult, by both the maiden as well as the Frenchman. He should have known better than to even ask her to dance after her championing of the knight on the jousting field today.

Even though it caused a pain in his heart he neither understood nor welcomed, Mathieu forced himself to face how Eva felt about him then and there: naught. The strange attraction he felt toward her, the tingling of his skin on hers, the wanton longing he felt whenever he was near her—it all meant nothing, if not returned by the lady herself.

Despite himself, his hopes had risen. She was a lady who not only stirred his blood but also seemed to share his interests. He'd been duly impressed by not only her willingness to handle the falcon this morn, but her lack of fear in doing so.

A life partner. Alas, 'twas not to be, at least not with the blonde maiden from Ghent.

Mathieu's ire simmered still, though, toward the Frenchman for his audacity on the dance floor. He rubbed his knuckles, still healing from the last time he'd taken out his frustrations by punching a stall board. The interruption this evening by Keegan had been a welcome one, to be sure.

The knight had complimented Mathieu by acknowledging his expertise with the horses. Respect. Unexpected, especially from one of Knape's group. But welcome, just the same.

'Twas a shame about the knight's charger, though. He feared the injury to the joint referred to as the *stifle* would never come right. At least, not right enough to render the stallion capable of the rigors of long-distance travel, let alone battle.

Mathieu had just folded his tunic over a chair and flopped onto his pallet when he heard a sound from beyond his door. He stilled, straining to hear. Closing his eyes, he sighed. 'Twas Kleine Uil, who seldom made much noise unless he'd gotten himself in trouble. More than once the tiny creature chased a rodent into the far end of a horse's stall, then found himself unable to escape without risking being crushed under a heavy hoof. Mathieu groaned and heaved himself to his feet.

The darkness in the stable was blinding, and Mathieu had not lit a candle or torch. He waited a moment to allow his eyes to adjust, training his ear to the sounds the bird made to locate him. Kleine Uil appeared from behind a heap of hay near the front entrance, flapping his wings and hopping up and down.

Kwiff-kwiff-kwiff. Kwiff-kwiff-kwiff.

The tiny owl was shrieking his warning call, a shrill sound of fear and fury. 'Twas not often the creature did this...

"What's wrong with you, silly bird? Encounter a rat twice your size again?" he murmured as he strode toward the front of the stable.

He then heard shouting and heavy footsteps out in the bailey. Mathieu rushed outside, oblivious to the fact that he'd fled his quarters barefoot, wearing only his braies.

Twenty paces from the stable, the giant Dutch knight he'd bid good evening to just moments ago was crouching next to a prone body on the ground.

Keegan looked up and saw him. "Mathieu. Come help me here. 'Tis a maiden."

Other men came running from the encampment behind Keegan bearing torches, some with blades drawn. Mathieu hurried to the spot and dropped to his knees, his heart clenching when he saw the maiden's face.

'Twas Eva, her face pale and eerily still in the torches' glow.

"What happened here?" Mathieu barked. "Last I saw her, this maid she was on the dance floor with Gaspard." Suspicion flared in his chest, and he flexed his fists.

Keegan's face was a mask of outrage. "I had barely gotten back to the camp when I heard a sound from the stable. I thought 'twas you, Mathieu. Then I saw him, a tall figure, all in black. The maid was flung over his shoulder. The man must have been drunk, and he staggered, losing his grip. The girl hit the ground, and then he was gone. Scuttled away like a three-legged dog."

"Alert the Captain," another knight barked. "We have a rapscallion in our midst."

The sharp blast of a horn echoed across the bailey—once, twice, three times.

Grumbles passed through the rank of men as they dispersed to search the yard. Mathieu did not move from the spot, however. He pressed his fingers to the side of Eva's cool neck and was relieved to feel a pulse. Even in the dim light, he could see a dark pool growing from under the maiden's head.

"A torch here, please," he asked of a knight near him. He passed the light over her body, finding the dark pool was, in fact, blood. "Call for the healer," he said, his voice tight.

Eva stirred then, moaning as she brought one hand up to the side of her head. When her eyes fluttered open, she belted out a scream that startled even the biggest of the giant men bending over her. They all staggered backward.

Mathieu caught her hand and squeezed. "Eva. Eva, it's Mathieu. What happened?"

Her eyes were wild, and for the moment he was certain she recognized no one, not even him. She batted his hand away and lashed out with both hands, fighting an invisible enemy.

Mathieu and Keegan held her down, one on each shoulder, to keep her from harming herself even further. She was quaking like the hull of a ship on rough seas. They were unable to reach her, break through her hysteria, for several of the longest moments of Mathieu's life. Then, just as suddenly as her flailing began, it ceased. Her eyes rolled back in her head and her body went limp.

Frighteningly limp.

Mathieu, down on his knees beside her, felt again for her pulse in her neck, then pressed his ear to her chest. Her heartbeat thudded, rapid and weak. He looked up, meeting Keegan's intense gaze. "Call the healer," he croaked again, his voice cracking.

The knights were all staring at him with venom in their eyes, and he realized in that moment how inappropriately dressed he was. How suspect he must have appeared. One of the big men's hands clamped down over his bare shoulder. Keegan stood and smacked the man's hand away, barking a curse.

" 'Twas not the ostler, you fool. I watched the scoundrel scurry off, that way." He pointed toward the kitchen garden. "Mathieu came from the stables a moment later." Then the knight swiveled to rake his gaze over his men. "Where is the Captain? Why has he not been alerted?"

At that moment two men appeared in the doorway to the Great Hall. One of them was the knight sent to retrieve his Captain. The other was the Duke, Philip himself.

"What goes on here?" the Duke called out. "Where is Knape?"

The knight beside him leaned in close to murmur something in Philip's ear. The Duke's oath echoed across the bailey.

Behind the Duke, the Duchess appeared. Outwardly, as always, she appeared calm and nonplussed.

"Bring the girl to my quarters, please, Sir Keegan. Send Gillette."

Isabella

An hour later, Isabella sat on a stool beside the pallet where Eva lay. She'd instructed the knight to bring the girl to a small room across the hall from her personal quarters. Frantic with worry, the Duchess had no intention to allow the girl too far from her sight. Eva had still not regained consciousness.

The healer, Gillette, was a stout woman dressed from head to toe in peasant brown. She arrived toting her basket of herbs and remedies. One look at the maiden and the elder's lips flattened. She ran her hands over the girl's arm, noting the bruising already coloring angrily on her skin where her sleeve had been torn away. Isabella urged her impatiently.

"She suffered a fall, Gillette. Her head... the scalp is torn, and it is bleeding."

Gently, the healer turned Eva's head and gasped. Beneath her was a swath of folded linen as thick as Gillette's beefy hand. The cloth was almost completely saturated, red with the girl's blood. She glanced up at the Duchess, shaking her head as she bent over her patient.

"Head wounds... 'tis not much I can do for them, Lady Duchess."

The healer pulled up Eva's eyelids, one at a time. The girl was completely insensible. "This could be serious, I'm afraid. And treating it is beyond my capabilities."

Isabella's chest clutched at the fear she saw in the healer's expression. "What can be done?"

Gillette folded her arms across her broad chest, her mouth grim. "There's a barber-surgeon in Brussels. He'd be the one to call, milady, if the girl doesn't regain her senses by the morn."

A knock at the door interrupted them, and Isabella called permission to enter. Duke Philip appeared in the doorway, his fists clenched at his sides.

"Is she recovered, milady?" The Duke's voice was high and tight, his movements jerky.

The Duchess bolted to her feet and stalked toward him. "Nay, and the healer feels the injury is serious. Her head... there's a gash and a huge swelling." Isabella's voice broke as she said the words. How could this have happened? Her grief was quickly overcome by anger. She turned on the Duke.

"How can one feel safe if a young maiden can be attacked thus? Within our own castle? With knights fairly swarming the bailey?" Isabella shouted, viciously glaring at her husband. "What says your fine Captain of this? Where was he when this occurred?"

Philip lowered his head. "In his quarters, my lady. Knape was already far into his cups when the dancing began. I sent him away shortly before the alarm sounded."

"Did no one summon him?" Isabella was now bellowing, her usual composure snapped.

"He could not be roused, my lady."

Isabella huffed and began pacing, her arms folded tightly across her chest. "Did the guards locate no one? No one to blame for this attempted—" The Duchess glanced over at Eva before tempering her words. "Abduction?"

Philip shrugged, which enraged Isabella further. He spoke slowly, as if speaking to a child. "The castle is filled with folk during the festival, dear wife. We questioned the guards, but they noticed no one unseemly leaving through the gatehouse. Only the peasants from the village, most so drunk they could barely walk."

The Duchess stared at him for a long, tense moment. Then she threw her hands into the air. "It seems the only thing that saved the poor girl's virtue was drink. Sir Keegan said the man staggered before he dropped her and ran." She pinched the bridge of her nose between two fingers and sank back onto the stool at Eva's side.

Isabella laid a hand on the young woman's cheek. "If, in fact, she can be saved at all." Her tears spilled over.

Mathieu

After Keegan carefully lifted Eva's limp form and strode off toward the keep, Mathieu remained, searching the ground. The memory of the maiden lying helpless in the dirt, her head bleeding, tore at his heart. He hovered the torch over the hard-packed earth where a rivulet of blood trickled. When he reached its source, he moaned.

A stone jutted up through the ground. 'Twas a granite stone, the part above the surface about the size of his hand. He could remember tripping on the damned thing more than once. It didn't protrude far, but what did was a sharp-edged wedge – sharp enough to cut her scalp, mayhap fracture her skull.

Of all the places where Eva's head might have broken her fall, this was the worst spot by far.

He'd watched Sir Keegan carry her off, unconscious still, to where he did not know. Worry consumed him, along with a feeling of helplessness he found maddening.

Should he inquire as to her condition? Ask to see her? Would she even consent to see him—or be asking instead for *her knight*? And why, even, should anyone honor his requests?

After all, he was merely the ostler.

Chapter Eighteen

Mathieu paced through the night, tracing and retracing his own steps through the stables, across the bailey toward the knights' camp, and back again. No news had come out of the castle since Eva disappeared into the keep in Keegan's arms. The big knight, who had exited the castle shortly afterward, shook his head and said he had no news.

The night was clear and cool, the sky an inverted, inky bowl pierced with pinpoints of light. The moon, just a day past full, glowered down at the ostler like a giant, knowing eye.

But not one willing to tell its secrets.

The cocks had just begun their pre-dawn serenade when the doors to the castle creaked open, and a hefty woman waddled down the stone steps. *The healer.* Mathieu spotted her and ran to catch her before she reached the gatehouse.

"Milady, please," he began, breathless, "how is the maiden? Does she live?"

Gillette stopped, shifting her basket of remedies up on her arm. Her face was grim. "Aye. She lives. But 'tis naught more I can do for her."

She started to move away, and Mathieu stayed her with a hand on her arm. "Please, healer. Can you tell me no more?"

At that moment the ostler heard his name called from the doorway. 'Twas the admiral, La Laing, his manner urgent.

"Mathieu, you must ride to Brussels. Take my charger—he is fast, and strong enough to carry you both back. We need the surgeon, Egbert van Bel. Right away."

"The surgeon." Mathieu's heart stilled in his chest. "But where do I find him, my lord?"

La Laing descended the steps and laid a hand on the ostler's shoulder. He looked older than he had just hours earlier, his skin ashen and his eyes dim. "Go to the Huyssen Inn. Ask for him there."

Mathieu had never saddled a horse faster in his life. The horse, seemingly annoyed at being disturbed so early in the day, did not make the task any easier. When he finally succeeded and ran with the reins in hand to the entrance of the stables. He swung into the saddle as the stallion skidded past La Laing in the bailey.

"Hurry, boy. The maid's strength is fading."

Brussels was a short ride from Coudenburg. As the glow of dawn splashed color on the horizon, Mathieu leaned over the neck of La Laing's streamlined red charger and gave the horse his head, the wind whistling past him. Eva's face appeared over and over in his mind—her smile, her laugh, her funny uneven gait, her pompous air when she felt threatened or insulted.

She could be taking her last breath even now, he thought.

She cannot die. Please, God, do not take her from me.

He remembered the place in the village, and he galloped through the streets until he reached it. The horse danced behind him as he pounded on the door of the Huyssen Inn. Long seconds ticked by, and Mathieu thought he would go mad, break the door down if no one opened it soon. Finally, he heard the bolts snap, and the door swung partway open. A face appeared in the crevice.

"Aye, what do you want?," the old man growled. "We are closed, our rooms are full. Go away."

When the man tried to close the door, Mathieu shoved his boot in the opening. "I have come from Coudenburg. The admiral... the Duke... Duke Philip sends me. For the surgeon. There's been an accident."

The old man squinted at him as if he didn't understand a word, then the lines on his face crumpled deeper. "Van Bel has a shop 'round back. Call for him there." Mathieu staggered back as he slammed the door in his face.

More precious minutes ticked by as the ostler tied the charger to a post and slipped between the buildings. He came upon another door bearing a sign: *Egbert van Bel, Barber-Surgeon.*

After several minutes of pounding on the door finally wakened van Bel, it took what seemed like forever for the drowsy surgeon to return to the door with a leather-wrapped parcel. He was a small man, slight of build, and balding. Shuffling through the alleyway, van Bel didn't seem at all hurried as

Mathieu led him to the street. The ostler clenched his fists. He wanted to scream.

"The maiden is Philip's daughter. Be quick, man."

The surgeon's eyes grew round. "Why didn't you say so?" he sputtered as Mathieu helped him aboard the stallion.

La Laing's charger was a powerful beast and lost no ground even bearing two riders. They burst into the bailey at top speed and skidded to a stop in front of the keep. Mathieu swung down and held out a hand to his passenger. But instead of returning to the stables with the horse, Mathieu called to his page, Rogier, who was stumbling sleepily out of his quarters. When van Bel scurried through the keep's doorway, the ostler waited not for permission. He was close on the surgeon's heels.

They climbed the great spiral staircase to the second floor. At the end of the hallway, Mathieu saw the Duchess standing, her gown rumpled and her face pale. She was wringing her hands.

"In here, my lord," she said, pointing to the quarters across the hall from her own.

Van Bel rounded the corner and disappeared into the room. Mathieu found himself face to face with Lady Isabella, who eyed him suspiciously.

He dropped to one knee before her, his head bowed. "I must see her, Your grace. Please... I know I am not her knight, but—" His voice broke.

"Her knight? I don't believe Eva's heart belongs to a knight." Isabella's voice was soft as her hand rested on his head. "But her condition is grave, Mathieu. She will not know you are here."

The ostler raised his eyes to meet hers. "Mayhap not. Still, I must see her. Please."

The Duchess hesitated only a moment before nodding and stepping out of his way.

The room reeked of tallow and sweat and pungent herbs. 'Twas so small a space there was barely room for a single pallet and half-barrel table, on which the candle flickered. Yet a single, stained-glass window was exquisite, taking up nearly the entire outer wall.

In the dim light, Mathieu leaned over the shoulder of the surgeon, who was on his knees beside Eva. He felt the maiden's neck, then laid his ear to her chest.

"How did this happen?" the surgeon barked.

"She fell from the height of a man. He dropped her."

The surgeon turned to peer up at him, questioning. "A wound such as this, it does not seem—"

"There is a stone. A sharp edge of marble," Mathieu blurted the explanation, but could not finish, his voice crushed in his throat.

Van Bel held the candle over Eva, running his fingers over the bruises on her arm. Then he studied the rest of her body, his gaze falling on her twisted ankle.

"She bears an injury here as well," he mumbled.

"Nay," Isabella cut in. "She was born that way."

Grunting, the surgeon nodded as he worked his way back up to Eva's head, which lay on a thick pad of cloth. Gently, he rolled her head to the side.

Mathieu's stomach lurched when he saw the massive swelling on the side of her head. A mat of her golden hair was dyed red, the blood already turning brown where it had dried. Van Bel got to work quickly, working to remove clumps of the clotted hair with a sharp rondel dagger. When he leaned back, Mathieu caught sight of the wound, now fully exposed. All the air rushed out of his lungs.

Protruding from Eva's scalp was a bump the size of a lady's fist. A small gash in its center was crusted over, but blood leaked out slowly in a pulsating rhythm. 'Twas the only sign of life about her. To look at her face, so still and grey, one might easily think she was dead.

Van Bel shook his head and made an ominous humming sound. "This is very bad. Very bad, indeed." He turned to look up at the Duchess, who stood next to Mathieu. "I must lance the wound, your Grace. The scalp must be peeled away to see if there is damage to the bone." His mouth flattened. "I cannot promise she will survive."

Isabel's voice was tight and small. "Do whatever you can, good sir. We are grateful you have come."

The next hours dragged on as Mathieu sat in the knights' encampment next to Keegan. 'Twas barely mid-morning and he'd already drank more ale than he'd ever drunk in a day. The big knight seemed to sense the ostler's pain and kept refilling both of their wooden mugs. The camp was strangely quiet this morn, with few other men moving about.

Gaspard nor Knape were anywhere in sight.

Mathieu glanced around. "Where is rest of the guard?"

Keegan snorted. "After feast day, our mighty knights are fit for naught. As for the Captain? We won't see Knape until the evening meal." He drained his mug and wiped the foam from his bushy mustache. "If I ever catch the devil who did this to her, I'll kill him with my bare hands," Keegan growled.

They waited as the sun rose over the castle, each moment lasting a lifetime. Every time a servant emerged from the keep, they both jumped to their feet. The Duchess promised she would send word when the surgeon had finished his task. Time and again, they were disappointed when the servant scurried off, heading elsewhere in the bailey.

Finally, as time neared the noon meal, a handmaiden came running across the bailey toward them.

"Lady Duchess calls for the ostler," she called flatly.

When Mathieu arrived in the doorway, the room smelled even worse than before. Now it brought to mind the stench from the butcher's stall on a hot summer day, and the thought turned Mathieu's stomach. There was no mistaking the tang of blood.

The surgeon was still leaning over Eva, wrapping her head with strips of linen.

"Your Grace, these wrappings must be changed at least two times a day. The wound should be dusted with some powder of myrtle, then wrapped in linens soaked in oil of roses and vinegar. This lambskin cap will prevent the dressing from drying and also keep insects away." The surgeon rose stiffly and turned toward Mathieu. "Are you the maid's man?"

Mathieu blinked, stunned. "Nay. I just... I simply care for her a great deal."

The surgeon handed him a bundle of clean linen strips and a bottle of the unction he'd described. "Then you should be the one to tend to the dressings. The wound is not pretty, and 'twill take one with a strong constitution—and who cares a great deal for the girl—to perform this duty properly."

Mathieu turned to look at the Duchess, who placed a hand on his shoulder. "If you wish, Mathieu, you may stay and tend Eva's wound. We will assign your stable duties to the knights' squires and pages."

He did not hesitate. "I do wish to tend to her. Very much, your Grace."

The surgeon rose to leave, and Mathieu voiced the question he was afraid to ask. "My lord... will she live?"

The man stared at him for a long moment before replying. "If she does, and regains all her faculties, 'twill be a miracle." He added, "If the wound festers, however, there will be no saving her."

Chapter Nineteen

Mathieu sat at Eva's bedside all through the afternoon hours. The air in the room grew close and warm as the sun beat against the castle's stone wall. Light splattered the space in many colors through the stained-glass window. As he sat slumped against the back of a small, hard chair, the ostler wondered absently why such an exquisite window dressed a room so small.

A servant knocked on the door at some point, offering a tray with bread, cheese, and a pitcher of wine. Mathieu motioned for her to leave it at the door. There was no way he could eat anything at all, but he sipped only at the tepid wine.

Holding her limp, cool hand in his, Mathieu stared at Eva, afraid she'd slip away at any moment. He watched her breathing, slow and shallow, but unceasing. Yet her skin remained cool. No fever yet. For that the ostler thanked the heavens.

As the light faded, a kitchen maid came again, this time bearing a basin and a small cup filled with a greenish powder. *The powder of myrtle.* Mathieu swallowed as he realized it was time to change the dressing.

On his knees, the ostler poured some of the unction the surgeon left into the basin and ribboned in two strips of linen. While they soaked up the concoction, he rolled up his sleeves and relit the tallow candle. He drew in a deep breath.

The lambskin cap slid off the oily cloths easily, and Mathieu began unwinding the bandage from around Eva's head. He did his best to jostle her as little as possible, though she did not stir at all. He was not sure if this made him feel better, or infinitely worse. When the last layer of linen came free, he stifled a gasp.

The injury was no longer a small gash. It was now an L-shaped flap, as long his thumb on each side. It had been sewn back into place with haphazard stitches. The surgeon said he would lance the wound, but Mathieu hadn't expected the treatment would leave a wound this severe.

Using a wad of linen, Mathieu dabbed the myrtle powder on the incision. He noticed the swelling had lessened, and the bleeding ceased. The wound did not appear angry or soured. A glimmer of hope flickered.

As he worked, Mathieu swore under his breath. He was clumsy, and his fingers were too big. The linen strips caught on his calloused skin. It did not help that he was trembling all over. He wondered if he was truly the best choice to tend Eva's wound after all.

By the time the ostler finished his task, his hands were shaking so violently he nearly sloshed unction all over the pallet. Sitting back on his heels, he dropped his head into his hands for a moment, trying to regain calm. Overcoming even his stalwart control, the sob issued up from the depths of him.

Mathieu jolted out of his reverie when a hand came down on his shoulder. Looking up, he saw the Duchess, studying him with a sad smile.

"Had ye trouble tending her wound, ostler?" she asked softly.

He nodded. "The dressing is new. I will change it again before the witching hour."

"Why don't you come to the hall? Eat something. Then go get some rest. I will have one of my handmaidens sit with Eva until you return."

Weariness and misery seeped into every inch of his body. And although it killed Mathieu to leave her, he knew he must. His biggest fear was not knowing if when he returned, the girl would still live. Yet he knew without food, without rest, he would be unable to perform his task adequately. He swiped a hand down his face.

"I should go to the stables first... the aviary—"

"It's all been taken care of, Mathieu. The stock have been fed and bedded down for the night." The Duchess paused, a twinkle lighting her eyes. "I even made sure the squires released Kleine Uil from your quarters. God knows, we can't have the tiny creature miss an evening of hunting."

Mathieu sighed, so many emotions swirling within him he dared not try to grasp at any one. His throat felt thick as he replied, "Many thanks, Lady Duchess. I will come to the hall."

The hall was already nearly deserted when he arrived, and the servants were busy clearing away the meal's leavings. Isabella motioned for him to join her on the dais. He felt out of place, since the only time he sat at the head table was when the admiral was present and requested it. Reluctantly, he settled into the seat beside her.

Isabella

The Duchess called for food and wine. While waiting for the meal to arrive, she turned toward Mathieu and studied him. Her watchful eye had missed naught over the past days since Eva's arrival. Something about the ostler had changed and judging by his emotional response to her injury, those changes held more importance than she had first thought.

"You have taken to the girl," she said softly. 'Twas not a question, but a statement of fact.

Mathieu avoided meeting her eye, staring instead at the goblet on the table before him.

"Aye. 'Tis a shame she has her heart set on a knight." He gripped the stem of the pewter goblet with both hands, a desperate hold. "I wish only happiness for her. If she lives."

The Duchess laid a hand on his arm. "The surgeon is skilled and wise, Mathieu. We will do all we can to ensure she survives."

The servant arrived with a pitcher, and a trencher filled with fragrant, steaming stew. After his goblet had been filled, he drained it by half before tearing off a chunk of bread. Isabella sipped from her own goblet before speaking again.

"The girl is an innocent, Mathieu. Her head is filled with the bards' tales of chivalrous romance. Yet truly, I think 'tis a sort of armor she wears over her heart. I've spoken to her at length. She realizes her station."

The ostler shot her a wry glance. "Aye, I believe you are right. But 'tis not wisdom, but her temper she wields as a shield." He speared a chunk of meat with the knife. "She reminds me of the little owl. Flawed, yet a fighter nonetheless." He raked his hair back from his face. "I hope her strength carries her through this tragedy."

Isabella blew out a breath. "I, as well. I cannot help but feel responsible, by bringing her here."

Mathieu shook his head. "Nay. In bringing her to Coudenburg, you made the dreams of a simple tailor's daughter come true."

As well, mayhap, those of a certain ostler, Isabella mused silently.

"Does Eva know how you feel for her?" she asked.

Mathieu shifted in his seat. "She knows I am drawn to her. Yet I believe she looks down upon me for my station. She hesitated not to allow the knight to replace me for the *bassadance*—"

"You know she had no choice in that matter."

" *'Twas* her choice to offer her token to the knight on the jousting field," he countered.

Isabella scowled. "As I said, she is but an innocent girl with dreams of grandeur. Besides, it did not appear she was too pleased when the knight collected his prize."

Mathieu blinked up at her. "What do you mean? I left the field before the joust ended." .

She narrowed her eyes at him. "So, you did not see? Gaspard was quite embarrassed by the girl's reaction to his kiss."

The ostler expression transformed, his lips quirking. "Is that so? Mayhap I shall renew my efforts to woo the maiden."

The Duchess leaned her chin on her hand and gazed off across the great room. "If she lives."

Sobering quickly, Mathieu snapped, "Did the guards ever find the man who did this thing?" An edge sharpened his tone like a blade.

"Nay. Whomever it was, they disappeared into the night like a phantom."

"If I ever catch the rogue, he shall die by my own hand," he growled, his fist tightening around the knife until his knuckles were white.

A figure appeared in the stairwell, and Isabella straightened in her chair. "Captain Knape. 'Tis about time you showed your face." Her voice was cold and accusatory. One of her thin eyebrows rose.

She felt the ostler stiffen beside her. The Duchess knew Mathieu despised the man, but not the reason why. Knape was a rough man, she knew, and stretched the codes of chivalry to their limits. But a knight needed to be so in order to survive on the battlefield. 'Twas one of the reasons she had never pushed Mathieu to continue his training and vie for knighthood. She knew 'twas not in his nature to be a warrior.

Not that the ostler didn't possess the bravery or weaponry skills—she knew he did. But sheer brutality and cold-hearted killing took a special kind of man. Mathieu would not be happy living such a life.

Still, she wondered about his hatred for Knape. Something specific must have happened between the men. Yet she knew not what.

"Shall I have the servants bring you food, Captain Knape?" she asked.

The tall knight shook his head, avoiding her gaze. He was unshaven and dressed in a rumpled tunic she guessed he'd slept in. The Duke had told Isabella that the Captain had drunk to excess the night before.

Knape made his way quickly across the room, pausing only briefly to bow before the Duchess. "Nay, Your Grace. I will sup with my men."

"You have heard, I trust, of the tragedy in the bailey last night?" she asked as he strode off, trying to keep her patience in check. She did not take lightly to being shunned which was, it appeared, his intent.

Knape froze with his back toward the dais. When he finally jerked around, he drew up, his whole body taught like a bow.

"Nay, your grace. What happened?" Knape's tone was strained.

Before the Duchess could relate the tale, Mathieu wiped his mouth and rose to his feet. "Lady Duchess, I will return to my quarters until 'tis time to tend the lady's wound again." He spoke low so only she would hear his words.

Isabella squinted up at him and paused before nodding her permission.

She must, she decided, take the ostler aside and find out what caused him such disdain for the Captain. Mathieu was a decent man, gentle and kind. There must be a very good reason for him to loathe being in the same room with Captain Knape.

Chapter Twenty

M^{athieu} Mathieu retired to his quarters but could not sleep. His mind kept whirring back across the bailey, up the spiral staircase, and into the small room where Eva lay. Was she breathing still? Could she possibly have woken?

Dressing in a fresh tunic and braies, the ostler made his way through the stables to the courtyard. He noted the pages and squires had done an admiral job in his absence. The stalls were heavily padded with fresh straw, and the horses munched hay contentedly. He did not see Kleine Uil, but 'twas not unusual. The owl typically hid behind the great mound of hay in a corner, waiting silently for an unsuspecting rodent to venture out.

Torches burned in the bailey, casting light where there would have otherwise been none. No moon tonight, nor were stars visible. The air felt heavy and carried the distinct scent of impending rain.

Mathieu was a natural-born loner yet was oddly gripped with the desire for conversation this night. There were so many worries on his mind, so much he was unsure of. He headed for the knight's encampment in search of Keegan.

He found the big knight leaning against the stone outer wall, a mug in one hand, speaking in low tones with, of all men, Sir Gaspard. Mathieu paused and turned to leave, but too late. Keegan had seen him.

"Ostler! Come here and tell us. You have news of the maiden?" he boomed.

He approached and nodded to both knights. "Sir Keegan. Sir Gaspard. I tended to the maiden this afternoon after the surgeon took his leave." Mathieu paused and tilted his head. "Do you know who took van Bel back to Brussels?"

"I did, ostler. 'Twas the least I could do," Gaspard said quietly.

The least I could do. And odd thing to say, Mathieu thought. Why?

Gaspard reached over and snatched a mug from the stack next to the barrel and drew some ale. Handing it to Mathieu, he added, "We both sent our squires, Sir Keegan and me, to the stables and aviary this eve as well. I trust they performed all the duties satisfactorily."

Mathieu drank deeply. "I thank you both, heartily. The Duchess asked if I would tend to the dressings on the girl's injury." He closed his eyes and shuddered. " 'Tis a ghastly sight." He gazed off into the darkness, sadness aching in his chest. "I pray she will survive this."

He filled the two knights in on the details of her injury and how the surgeon had treated it. Both men scowled and shuffled in place as he described the gory wound.

" 'Tis no wonder the Duchess asked you to tend the injury. I doubt any of the servants or handmaids could stomach it," Keegan muttered.

"I'm not sure I could," Gaspard added.

Mathieu shrugged. "I've tended battle wounds on the horses, and rest assured, some of them have been nearly as difficult to see as Eva's injury. 'Tis worse when the maggots set in."

Both knights, huge and powerful men, winced and groaned.

"No news as to who was responsible?" Keegan asked.

"Nay. The Duke believes 'twas someone from outside the castle who was here for the feast. I guess now we'll never know," Mathieu said. He turned toward Gaspard. "Sir Knight, in all the confusion, I neglected to congratulate you on your jousting victory." He caught the leer Keegan threw his way and ignored it.

"Thank you. I am proud of the win." He paused, studying Mathieu with narrowed eyes. "But my victory favor from the maiden didn't turn out exactly the way I'd hoped."

Mathieu lifted an eyebrow. "Oh? I had left the field for the stables."

Gaspard drained his mug and then glared at Mathieu. "I will tell you this, ostler. The lady likes the attention from the knights, the dancing and the flirting. But it's just as well I have no ideas of pursuing her. I believe her heart already belongs to another."

The courtyard was dark and silent as Mathieu crept through into the castle. He had waited as long as he dared, knowing the dressing needed changing, but dreading the task just the same. Two mugs of ale shared with the knights bolstered his courage enough to drive him up the stairs to where she lay.

A single candle flickered on the table, and a handmaiden sat near the window on a chair. Her chin rested on her chest, and she was dozing. Mathieu cleared his throat so as not to scare the wits out of her. She jerked awake, confusion clouding her face.

"I am the ostler, milady. I have come to tend the maiden's wound."

She rose, saying, "I will wait in the hall, my lord. Unless you need my help..."

The way her voice trailed off, Mathieu could tell the girl definitely did not want his reply to be "aye."

"Has there been any change?" he asked.

"Nay. I will wait outside, my lord," she repeated, scurrying for the door.

A fresh bowl of myrtle powder stood beside the linen wrappings and bottle of unction on the table. Mathieu sucked in a deep breath and knelt next to the pallet.

Her pose and ghostly white pallor made her look so much like a corpse, he shuddered. Folded neatly across her middle, her fingers felt cold to his touch. But a pulse beat still in her neck. Hope flared in Mathieu's mind when he determined 'twas even stronger than before.

Spiraling two strips of linen into the bowl of unction, he got to work unwrapping Eva's head. As the bandages fell free, he held his breath. He prayed the ugly incision had not swollen, turned angry, or showed signs of infection.

It did not. A bald spot the size of his palm, where the surgeon had cut away her beautiful blonde hair, surrounded the stitched skin. The tan myrtle powder had absorbed some of the oozing, turning it a sickly dark green. But the wound was dry and did not appear to be bleeding.

Mathieu did better this time. His fingers weren't shaking so badly—probably thanks to the ale—but he also knew now exactly what had to be done. The task took him half as long as the first time. Still, Eva did not stir at all.

After he'd reapplied the calfskin cap over the dressing, he rested his elbows on the pallet, gazing at her face. If not for the ghoulish cap, one might think she were simply sleeping, peacefully. Her golden lashes fanned across ivory cheeks, and Mathieu felt his throat fill with emotion.

"My lord? How is she?" The Duchess' voice reached him from the doorway.

"She sleeps still, Your Grace. There is no change in the wound."

Isabella came to crouch beside the pallet. "She sleeps still—better to bear the pain. The surgeon's work was harsh." She wrinkled her nose at the memory. "There were slivers of bone... he removed them. It is a blessing she sleeps."

An involuntary shudder racked Mathieu's shoulders. He could not begin to imagine the pain such a wound would cause, if the girl was conscious. Yes, better she sleeps.

The Duchess patted his shoulder. "My private quarters are across the hall. If you have need of me, alert the guard outside my door. He will rouse me."

Mathieu remained after the Duchess left, kneeling next to the pallet. The pain in his heart throbbed in rhythm with his heartbeat, a heart that felt as though it were breaking. How had this happened?

Less than a fortnight ago, he had begrudged retrieving the girl from Ghent.

He'd found her to be snobbish and aloof, almost to the point of insulting. Her pride was definitely her strongest suit—a suit she wore like armor. He wondered if what she kept hidden was more than just her illegitimate birth and her defect.

He wondered if he'd ever get the chance to ask her. Rubbing his eyes and blaming the moisture there from exhaustion, he rose to leave. Unable to help himself, he feathered the back of his hand over her cool cheek.

"Sleep peacefully, princess, until your pain has ebbed. But please, please come back to me. Back to the world of the living." His voice broke. "Give me the chance to win your love," he whispered.

As he stood he caught sight of her hair, the long, golden ribbons the surgeon had cut away. They had fallen between the pallet and the table. Reverently, he lifted the strands and ran them through his fingers. Stuck together near one end with crusted, dried blood, the remainder of the strands were still as soft as the finest silk. They still smelled like her—fresh and clean, scented with lavender.

A knot formed in his throat, and he swallowed hard. Curling her hair into his fist, he left the chamber.

The next two days passed in a blur for Mathieu. His fatigue increased as his inability to sleep took its toll, and soon he felt as if he was trapped in a terribly bad dream. In more lucid moments—like when he stared down at her horrendous wound—he knew 'twas no nightmare.

On the third night, he came to check on her after the evening meal. Nothing had changed. Like one who was already dead yet continued to breathe, Eva remained still, growing paler. Her full cheeks, Mathieu noticed with horror, had begun to take on a hollowness.

As the evening light faded from the colorful window, the ostler sat beneath it, his back against the stone wall. Exhaustion overtook him. When he closed his eyes, his mind whirled into the recent past, where his Eva was alive and well and feisty.

The afternoon in the aviary, when she'd so delighted him with her interest and bravery with the falcon. When she melted into his arms as though 'twas where she belonged. The scent of her hair, lavender filling his senses. The taste of her lush mouth, hot and warm on his own.

He could see her clearly, in his mind's eye, dancing down the length of the Great Hall, their hands joined. The look of sheer delight and joy on her face was one he'd never forget. One, he prayed to all that is holy, he would see again.

His Eva.

His mind whirled back to the night of the bonfire, when he'd stolen their first kiss. When she'd come to the stable and met his little owl friend. How enchanted she had been with the flawed creature, stroking its feathers as Kleine leaned into her hand. She identified with the damaged owl. Eva also recognized, and acknowledged, the part of Mathieu he tried to keep hidden. His softer side. The one that drew him to pamper the infirmed yet not pity them.

His Eva.

Then the memory of her attack crashed down on him like a guillotine. Kleine Uil's screeching. Keegan stooping over her body on the ground. The rivulet of blood trickling off the wedge of granite in the bailey.

He jerked awake to a sound. In the dim light of the almost-spent candle, he could see she had not moved. Did she breathe still, or had the relentless hand of death claimed her?

But he had heard a sound. Had he dreamed it?

A moment later she stirred, moaning, and his heart leapt. He rushed to her side.

When he laid his palm against her cheek, dread washed over him in an all-consuming wave. Her skin was as hot as a kettle on the hearth. She was burning up with fever.

Mathieu stumbled out the door, jarring awake the dozing guard in the hall.

"Please. Rouse the Duchess. The maiden worsens."

Within moments Isabella was at his side. She touched Eva's head and gasped. "Bring us water," she shouted to the guard.

They bathed her with cool water until her chemise and the pallet beneath her were soaked.

She fought them, moaning and pushing their hands away in a frenzied battle against the chill. Two handmaids held her down, and between Isabella and Mathieu, they continued until Eva stopped thrashing and went limp. Frighteningly so.

Isabella's fingers went to her neck as Mathieu pressed his ear to her chest. Still beating, rapid now but still weak. They looked at each other, and the ostler saw the haunted look in Isabella's eyes.

"I'm sorry I brought her here," the Duchess whispered, a tear leaking from her eye.

"Nay, Lady Duchess. I am not. Even if it be selfish. Meeting Eva of Utrecht was one of the most magical events of my life."

"But if she dies—"

"If she dies, I will have the brief, wondrous memories of my time with the maiden. Grief could never erase them." He held the Duchess' gaze. "Eva is special, Lady Duchess. She has touched my soul as none other. I believe she was sent to us for a reason. I also believe her pride—her stubborn pride—will help her weather this storm. I pray it, verily."

Unable to speak, Isabella's mouth quivered, and she looked away. With a parting glance at the girl, she quit the room in silence.

Mathieu changed Eva's dressing again later that night. When he removed the lambskin cap, heat rose off the oil-soaked bandage in a steamy cloud. The fever had not abated. His heart clenched in his chest.

Then a haunting revelation washed over him.

The cap was holding in the heat of her fever.

After redressing the wound, the ostler left the cap off. He bathed her again with cool cloths, over her face and arms, laying a wet strip over her forehead when he was through. She made no sound, no movement as he worked. The pulse in her neck fluttered like Kleine Uil's heart yet felt weaker than before. Even though her skin still burned hot, she'd begun to shiver violently.

Agony twisted in his gut as the ostler struggled with the grim reality—the maiden was dying.

There was naught more he could do for her. That anyone could do. Mathieu prayed for a miracle, wishing he could infuse the young girl with his own strength. If only he could transfer some of his life's force upon her broken body...

Around the time of the witching hour, Mathieu cast prudence and propriety to the side. He carefully climbed onto the soggy pallet, positioning himself to sit above her head. With his back against the wall, he rested one leg on each side of her body. Then he lifted her until her battered head rested against his chest. He wound his arms around her and lowered his cheek to rest against hers.

Entirely inappropriate, yet entirely essential.

If the maid's soul was to leave her body this night, Mathieu wanted to be the last to hold her while she lived.

As he held Eva's limp form, her shivering lessened. Her breathing slowed and grew shallower. His tears flowed unchecked down his own cheek onto hers. Mathieu felt sure she was nearing the end. He knew he should call for the priest to administer the last rites.

But that, he decided, would be giving up hope. That, Mathieu refused to do.

He began to speak to her softly, hoping that somehow his words were penetrating her mind.

"Eva, you have touched a part of my soul I knew not existed. Your beauty, inside and out, has changed me. I could never have earned your love, but I prayed someday I might. I have never known love, but you taught me its magic. I love you, Eva of Utrecht. If ye enter heaven this night, ye shall know it to be true."

Now facing the colorful round window, the ostler tried to make out the images in the stained glass. 'Twas not one single pane, he realized, but many smaller panels set in a circular pattern. They radiated out from the center like the spokes of a wheel. Or the petals of a flower. Like wildflowers. He recalled Eva's mention of her love for wildflowers.

Mathieu wondered again at the placement of such an exquisite window in this tiny room.

The moon's cool rays radiated through the complex design, causing the air around them to glow. The effect was mesmerizing. As he gazed upon it, a strange peace settled over him as he succumbed to exhaustion.

Chapter Twenty-One

Isabella

The Duchess crept into the room at dawn's first light. After helping the ostler deal with Eva's raging fever, she had gone back to her quarters with a heart heavy, certain the girl would not live until the morn. Sleep eluded her. Finally, she rose and dressed, then made her way across the hall.

Shock and pity washed over her at the scene. Mathieu lay in the bed with the girl, holding her in his arms on the sodden pallet. The ostler's scarred cheek rested against Eva's, on the side opposite her wound. He was deeply asleep.

Two damaged creatures, clinging to one another. Her heart clutched.

The girl, she feared, had ceased breathing. She knelt beside them and laid her fingers on Eva's arm. 'Twas cool and damp, and the Duchess' stomach lurched. It was then she noticed how the girl's hand clutched Mathieu's wrists. It looked as though she'd been hanging on as one drowning to a floating branch.

Isabella laid her fingers on the girl's neck and was shocked to feel a pulse. 'Twas stronger now, no longer fluttering like a captive bird. Her fever had broken, and she lived still. A burst of hope bloomed in her chest.

The Duchess hurried into the hall and summoned the guard.

Mathieu

Mathieu awoke to a throbbing pain. Cocked at an odd angle against the wall, his neck was so stiff he could barely move his head. His arms felt empty and cold. His clothing was soaked through to the skin from the soggy pallet beneath him.

Eva was gone.

Bolting to his feet, Mathieu nearly collided with the Duchess in the doorway.

"Is she...?" He could not bear to say the words he knew to be true.

The expression on Isabella's face first confused and then angered him. Her mouth was quirked, as though trying to suppress a smile. 'Twas funny? His fists clenched as he croaked out the question.

"Where is Eva?"

The Duchess took hold of Mathieu's arm and led him, silently, across the hall into her personal quarters. There, on a padded bench with a tall, carved back, lay Eva. Dread consumed him. Her body was laid out, like one in death. But on a settle in the Duchess' private quarters? This was odd. The Duchess had apparently loved the girl too.

He hurried to Eva's body and dropped to his knees, sobs racking his chest.

"No, Mathieu. Do not grieve. She lives." Lady Isabella's voice penetrated his sorrow and for a moment, the ostler was befuddled.

It was not until he laid his ear to Eva's chest and heard her heart beating, steady and strong, that he believed the Duchess' words. She slept still, yet her skin was cool. No fever. The Duchess' handmaids had stripped her wet chemise and replaced it with a clean, dry frock. He looked up at Isabella, who was now smiling openly.

"I had to get her off the wet pallet and into fresh clothes," she said.

Mathieu cringed, realizing how it was Isabella had found him. In the bed, holding the maiden.

"I am sorry, milady. I know what I did was improper. But she was shivering. I hoped only to warm and comfort her."

Isabella closed her eyes, shaking her head. "You did naught wrong, ostler. For all we know, yours may have been the life force holding her spirit within her body."

" 'Twas my hope," Mathieu choked out.

"She is past the danger of the fever. A miracle," she said. "Now we need pray for yet another—that she wakes. Wakes to see and recognize the man who truly loves her."

The ostler stood, dumbfounded. He did not know what to say.

The servants entered the room carrying the bandages and unction.

" 'Tis time to change the dressing, Mathieu. If you would, please," the Duchess said. She eyed him up and down, standing there in his soaking garments, dripping on her solar floor. "But first, you should go change into dry clothes."

Isabella

While Mathieu was gone, Isabella ordered a new, dry pallet to be placed in the small room, along with rations for the ostler to break his fast. She knew he wouldn't want to leave her yet again to dine in the Great Hall.

Mathieu returned shortly after, and the Duchess met him in the hall.

"How is she, Lady Duchess? Still no fever?" he asked, rubbing his hands, one over the other.

"She is the same, Mathieu. We have moved her back into the oratory, onto a dry pallet." She sobered. "Still, she has not awoken, I'm afraid."

The Duchess motioned for him to follow her. When they entered the room, as before, Eva lay in a corpse-like pose, her hands folded on her middle. Isabella was pleased to notice the room smelled much better now, with the fresh pallet and a new layer of scented rushes covering the floor. He watched Mathieu kneel at the girl's side to check the pulse in her neck. His sigh of relief clutched at her heart.

"I have left you bread and cheese, with a little wine, Mathieu. You are welcome to break your fast here, if you wish."

"Many thanks, milady." Mathieu pulled the single chair closer to the pallet and settled into it. He glanced about the small room. "What is this place, Lady Duchess? It seems an odd room for such a wondrous window." He motioned to the round, stained glass, glowing brilliantly now in the morning sun.

"This was intended as my private chapel. When my husband, Philip, took over the conversion of the castle to a residence, he ordered this room be built for me." Tears blurred her vision. She motioned toward the window. "The colorful window amplifies the light pouring in, like divine light from heaven."

" 'Tis most powerful." He laid a hand over Eva's, and she could see he was fighting back emotion.

"I thought 'twould be the best place for Eva. Here, I pray, the heavens will shine their light down upon her and mayhap heal her." She gathered her skirts and turned to leave. "Eat, Mathieu. You must keep up your strength."

The ostler stood and bowed before her. "I know 'tis most irregular to ask I be allowed to remain, Lady Duchess. You may assign a handmaiden to join me if you wish—"

She waved a hand in the air. "The handmaiden who was here last night waited outside the door until you had finished with Eva's bandage. I then sent her away." She placed a hand on his shoulder. "I have no doubts your intentions with the girl are honorable."

Mathieu heaved a deep sigh and raked a hand through his hair. "If she awakes... no, *when* she awakes, I intend to ask Eva for her hand in marriage." He hesitated before adding, "I will ask the Duke for her hand."

The Duchess was not surprised at his words. She had witnessed, firsthand, how the relationship between the two had flickered with promise. 'Twas true, Eva had met Mathieu less than a fortnight ago, yet some things, she knew, were simply meant to be.

To Isabella's mind, Eva and Mathieu were meant to be.

"She will most likely refuse me," he added sadly. "She has set her sights higher."

"You may be surprised, ostler. Eva has learned much since she's come here to the castle. She's also, I daresay, matured a great deal in her thinking."

Isabella found Philip in the Great Hall. He was sitting with his arms crossed on the table, staring into his goblet as the servants cleared away the morning meal. When she stepped up onto the dais, he greeted her with a wan smile.

"Milady. How does the maiden fare?" he asked.

"She breathes still but has not awoken." Isabella took the seat next to her husband. "Do you still intend to travel to Ghent this day?"

Philip nodded. " 'Tis not much I can do for the girl, even if I stay." He met her gaze, concern pinching his brows. "Shall I inform her family of her fate while I am there?"

Her family. The Duke's indifference roused ire in Isabella's chest. "Her family? I believe *you* are a member of her family as well, are you not, Philip?"

His scowl spoke volumes. "Aye. I am her father, but I did not raise the girl. I am not one who has grown to love her, and who will miss her if she does not live," he added quickly.

The Duchess snapped around in her chair to glare at him. "We do not yet know if the girl's life is forfeit, do we?" Isabella took a sip from her goblet the servant had just filled. Quietly, she added, "The fever broke during the night. She may have a chance at life after all."

Philip looked up and smiled. "Good news! So, I shall send word to... her maman that she may be coming home soon?"

"Nay. Eva may not be going home soon, even if she recovers. Do not send word. Not yet."

"Why so?"

Isabella set down her goblet, her eyes boring into his. "The ostler has expressed interest in the maiden. We may have, inadvertently—and with no help from you, I might add—found a marriage match for Eva by bringing her here to Coudenburg."

The Duke's mouth flattened, and Isabella wasn't sure if it was due to her insult or to the proposed match. Until he spoke.

"I received a missive this morn, milady," he began, "from Master Arnolfini in Ghent. He has an apprentice, an Italian called Stefano. He has expressed interest in the girl as well."

Isabella tipped up her chin. "Eva mentioned this man to me. She has no interest in the Italian."

Philip sat back and crossed his arms over his chest. "That may be so. But a merchant's wife lives much more comfortably than an ostler's. Do you not agree?"

Isabella bristled. "Marriage can be more than a domestic arrangement," she said through clenched teeth.

"Oh. Is it *love* to which you refer? Have the bard's tales tainted your mind with the ridiculous idea of romance?" Philip hissed, his tone as sharp as vinegar.

He jumped, however, when the lady's fist came down on the table, rattling everything on its surface.

"To you—as to most men—love is synonymous with lust, nothing more. Pleasures of the flesh, fleeting and inconsequential." She glared at him, narrowing her eyes. "Love does exist, dear Philip. Mayhap not for me or you. 'Tis true, 'tis a rare find in this world. But I believe Eva has a chance for this wondrous thing, with Mathieu. As Alys has with Rutger," she added.

Philip ran his hand through his short, dark hair. "I had forgotten. Alys is to marry the blacksmith's apprentice soon, is she not? He asked for her hand on May Day."

"Aye. The union was to take place before you left for Ghent, but Eva's injury changed those plans. When do you intend to return? We will schedule the wedding for then."

"I should return within a fortnight. The business I have there should not take long."

Isabella couldn't help but wonder exactly what "business" Philip referred to. Would his short trip result in yet another bastard? She dared not ask.

At this point, she had come to where she did not care.

Chapter Twenty-Two

E*va*
    Eva was in her room at home, in Ghent, that which she shared with her two siblings. Young Tomas was awake early, again. Even on the days when she was permitted to sleep late, her younger brother would not allow it. He was trying to wake her, this time by pulling on her hair. A sharp pain throbbed on the side of her head as he tug, tug, tugged. If she didn't stop him soon, he would pull out her hair by the very roots.

Her eyes fluttered open and she raised a hand to swat him away. But a swirling light of many colors accosted her eyes, making her dizzy. Clutching one hand to her head, she felt not her hair, but a wad of cloth. Confusion swept over her, and her stomach twisted. She was going to be sick, she was sure of it. But when she tried to roll over so as not to soil her pallet, a strong, warm hand caught hers. She struggled to focus on the face hovering above her.

'Twas not Tomas. 'Twas Mathieu.

He was... smiling. Beaming, in fact. Yet there were tears running down his face, over his puckered scar and into a beard that had grown quite full. She stared at him, thoroughly confused.

"Wha—what happened?" she asked. Her throat felt as dry as pressed linen, her tongue a sticky, starched board.

Mathieu dropped to his knees beside her, grasping both of her hands in his. He laid his forehead on them, and she could feel his body shuddering. Was he ill too?

By God's bones, she needed some water. "Ostler... Mathieu. Water. Please."

He stumbled to his feet and shouted toward the door. "Bring water for the lady, please. She wakes!" He returned to her side, cupping her cheek in his hand. "Praise God. You are still with us."

She raised her hand to her head once again. The tugging on her scalp had not ceased, and now the pain was threatening to pop her eyes out of her head. "Can you untangle my hair, please, Mathieu. It must be caught on something."

"Nay, sweet girl. You have an injury. Your pain comes from that." He turned to the servant who had entered with a pitcher and a cup. "Please, summon the healer. The lady needs something for the pain."

Several hours later, Eva lay on the pallet, propped up by great, soft pillows the servants had carried in from the Duchess' solar. Her head pounded still, but a potion the healer made her drink was beginning to soften the pain. Many faces had drifted in and out of the small room since she'd awoken, ever-changing.

Except for Mathieu's. He had not left her side one time.

Now it was Isabella who sat near the pallet, holding one of Eva's hands. "What is the last thing you remember, Eva? Do you remember who accosted you in the bailey?"

Eva blinked, clawing through her befuddled brain to remember. It seemed a lifetime ago, and yet, just moments. Finally, a memory stirred.

"The tiny owl. Kleine Uil. He was screeching. I had come to speak to Mathieu, to thank him. For the dance." She smiled up at him where he stood behind the Duchess.

As the scene formed itself in her mind, her smile faded. "Someone grabbed me. My arm. He tore my beautiful gown. A great gauntlet covered my face. I could not breathe." Her gaze drifted off toward the window. "That's all I remember."

Isabella sighed and patted her hand. " 'Tis fine, Eva. Do not worry on it any longer." She turned to the servant by the door. "Can you please bring more broth for the maiden? She's finished what was here."

Eva was, truly, starving. Her stomach made odd noises as it turned over on itself, empty as it had been for—as she discovered—four days.

She had been unconscious for four, entire days.

Just then a loud, gurgling came from her midsection. Feeling her cheeks warm, she raised a hand and asked, "Your grace, may I have some bread as well? My stomach demands it."

Warm laughter from all present felt like an invisible embrace.

" 'Tis good to hear you are hungry, Eva. I will send up bread, and perhaps a little cheese."

When all had left the chamber save Mathieu, she asked, "Alys' wedding. Did I miss it?"

"Nay. They have postponed the marriage until you are well. Now 'twill occur when the Duke returns from his business in Ghent."

Eva tensed. The Duke had left for Ghent. Why did that frighten her so? Her thinking remained clouded, whether from the injury or the potions, she knew not which.

Think, Eva, think. The Duke will tell her mother of her injury, certainly but...

Her eyes flew wide, and she struggled to sit forward. "Mathieu, the Duke must be told. The clothier, his apprentice. Stefano intends to ask for my hand."

She watched the ostler's face pinch with concern. "Your hand?" He swiped a hand down his face, a mask of anguish. "Are you promised to another, milady?" he asked, his voice a tremulous whisper.

"Nay! The apprentice, he pursues me. But I do not want to marry him. Please."

Isabella came in through the door carrying a tray of food and drink. "Lady Duchess, the Duke must know—I do not want to marry Stefano."

Isabella set down the tray and clasped Eva's hand. "Worry not. I have spoken with the Duke before he departed. No decisions will be made until his return."

Over the next days, Eva's strength returned gradually, though the pain in her head persisted. The healer instructed the cook to prepare great pots of tea with ginger, peppermint, and feverfew. Although the taste was rather unpleasant, she found the brew did ease her head from aching for a short time.

'Twas a glorious spring day when the healer first allowed Eva out of the castle. Mathieu held her arm securely as they strolled in the garden, now a riotous mass of color and scents. He led her to a turfed bench to rest in the shade, as the sun had risen high.

"Are you well, milady?" Mathieu asked.

Eva breathed in the floral-scented air and smiled. "I am. The healer's tea works its magic. And you," she reached up to cradle the ostler's cheek in her hand, "your gentle ministrations cause my wound to heal quickly, I believe." Her hand touched the bandage. "I fear, though, what I shall look like when the wrappings come free. My hair..."

"I would think you beautiful if there was not a hair on your head."

"Would you?"

He gazed into her eyes. "Aye. And I would do anything for you, Eva. I just wish I could find the man who did this to you." His fist clenched and unclenched. "I would kill him with my bare hands."

"Nay. You have it not in you, Mathieu. You are not a killer. 'Tis why a warrior's life would not suit you."

He stared at her silently for a moment. "Does that pain you? You had your heart set on a knight, did you not?"

Eva lowered her head. "Aye, I did. I was a silly girl who did not understand what is truly worth seeking in this life. The Duchess has taught me well since I arrived here at Coudenburg."

"I feel sorry for the Duchess," Mathieu said. "She has many riches, but not what she truly desires."

"She told me. Isabella made me realize the difference between marrying for title and marrying for love." Eva leaned her head—the side not injured—on Mathieu's shoulder and breathed in his musky scent. "I think, mayhap, I am discovering what it is to love."

He caught her hand in his and squeezed it. "I believe, mayhap, I am as well."

A warm rush of emotion washed over her, sending her heart to flutter. She looked up and studied him. His warm brown eyes were intense on hers, and his hair was loose around his shoulders, stirring in the warm breeze. He'd shaven since she'd first awoken, and she couldn't decide whether she preferred his handsome jaw clean or bearded. Either way, looking at Mathieu, surrounded by his scent, feeling his warm skin on hers—all made her heart dance in a way she'd never known before. There was something about his gaze that stirred embers inside her chest.

When he looked at her this way, she felt she could almost hear his thoughts. Eva had never known a man—nay, anyone—who spoke to her with their eyes.

Mathieu did. And what he was saying to her right now made her whole body feel as though it was melting into the turf atop the bench seat. When he lowered his mouth to hers, she welcomed his kiss.

Twining her fingers into his hair, she gave herself up to him, this man who was quickly claiming her soul. He did not wear armor, nor did he hold a title or lands. What Mathieu possessed was something Eva decided was even more valuable—a brave yet kind, gentle heart. He had not left her side, she was told, the entire time she was near death. He had held her close the night the fever nearly stole her life away.

Isabella swore 'twas Mathieu's presence, his infusing his life force into hers, that saved her. At this moment, she knew 'twas true.

Their tongues tangled in a sensuous dance that went beyond the physical. Eva quivered down to her very soul. When they finally drew apart, she held his face in both hands.

"I love you, Mathieu of Liège. I know not whether I am worthy of you, or if you can find it in your heart to love one as imperfect as I, but I pray it can be so." His image blurred in her eyes as she held her breath, waiting for his reply.

He stroked her cheek and pinched her chin between his fingers. "I don't know when you wormed your way into my very being, Eva of Utrecht. But you are there. I do not intend to ever let you go."

She wrapped her arms around him, laying her head against his broad chest. It felt so good to hold him, and to be held. His unique scent, leather and lye soap and musky male, did things to her insides she did not understand. Desperately, she yearned to understand this magical feeling more.

Mathieu ran his hand down her head gently, skimming over the linen bandage that still encircled her crown. "I wonder how long before the healer removes this."

She tensed and closed her eyes. "I will rue the day. I'm certain 'twill be the day you reel away from me in horror. My hair, I'm certain 'tis ruined."

He pushed back and looked into her eyes. "Remember, milady, 'twas I who tended your wound. I have seen it at its worst." Reaching into the pocket of his braies, he extracted what Eva at first thought was a length of rope. She gasped when she realized 'twas a plait of her own hair.

"I found this after the surgeon left. This is what he cut away from your wound. You see? 'Tis not much." He ran it through his fingers. "I washed the blood away and braided it. I'm going to ask the goldsmith to add a ferrule and clasp. I want him to fashion for me a bracelet. I want to carry a part of you with me, always."

Chapter Twenty-Three

M*athieu*

    Mathieu watched as the barber-surgeon unwrapped the linen bindings from Eva's head. It had been almost a fortnight since the injury, and van Bel rode in on his own horse to check on his patient. 'Twas time, he said, for the stitches to be removed.

The look of terror in Eva's eyes made Mathieu's stomach twist. He wasn't sure what pain she might have to endure for this procedure, but he had assured her he would be with her throughout. The healer had given her a strong potion when they discovered the barber-surgeon had arrived. Hopefully 'twould get her through the worst of it.

"I will try to be gentle, Lady Eva. But the stitches must come out. The incision is healed now, quite nicely." The surgeon smiled down at her. "Even your golden hair has begun to grow back around the wound."

Eva flashed a tremulous smile at Mathieu but said nothing. He squeezed her hand, which was trembling like a leaf in the wind.

'Twas all over in a few moments and with nary a tear shed. Van Bel worked quickly, snipping the stitches and jerking the twisted lengths of silk gently to free them. Like a hawk, Mathieu watched his lady's face, which remained scrunched into a tense mask the entire time.

When the last stitch pulled free, Mathieu murmured, " 'Tis all over now, milady. You can open your eyes."

In that moment he was so incredibly proud of her, his heart filled to bursting. Love washed over him in a hot wave. *I must ask Philip for her hand,* he thought, *as soon as he returns from Ghent.*

The Duke did arrive, later on that very day. He did not, however, arrive alone. Mathieu was sweeping out the stables near noon when he heard the trumpet sound.

Not that the Duke ever traveled alone. Philip had taken a dozen of his knights with him on his journey, and they surrounded him as he made his way into the bailey. But this day an additional rider accompanied them. The man was tall, angular, and dark-haired, much like Philip himself, yet he wore no armor nor even a mail tunic. For a moment Mathieu wondered if this might be yet another of the Duke's bastard sons.

Pages and squires scurried to help the men with their mounts, and the ostler headed straight for the Duke. He kneeled at the horse's head and bowed before him.

"Welcome, my lord. Good to have you home. Did your journey go well?" he asked as he helped Philip dismount.

"Aye, it did. I accomplished much. And I hope to have tied up yet another loose end." He turned to the tall man, who now stood beside him. "Mathieu, this is Stefano de Lucca. He is the apprentice of my good friend, the clothier, Giovanni Arnolfini."

Stefano. The man's name struck Mathieu in the chest as painfully as an arrow. 'Twas the man Eva mentioned when she first recovered. The man who intended to ask for her hand.

The ostler shook Stefano's hand briskly. He was taller than Mathieu, with the chiseled good looks of a nobleman. His black hair was curly and hugged his head like a cap. Dark eyes of almost the same color scrutinized the ostler. He did not smile.

"I understand you are the man I should thank for tending to my Eva. The Duke speaks highly of you, ostler."

My Eva.

With those two words alone, a fire blazed to life within Mathieu's chest. The slight quirk at the corner of the man's mouth said more than mere words. This Italian knew, somehow. He knew Eva was special to him. Stefano was also well aware that with his status as a nobleman, apprentice to one of the Duke's comrades, he definitely held the advantage.

Pulling his hand free, Mathieu said nothing. He simply nodded and took the reins of Philip's horse, heading for the stable.

When the time came for the noon meal, Mathieu was in the middle of setting out his hunting birds in the yard. He thought to ignore the call, but curiosity and dread pushed him to tether the last two falcons quickly and head for the Great Hall.

Immediately upon stepping through the doors, he regretted coming straight from his work. On the dais, Isabella and Philip were flanked by the usual occupants, Captain Knape and Admiral La Laing. Next to the admiral sat the newcomer, Stefano de Lucca, dressed in clean clothes after his journey, looking every part the nobleman. Mathieu glanced down at his own dust-covered tunic. Stopping short, he took a step backward. The least he could have done was to wash his hands and face.

But too late. Isabella had spotted him and called him by name.

"Mathieu, welcome. Would you please go to the girls' quarters and retrieve Lady Eva? You can tell the guard outside her door I have sent for her."

Wiping his hands on his braies, Mathieu nodded and headed down the hallway. At least the Duchess had acknowledged him as Eva's escort. He couldn't help wondering if 'twas all he would ever be to her.

Alys met him at the door of the dortour. When he asked for Eva, she held a finger to her lips.

"The lady sleeps, ostler. I do not think the Duchess wants her disturbed."

"Aye, she does. Lady Duchess herself sent me to retrieve her." He shifted from one foot to the other. "Eva has a visitor," he mumbled.

Mathieu waited in the hallway, his stomach churning. The very last duty he wanted to perform was to deliver Eva—*his* Eva—to this man who arrived with such lofty assumptions. Yet in his heart the ostler knew the truth of the matter. 'Twould be Philip, the maid's father, who would decide her fate when it came to a betrothal. The very thought made the bones of his chest feel as though they were cracking in two.

Within moments Eva appeared. She was fresh-faced and smelled of lavender. A bandage no longer necessary, one of the handmaids had fashioned her hair in a braid that wrapped around her head, covering her wound. Tiny white flowers adorned the braid, giving her the look of an angel.

Wearing a kirtle of dark green, her eyes shone as she smiled up at him.

"Mathieu. Is it time for the noon meal? I am famished."

"Aye, milady. But the Duchess herself calls for you. The Duke has returned from Ghent."

He watched as she wilted, a flower in the hot sun. "In truth, I've been dreading his return."

"As have I."

"I hope..." Eva began the thought, then allowed it to fade, hanging in the air between them.

Without another word, Mathieu closed his hand over hers and led her down the hall toward the Great Hall.

He wanted to scoop her into his arms and head straight for the stables. Once aboard horses, they could be far away from this place in a matter of minutes. He would take her to a place where no one could find them, to a small church, and marry her before any man could stop him. Surely with his experience with the horses and hunting birds, he would find work somewhere.

But then what? Dread dropped over him like hot pitch. There was nowhere to go, and no way to get there. Mathieu didn't even own his own horse.

When they reached the hall, Eva stopped short in the entrance, jerking the ostler to a standstill. Her panicked gaze flashed from the dais to Mathieu and back again. "Stefano," she muttered.

"Aye."

After helping her up onto the raised platform, Mathieu watched as Eva took her seat next to the Italian apprentice. His skin prickled as he clenched and unclenched his fists. When he realized there was no place for him at the head table, even though La Laing was present, he turned to take a seat at one of the common ones.

'Twas the longest and most uncomfortable meal he'd ever sat through. Although the fare smelled delicious—roast hen and spring pottage—Mathieu found it all to taste the same. Bitter, like resentment. Cold, like the icy claw wrapped around his heart.

Philip and the Italian's lively conversation did nothing but aggravate him further. Eva seemed detached, offering little to their talk of fine silks, tapestries, and bejeweled velvets. The words all blurred into a monotonous hum in Mathieu's mind as he spent more time with a mug in his hand than a knife on his plate. Until two words pierced his brain.

Wedding attire.

He watched Eva stiffen, her mouth flattening into a line even as her eyes rounded. She didn't appear to be eating much either, even though she'd claimed to been starving. The appearance of the Italian apprentice had extinguished more than just the ostler's appetite.

When Stefano's hand closed over hers, it was all Mathieu could do to keep from launching himself up onto the dais at the Italian. He ground his teeth and sucked in a shaky breath, waiting.

Eva leaned forward and shot a panicked glance toward the Duchess, whose eyebrow had risen at the mention of wedding attire. She blotted her mouth with a napkin and laid it on the table before she spoke.

"I'm aware, Philip, that the clothier possesses a fine array of imported fabrics for any special occasion. But Alys, as you know, has already fashioned the gown for her wedding day. Which, by the way, will now be held five days hence. Since Eva is now well, and you have returned home, Your Grace."

Philip began shaking his head before Isabella had even finished speaking. "I have spoken much with Stefano on our journey back from Ghent, dear lady, and I think mayhap we should push the betrothal back a few days more." He glanced toward Stefano and winked. "We may, in truth, have a double wedding to plan for."

Eva's goblet slipped from her fingers and clattered to the table, splashing red wine everywhere. Stefano jumped to his feet, brushing frantically with his napkin—*at his own tunic*. With no regard in the least for the lady's welfare.

Mathieu leapt up and, knowing he was breaking with tradition, climbed onto the dais, heading straight to Eva's side.

"Are you well, milady?" he asked, his voice soft. "Here, let me help you."

Eva pinned him with tear-filled eyes. She sat as still as stone as he blotted the wine from her kirtle and lap. Philip's sharp retort shot through him like a hot blade.

"That's quite enough, ostler. How dare you touch the maid in this way?" The Duke called for a servant girl. "Bring wet cloths, wench, and help the maiden clean her dress." Then Philip stood so abruptly, his chair toppled to the floor behind him. He pointed a long, bony finger at Mathieu. "Out, ostler. You belong not here at the high table. Begone to your duties in the stable."

Mathieu's pulse pounded so violently in his head, he heard nothing else as he headed across the bailey. Philip had never—*ever*—belittled him so.

In front of everyone, no less. Mortified, he was angry beyond bounds. His shattered pride, however, was the least of his pain.

'Twas his heart that bled freely in his chest. At least, that's how it felt.

So engrossed was he inside his own seething mind, he jumped when a hand clapped over his shoulder. Spinning around, fist raised, he nearly landed a punch squarely in the man's face. When he saw 'twas Admiral La Laing, all the air whooshed out of his lungs.

"Sorry about the scene, Mathieu. I think the Duke is pretty puffed up thinking he's outsmarted the Duchess and found Eva a husband before she did." The admiral fell in step beside Mathieu, shaking his head.

"I wish I'd gotten to him first, Admiral. In fact, I've already told the Duchess I intended to ask for Eva's hand when he returned." The ostler swiped a hand down his face. " 'Twould seem I am too late."

"Don't be so sure about that. As you know, the Duke may be in charge of such things, but he's oft swayed in his decisions by the Duchess. Ask for an audience with him." La Laing stopped at the stable door and faced Mathieu. "And speak again with Isabella."

As the admiral turned to leave, Mathieu asked, "Admiral, what of your trip to look at horses? Was that cancelled?"

La Laing replied quietly. "I wasn't about to ask you to leave while Eva's life hung in the balance, boy. And now that her future does as well, I won't ask you to leave now. It can wait. The colts aren't going anywhere."

Chapter Twenty-Four

E*va* "I should like to take a walk with you, milady. The Duke says the castle gardens are lovely this time of year."

Eva sat rigidly, still at the table on the dais. The meal was long done, with the only ones remaining the hall she, the Duchess, and Stefano. The Italian had been trying to make conversation with her since she first arrived, but didn't take the hint very well when all she offered were one- and two-word replies. When his hand closed over hers, multiple times, she deftly slipped it away to hide in her lap. She found the mere touch of this man's skin on hers repulsive.

Even before, she remembered. Before she'd ever left Ghent to come to Coudenburg. Before she'd met Mathieu, a man who stirred very different emotions within her.

Now, the revulsion toward Stefano was even worse. Now since she had experienced such opposite emotions. With Mathieu.

Anxiously, she glanced again and again toward the Duchess, who was observing her and the Italian with a detached expression. Philip and the admiral had left long ago, leaving the Duchess, so it seemed, to act as chaperone.

When Stefano mentioned the gardens, the Duchess tipped up her chin.

"They are lovely, Stefano. If you would like to take Eva out for a short time, Adrian would be happy to accompany you." She motioned for the guard who'd been assigned to watch over Eva since her recovery. The huge man stepped forward and nodded.

Isabella added, "Just don't keep her out too long, my lord. She's still quite weak from her injury."

Eva wondered, at that moment, where the guard had been while she and Mathieu sat in the garden earlier. Numerous times, in fact, since her recovery.

I guess the Duchess trusts me with Mathieu. That in itself should be a telling sign of what's meant to be.

"Oh, and Eva? When you return, please join me in my solar." The Duchess turned and disappeared into the stairwell.

Stefano offered his arm as he rose from the table, then helped Eva down from the dais with hands clasped firmly around her waist. Eva fought a wave of nausea at his intimate touch. When his grip lingered a bit longer than necessary, Adrian stepped forward, eyeing the man warily. The Italian shot him a resentful glare.

"The lady has difficulty walking, my lord. I am simply ensuring she is steady before we proceed."

'Twas true, Stefano knew all about Eva's affliction. He'd been coming around to the tailor shop for nigh on five winters, since Eva was just a girl. At first, she'd been fascinated with the handsome Italian, whose accent and dark good looks were so different from the other men in her life. Her stepfather, like her maman, was blond and fair. Many of the Dutch who did their business with them were also light of hair, skin, and eyes.

In a playful puppy sort of way, Eva guessed she had unknowingly encouraged Stefano's interest in her, early on. He'd already been of marrying age, nearly ten winters older than she. Her teasing and flirting with the man, though, had been in innocence and for the attention, which Eva got little of in her very sheltered existence.

She chastised herself now for setting herself up for the difficult situation in which she now found herself.

How to deal with it? Should she simply be honest with Stefano and tell him she held no romantic notions with him? How, she wondered, would he react to that kind of news? After waiting five years until she came of age, and then traveling all this way to speak with the Duke?

Logically, her choice made no sense. Stefano, although not a knight, was of noble blood. Noble *Roman* blood. He also stood on the threshold of his own clothier business in one of the busiest trading centers in all of Flanders. To marry Stefano meant living a life of wealth and luxury, and near to her dear maman and beloved siblings.

Her maman and stepfather, she knew, had been encouraging the Italian's intentions all along. A match with him truly did make perfect sense.

Except her heart now belonged to another. Her breath came in rapid, shaky bursts as she accompanied Stefano out of the Great Hall and into the garden. Somehow, even though the sky above was flawless blue and the sun warm, the garden did not seem nearly as lovely to her as it had when she was with Mathieu.

What was she to do? Had Philip already consented to the match? She prayed 'twas not true.

"Tell me about your stay here, milady. I understand the May Day Feast was wondrous. I regret I was not able to break away until now. I would have loved to enjoy the celebration at your side."

Eva dipped her head, avoiding his gaze. " 'Twas wondrous." Remembering her victory on the dance floor, she smiled up at him. "I even danced the bassa. With Mathieu. 'Twas a most memorable event in my life."

She felt Stefano stiffen beside her. "Yes, Mathieu. He was the one who brought you here, was he not? I trust he was a gentleman on the journey?" One of his dark eyebrows rose.

"Of course," she snapped. "Besides, we were accompanied by Blanche, Lady Duchess' handmaid. Mathieu has been nothing but kind to me since I arrived at Coudenburg." She sniffed.

A long beat of silence shot tension through the air like lightning. His voice was terse when he said, "I do not wish to speak of the ostler this day, Eva. I wish to speak of us, you and me." He motioned toward the turfed bench, the same one where Eva had shared a passionate kiss with Mathieu just hours ago. She swallowed hard to keep her thoughts to herself as she settled onto the seat.

Eva clasped her hands in her lap so tightly, her knuckles were white. She needed to set this Italian straight, and right now. The final decision for her betrothal may belong to the Duke, but she could not believe her father would force her to marry a man for whom she felt nothing.

Even less than nothing.

She straightened her shoulders, summoning the courage to speak. "Stefano, you are a handsome man and a fine prospect for any woman seeking a husband." Turning to look directly into his eyes, she went on, her voice trembling. "But not for me. I do not love you. I intend to seek a marriage for love."

He reeled back as though she'd slapped him, his dark eyelashes blinking so fast she thought for a moment he'd break into tears. But then he began to laugh. Eva sucked in a breath, horror filling her.

He is laughing at my rejection of him?

"I can see, young Eva, that childish notions still live on in your head. Your wish to marry for love?" He barked out another burst of laughter. But quickly, he sobered and pinned her with a terrifying glare. "Andries and Marisse highly approve of our marriage, Eva. They encouraged me to ride out with the Duke on his return."

Eva's guard, Adrian, was standing near the garden gate with his arms crossed and had appeared to be dozing when Stefano's laughter roused him. Eva shot him a desperate look, but Stefano simply smiled at the guard, nodding to signal that there was no need for alarm.

When he turned back towards Eva, though, Stefano narrowed his eyes, and his voice lowered to a threatening rumble. "I have waited a very long time for you. And remember, milady, you are far from perfect. 'Twill be a generous man indeed who will accept you," he motioned toward her ankle, "as you are."

Enraged, Eva tipped up her chin and hissed, "It matters not, Stefano. I do not love you, nor do I intend to share the rest of my life with you. Nor to ever share your bed."

The spark of anger she saw in his eyes frightened her. But she was desperate now to end this. "You are, as I said, a very handsome man who would delight most any woman as a husband. But not me."

One of Stefano's eyebrows lifted. "This wouldn't have anything to do with your esteemed ostler, would it?"

Eva turned to stare straight ahead, keeping her hands bound together in her lap. "As a matter of fact, it does."

"I suppose a lowly stable boy would be most happy to take you on, no matter what your condition. He must be used to dealing with lame beasts all the time."

Shocked, Eva snapped her head around to glare at him. "How dare you speak to me this way? You obviously have no respect for me at all, and still, you expect me to consent to be your wife?"

Her raised voice had finally raised the alarm for her guard. Adrian took a step towards them.

But Stefano's ire was beyond his control now. "You obviously need someone to keep you in line. To keep an eye on you, to keep you safe," he ranted. "Look at you. Here you are at the Duke's castle, with knights at every corner, and still you managed to place yourself in a position of danger. Where was your not-a-knight on the evening you were attacked? How was he protecting your honor then?" Stefano's tone had turned acidic, like spoiled wine.

At that moment, a servant girl came to the garden gate, her gaze flashing from Adrian to Eva and back. Then she addressed the guard.

"The Duchess wishes to see Lady de Lucca in her solar," she said.

Adrian nodded and approached them with long strides. But Stefano stepped forward, defiant.

"You have delivered the message, guard. When we are finished here, I will escort Lady Eva to the Duchess' solar."

The guard shook his head, his expression flinty. "Lady Isabella asks for the lady *now*. Milady?" Adrian stepped forward and offered his arm. Eva wasted not a single breath before sliding down off the seat. She took the guard's arm and hurried out of the garden without a glance back at Stefano.

She knew how angry he must be. But she was relieved, just the same. Until she heard the words he tossed in her direction as she passed through the garden gate.

"Remember, Lady Eva, the decision on your betrothal belongs not to you. It belongs to your father, the Duke."

Mathieu

After the admiral left him at the stables, Mathieu paced up and down between the stalls, temper sizzling just under his skin. He wanted, as usual, to punch something. Mayhap he could imagine the Italian's face as he plowed a fist into a stall board. But there were pages about, so he couldn't do that. Not now.

He decided to head over to the knight's encampment and seek out Keegan. He'd come to feel a sort of camaraderie with the knight since the night Eva was attacked. Right now, a friend was exactly what Mathieu needed.

Mathieu found the knight deep in discussion with—who else?—Gaspard. Once again, he halted as soon as he recognized the Frenchman, but not soon enough. Keegan's booming voice echoed across the yard.

"Ostler! Come hither and join us for mug of ale."

Begrudgingly, Mathieu took the cup from Gaspard and drained it by half. Frustration, even panic, surged in his chest, and he felt as helpless as a kitten. Was there nothing he could do to stop this charade from playing out?

As he wiped the foam from his lip he noticed Gaspard's smirk. "What's the matter, stable boy? Been bested by an Italian merchant?"

It was a reflex. The thought didn't have time to transmit from Mathieu's fist to his brain. The ale mug flew away as he made contact with the sneering knight's face, landing a solid punch to his jaw. Shocked, the Frenchman stumbled backwards, landing on his arse in the dirt, his face splattered with ale and blood.

Keegan was on his feet, stepping between the men in one swift movement. Trembling with rage, Mathieu stood his ground, glaring up at the massive warrior.

"He deserved that," Mathieu muttered through gritted teeth, "and you know it."

Keegan had his huge paw firmly planted on the ostler's chest to prevent him from swinging again. But turning to Gaspard as he struggled to his feet, Keegan echoed, "He's right, Frenchman. Ye deserved that."

Gaspard wiped his hands on his breeches, then spat blood into the dust. He studied the ostler through narrowed eyes for a long, tense moment. Then, rubbing his jaw, he turned to grab two more mugs from beside the ale barrel.

"You're right," he said, his back to both men as he drew from the tap. "I deserved that." He faced them, handing one mug to Mathieu. "Now, with that behind us, we need to put our heads together and figure out how we're going to stop this betrothal from happening."

Mathieu stared at the Frenchman for a moment, disbelief stunning him. Gaspard was on his side in this? He'd been under the impression the knight was his opponent in what seemed to now have become a race for the lady's hand.

But wait. That still could be Gaspard's meaning. Mayhap *he* was the one who wanted Eva, and the Italian's appearance would prevent his plans from materializing.

As though he'd read Mathieu's mind, the Frenchman scowled at him. " 'Tis not for me I want the betrothal stopped, you fool. I have no interest in taking a wife. At least, not yet." He took a long swig of the ale and levelled his gaze on the ostler. "You, on the other hand... it's written all over you, man. You love the girl. Don't you?"

Mathieu slid his eyes away and felt a hot flush rise into his face. Was it that obvious? Had he made that much of a fool of himself over this woman?

Keegan's huge paw clamped down over his shoulder, and he turned to look up at the man. God, he was a monster. The Scottish knight stood a head taller than Mathieu, and with his golden-red hair and beard, brought to mind a lion.

A gentle one, though. The ostler sensed that in Keegan. 'Twas why he liked him so.

"There's nothing to be ashamed of, Mathieu. Every man loses his heart eventually to a warm, soft woman. Every man who has a heart, anyway."

Mathieu sighed. "At first I was sure it was just physical. I'm a loner, and don't pay much mind to such affairs of the heart. But I am a man, too." He shook his head, staring into his cup of ale. The way it sparkled bright gold in the sun, it brought to mind the color of Eva's beautiful hair. He reached into his pocket and felt for the lock he'd salvaged from the floor near her sickbed. He raised his eyes to Keegan's sharp blue ones. " 'Tis more. 'Tis definitely more than lust. I want her for myself. For all time. But now—"

"But now nothing. You have to fight for her, man. I wouldn't let this pompous merchant waltz in and claim her out from underneath you." Gaspard stopped short, a mischievous quirk lifted one corner of his mouth. "You haven't had her underneath you yet... have you?"

Keegan kicked the Frenchman's boot so hard the smaller knight almost hit the ground again. Gaspard hopped a step away. "God's bones, Keegan, you could break a leg with that hoof. I'm just saying, if you've already claimed the girl's maidenhead, mayhap the Italian won't want her anyway."

"I have not," Mathieu said solemnly. "I have too much respect for her. Though I have the feeling she'd be willing. Nay. If I take Eva, it will be after we are bound by marriage."

"No *if* about it, ostler. Does the lass feel the same about you? Are you sure she's not just been toying with ye until her rich Italian came riding in to claim her?" Keegan squinted down at him, scratching his beard.

Mathieu shook head. "Nay. She's already spoken to Isabella about this Italian merchant. He's been pursuing her for a while, I guess, but Eva does not favor him."

Keegan drained his mug and tossed it over into the basket next to the barrel. "Then I would say, Mathieu of Liège, ye need to take action, and quickly. Don't give this a chance to go any further."

Mathieu tipped his head. "But how?"

"Take her away. Make her yours before anyone has the chance to stop ye. There's a cleric in the little church in the village, just down the bottom of the hill. His name is Brother Michael. Tell him I sent ye."

Blinking, Mathieu considered this. It was sudden, and it was rash. "Do you think the Duke will send me away if I do this? 'Twould be in direct defiance to his decision about the girl's betrothal."

"Go talk to Isabella first, then. She is a woman with a kind and virtuous heart. Surely she will side with ye and Eva on this."

Chapter Twenty-Five

E *va* Accompanying the guard to Isabella's solar, Eva dreaded the news she would hear. She had told Isabella of her feelings—or lack thereof—for the Italian. But she knew in the end 'twas the Duke who made this decision. He was, after all, her father.

Isabella was standing before her colorful arched window looking out over the bailey. After the door clicked shut behind her, Eva stood, wringing her hands. The Duchess did not turn to face her.

"I have done what I can, Eva. But Philip seems to have his mind made up on this. This man, this Stefano, is apprentice to his very good friend, Arnolfini. A very powerful merchant, indeed. And one who gets what he wants, at any price."

Her heart seized in her chest. Isabella was her last hope to save her from this loveless match. Sadly, it seemed even a Duchess could not change her fate. Eva's throat closed and she stifled a sob, bringing both fists to her mouth.

Isabella turned to face her, a mournful expression drawing down her noble features. "You will have a good life with this man, Eva. He is almost finished his apprenticeship, and Philip tells me he has already arranged for him to set up shop in Antwerp—"

"I do not love him," Eva choked out. "In fact, I cannot even stand the man's touch on my skin."

Isabella winced as though the words had struck her. Then her pale eyebrows rose. "You are but a girl. What do you know of love?"

Eva sucked in a breath and closed her eyes. "I know how I feel about the ostler, your grace. I know Mathieu feels the same about me."

Isabella sighed. "Many times, we mistake physical attraction for true devotion, Eva. Especially at your age, it's an easy mistake to make. Lust fades. True love, however, never does. At least," she paused, lowering her gaze, "from what I'm told."

Eva was shaking her head, tears running unchecked down her cheeks. "I tried not to love him, Lady Duchess. I had my heart set on a knight. One brave and strong and powerful. But Mathieu has shown me there are many ways to be strong." She lifted her hand to her wound, hidden beneath the braids the handmaid had fashioned to hide it. "Was it not you who said it was Mathieu who kept my spirit within my body the night I almost died? Isn't that love?"

When the Duchess looked up, Eva saw the sheen of tears in her eyes. "Yes, I believe it is."

"Then help me," Eva begged. "Help us."

Isabella turned back toward the window. "I cannot. I tried, but I failed. Philip has set the weddings—for both you and Alys—for this Saturday next. I will send the seamstress to measure you for a gown—"

A knock on the door interrupted her, and they both turned the sound. "Who is there?" Isabella called.

"It is Mathieu, Your Grace. I know I come unannounced, but it is urgent."

Twenty minutes later, Eva and Mathieu sat side by side on the high-backed bench in the Duchess' solar. Their hands tightly clasped, Eva felt some of the tension draining away from her, just having him so near. In her heart, she knew this was the right path. Even though it was one putting all of them—herself, Mathieu, and the Duchess—at risk for the Duke's ire.

"You are both absolutely sure this is what you want to do," Isabella pressed. She sat by the window, her bejeweled fingers folded tightly in her lap. She pinned her gaze on Eva. "You will have no grand home—not even a cottage like Alys and Rutger. All Mathieu has is his small quarters in the stable. His room at Germolles is not much bigger."

In reply, Eva gazed up at Mathieu, feeling her heart swell in her chest. "As long as it is beside Mathieu, I will sleep in the straw with the horses."

"Do you think Philip will cast me out?" Mathieu asked.

Isabella sighed. "He may. But I know how he respects your expertise with the horses and the birds. I do not think he would send you away, if only for his own selfish reasons." She rose and slanted them both a look. "Philip must never know I knew of this plan."

"Never," they declared in unison.

"So 'tis settled then," Mathieu said, lifting his hand to Eva's cheek. "We will go to the village. Tonight. Keegan has already sent word to Brother Michael. By the witching hour, you will be my wife."

Mathieu

That afternoon, after Mathieu had finished his duties in the stables and aviary, he drifted again toward the knights' encampment. He wanted to be sure the plans were set... to ensure Keegan had, indeed, arranged their meeting with Brother Michael for that evening. He found Gaspard and one of the other knights sparring with wooden swords, and he stood watching them for a spell.

He could have gone this route. He could have earned his spurs and sword. If he had wanted to.

After the larger knight knocked the weapon from Gaspard's hand and effectively "killed" him, the Frenchman swore and swiped a hand across his mouth.

"You got me again, Alexander. Remember, brother, how many years you have on me with regard to swordplay." Gaspard pointed at the older knight, smirking. Alexander waved him away and headed toward the tents.

"You may have lost, but you're very good with the sword," Mathieu said. "Who trained you, Frenchman?"

Gaspard flopped down on the bench along the outer wall. "Believe it or not, an Italian." He shot Mathieu a wry look. "Not what you'd like to hear about now. But the Italians are excellent warriors. And they don't always need a weapon to win a battle."

Mathieu sat beside Gaspard and cocked his head. "How so?"

"They train in hand-to-hand combat, without weapons, more than we do. I believe the influence traveled to Rome from the East." The Frenchman studied Mathieu. "Being you don't have access to your own sword, learning some of those tactics might come in handy for you. Someday."

Mathieu jumped to his feet. "Teach me. I spar with the apprentices all the time, but 'tis not the same as battle with real weapons. And fighting on horseback is far different than face to face, on the ground."

Without saying a word, the Frenchman moved so fast Mathieu had no chance to defend himself. Bringing one arm up to knock Mathieu's right arm away, Gaspard used his other hand to chop the ostler in the side of the neck, stunning him. Before Mathieu knew what had happened, Gaspard had hooked his foot around the ostler's leg and pulled it out from under him. He was flat on his back, stunned, the breath knocked out of him.

"By God's bones, you're fast," Mathieu choked out as he struggled to his feet. "Teach me some of these moves, Gaspard."

For the better part of the next hour, the French knight patiently taught Mathieu what he knew about what he called "grappling," which was what the Italians called battle without weaponry.

"There's little use to your fists in situations like this," Gaspard explained. "You end up risking damage to your hands, which then renders you powerless. An upward palm to the chin and nose, now... a strike like that could actually kill a man. The goal is to get him on the ground, where you can use your own arms and legs to bind him, like chains." He scanned Mathieu from head to toe. "You're not beefy, like Keegan, but you've certainly got the height advantage. I'll bet you're fast as well."

Mathieu had never heard of this kind of combat, but he was an eager student. He realized his disadvantage if ever he did find himself in a position where he had to defend himself—or now, his lady—lacking the advantage of either armor or weapons. Who would have guessed the man he scorned so on his arrival, and on the day of the joust, would become such a valuable friend to him?

The two were sweaty and covered in dirt when Keegan came stomping into the encampment. His bushy eyebrows rose. "What's this, now? Has there been a disagreement I'm not aware of?"

Gaspard laughed and slapped Mathieu on the back. "Not hardly. Mathieu wanted to learn some of what I learned from Antoine. You remember, the Italian knight we met back in Nice?"

"I do," Keegan said. "Crafty bastard, 'twas he. Took me to the ground before I had a chance to unsheathe my dagger." He turned to Mathieu and lowered his voice. "It's all arranged. Brother Michael will be expecting ye at the church soon after the sun sets."

Eva

The evening meal was delayed, Eva was sure of it. Why tonight, of all nights? She had spent the afternoon in the dortour, all alone, watching the activity in the bailey through the slit window. Isabella advised it was best for her to keep out of sight, especially from Stefano, for the remainder of the day. She also did not want to be caught gathering her things in the bag she'd brought with her from Ghent. No one could know of this plan. After it was done, she could come back for her belongings without worry for explanations.

If Philip didn't bar her from entering the castle. Tension wound tight in her chest, and her heart beat just a little faster than it should all through the long hours. As the sun began its descent behind the mountains beyond the curtain wall, Eva's entire body felt drawn as tight as a bow.

In reality, though, how angry could the Duke be with her? He'd ignored her existence up until just a few months ago, hadn't he? What right did he have to waltz into her life and make monumental decisions about her future at this late date?

Because he was her father, she reminded herself. Because he was the Duke. Because she was only a girl, a woman with no voice, no right to an opinion of her own. Eva had watched her mother, her entire life, bow to her stepfather's will. Many times, she could see the flash of anger in Marisse's eyes when Andries overrode her opinions or simply ignored them. But Eva had accepted this was the way life for a woman. A wife.

Would it be that way between her and Mathieu? 'Twas a question she'd not asked herself until this very moment. Just the thought of it made her heart flutter even faster.

No. 'Twould be different between them, because they were in love. 'Twas no love between Marisse and Andries, of that she was certain. Her mother had been granted a husband, by the Duke, as reparation for leaving the woman alone in the world, one having borne his child. Marisse had no choice but to accept her fate.

Eva tried, just for a moment, to imagine what it might be like to be married to Stefano. 'Twould be the same as with her mother, she was certain. Even worse. The Italian merchant had a much higher social status than a mere tailor. His haughty attitude spoke volumes about his personality. Surely, he would treat her as a possession, and a damaged one at that.

She shuddered at the thought.

From her perch at the window, she finally saw the knights and craftsmen trickling away from their stations toward the keep. The meal must finally be ready. Not that Eva had an appetite. She was certain she wouldn't be able to eat a bite.

But she must. She must do nothing out of the ordinary to draw attention to herself. The plan was set, and it must go through.

She would eat a light supper, then excuse herself early, complaining her head wound ailed her. Surely, with her injury still so fresh, no one would question her behavior. The worst that could happen would be someone would send the healer up to check on her. But Isabella would be the only one to do this, and unless prompted by the Duke, she knew the Duchess would not send the healer to the dortour tonight.

Eva would slip out and meet Mathieu, as they had planned, in the stable before any of the other girls had a chance to return to the dortour. Then, they'd be on their way. To their future, together as man and wife.

Eating light was no challenge for Eva, as lamb was the main course this evening. Of all the meats served, lamb was Eva's least favorite. The animal they butchered must have been a mature, male sheep, because the aroma was very strong, hanging in the smoky air throughout the hall. Even the gravy reeked, and at one point, Eva feared she may well have to leave the table to be sick.

She sat beside Beverielle at her sisters' table. Chatter was hushed and tentative tonight, at least for all the girls except Alys. With the May Day festival over, the future of the others hung in the air between them, uncertain. Would they be sent back to their mothers, to their old lives? Or would Isabella invite them to stay on with her, and travel to Germolles when she traveled back there in the fall? No word of their futures had been discussed.

For Alys, the future was known. Eva watched as she and Rutger sat close beside each other, him feeding her from a trencher they shared. A glow surrounded them, like something magical and rare. Just three days from now, Alys would be Rutger's wife. Philip had given his permission before Eva's injury. With Eva recovered, their wedding could be celebrated along with her own to Stefano.

At least, that was the Duke and Stefano's plan.

She was infinitely relieved the Duke had not appeared in the hall for the meal tonight. Nor Stefano, for that matter. She'd been so afraid Philip would make his "big announcement" of her betrothal. Besides the part of her that was relieved, though, there was another writhing with worry—where had the two men gone this night? Isabella, sitting alone on the dais with only Admiral La Laing for company, had seemed surprised the Duke had not appeared to sup with her as well.

Captain Knape was also missing. Where had they gone, unannounced and unplanned?

This was a good thing, Eva reminded herself. Without the three powerful men in the castle, at least nowhere anyone could see, her plan was much more likely to go smoothly.

Just as Eva had laid her linen on the table and was preparing to leave, Beverielle leaned toward her to whisper in her ear.

"Has the Duchess said anything about us going home?"

Eva shook her head. "I've heard nothing. I know Alys will be staying, of course. But the Duchess has not yet announced plans for any of us others."

"Do you know this man?" Beverielle laid her hand over Eva's and tipped her head toward the table where some of the knights sat, still spearing chunks of meat onto their knives and laughing over their meal. "That knight there. Do you know his name?"

Eva squinted, trying to make out the man's features in the smoky room. The air had grown chilly as the sun set, so the servants had lit fires in both hearths. But the wood must have been wet, because it seemed to Eva more smoke was billowing out into the room than rising up the chimney.

The knight Beverielle was indicating was sitting right beside Mathieu. She'd been trying to avoid meeting the ostler's gaze all evening for fear of someone noticing the sparks passing between them. Her skin tingled now, just watching him converse with a serious expression with the huge knight beside him.

"I do not know the knight's name, Beverielle," Eva said. "Why?"

"He looks Scottish. I've heard him speak, and his brogue gives him away." A smile played around the edges of her pouty lips.

Eva studied the girl beside her, then glanced again at the knight. They both bore the same ivory complexion and bright hair, more copper than gold. "Are you Scottish?" she asked.

As though she'd thrown cold water on the girl, Beverielle withdrew her hands and folded them in her lap. Staring at the table before her, she mumbled, "My mother is."

Eva was just about to question her further when the huge, oak doors to the hall burst open. Everyone jumped, and silence hushed the room like a sodden blanket.

Chapter Twenty-Six

M*athieu*
Mathieu was deep in conversation with Keegan when a cool blast of air swept the smoky air into swirls around them. Everyone turned and stared as the three men came tumbling through the door, carrying paper-wrapped parcels and laughing boisterously. 'Twas the Duke, Captain Knape, and Stefano.

They were drunk, Mathieu realized. 'Twas plain enough to see. One could almost smell the spirits on their breath from across the room. They were sharing what must have been a crude joke between them, judging by the lewd glances and snickers they shared. Before they'd even made it over the threshold and slammed the doors shut behind them, Knape slapped Stefano on the back so hard he stumbled forward, catching himself on the edge of the long wooden table nearest the door.

Squinting up at the crowd as though he'd just awoken, Knape perched both fists on his hips and bellowed, "Quit gawking, fools!"

Immediately, low conversation resumed, and the castle folk continued their meal, casting furtive glances toward the newcomers. Isabella, however, was not one to ignore such bad behavior, even of the Duke. Rising to her feet and drawing herself to her full height, accentuated by the tall double-horned headdress she wore, she mirrored Knape's stance and narrowed her eyes.

"My lords. You are expecting to sup, even at this late hour?" Her voice resonated through the hall, shrill and sharp.

"Why, yes. And why not? 'Tis my castle and court, is it not, fine lady?" The Duke swayed where he stood, spreading his arms in a gesture Mathieu wasn't sure was meant for emphasis, or to help him keep his balance. He turned to his companions and slurred, "Join me on the dais, my good men. We have an announcement to make!"

Oh, no. Were they too late? Was the deed already decided? Mathieu's dinner curdled in his belly as he slid a glance toward Keegan.

"Ye need to get out of here, now," Keegan muttered. "Take my horse. He's sound now, is he not? Take your woman, mount up, and ride, my boy."

Stefano was the only one of the three who appeared tentative, and perhaps slightly more sober than the other men. He clutched to his chest a bundle about the size of a baked loaf, wrapped in plain paper and tied off with cord. Keeping his head down, he followed the Duke and the Captain along the wall of the hall toward the dais. He paused when he passed behind the place where the girls sat, studying the group as if he wasn't quite sure what he was looking for. The minute his eyes met with Eva's, though, a slow, stupid grin spread his features.

"My beloved Lady Eva. Soon, you will be mine," he sputtered. He held out the package he carried. "I come bearing gifts. For you." Grinning like a fool, he then stumbled onward toward the front of the room.

Isabella's eyes grew wide, and she caught Mathieu's eye, surreptitiously waving him out of the room with her linen cloth. Eva, seeing this, quickly rose to her feet and slid out from between her sisters.

"And where do you think you are going, my fine young lady of Utrecht?" the Duke boomed as he plopped into his seat beside the Duchess. "You cannot go now. You are the reason for our celebration this fine evening!"

Panic filled Eva's expression as she flashed a glance toward Mathieu. He nodded, shifting his gaze toward the door. His prodding was all she needed.

Placing a hand to her stomach, Eva swayed, grabbing onto Beverielle's shoulder to steady herself. "I'm so sorry, my lord, but the lamb... I'm afraid it's not agreed with me. I think I may be—"

Mathieu, even in his panicked state, couldn't help but admire the lady's acting skills. Grabbing a linen off the table, Eva pressed it to her mouth and made the most convincing gagging noises he'd ever heard. Several people winced and stopped eating. Stefano, who was apparently not used to imbibing as much as he had that evening, promptly turned and vomited over the back of the dais.

"Go, man. Now!" Keegan growled.

In the confusion that followed, Alys hurried to Eva's side and wrapping her arm around her shoulders, led her from the hall undeterred. Once they'd slipped out of the hall, and Eva was sure they were out of earshot, she turned to Alys with wide eyes.

"I am not ill, Alys. I am in love."

The red-haired girl blinked at her in shock, then took a step back. "Are you sure? You're sweating, your color's a bit green, and I know you dislike lamb—"

"I'm green at the thought of having to marry that arrogant Italian merchant. We're escaping tonight, Alys. Mathieu and me. We're going to the village to be wed," she rasped, hurrying her companion down the hall toward the side exit to the bailey.

Now it was Alys' turn to stare wide-eyed. "The ostler? You're going to marry the ostler?" she sputtered. "I thought..." Realization sparked a light in Alys' eyes. After all, blacksmith or not, Alys had fallen hard for Rutger. No matter what his station in life.

Her slow smile warmed Eva from the top of her scarred head to her twisted foot. She nodded. "I am. We are in love. Like you and Rutger. But we're doing it now, tonight. Before anybody—the Duke, the merchant, anyone—can stop us."

Alys returned her smile, then wrapped her in a quick hug. "Godspeed, Eva of Utrecht. I am happy for you both."

Eva turned to leave when they heard hurried steps coming down the passageway. The two girls froze and held their breath. Would they be caught out? Would Eva be dragged back to the Great Hall to face her worst nightmare, betrothal to Stefano? But the steps were soft and light. It sounded like a small person. A handmaid, perhaps.

When the young woman appeared, Eva recognized the girl as one of Isabella's personal ladies. She ran up to them, breathless, glancing back nervously over her shoulder. Scooting them all closer to the wall near the door, the girl—her name was Moira, Eva remembered—pulled them into a close huddle.

"Her lady grace sent me to fetch this for you, Eva. You are to take it with you and wear it for your wedding ceremony."

The girl held out a length of the finest lace, sparkling white and lovely in its intricate pattern. Eva had never seen such a fine piece of cloth in all her life, even working as she had in the tailor shop. Lace of this value, probably imported from the faraway East, was a rarity indeed.

She hesitated, almost afraid to touch the cloth that it might burst into flames. "I cannot, Moira. This is too valuable—"

"Lady Duchess said that's what you'd say. *Make her take it*, she insisted. She is not to be a virgin bride without a veil."

Tears blurred her vision as she reached out to take the length of lace. "I do not know what to say," she choked out.

Moira laid a hand on her arm. " 'Tis nothing to be said. Blessings be on you and your beloved, Eva of Utrecht. May God speed you to your destiny."

The maid then kissed Eva on both cheeks and scurried away.

As Eva slipped out of the giant wooden door leading to the bailey, she heard the clatter of hoofbeats. Even in the fading light of evening, she saw the cloud of dust behind the horse as it careened around the side of the stable and headed straight for her. Mathieu was aboard a giant, faded red horse Eva had not noticed before.

Where did he get a horse? And how on earth did he expect her to climb aboard the monstrous beast?

"Stay there," he called. "On the steps!"

She had little time to ponder. The horse barely broke stride as Mathieu galloped up so close Eva feared she'd be crushed under its thundering hooves. As the charger swooshed by, the ostler—obviously also an expert horseman—reached down and snagged her around the waist. With a bounce and a swoop, she was aboard, straddling the saddle in front of Mathieu, his strong arm snugging her to his chest.

Mathieu

"Open the gates!" Mathieu called to the stunned guards who watched from the portcullis.

The two men looked at each other, then scowled. "By whose authority do you take this maiden from the castle?" one of them barked.

"By God's decree," Mathieu snapped. "Now open the gates or Lady Duchess shall have your heads."

Confused but sensing his urgency, the guards shrugged as they hurried to raise the bar and swing the gates open. They had barely opened wide enough to admit Keegan's broad horse before Mathieu and Eva swept through. Through to freedom.

Mathieu gave the big horse his head and gripped Eva even tighter as the charger's gait gobbled up ground in the direction of the village. 'Twasn't far, and even from this distance Mathieu could see candles burning in several of the cottages' windows. The tower of the small parish church stood out in sharp relief against a sky still tinted with the afterglow of the sunset. Mathieu turned his mount in that direction.

"Are you sure this is what you want to do?" he rasped against Eva's ear. She felt small and warm against him, trembling with either the chill of the evening air or excitement, he knew not which. Her one hand gripped his with white-knuckled intensity, while the other she'd intwined into the shaggy red and white streaked mane of the roan horse.

When she dipped back her head against his neck, fire erupted inside his chest. Nay, this was more than lust he felt for this girl. This fire leapt at the edges of his heart and threatened to burn it to ash. If, heaven forbid, she changed her mind now.

But no, he knew, there would be no turning back. For either of them. The die had been cast.

Turning her face as best she could, Eva burrowed into Mathieu's neck, humming some words he could not hear. Then, unexpectedly, the wench reached up and grabbed his earlobe in her teeth, nipping it a little more than softly.

Now the fire dropped lower, into his belly and beyond. He urged the roan faster. The sooner they were joined in the eyes of God, the sooner they could be joined, in all ways.

Mathieu's heart sank when he skidded the horse to a stop before the tiny church, seeing it was dark and seemingly empty. A sick fear prickled his skin. Had Keegan not gotten his message to the parson? Were they too early?

He was sure they had little time before a cavalry of the Duke's men would be hot on their heels. They must not, they could not, stop this joining from happening. He would sooner die than see their story end so.

The creak of the old wooden door startled them both as he jumped down and reached to help Eva to the ground. Ah, but the parson was a wise one.

Aye, darkness reigned still. But darkness kept things hidden. A lighted church on an ordinary evening would send a beacon to those who would try to stop this marriage.

Brother Michael—Mathieu assumed it was he, as he'd never met the man—held a lone candle, flickering wildly in the open air. Holding his finger to his lips, he ducked his tonsured head toward the doorway and motioned for them to follow. With one arm firmly around Eva's waist, Mathieu steadied her climb up the old stone steps.

The sanctuary was as black as the deepest night in a forest, cloaked by a hush that made Mathieu's ears ring. Silently, they followed the parson and his sputtering candle through the main chapel, past the meager altar, and into a small room Mathieu guessed was the sacristy. It was here, he'd heard, the men of God prepared for the services. It was a small room, and one without a single window.

This room, in contrast to the blackness of the chapel, was aglow with warm light. Candles burned everywhere, several on each of the small tables and chests dotted around the space. In the center, a taller desk had been spread with white linen embroidered in gold. The cloth draped gracefully over its sides to the stone floor. Three candles perched there behind an open book, along with three lengths of cord: one burgundy, one ivory, and one gold.

Eva glanced up at Mathieu, whose hand she was gripping so tightly, his fingers were numb. "What are the cords for?"

Before Mathieu had a chance to reply, even if he had known the answer, the parson explained.

"Since this is a rather... unconventional wedding, we're going to perform the rite twice. To make sure 'tis no doubt should someone question the union." The short, round man robed in brown pointed to the book. "Mathieu, you will recite the vows as the man in this joining, according to traditional Christian religion. We will also perform a Celtic handfasting."

He grinned at Eva, revealing a row of stained, crooked teeth with several gaps between. "That's what the cords are for. The burgundy symbolizes your partnership, filled with romance and happiness. The ivory signifies purity, peace, and devotion. The gold promises a prosperous, long life. I wish that for both of you. I truly do." The parson smiled up at them.

The sound of hoofbeats outside the chapel caused them all to freeze and turn toward the door. Mathieu held his breath. Surely, the Duke's men couldn't have rallied and found them so quickly. Philip and Knape were stumbling drunk when they'd left.

They both whooshed out a breath when the sound faded in the distance. Mathieu turned to the parson. "Brother Michael, let's get this done. I don't think we have much time to spare."

"Very well," the parson said, hustling around to the back of the makeshift altar he'd set up in the sacristy. A pair of round, metal-rimmed spectacles lay beside a white satin collar on the table. He donned both and picked up the book.

"Wait," Eva said, and Mathieu's stomach turned over. Had she changed her mind... now?

Eva drew out the length of lace from her sleeve and handed it to the parson. "The Duchess said I should wear this," she whispered.

Brother Michael smiled, setting the book down and draping the luxurious length of lace over Eva's golden hair. He smiled at her for a long moment before retrieving the book and starting to read.

"Blessings, gentle lord and lady. We are here today to join..." He paused, leaning over to glance at a piece of parchment lying beside the prayer book, "the fair Eva of Utrecht with Mathieu of Liège." The parson peered at Mathieu over the black iron frames of the glasses. "No banns were posted?"

Mathieu shook his head, and a frisson of fear flared in his chest. Would the parson insist on all the particulars? Keegan seemed to think 'twould be a simple matter with Brother Michael.

He breathed a sigh of relief when the parson waved a hand in the air dismissively. "No matter. We shall proceed."

Mathieu became aware of Eva's violent trembling as she stood close beside him, still clutching his hand as though she were in fear of being torn away by a violent wind. He rubbed his thumb over her icy knuckles and squeezed her hand.

Just get on with it, Brother Michael!

Almost as if he'd forgotten it, which he apparently had, Brother Michael held up one finger and stooped to reach behind the table. When he rose, he held in his hands an ornately bejeweled... *sword.*

Eva gasped as both she and Mathieu stumbled backwards. Was this a trap? Had Brother Michael been plied by the Duke to intercept their union—by ending their lives?

Seeing their fear, the parson again made a dismissive gesture with his free hand. "Nay, nay," he jabbered as he laid the blade flat on the makeshift altar. "I do not intend to harm you. 'Tis is a sacred blade. 'Tis another symbol of Celtic origin. Mathieu, Eva, lay your right hands atop the blade."

Timidly, they both stepped forward, but Mathieu had to actually fold Eva's hand within his own to get her to touch the blade. The parson grunted his approval and continued.

"Lord Mathieu, Lady Eva. Is there any reason known to you why this partnership should not be made?"

They both shook their heads. Brother Michael whispered, "You must reply, *There is none.*"

Sweat had begun to trickle down the back of Mathieu's neck and between his shoulder blades. Eva continued to quake next to him as though she were standing in a snow drift. Was getting married really supposed to be so painful? Did it always take an age?

Or did it just seem that way because what they were doing, they both knew, went against the will of the Duke?

"There is none," they answered in unison.

After Mathieu recited his vows, the parson looked up at him. "Do you have a ring?"

A ring. He'd never thought of that. Mathieu was so intent on getting Eva out of the hall, away from the Duke and Stefano and anyone else who might prevent this from happening, a ring had never crossed his mind. He shook his head, frowning.

"I do not."

Brother Michael closed his eyes and nodded. Reaching into a pocket hidden in the folds of his coarse brown cloak, the parson drew out a circlet of iron. "I always keep a few of these on hand, just in case."

It was rough-hewn nail used by the blacksmiths to attach horse's shoes. It had been fired and bent into a rough circle. Mathieu frowned as he glanced down at Eva. "I wish I had better for you."

The way she was gazing into his eyes made him feel ten feet tall. "I need no better than you, Mathieu of Liège."

When the iron circlet was slipped over Eva's finger, Mathieu blew out a breath. It was done. They were married. Weren't they?

"Now we must perform the handfasting ritual."

Mathieu groaned. From beyond the sacristy door, Mathieu could swear he heard footsteps. Voices, though muted and muffled. He cast a panicked glance at Brother Michael who, although his eyes widened, continued as if he'd heard nothing.

Mathieu knew they were running out of time. He measured his breaths as best he could as Brother Michael wrapped the three cords around their joined hands, reciting the significance of each one as he did. The ostler noticed that now, too, the parson's hands were shaking. Fumbling in haste, he tied the loose ends of the cords into a knot.

"May this knot remain tied, drawing your hands together in love." The parson wrapped his own hands around theirs and held their gaze. "Hold tight to one another through good times and bad and watch as your strength grows."

The voices outside the door grew louder. Heavy boots stomped closer. Eva turned her face into Mathieu's chest and began to weep.

Sliding the knotted cords off their hands, Brother Michael recited the conclusion with a rapid, hastened decree.

"May what is done before the gods be not undone by any man."

It was at that moment the door to the sacristy crashed open, the whoosh of wind snuffing out all candles save one.

Chapter Twenty-Seven

Mathieu spun around, fingers closing on the hilt of his dagger, expecting the worst. 'Twas Knape, most likely, joined by a small army of his men, against whom he would be powerless. Would they kill him first before whisking Eva away? He dearly hoped he wouldn't live to see her dragged off—out of his arms, out of his life. Especially now, finally, when they were joined before the law and gods.

One sure way to annul a marriage was to render the bride a widow.

A massive form literally filled the doorway. In the dim light, at first Mathieu could make out only bright, white teeth, rimmed by a decidedly auburn beard. When Keegan spoke, the ostler nearly melted into a heap on the floor.

"So here ye are. 'Tis done yet? Ye do not have much more time, ostler."

Mathieu's gut clenched. "Are they coming after us? Were you followed?"

Keegan guffawed and slapped the Mathieu on the back. "Nay, ye fool. Do ye think I'm that ignorant a knight? Aye, they were coming after ye. We watched them leave the bailey, then waited a few minutes before taking off ourselves. With no lights on in the chapel, they rode right on by."

So that was the hoof clatter they'd heard earlier. A chill slithered down Mathieu's spine. "Who is with them?"

"Knape, some of his favored few, and Stefano, of all men. They sobered up pretty quickly once they realized ye both were gone."

Mathieu clutched Eva closer to his side. "And the Duke?"

Keegan shook his head. "Lady Duchess snagged him before he'd even left the high table. Last I saw them they were both headed to their quarters. I have a feeling the Duchess will do whatever she can to save ye both."

Eva's fingers dug into Mathieu's arm. "Where shall we go? We can't go back to the castle."

Keegan fisted both huge paws on his hips. "Nay, that's true, ye can't. But Gaspard and me, well, we've come up with a sort of wedding gift for ye."

"We've got coin," Gaspard stepped forward into the dim light from behind Keegan, whose bulk had completely obscured him from sight. "Not much. But if you'd like to spend your wedding night at the Lady's Raven, we'd be honored to pay for the room."

In that moment, Mathieu felt the cold, hard shell on his heart, that which he'd formed in regard to the Frenchman, fall away. How wrong he had been to despise the man so, not even fully aware of his intentions.

"But won't the inns be the first place they will look?" Eva asked in a small voice.

Keegan shook his head. "They've been there already. We saw them go in and out of both inns leading out toward Brussels. They're convinced ye two are headed to hide in the city."

Eva gazed up at Mathieu, the fear in her eyes making his stomach lurch. He squeezed her hand. "I promised to take care of you, and I will. But we did this so suddenly, I had no time to make any other preparations."

" 'Twon't be the first wedding night spent at a common inn. But once the marriage is consummated, well, there will be little any of them can do about it."

Mathieu blinked. *Consummated.* He had a big responsibility lying before him, and very soon. Eva, he knew, was a virgin. He wanted with all of his heart to make this a most special night for her."

"Come on, now," Keegan grabbed Mathieu's arm, tugging him toward the back of the sacristy. "Brother Michael won't mind if we slip out the back, will ye?"

The parson shook his head and began to unbolt the numerous fastenings securing the back door of the tiny room. "It leads through the graveyard, you know," he said, casting a worried glance toward Eva. "That won't bother you, I hope?"

"Nay," Mathieu said, pulling Eva closer to his side. "*We will walk through the valley of the shadow of death—*"

"Alright, alright," Keegan snapped. "Enough proselytizing. Let's get you two up to the Lady's Raven and secure in your nuptial nest."

As they slunk between the tilted headstones and through the rusted iron gate, Mathieu whispered, "What about the horse, Keegan? Your horse?"

"We'll meet Knape's party when they come back through the village, telling them we couldna find you. I'll tell them we found my charger tied to a post near the stables. The mare I rode in on, I'll put in Lady Raven's stable. Ye can ride her back in the morn."

"Return to the castle? What happens when they realize what we've done?" Mathieu asked, his voice shaky.

They'd arrived at the side door to the Lady's Raven. Keegan laid a hand on Mathieu's shoulder and looked directly into his eyes. "Ye have got the lady Duchess on your side, both of ye. By the morrow I'm sure she'll find a way to defuse the Duke's anger. She's pretty crafty that way. The lady is an expert at negotiations. Ye both know that."

Chapter Twenty-Eight

I *sabella*

Candles and torches blazed in the Duke's bedchamber, matching the anger he barely contained. Pacing up and down the length of the room, he ranted, hands waving, spewing words a lady—particularly a Duchess—shouldn't hear. But Isabella was used to Philip's tantrums. She'd been dealing with them for long enough to know it was pointless to say a word until the raging subsided.

It didn't take long.

Philip halted directly in front of the Duchess, who sat on the opposite side of his oak desk, her hands folded before her. Not a shy one by any means, Isabella's chin was raised, and she met his gaze with confident intensity. After a moment of silence passed, she spoke.

"Are you quite through?"

Philip threw both hands up in the air and recommenced pacing. "No, I'm not. Although yes, I am. This debacle will bring much turmoil to our business dealings in Ghent, Isabella. We both know that. You are well aware of how insistent Giovanni Arnolfini can be in getting his own way."

"Philip, please." The Duchess rose and drew the tray holding a pitcher of wine and two metal cups closer. "Have a drink to calm your nerves. Sit down and let us discuss this situation. You know I always find a way to heal a rift."

The Duke paused and swiped both hands down his face. "True, yes. I cannot deny it. You are a wise and shrewd negotiator." He took the cup she'd poured for him and sat heavily across from her.

Isabella raised her cup. "First, I want to toast yet another success accomplished—at least, it should be by now. Another of your bastard daughters married off, and happily."

Philip winced. Isabella knew this was his Achille's heel, his many illegitimate offspring littering the Flemish towns and countryside. If there was ever a way to douse his ire, 'twas reminding him of his many sins.

205

His weakness. For all the power his position commanded, his "weakness of the flesh," as the Bishop of Tournai had dubbed it, was no secret. He couldn't help it. He never tried to hide it. But Isabella knew she'd elevated her own position—and power—by accepting this weakness and helping him to make things right.

It only took a moment for the realization to seep through his anger. He narrowed his eyes to slits at her over his cup. "You knew this was going to happen. Didn't you?"

Isabella shifted her gaze to the purple clouds swirling in the wine. "I won't deny, I had some inkling of the children's plans. I did not, however, do anything to aid them."

Philip tossed back the wine and wiped his mouth on the back of his hand, inadvertently scoring his cheek with one of his ornately carved gemstone rings. Apparently he was still not quite sober from his night with Knape and Stefano. He swore under his breath as he grabbed a linen to blot the blood oozing from the scrape.

Isabella rose immediately and grabbed the washing bowl and cloth from the sideboard. Kneeling beside his chair, she proceeded to gently cleanse the scratch. The gesture, she knew, would soften Philip's resolve even further.

She was right. He sighed as he tilted his head toward her gentle ministrations. "Oh, my lady, you do know how to ease my troubles."

If only you didn't get yourself into so damned many of them.

When the bleeding stopped, Isabella sat back on her heels. "Now," she said, "why was it so important to Arnolfini that this Italian apprentice wedded Eva?"

He opened his eyes, his eyebrows drawing together. "You know Arnolfini. He owes some debt to Stefano's family in Rome. It must have been an impressive one, because mentoring the young man alone should have been enough to satisfy any debt." He snorted and shook his head. "When I spoke to him, just days ago, he made it clear he wanted the Italian to be wed by Christmastide. The tailor's daughter was the maid the lad had his heart set upon."

"Yes, but Eva—*your daughter*—does not love Stefano. Cannot stand the sight of him, from what she told me."

She saw Philip wince again at the mention of his relation to the girl, before forging on. "Eva has fallen in love with our ostler. There isn't much anyone can do to change that."

Philip snorted again. "Especially not now! God's bones, he's probably already bedded the maiden by now. She wouldn't do for a bride in Arnolfini's eyes, even if Knape's men do find her."

Isabella patted Philip's arm, noticing how the clarity was returning, but slowly. He'd been pretty deep in his cups when he and the other two men arrived in the hall. "Where were you tonight, by the way? You, Knape, and Stefano?"

Usually, Philip would have leapt to his feet, reminding his wife that his goings on were none of her affair. Tonight, though, she knew he needed her help with this Arnolfini situation. He met her gaze. "Stefano wanted to buy his bride some gifts. We shopped in Brussels, then stopped at the Lady's Raven on the way back to celebrate the Italian's upcoming betrothal." He scratched his head and yawned. "We might have gotten a little carried away with the spirits."

Isabella cocked an eyebrow. "You might say that. How angry do you think the Italian will be over this change in plans?"

Philip yawned again, and Isabella knew she had worn him down sufficiently. "Not a clue. I don't think he loved the girl, that's pretty apparent. He just wanted the right to say his bride was of royal descent."

Isabella rose and returned the wash bowl and bloodied cloth to the sideboard. With her back turned to him, she murmured, "It shouldn't be too much of an issue to find him another *bride of royal descent*. Should it?"

She didn't have to see Philip's wince. His groan said it all. She heard the chair legs scrape along the stone floor and felt his arms close around her from behind.

Shock pulsed through her. Tenderness from her husband? She'd rarely seen it, at least, not when there wasn't a clear need to spawn a male heir over their heads.

But Charles was nearly three years old now, and seemed a strong, if not willful and undeniably spoiled child. No, there was no immediate need to spawn another male heir. Besides, Isabella was at an age when that event was all but impossible.

Still, she could not stifle the sigh that escaped when his lips pressed warm beneath her ear and trailed down her neck.

"Surely, dear wife, there must be some other young lady here at Coudenburg who might serve as a suitable replacement for the tailor's girl?" he whispered.

Isabella's mind sifted through the girls she'd gathered for the festival. Many would be returning to their own homes soon. Only Alys, and now Eva, would remain. And many were far too young to even consider for betrothal. Except for...

"There is Beverielle. She's almost the same age as Eva. Only a few months younger, I believe." A dark chuckle rumbled deep in her chest. "You didn't waste much time between those two liaisons, did you?"

She felt Philip stiffen, but reached up to run her fingers through his short-cropped hair before he could pull away. "It's alright. 'Tis all in the past. Nothing to be done to change it now." She turned toward him, lacing her fingers around his neck. "Would the Italian have a problem accepting a Scot for a wife?" she asked, her voice honey sweet.

Philip was busy dismantling the pins holding Isabella's headdress in place, his fingers fumbling at the task. "She's a comely lass, is she not?"

"She is. Many men are enchanted by a woman with the red hair of the Scots. Beverielle has yards of it," she said as she slipped off her wimple and shook free her own dark tresses. They cascaded down over her shoulders, and Philip groaned.

"You may be my wife, Isabella of Portugal, but that does not lessen my craving for you."

Isabella blinked, then laughed out loud. "Why don't we pretend we're not wed this night, Philip. Let's engage in a little role playing."

With those words, Isabella stepped away from him and pulled the ribbons holding her surcoat closed. The heavy velvet dropped to the floor. "I can play the temptress as well as any tavern maid." She slipped her rich, burgundy tunic over her head, leaving only her thin chemise. Quickly, she turned and extinguished all the candles on the table and the windowsill, along with the torch on the wall. The one candle remaining lit was beside Philip's regally appointed canopy bed—behind her.

She knew, at her age and having borne three children, revealing her body with intention to seduce him was better off in muted light. Finally, she slipped her filmy, silk chemise over her head and stood before him. Still, however, he did not touch her. Although she could see the fire in his eyes, his arms remained at his sides.

Tossing her long, dark hair back over her shoulders, she crossed her arms as she cocked her head coyly.

"Shall ye like to bed the wench, your lordship? I can make ye wildest fantasies come true. Nary a soul shall be the wiser."

An hour later, as Isabella lay staring into the darkness with Philip snoring beside her, she wondered how on earth she would break the news to Beverielle. Poor child, she was not yet even of age, and her future husband had already been chosen for her.

A fate the Duchess herself had lived. 'Twas not one she wished on any other.

Chapter Twenty-Nine

M*athieu*
The Lady's Raven wasn't the nicest inn in which Mathieu had lain his head, nor was it the worst. In truth, he'd only seen it from the exterior, never even having ventured into its tavern for a pint. According to Keegan, it was the better of the two in the small village on the outskirts of Brussels. The bedclothes, he claimed, were changed weekly, and there were fewer of the tavern wenches who plied their business within its walls.

Still, he wished it could be finer for Eva. This was her wedding night, by God's bones. But between what he wished for his bride and what he would be able to provide her lay a chasm so wide, Mathieu wondered if he'd ever cross it.

As they slipped through the heavy oak door, Eva clung to Mathieu's arm as if her life depended on it. Her eyes were wide with worry, darting quickly from one person's face to the next as they crossed the tavern. It wasn't until the keeper had directed them to the room Keegan and Gaspard had paid for, and they traveled down a hallway off the main room, that she relaxed her nearly painful grip on his arm.

"They won't find us here?" she asked, her voice breathy and haunted.

Mathieu shook his head and lifted a strand of her hair off her forehead. "Nay. They've already looked for us here. They believe we headed clear through to Brussels, mayhap beyond."

The room was a surprise, and Mathieu blinked as the door sighed open. This was no transient's bedchamber. It was an elegantly appointed suite.

Eva gasped and held her hand over her mouth. "Oh, this must have cost them many, many coins."

Again, Mathieu felt the twinge of guilt in his chest for the way he'd thought of—and treated—Gaspard. Keegan he knew was his friend. But renting a room of this caliber went above and beyond a friendly gesture, even from the closest of comrades.

The dark wood walls had been whitewashed, making the space appear even larger and brighter than it was. The broad window, though tightly shuttered, was draped with colorful fabrics that cascaded to the floor. A small table with two chairs bore a single, fat candle, beside which had been laid a pitcher with two metal cups. In the center of the room, an oversized bed reigned—one that made Mathieu's narrow pallet seem like something meant for the animals to sleep on, not a man.

A man *and his wife*. Mathieu cringed inside to think that after this one night of pampered bliss, he'd be bringing Eva into his own meager quarters. She would feel like the fledgling that falls from its cozy nest into the manure pile. He sucked in a breath.

"This is wonderful, Mathieu," she said, running her fingers along the hand-stitched quilt covering the bed. She turned to him with wonder in her eyes. "I've never slept in a bed like this one."

Nor will you again, at least not for quite a while. Not after this one night.

But he wouldn't spoil it for her. Not yet. Let her live the dream of a princess for this one night. They would deal with the realities of tomorrow when the day dawned.

Now, Mathieu had an even more important task on his mind. To make his bride's wedding night as memorable, and as pleasurable, as was humanly possible.

He bent to kiss her, brushing his lips softly across hers as he drew her body to him. She was soft and warm and willing, but he also knew how innocent she was. Did she know what would happen between them tonight? Kissing was one thing, but...

He drew back and lifted her chin with two fingers. "Do you know what happens between a man and his wife, Eva? Has your maman ever explained—"

Her wide eyes and quick shake of the head were his answer. "I've seen the dogs in the spring, but surely it can't be as crude and violent as that... can it?"

Mathieu blew out a breath and cupped her face in his hand. "No, sweet Eva. It's not like that. But 'tis not without pain... at least, the first time."

He expected her to gape at him with fear in her eyes, back away perhaps. But she surprised him by nestling closer, entwining her fingers in the folds of his tunic. "I'm fear not. 'Twill make us truly man and wife, right?"

He nodded. " 'Twill. Then no one can say the marriage is null."

The smile that lit up her face warmed him to his toes. "I'm ready, then. Make me your wife, Mathieu of Liège."

Eva

Eva was living in a dream world. Here, in this magical room with candles flickering all around them, truly did seem like a fantasy come true. She knew not what was about to happen to her, to her body, but she knew 'twould be something that would change her, forever. She would cross the threshold from child to woman. She would—"

Suddenly, she froze and laid a hand on Mathieu's arm. "Will we... I mean to say, can we conceive a child this night?"

Mathieu's brown eyes waxed softer as he brushed his knuckles on her cheek. "Mayhap. 'Tis not often it happens the first time, but—"

"Is there a way to keep that from happening? I mean to say, is there a way for us to be joined without risk of creating a child?"

She was stammering now, and cold fingers of dread began creeping up her spine. Mathieu tilted his head, studying her in confusion. "Why? We are married now, Eva. Children are a natural product of the union between a man and a woman."

Abruptly, she turned away from him and crossed the room to lay her fingertips on the windowsill, her steps even more uneven than usual. Although she could not see through the planked shutters, it was as though in her mind she could see glimpses of what the future might bring them. The images she conjured made her shudder.

Another imperfect child. Another babe born with an ugly, twisted foot. Mayhap a disfigurement even worse.

Mathieu was behind her, gripping her with both hands on her trembling arms. "What are you afraid of, Eva? Does childbirth worry you so?"

She spun around and faced him. "Nay. Not childbirth. What I do fear is producing a babe with my disfigurement, Mathieu. Another misfit. Another creple. 'Tis something can be passed on from mother to child, the healers tell me."

He folded her into his embrace so quickly she had no chance to resist. Stroking the back of her head gently, he shushed her and rocked her from side to side. "Nay, do not fear this, Eva. What are the chances? Your sisters, the other girls with you in Coudenburg, were they born impaired?"

She shook her head, burying her face into his chest, her tears soaking his tunic. Then, through a muffled sob, she croaked, "But what if I do? What if I bear you a son or a daughter with a disfigurement like mine? Or worse?"

He pushed her from him and held her at arm's length. With one finger, he tipped up her chin, forcing her to meet his eyes. "Then I shall love the babe as I love its mother. With all of my heart. With all of my soul. In my eyes, Eva of Utrecht, you are not imperfect. You are not maimed, or twisted, or ugly. You are special. The most special and precious person who has ever come into my life."

Time slowed then until Eva was sure she'd fallen into a coma, like the one after her injury. Mathieu led her to the bed and bid her to sit, then knelt at her feet, sliding off her slippers one at a time. With excruciating gentleness, he proceeded to use his strong fingers to massage her feet, both of them, until little gasps of pleasure escaped with her breath.

She never realized how pleasurable it could be to have someone rub her feet, especially the one crooked and twisted. The muscles ached her sometimes, keeping her awake in the night. As though he knew this, Mathieu spent an extra-long time kneading that ankle and foot until something else—another feeling, entirely new to her—crept up her leg and into other parts of her body.

But when he stood and reached to unlace her chemise, she felt suddenly afraid. She began to tremble and whispered, "Hold me, Mathieu."

He pulled her to him and gently ran his hand down her hair. "Fear not, sweet wife. I will be gentle. I promise, I will try not to hurt you any more than is necessary to make you mine."

Chapter Thirty

E *va* Morning, of course, came far too quickly. As the fingers of dawn slipped in around the edges of the shutters, Eva opened her eyes and, for a moment, did not know where she was. The warmth of Mathieu's body spooned up behind her, however, quickly brought back memories of last night. *Her wedding night.* She was no longer a child. Now, she was, truly, fully, a woman.

Mayhap that knowledge would help bring her the strength to face what she knew today would bring.

Mathieu stirred behind her, groaning as he stretched and drew her closer against him.

"Are you well this morning, dear wife?"

How could she put into words how "well" she truly felt? There were no words. She was in love, and she was married to a most wonderful, caring man.

"I am complete," she whispered.

They stole the time to nestle a little longer before the innkeeper began bellowing in the halls. A cruel reminder. Their time in this perfect nest was temporary. Now, it was time to face the realities waiting for them at the castle.

The day was grey and drizzling, chilly for this late in spring. Eva was glad she'd worn her cloak last night, though for different reasons. Today, she would not need hide behind its voluminous folds and hood. Today, it might protect her from arriving at the castle soaked and shivering.

She waited at the back door of the inn while Mathieu retrieved the horse Keegan had left there for them. And then, they were off, Eva's back snugged up against her husband, his arm wrapped tightly around her waist. The ride back to Coudenburg was not long.

Not nearly long enough.

They heard the guards shouting when they crested the last hill through the meadows. Surely, no one suspected they would be returning. Except for Keegan, Gaspardd, and Isabelle, who were all well aware neither had the means to start a new life elsewhere. At least, not yet.

The gates swung open, and standing there in the center of the bailey, hands on his hips, rain running down his face, was Captain Knape. Eva felt Mathieu stiffen.

"Why," she asked softly, "do you and the Captain hate each other so?"

"A story for another time, sweet lady. For right now, we'll deal with the rage attached to our more recent actions."

"Well, well. The wayward children come home," Knape boomed. "Dost though return with heads hanging in shame?" He pinned his gaze on Eva. "Did he kidnap you, milady? Shall we lock him in the dungeon?"

Eva sat up taller and lifted her chin. "Nay, Captain. This man, this *good* man, is now my husband."

Knape's face contorted into an even more ugly visage. "So, he's violated you, then."

To her surprise, two knights stepped out from under the tent in the encampment. Keegan and Gaspardd.

"We witnessed the union, in the church, before the eyes of God, Captain. 'Tis done. 'Tis naught can be done to change it," Keegan called.

Knape fisted one hand at his side, curling his other fingers around the hilt of his sword. "Aye, 'tis one thing can be done to undo the damage."

Gaspardd stepped forward. "And that would be murder, Captain Knape. With multiple witnesses. I beg thee, do not allow your anger to overrule your good judgement."

By now, all of the knights had gathered in a group near the edge of their camp, and watched as Mathieu dismounted, helping Eva down to stand beside him.

"We request audience with the Duke," Mathieu said.

"The Duchess as well," Eva added.

The Great Hall was nearly empty, with only a few servants cleaning up the last of the morning meal. At the high table sat the Duke, his hands wrapped around a cup. Glaring at them both as they entered, Philip raised a bony finger and pointed to a place at the table directly at the foot of the dais.

"Sit, both of you." He then called to one of the servants. "Fetch the Duchess. The Italian, as well. We have much to discuss."

Isabella appeared in the doorway a moment later. Eva met her eyes and searched them for some inkling of what was about to happen, but the Duchess lowered her gaze as she stepped up on the dais. Had she succeeded in intervening on their behalf? Or would they be cast out? Eva wondered briefly what her maman would say if she and Mathieu came riding into Ghent, seeking shelter.

She doubted her stepfather would have any more sympathy for them than the Duke. Mayhap less.

Stefano's arrival caused Eva's entire body to tense. He glared at her as he climbed up and took a seat beside the Duke, at the high table. That in itself was not a good sign.

Philip drank from his cup, then slammed it onto the table. "What have you done, ostler?"

Mathieu clasped Eva's hand tighter in his own. "We have married, Your Grace. Brother Michael wed us last eve. We are man and wife—in every sense."

Fire flashed in the Duke's eyes. "I am the girl's father. You did not seek my permission. I could have you flogged. Truly, I could have you put to death for this act of betrayal. At the very least, cast you out. Both of you!"

Eva felt Mathieu's body sag beside her. He lowered his head. "I did not ask your permission, Your Grace. For that, I am sorry. But I love this woman, and she loves me. I will, however, as your loyal servant, suffer whatever punishment you decide to inflict." Eva was shocked to see tears in Mathieu's eyes as he looked up. "You have been like a father to me, and the Duchess as a maman. I cannot imagine leaving your service. But if that's what you desire—"

Isabella placed a hand over Philip's then, to Eva's surprise. She'd never seen the Duchess display any kind of affection toward the Duke at all since her arrival. The Duchess cleared her throat, then spoke.

"Mathieu of Liège, Eva of Utrecht, you have both violated custom. For that ye shall do penance. But we shall not cast you out." She looked at Mathieu. "You, ostler, shall have your wages cut by half until Christmastide.

If you require more coin for your needs, ye shall have to seek other employment, either inside or out of the castle. On your own time."

She turned to Eva, and her eyes softened. "Eva, you shall become one of my handmaidens. Blanche will train you. You shall serve in this capacity until Christmastide as well."

Blanche. The grouchy old biddy who chaperoned her from Ghent. Of all the handmaidens Isabella could have chosen to train her, why did it have to be Blanche?

Although she might have been imagining it, Eva thought she saw a hint of a smile struggling to escape from the Duchess' lips. "In the meantime, you shall both cohabitate in the ostler's meager quarters. After all, you are now husband and wife."

"And what of me?" Stefano jumped to his feet. "What retribution shall be granted for my loss? The Duke promised the girl's hand to me. Now she is," he motioned frantically toward Eva and Mathieu, scowling, "Soiled. Spoiled, like curdled milk. I wouldn't want her if you granted me her hand here and now."

Isabella turned to face the irate Italian. "We regret that circumstances have prevented Philip from fulfilling his promise to you. We will, however, offer a compromise."

A compromise? What on earth—

At that moment, the lovely, shapely form of another girl appeared in the doorway. Her copper red tresses flowed like golden fire over her shoulders. Unfortunately, Eva quickly saw that the lass' eyes were as red as her hair.

"Stefano, we would like to present another of Philip's daughters for your consideration. Beverielle of Flanders, please come forward to greet your betrothed."

Eva closed her eyes, a wave of sickness washing over her. Why was it this way? Why were women traded and sold like horses? Like chattel? She had come to know Beverielle over the past weeks, and knew of her attraction to Keegan, another from her homeland of Scotland.

Beverielle, dressed in virginal white from head to toe, made her way across the room to the edge of the dais. Stefano, whose ire seemed to quell amazingly fast on the maid's appearance, rose and took the girl's hand, kissing it. Then he turned to the Duke. Eva noticed, even now, he looked past the Duchess and spoke expressly to the Duke.

A woman's say meant little.

"Is this true, Your Grace?" he asked.

Philip nodded, begrudgingly, before refilling his cup. "Aye. If you desire her for your wife, she will be yours."

Stefano, still holding Beverielle's hand and standing high above her on the dais, studied her for a long moment. This was, Eva realized, symbolic if anything ever was. Stefano was establishing, right from the start, his position as far above her.

"She is lovely, Philip. Truly." He reached down and fingered a strand of Beverielle's copper hair, and she flinched. Stefano seemed not to notice. "She cannot be of Flanders. Not originally. Not with this glorious crown of hair."

"Her mother was from Scotland. Brought to Antwerp, where she made her life in a tavern." Isabella related the facts of Beverielle's lineage flatly.

Stefano's eyebrows shot up. "Ah. So, she grew up in a tavern. She is still pure, though?"

"Aye. I swear it," Philip growled.

"And she is of age?" Stefano asked, his eyes never leaving Beverielle's face.

Isabella was the one to answer. Not one to stand down, no matter what the situation. "She will come of age a week before Christmastide. In the meantime, ye can get to know her, since she will remain here, then travel with us to Germolles in the fall. I hope the two of you will find pleasure—of the purest and most innocent kind—in each other's company."

Eva's heart clutched for her sister, whose face was now entirely splotched with red and wet with tears. Yet she said not a word. There was nothing she could say. Nothing that could change her fate.

A fate Eva had barely escaped, thanks to Mathieu. Yet the guilt that consumed her heart was like a wasting disease, one she felt quite certain would eat at her conscience for a very long time.

"She's even lovelier than the Flemish girl," Stefano muttered, flashing a scowl in Eva's direction, "and with her background, may make an even more interesting companion. Come, Beverielle. Let us retire to the hearth. I will warm you with a cup of the Duke's finest mead."

Chapter Thirty-One

Mathieu

Mathieu threw himself into his work as soon as they quit the hall. Grateful! He was so grateful the Duke had shown such leniency. He knew the Duchess was the one responsible, but still. It could have gone much worse, for both of them.

It pained him to see Eva take on the role of handmaiden. She deserved much better than that, but truly, how much better could he give her? Especially now, with his already meager wages cut in half until Christmastide. He had need to spend little, and had saved a small sum for someday, but now he would have nothing to spare.

The knights and their pages had done an admirable job tending to the horses and hounds, as these were duties familiar to them. But the aviary? It was a mess. The raptors' cages were deep in their own waste, and the smell permeated into the bailey. In one sense, he was glad they had not tried to do much more than feed the birds. Who knows what might have happened if a falcon had escaped, or worse yet, attempted to attack the handler? No, it was best this way, even if it did mean he would have a very messy couple of days' work ahead of him.

Mathieu was relieved to find the tiny owl, Kleine Uil well, if not a wee bit perturbed at him. The creature gave him a good chattering to when he opened the door to his quarters, even though the bird usually was asleep during the day. After an intense lecture, followed by the owl perching on his shoulder to nuzzle his neck briefly, Kleine Uil returned to his sleeping place beneath the pallet.

Mathieu donned his oldest, grimiest work clothes before heading to the aviary, knowing that to remove the smell of bird excrement from them would be all but impossible. Before he left the small room, he perched his hands on his hips and scanned the space. It was little more than a closet, with just enough room for his sleeping pallet, a sideboard where he kept a washbowl and pitcher, and a table next to the bed which held the candle—the only light in the room. This was not much to offer a new bride, he thought with a sinking feeling. If the Duchess offered her a room with the other handmaids, it might well put this place to shame.

Still, he could not bear to think of sleeping apart from his bride. He hoped she would stay with him here, and share with him his hope for the future, when he might offer her much better.

Mathieu's skill with the horses and birds was a gift. He knew that, and as Isabella had said, the Duke knew it as well. Once the ill feelings from his disobedience had faded, he hoped to ask the Duke, mayhap Admiral La Laing, for an increase in position. Surely, after so many years of loyal service, he was deserving.

As he pulled the door to his room closed behind him, he caught sight of Keegan standing just outside the stable door. He was arguing with someone not in Mathieu's line of vision. When the other man spoke, however, he knew who it was. Captain Knape.

"You lied to me, Keegan. You told me you found your charger tied to a post in the village. You knew all along what those two adulterers were up to, did you not?" Knape sounded angry, but eerily calm, too. He must be sober, a rare condition for the Captain. Still, hearing the man's voice unfettered by the slur of drink sent chills up Mathieu's spine.

What was he up to? Here was a man who could be much more dangerous sober than in his cups.

"I told ya once, and I'll tell ye again, Captain. We found Dirck tied to a post. I wasna about to leave my prize charger standing alongside the road for anyone to steal." Keegan stood towering over the Captain, with his arms crossed over his massive chest. His tone, though, held a pleading note.

This, too, sent chills through the ostler. He hoped he had not brought his friend trouble he did not deserve.

Mathieu stepped out into the open and both men turned. Knape narrowed his eyes and took a step toward him.

"So, you slipped free of the noose again, I see. I thought surely the Duke would toss you in the dungeon for what you did."

Mimicking Keegan's stance—though on a much smaller scale—Mathieu crossed his arms and planted his feet wide. "I do not regret what we did,

Captain. If it displeases you, I am sorry. But you had no claims on the girl. I see not why it should matter to you anyway."

Knape shook his head and spat on the ground. "If it had been up to me—"

"That's the point, Captain. It wasn't up to you. Leave it be." Mathieu shocked himself with his boldness. But he'd had just about enough of this arrogant, evil man.

"I hope you both burn in hell," Knape snarled, turning on his heel. As he stalked away, his muttering echoed across the bailey, torching Mathieu's blood to boiling.

If I hadn't been so damned clumsy, 'twould have been me taking the maid's virginity.

Mathieu locked gazes with Keegan, who had heard the Captain's words as well. Realization turned quickly to rage.

" 'Twas him that night. He almost killed her, the evil bastard." Keegan's already ruddy face reddened further. "The Duke should be told of this."

Mathieu heaved in a deep breath, then blew it out. He was in no position to rile the Duke any further. Besides, Knape would never admit to what he'd done, not in front of anyone who mattered.

"I will have my day with Captain Knape, Keegan. Mark my words. One way or the other, Knape will pay for his sins. Not only for nearly killing my Eva, but for other evil deeds I've witnessed. The man is a heathen. His heart is as black as his cloak." He locked eyes with Keegan. "I will have my day with Captain Knape," he repeated. "As God is my witness."

Eva

Alys was crying as she headed to the dortour to help Eva pack her few belongings.

"I can't believe they're making you a handmaid! You'll have to wait on the ladies, help them dress and undress. Comb their hair. Clean out their chamber pots! It's below you, Eva. You're a Duke's daughter!" Alys wailed.

"And with Blanche! Your days and nights will be torture, Eva. She'll make you do all the really nasty chores. I hear the old bat snores like thunder."

Eva shook her head. "I won't be sleeping in Blanche's room. The Duchess said I can stay with Mathieu, in his quarters."

Alys' eyes widened, but she said nothing. The look on her face made Eva wonder, was Mathieu's room really so bad? Worse than a cramped maid's quarters? But she remained somber, keeping her worries well hidden. " 'Tis the Duke's will. We disobeyed him, Mathieu and me both. We violated custom. We deserve to be punished."

"For how long?" Alys asked.

"The Duchess said until Christmastide."

As they turned the corner into the girls' room, they heard weeping. Eva knew immediately who it was, even before she saw Beverielle's ginger mane spread out over her pallet. Guilt singed Eva's heart as she went to sit beside her.

"I am so sorry, Beverielle. I had no idea this would happen. If I had known—"

Eva stopped short. Would she have done anything differently had she known her running off with Mathieu would destroy her sister's future? It pained her to admit the fact, but nay. She would not have changed a thing.

Beverielle sat up and glared at Eva with hatred in her eyes. "You have what you wanted. Both of you do," she spat, shifting her gaze on Alys. "I have no chance at making a choice for my future. Not now."

"There's still time," Alys offered. "Mayhap the Italian will not favor you."

"Ha," Beverielle snapped. "He's already making all kinds of suggestive comments, making me feel like a cheap tavern wench." Her sobs bubbled up anew. "Which is what I am, is it not? Nothing but a common tavern wench."

A clapping noise made them all jump and turn. There in the doorway stood Isabella, her lips pursed.

"What is this I hear? Why do you speak of yourself in such a way, Beverielle?" Lifting her voluminous skirts, Isabella made her way to the pallet and sat. She smoothed her hand down the girl's coppery hair. "I don't want to ever hear those words out of your mouth again, do you hear?" She tipped up Beverielle's chin. "Look at me. Don't you ever forget—you are of royal blood. You are the Duke's daughter."

Tears continued to stream down the girl's face. " 'Tis true, though, Lady Duchess. But my maman, she was—"

Isabella pulled Beverielle to her chest and held her like a small child. "Your maman did what she had to do to survive." She glanced up at Alys and Eva. "It's what we all must do, we women of this world. We must do what is necessary to survive. Of that, we should be proud. It takes great strength to do things not of our choosing, and to survive the consequences."

Eva hung her head. " 'Twill be hard for me to be a maid, Beverielle, but I will do it. And I will do it well."

"I will work beside my beloved in a man's trade," Alys added. "In the blacksmith's shop. My skin will be roughened and red and I will be covered in soot by days' end. But I will do my best to make him proud."

Isabella held Beverielle at arms' length and held her gaze. "Remember too that you are not your maman. You are your own woman. You will make your own way in life."

"But I've been given away to a man I do not love," she wailed.

The Duchess wiped a tear off her cheek with her thumb. "You may, in time. Besides, there is still time for things to change."

But Eva could tell by the somber expression on the Duchess' face that even she doubted the girl's fate stood a chance of change.

Chapter Thirty-Two

M*athieu*

    Mathieu opened the door to his quarters and stepped aside to let Eva pass. The servants had brought her things earlier, which he had piled neatly on the chair in the corner. There was nowhere else to put them.

Eva said nothing as she crossed the threshold, glancing about the space. There wasn't much to see. Mathieu waited with his heart pounding so hard he could barely hear her words when she finally spoke.

"It's cozy, Mathieu. Does it stay warm in the winter?"

It was true, there was no hearth. But snugged up to the stables, the room did stay fairly comfortable, even when the winter drew near.

"We will not be here for the worst of the winter months. I... we will travel with the Duchess to the chateau at Germolles. My quarters there are a little larger. There is a small hearth, and even a privy off the back."

Eva plopped down on the pallet and lifted her twisted ankle to rest on her knee. "I have spent much time on my feet today. I'm afraid my foot pains even worse than usual."

Again, guilt washed over Mathieu. A Duke's daughter had been lowered to the level of a handmaiden. All because of him.

"Are you sorry? Do you feel you have made a mistake?" he asked, afraid to hear her reply.

She simply smiled and reached out her arms to him. "I know you knew me as a spoiled, willful child when I came here, Mathieu. But 'twas not true. Not really. I was shielding myself. I knew not what I would face here at Coudenburg. 'Twas easier to play the strong one and protect my heart."

He knelt before her and lay his head in her lap. "I want so much more for you, dear Eva. I promise, someday, life will be easier for us. You will sleep in a finer place—"

"Shh," she cooed. "Truly? In Ghent I slept on a pallet not nearly as big as this one. And I had to share it with my stepsister, who kicked in the night like a rank horse!"

The evening meal was tortuous. All eyes were drawn to them, again and again, with unspoken questions and silent accusations. The only one who seemed happy for them was Admiral La Laing, who greeted Mathieu with a hearty handshake and embrace as they entered the hall.

"Mathieu! I hear congratulations are in order. You have chosen wisely, my man. Your lady is lovely, indeed." He took Eva's hand and kissed it before folding it into Mathieu's. "I wish you both a lifetime of happiness and contentment. Here, you two sit close to me." They took the seats he indicated at the table just beneath the high table.

There was no festive banquet, no celebration—not that either of them expected it. Still, Mathieu wished there could have been some sort of acknowledgement of their union. Instead, they supped on simple fare, roasted pigeon and quail, along with a pottage of summer vegetables.

"Now that your future is somewhat... altered," La Laing smiled and winked at Mathieu, "I won't be asking you to go with me to pick out those colts. The Duke wants to go anyway, and I don't think the two of you would be very friendly traveling companions. At least, not until some of Philip's ruffled feathers smooth."

Mathieu sighed. "I had so wanted to see Barreau's crop. How many will you bring back?"

"I'm not sure how many Philip is interested in, but I'd like to add at least a four or five to our string. Can you handle that many for training come spring?"

"Oh yes. Easily. It's my passion, Admiral. 'Tis what I do."

La Laing drained his goblet and wiped his mouth. "Good. It's settled then. Philip and I will leave in a few days, right after Alys and Rutger's wedding. We'll take just a few of the knights. The road between here and there is peaceful these days."

Eva

The next weeks passed quickly for Eva, though not without trial. Blanche, it seemed, had mixed feelings about taking her on as an apprentice. On one hand, she scorned the girl for having violated tradition and defying the Duke's will. On the other, the old woman was relieved to have another on which to pile all of the tasks that had become difficult for her, at her age.

And distasteful, no matter what one's age.

Eva was no stranger to domestic duties. She had emptied chamber pots back at home. She had helped care for her siblings and her parents' clothing, washing and hanging and beating the creases out. But keeping up with the needs of a small family and caring for a veritable fleet of ladies-in-waiting, were very different kinds of responsibilities altogether.

Eva spent most of her time worrying she would ruin the fine, fancy garments Isabella and her ladies wore. She knew how to handle fabric—new fabric, and fashion it into a garment. But caring for the clothing once soiled? She had not a clue.

The bright spot was the day of Alys and Rutger's wedding, which took place in the same building where Eva herself had been wed not a week earlier. Their nuptials, however, were held on a bright, sunny morning with all the castle folk and many villagers there to witness, and in the main chapel, not hidden away in the sacristy. Eva was surprised she had even been allowed to attend, but the Duchess herself asked her to accompany her and her ladies-in-waiting to the village.

Eva's heart warmed to see how happy the couple were as they entered the hall that night for the wedding feast. Their joy reminded her of how grateful she should be for having a good husband of her own, a man she loved, and who worshipped her. As she and Mathieu shared their meal from a common trencher, their bodies so close they were touching from hip to ankle, Eva couldn't help the heady thrill of sheer joy humming through her.

The Duke took six of his knights with him when he and Admiral La Laing left the next morning for Barreau's farm in France. They would be gone a fortnight, at the very least, they told Mathieu. With both Philip and La Laing gone from the castle, the man in charge would be Captain Knape.

Little did anyone realize how perilous a situation this would leave the unfortunate soul who stumbled into the Captain's path.

Mathieu

Mathieu was grateful the Duke had taken neither Keegan nor Gaspard with him. At least there were two of the guard whom the ostler trusted. The Captain, however, made himself scarce, at least for the week. The ostler witnessed him stumbling back from the village on more than one occasion, late in the night when he did his walk-through of the barn to be sure all was well.

Drink, he was certain, would be the evil man's downfall. But, in truth, when the Captain was in his cups, he was less dangerous than when he was sober. Mathieu hoped Knape continued his bingeing until the Duke and the admiral returned.

A fortnight passed quickly, and the Duke was due home any day. Mathieu was excited, eager to see the fresh, unbroken colts he would add to the Duke's string of horses. He liked working with the young animals. Unspoiled, and although sometimes full of spirit, they presented a new challenge for the ostler which he genuinely looked forward to.

Eva was working harder than she ever had in her life, and Mathieu could see how it wore on her. Every night, she came to their quarters with her feet tender and swollen, particularly the twisted one. Mathieu did his best to comfort her, massaging the tender joint and once, even wrapping it in the same kind of poultice he used to treat the horse's leg injuries.

"So, I'm no better than a palfrey now?" she asked as he wrapped her leg in what looked like muddy linens. "I'll smell like one, too," she said, wrinkling her nose.

Mathieu smiled up at her. "You know how I love the smell of horseflesh, so don't expect that to keep you out of my bed."

Eva promptly stuck her tongue out at him, and he reached up and pinched her bottom.

"Now, I want you to lie down and keep your foot atop those sacks I've piled on the end of the pallet. 'Twill help drain the excess fluid out of the joint. I promise, by morning, you'll feel much better."

He bent to kiss her sweetly before leaving her to rest. "I won't be gone long. I'm going over to see how the knights are faring with the Captain in charge. I haven't seen either Keegan or Gaspard in a day or two."

Eva's eyelids had already fluttered shut. "I will rest here for just a minute." She was asleep before Mathieu left the quarters.

He found the knights' encampment alive with light and noise. They had a bonfire burning, even though the night was warm. A fresh barrel had been rolled up from the cellar, and several men were already filling their mugs with frothy ale. He spotted Keegan first, who stood half a head taller than most of the other men, his coppery hair flashing in the firelight.

"Yo ho, ostler! Come join us. We've having one more, grand get-together before the keepers return," Keegan shouted, raising his mug.

Mathieu tipped his head. "You still have one keeper here, do you not? The most brutal taskmaster of all."

Gaspard strolled up beside Mathieu and handed him a mug. "Knape's been in the village most of this past week," he muttered. "Only comes home every couple of days to sleep off his poison. Seems he's found a wench at the Rusted Arrow he favors. Poor damsel. I pity her."

The image of Knape pawing a tavern maid touched a raw spot in Mathieu's memory. He felt the bile rise in his throat, and he washed it down with ale. "Poor damsel is right. I've seen what Knape is capable of. She'll be lucky if she comes out of this with her life."

Both Gaspard and Keegan stopped short and stared at him. "We know you have something on Knape, but you won't share it. Why?" Keegan asked.

Mathieu ducked his head and stared into his mug. "Because, my friends, I'm afraid if I do, the Captain will finish what he started all those years ago. He'll kill me."

Chapter Thirty-Three

Mathieu stayed with the knights far longer than he'd intended. He'd gone back to check on Eva several times, but he could not find the strength to disturb her. She had fallen asleep right in the middle of the narrow pallet, her bandaged foot still propped on sacks. If he crawled into bed beside her, he'd surely waken her. He decided on his third trip that it wouldn't hurt for him to enjoy one more hour and one more mug of ale with his friends.

What no one expected was that Captain Knape would return again that night.

But that's exactly what he did. As the embers of the bonfire faded and most of the knights had straggled off to their cots, a lone figure staggered through the bailey and into the encampment. Mathieu's heart leapt when Keegan peered over his shoulder and said, "The taskmaster returns."

The three men struggled to their feet, tossing back what was left in their mugs. Mathieu's hope was that Knape would fill a last mug with ale before making his way back to his room in the castle. He was the only knight granted a real bed in the main hall.

Knape, however, had apparently come home looking for a fight. Mathieu bid his friends good eve and headed toward the stable, but when he passed Knape, he didn't keep enough distance between them. The Captain stumbled into him, slamming him hard on the shoulder. Mathieu almost lost his footing and turned on Knape. Although his quick temper nearly overtook him, he swallowed hard and barked, "Sorry, Captain. I beg pardon."

Knape already had his hand on the hilt of his sword. "You're damned right, you're sorry. You are the sorriest excuse for a horseman this court has ever seen." Knape pushed Mathieu again, a hand flat on his chest, but the gesture caused him to lose his balance more than the ostler. This incensed him.

"You have no place in my knights' camp. You are no knight. Never could be. Ye tried and ye failed. You aren't worthy of licking the boots of any of my men."

Mathieu held his tongue, swallowing the rage building within him. He hated this man, and for more reasons than one. It wouldn't take much, especially after all the ale he'd downed this eve, for him to lose control.

Still, he simply sidestepped the Captain and continued on toward the stable.

"Off to plow the bastard whore you were fool enough to marry, are ye? I shall like to witness that, ostler. Do you ride her like a horse?" Knape's maniacal laughter rang through the bailey.

Slowly, in the dim light, Mathieu could see a number of the knights emerging from their tents.

"She's a lame horse, though. With that twisted foot, a good horseman would have put the bitch down the day she was born." Knape coughed and spat into the dirt. "But no, not you, Mathieu of Liège. You deigned to take the wench as your wife. I cannot wait to see what manner of crooked monsters the two of you spawn."

Clenching his fists, the ostler turned and continued out of the camp. With his back to Knape, Mathieu could feel the hair rising on his neck. How much was he expected to accept from this evil, arrogant man?

But Mathieu was no fool. He was unarmed, and Knape had not only his broadsword, but who knew how many daggers hidden on his person. To fight him would mean certain death. It took every ounce of his willpower to keep walking, albeit slowly, toward the stables.

But Knape was not to be avoided. Not this night. Who knew what had happened in the village to stir his anger so, but the Captain was angry—crazy fool angry, and deep in his cups to boot? When Mathieu felt the man's gauntlet clamp on his shoulder, sparkles of ire burst behind his own eyes.

He wanted to punch something, and hard. Knape's face would be perfect.

Gaspard's words from the day he taught him weaponless combat echoed in his head then, causing him pause.

There's little use to your fists in situations like this. You end up risking damage to your hands, which then renders you powerless.

Mathieu closed his eyes and sucked in a breath. His temper was about at its limit. He turned to face the Captain, fists balled at his sides.

"I do not want to fight you, Captain. Please do not provoke me any further. I am unarmed. If you mean to run me through, then do it now, with all your men as witness. You shan't get away with murder. Not this time."

By now the entire encampment was awake, the knights gathered in a gaping crowd up against the outer wall. It was true, anything to happen this night would bear plenty of witness. Mathieu searched the crowd but could not locate Keegan or Gaspard in the darkness. But the ostler's words had touched a nerve in the Captain, who lunged for him, swinging a fist that Mathieu easily ducked to avoid.

"How dare you? I put that scar on your face for a reason. You are a coward, and the scar on your cheek proves the fact. One little scratch and you ran away from knighthood with your tail between your legs."

Mathieu folded his arms across his chest and squinted at the Captain. "Is that why you cut me? I thought it was so you could keep the poor maid on the table all to yourself." He barked out a wry laugh. "Even with that, you needed help, though, didn't you? Needed two of your henchmen to hold her down so you could—"

Knape swung again, and with a simple step to the side, Mathieu sent him reeling. He landed in the dirt but came up just as fast, a dagger glinting in the torchlight from the keep.

"I will kill you, Mathieu of Liège. Say one more word and I swear, I will kill you."

Mathieu took a step toward him, causing Knape to stumble backward. "Kill me? In cold blood, in front of all your men? I think not. Although, it didn't stop you that night, did it? Didn't stop you from raping that poor girl, almost to her death. But no. Still 'twas not enough. You had to finish the deed, carrying her limp body to the stable, then slitting her throat to bleed out in the hay."

Knape's roar curdled Mathieu's blood as he raised his dagger to strike. But before he did, a huge man tackled him from behind, both of them landing hard at Mathieu's feet. Keegan had just saved Mathieu's life. At least, temporarily.

As Knape struggled against the Scot's powerful grip, he spat out an oath. Then, he ripped off one of his gauntlets and threw it on the ground at Mathieu's feet and issued his challenge.

"Tomorrow, at dawn. We will settle this, once and for all between us, ostler," he growled.

"Mathieu owns no armor, no chainmail, no sword," Keegan shouted. "Ye cannot fight an unarmed man."

"Oh, aye he can. But he shall come to the challenge the same as me," Mathieu shouted. "I will fight you, Captain Knape—with no armor, no weapons. Hand to hand, man to man. Let us see who comes out the victor when you can no longer hide behind your weaponry."

Eva

Kweeo! Kwiff, kwiff, kwiff!

Kleine Uil's shrieking woke Eva with a start. She bolted upright, then nearly fell off the pallet since her one foot was still propped up on sacks.

"Mathieu? Mathieu!"

He was not in their quarters. With Kleine Uil making such a stir, he must be in the stable. The creature didn't do this often, but when he did, he'd usually put himself in a position of real danger.

As Eva hobbled through the darkened stable, she could hear voices, shouting above the ear-splitting screeching of the tiny owl. Torches blazed over by the knights' camp. Two men were facing off, bellowing at one another.

She recognized Mathieu's voice, and her heart shattered. What trouble now? Then she recognized the slurred words of Captain Knape.

Eva knew Mathieu hated the man, but he'd never told her why. Still, she had been afraid it would come to this, any day. As gentle a heart as her husband possessed, she knew Mathieu also had a volatile temper.

Within moments, it was over, and she could see him returning to her. She whooshed out a breath. Good. No fight. No bloodshed. He was safe. She hobbled to him and threw her arms around his neck.

Her husband was shaking all over, and she knew 'twas not with cold nor fear. For the longest time, the ostler could not even speak. He simply swept her off her feet and carried her back into their quarters.

After kicking the door to their quarters shut, he set her down and held her to him with such force, it took her breath away. She'd not seen this side of him, and she wasn't sure if his savagery frightened her, or excited her.

Before she could say a word, ask him anything, his mouth came down hard on hers. This was more than passion, she felt. This was desperation. After a moment, she met his harsh kisses, fisting her hand in his hair. In the next moment, his body went limp.

She felt him shuddering and realized with anguish that he was crying. With his face buried in her neck, the ostler sobbed like a child for long moments. Finally, he lifted his head and looked into her eyes.

"Did I hurt you?"

"Nay. Did you want to?" she asked, her lips quirking.

"Nay. I love you too much to ever hurt you. But I've done a bad deed tonight, dear wife."

Eva studied his face in the dim light. "What, husband?"

"I accepted a challenge."

Eva blinked, waiting. She was afraid to breathe.

"At dawn, I fight Captain Knape."

A cold chill washed through her, the dread sapping every ounce of her strength. Closing her eyes, Eva began to pray.

Chapter Thirty-Four

M*athieu*
A multitude of emotions surged through Mathieu's mind as he lay there in the darkness, holding Eva close. Sleep eluded him, as he'd known it would. This day was inevitable, with many years brewing and made certain by him living his life in such close proximity to the man whom he hated with every fiber of his being.

The personal insults, he bore for years. He'd become all but immune to Knape's verbal assaults. But the harsh words aimed at his beloved, in front of all the Duke's knights, was too much. The shield he'd wrapped around his heart the day he witnessed the horror served its purpose well. Now, however, he had another to protect, and as he'd vowed on their wedding day, he would protect Eva with all of his being until the day he died.

He hoped that day had not arrived so quickly.

Eva stirred in his arms and when she voiced her question, his entire body tensed.

"Will you tell me now why it is you hate the Captain with such venom?" Her fingers brushed his scarred cheek. "He gave you this, did he not?"

Mathieu took a deep breath. The tale was one he tried to forget. Yet he knew as his wife, she deserved to know. After dawn came, he may never have another chance to tell her.

"I was seventeen, working with my maman and my stepfather in his tavern, The Raven. The Duke had just arrived to spend the winter months at his castle on the Rhone. Of course, his Royal Guard accompanied him."

Mathieu pushed himself up to sit, his back resting against the hard, planked wall. Eva laid her head on his lap and waited. He was pleased with her patience. These memories were tortuous. Retelling the tale, as he'd never done before—not like this—would be like living it all over again.

"My father was a knight, fighting in the Flemish army at Othée when he died. 'Twas before I was born, but I dreamed of someday following his lead.

My maman was not of royal blood, but she begged audience with Admiral La Laing, being my papa had served. She secured me a position to foster with the Duke's army. Even though I was at such at advanced age."

Most young men started their journey to knighthood when they were just babes, seven or eight years old. Mathieu had not had that advantage. He spent his days in the stables, working with the horses, and his nights scrubbing mugs and tapping barrels in the alehouse.

"There was a young maiden of about my age, and just the sight of her swept me away the day she came to work at the tavern. Her name was Meadows. I was a foolish lad and set my sights on the girl. She never knew how I felt. In truth, I don't think she ever acknowledged my existence."

Mathieu slipped out from beneath Eva and went to the sideboard, where a little sloe wine remained in the pitcher. He lifted it and drank, not bothering with a mug. Then he crossed his arms and stared out through the tiny window at the moon, nearly full and lighting the courtyard with an eerie glow.

"I had just finished putting the knights' horses up for the night. A half-dozen of the Duke's men had straggled in, though it was late, and asked for a meal and beds. Maman knew better than to deny the Duke's Royal Guard. The men ate, and drank, and all but three retired to their rooms."

Mathieu closed his eyes against the memory, but it played out in his mind anyway. 'Twas not a sight he'd ever been able to erase from his mind. 'Twas the kindling that kept his hatred for the Duke's Captain ever-glowing, ever ready to burst into flames.

With his back to Eva, he continued.

"Knape flirted all evening with Meadows. He'd had his eye on her since the moment they arrived. The other men, they picked their quarry from the wenches who plied their trade under my stepfather's roof. But Meadows wasn't one of them. The daughter of a local sheep farmer, she had her sights set higher. She hoped for a better life.

"The more Knape drank, the bolder he became. The last time he smacked Meadows on her bottom and pulled her to him, she'd had enough. She turned and let fly, slapping him flat palmed across his face. That was her fatal mistake."

He turned to face Eva, unashamed of his tears. "One does not humiliate Captain Knape and live to tell of it."

Eva sat on the edge of their pallet, watching him with wide eyes that flashed in the moonlight. With his last proclamation, she covered her face with her hands.

"Knape grabbed Meadows around the waist, lifting her off her feet as he swept the table clear. When he threw her down, I heard her head hit the wood so hard, I felt certain she'd been knocked unconscious. 'Twould have been better if she had.

"He barked orders to his companions, also *gallant knights*." He spat the words as though they were poison. "To their credit, they seemed reluctant, but they had no choice. He was their Captain. To deny his orders would mean certain severe punishment, if not death.

"They held Meadows down, one man on each shoulder, as she twisted and screamed for mercy. Knape knows not the meaning of the word. He tore her dress from her body and cast it on the ground. Then he abused her body with such brutality, he brought to mind a wild boar. And poor Meadows fought back. But when she caught him in the groin with her knee, he slapped her so hard, I thought for certain he'd broken her neck.

"I tried to help her," he choked through a sob. "He turned on me, dagger in hand, so fast I did not see it coming." He reached up and covered his cheek with his palm. " 'Tis the Captain who marked me that night."

Mathieu was shaking now. He clenched his fists before him, and his words sputtered out from between clenched teeth. "Meadows lay still, helpless, until he was finished. But even then, having stripped her of all dignity, he wasn't finished acting out his evil.

"After the beast had fastened his braies, he tossed her half-naked body over his shoulder and headed for the stables."

Eva was on her feet, wrapping her arms around him, but he pushed her away. Sympathy, comfort was not what he wanted. 'Twould not even the score for an innocent life taken so savagely.

He caught her wrists in his hands and stared straight into her eyes. "Don't you see? The Captain is a murderer. Killing on the battlefield is one thing. Taking another's life... a girl, an innocent who'd done him no harm, for his own evil pleasure—that goes against the laws of God and man. Is that how the code of chivalry is carried out? Is that how a knight abuses his powers?"

Eva took a step back and wrapped her arms around herself. She, too, was trembling all over. Now, at least she understood. She knew the reason for his hatred and hidden rage.

" 'Twas what kept you from your sword and spurs." It was a statement, not a question.

Mathieu threw his hands up and began pacing in the tiny space. "What I saw that night proved to me that a man who gains the title—a knight—can wield his power in whatever ways he chooses without punishment."

"But not all knights are evil, Mathieu," Eva murmured. "Are they?"

He stopped and dropped his head. "Nay. Not all knights are evil. But the one who leads the Duke's Royal Guard is. And this day, his reign of terror will end. By God's breath, I swear 'twill be true."

Eva ran to him and again wrapped herself around him. "But how can you win against a man armed with dagger and sword? Surely, you will be killed," she sobbed.

He faced her and gripped her arms. "Nay. We will fight without weapons, my love. The conditions of the challenge were spoken before Keegan and many more witnesses." Mathieu pulled her to his chest and pressed his lips to her hair. "We will see just how mighty the powerful Captain Knape is when stripped of the armor he's hidden beneath for all these years." Then, in a whisper, he began to recite the Prayers of a Knight:

"Grant me the gift of Divine Grace and conquer my five senses, that I may carry out the seven works of mercy..."

Chapter Thirty-Five

Mathieu

What does one wear to face another man in battle? Traditional garb—chainmail, armor, a helm with shield—none of these would be allowed this day, even if Mathieu had access to them. The belt holding the sheath for his dagger 'twould be banned. So how to go into a match such as this properly garbed for maximum protection?

Although he usually did not wear his leather braies in warm weather, they would, he reasoned, provide him with the most protection against scratching nails or biting teeth. He also had a sueded tunic with long sleeves—another smart choice, he wagered. Sweat he could bear, but at least his skin would be protected. He dug these things out from under the pallet as Eva slept.

He stood over her for a long moment, watching her, lost in her dreams. Better she remains unaware as long as possible this morn. Her anguish would do nothing but heighten his anxiety.

As he stood peering out of the window, fumbling with a strip of leather with which to secure his hair, Eva woke.

"Aye, husband. That glorious mane of yours could provide a handhold for your enemy this day."

She rose and helped him, combing her fingers along his scalp as she gathered the long hair to his nape. It sent tingles down his spine. If only he could turn and face her this moment, claim her lush mouth with his, and allow his hands to roam wildly over her soft curves. Just one more time.

But there was not time. The horizon had already gone pink over the mountains in the distance. Energy he sorely needed to face the challenge ahead of him should not be wasted on satisfying his carnal desires.

Still, he yearned for it. Yearned for her. She seemed to sense this and, after binding his hair securely, placed a kiss at the base of his neck. Then, she proceeded to rent his heart in two.

"Please, Mathieu. Do not do this. Do not fight a battle you cannot win."

With his back still to her, he closed his eyes. The emotions flooding him warred against one another. One part of him knew she was afraid, afraid of becoming a widow before she'd long been a wife.

Another part of him coiled in resentment. Was she so sure he could not win this battle against Knape? He'd explained they would be fighting on equal ground—no weaponry.

He turned and glared at her. "So, even you, my wife, has no confidence that a common ostler can win against a knight." He spat the words, feeling his pride ooze with the fresh wound. "You chose me. I thought you understood my strength did not require the use of daggers or swords. I thought you had more faith in my abilities."

Eva twisted her fingers in his tunic. "I do have faith in you. I know your strengths are far greater than a man who wields weapons—"

"Then why do you try to dissuade me from this fight? Whether you believe in my chances for victory or not, Eva, I will win this day. I may not be a knight, but I am a warrior. My father died on the battlefield. I may not have earned the trappings of a knight, but I possess the heart of one. 'Tis in my blood."

He pushed her from him then, and she landed hard on the pallet. Covering her face with her hands, she sobbed, "I love you, Mathieu. I do believe in you. But I cannot bear to lose you."

Crouching to meet her eyes, he took both of her hands in his. "As God is my witness, I shall conquer the evil Captain Knape. I will either conquer him or die trying."

The bailey was alive with people, an oddity for this early an hour. All the knights had gathered along the outer wall, a few bearing torches. Most wore chainmail. Others had strapped their swords at their sides.

Whose side would they be on, Mathieu wondered? Which man would the knights be cheering on? A commoner, a man with no position or title who tended to horses and hounds and hawks all his days? Or their Captain?

He was afraid to venture a guess.

The castle folk had heard of the challenge as well, it seemed. Everyone, from the lowliest servants to the Duchess' handmaidens, were spilling out onto the steps to the Great Hall. Combing the crowd for Isabella herself,

Mathieu did not see her at first. 'Twas only when he lifted his gaze to the window of her solar on the second floor that he saw the colorful, multi-paned window had been flung wide. Isabella stood watching, her expression unreadable. A chill slithered down Mathieu's spine.

Did the Duchess disapprove of this challenge taking place? Especially in the absence of the Duke?

His answer came in the next breath, when he saw her close her eyes and nod, once. Unspoken permission to proceed. Mathieu realized at that moment he would not have engaged the Captain if Isabella had voiced objection. His respect for this lady knew no bounds.

Keegan stood in the center of the bailey, feet planted wide, arms crossed across his chest. He also wore chainmail, along with his sheathed sword. Mathieu wagered he had a dagger hidden in each of his tall, heavy boots as well, not that they would be of much help to him.

No, this day he would be facing his lifelong enemy nearly as helpless as a newborn babe. Another chill gripped his chest. Eva's words had shaken him. Was he man enough to do this? Could he possibly win?

Everyone paused and turned as the thunder of hoofbeats reached them through the gates, which swung open to a lone youth aboard a sweat-flecked palfrey. The boy's eyes were wild. He couldn't have been much older than Mathieu had been that day long ago. The fateful day that brought him here to this moment in time.

"What brings ye here, boy?" Keegan shouted.

The boy jumped down and started toward Keegan before Mathieu noticed his face was covered in dirt and streaked with tears. He fell at Keegan's feet, croaking out, "The Duke. I beg audience with the Duke."

Keegan raised one bushy eyebrow as he hoisted the boy to his feet. "The Duke is not here. What manner of trouble requires the Duke's attention?"

"My sister," the boy choked out. "Meri Anne. My sister. She is dead, my lord."

The big knight glanced around him to the crowd with a quizzical expression. "Who is this Meri Anne? Is she one of our court?"

One of the knights stepped forward, his head bowed. "She is not, my lord. Meri Anne works at The Raven. She is a tavern wench—"

Mathieu's stomach twisted. Was this the woman Knape had been spending his time with these past weeks in the Duke's absence?

At that moment the Captain appeared on the steps of the keep, his clothes rumpled, and his face swollen and creased. He pushed roughly through the crowd, causing one of the kitchen maids to fall to the ground.

The boy stiffened and stood taller. Narrowing his eyes, he raised his hand to point a wavering finger at Knape. "There he is. He is the man who paid her coin to go with him last eve. When we found her in the bedchamber this morn..." The boy's voice broke.

So the bastard had done it again. How many times was this, Mathieu wondered? How many lives had been ended to satisfy a sick and twisted bloodlust no man should possess?

Knape wasted no time. He bolted across the bailey with long strides and had nearly reached the boy when Keegan stepped into his path—so suddenly Knape bounced off the big man's chest. Stumbling backward, the Captain grabbed for his sword before Keegan locked his wrist in a vice-like grip.

"Nay. There will be none of that this morn, Captain Knape. Ye will answer for this wench's life later, when the Duke returns. First, ye have another battle to wage."

The boy's tale sent Mathieu's rage to a blinding fury. Clenching and unclenching his fists, he took a step toward Knape, ready to tear the man's head from his shoulders. 'Twas only Keegan's giant hand on his chest stopping him.

"First, the field shall be levelled. Knape, ye shall throw down your weapons and engage in the challenge ye, yourself claimed, under the terms agreed upon."

While two of the ladies bustled the boy off toward the castle, a page came running from the stables to tend to his horse. An eerie silence fell over the crowd for long seconds. Then, one by one, Captain Knape began to drop his weapons to the ground.

When all visible weaponry lie in a heap at Keegan's feet, the big knight nodded toward Gaspard and another knight standing nearby. "Search him. Make sure he has no daggers hidden." He snarled at Knape, "The chainmail goes as well."

Keegan turned to Mathieu. "The men will search ye also, ostler. This needs to be proven a fair fight to all who bear witness."

Mathieu nodded and stood with his arms and legs spread, allowing the knights to inspect his person. He had nothing to hide. As they did, his gaze bore down on his opponent. For just the briefest moment, Mathieu thought he saw an emotion pass across the Captain's face he'd never seen there before. Could it be fear?

Eva crossed his line of vision, scurrying unevenly to the steps of the castle, where she was enfolded within the arms of her sisters. She was trying to be brave, Mathieu could tell. Yet although she stood tall and her jaw remained set, he could see the anguish in her eyes.

Were her fears well founded? Would he make her a widow before she'd been a bride long enough for joy's blush to fade?

As Gaspard's hands searched him, the Frenchman leaned close to his ear. "Don't forget the moves I taught you. No fists. It's essential you say balanced. On your feet. Surely, you will triumph."

Silence fell over the bailey as Keegan stepped between the men and called for the match to begin.

"Fellow knights, men and ladies of the court, and Your Grace, Lady Duchess," he glanced up at the solar window. "Last eve, the Captain of the Royal Guard threw down his gauntlet to challenge Mathieu of Liège, our ostler and falconer. The battle will take place on even ground. No weapons, no armor."

Everyone started and turned when the Duchess' voice rang out from her second-floor view.

"Is this a battle to the death?" she asked.

Keegan set his lips in a grim line. "Aye, Your Grace. Either to the death, or until one warrior grants mercy."

After her nod of approval, Keegan took a step back and held out his arms. "Let the challenge begin."

Chapter Thirty-Six

Mathieu had never seen Knape move so fast. The Captain came at him the instant Keegan's words rang out, screaming a war cry that echoed across the bailey. Before the ostler could take a breath, Knape had grabbed one of his wrists in one hand and thrown his other arm around Mathieu's neck. He was trying to use his weight and momentum to throw Mathieu to the ground. There, he knew from what the French knight had taught him, he would be all but helpless.

In that fleeting moment, the ostler was grateful for the schooling Gaspard had given him.

Mathieu quickly countered with a shoulder throw, taking two quick steps directly at Knape, pivoting so his back crashed into the man. With their arms locked in a stranglehold, Mathieu twisted and lifted Knape's body, up and over his shoulder. When the Captain hit the ground, flat on his back, it was clear he was not only shocked, but the breath had been knocked out of him.

This served two purposes, as far as Mathieu could tell. For one, it gave him a brief moment to regroup, breathe, and think about his next move. For Knape, it served only to fuel his ire to a frenzy.

Back on his feet, he came at Mathieu again, lunging head down like a bull. He hit the ostler hard, but Mathieu's wide stance was stable, with one foot in front of the other. Although the move knocked him off balance, his position kept him from going down.

Mathieu took this opportunity to reach down and hook an arm under Knape's leg, lifting him up and throwing him to the ground once more. This time, though, Knape was ready, rolling away in a flash. He was back on his feet within seconds. It was then the Captain decided to change his strategy.

Knape reeled back a fist and hit Mathieu in the face with a brain-jarring blow that almost took him down. Pain exploded behind his eyes, and the coppery tang of blood filled his mouth. He was resorting to fists, the tactic

Gaspard had warned the ostler to avoid. Mathieu's only choice now was to stay quick enough on his feet to stay out of the Captain's reach.

This proved to be a difficult task when the world was spinning around him. Mathieu had been knocked in the face more than once by a rank young horse, a beast whose head was surely harder than Knape's fist. But he'd taken the ostler by surprise and hit his nose just right. Mathieu felt sure it was broken.

Swinging wildly, Mathieu tried to counter Knape's punches with jabs of his own. Dizziness and nausea was quickly consuming him, however, and every time his fist whooshed through empty air, the Captain lunged in with another blow to his head. One to his ear made it sound like the church bells were ringing. Another to his jaw caused him to bite his tongue.

A feeling of dread consumed him as he realized Knape was fighting in a way Gaspard had not trained him.

There's little use to your fists in situations like this.

Well, they were working quite well for the Captain, it seemed. Mathieu did not know how to defend himself from an attack of this nature. Why hadn't Gaspard given him some strategy for a situation like this?

Then, from somewhere in the back of Mathieu's brain, Gaspard's words came back to him.

An upward palm to the chin and nose... a strike like that could actually kill a man.

Mathieu was on his knees now, the world growing darker and fuzzier around him with every passing second. But those words resonated in his head, like a mantra. Like a prayer.

Like a miracle.

He waited until Knape came at him again. From his lower vantage point on the ground, the angle was perfect. As the Captain ducked in to punch him again, the ostler drew back his elbow and threw his hand up, open and flat. Straight at Knape's face.

The pain in his palm told him he'd hit his mark—teeth had slashed his skin. He looked up to see the Captain go down, blood spurting from his nose and mouth. Long seconds passed. Knape lie there, very still.

Had he killed the man? Gaspard said it was possible.

Staggering to his feet, Mathieu straddled the Captain's prone body and placed two fingers on the side of his neck. Still a pulse. Still alive. Still—"

"Mathieu! Watch out!"

Keegan's shout cut through the fog in Mathieu's brain but for a moment, his words made no sense. Knape appeared to be alive still, but unconscious. One arm was twisted up over his head at an unnatural angle, and the other lay down along his side.

Until it didn't any longer. Eva's scream from somewhere far off pierced his heart. What was happening? What was the danger? Instinctively, Mathieu slipped off the Captain, who rolled with him, ending up on top. Knape's arm was raised above him, and sunlight glinted off the blade in his hand. As the Captain brought the dagger down toward his neck, Mathieu's quick reflexes revived just in time.

He caught Knape's wrist and straightened his own arm, using leverage to twist the Captain's arm. Savagely, he threw all his weight into the move, cranking Knape's arm at an angle not naturally possible. He heard the bone break. He heard the man's anguished scream. He felt him go limp on top of him as the blade clattered to the ground.

Pushing Knape off him, Mathieu dove and grabbed the hilt of the dagger, turning to end this battle. The man was evil, through to his black soul. The ostler had never killed a man in his life—didn't know that he could. 'Twas one of the reasons he never wanted to earn his spurs and sword. 'Twas not man's right to take another's life. But this hatred had been building too long and too hard for him to stop himself now.

For years, whenever the rage overtook him, he pictured in his mind the sneering face of the Captain, there on the surface of the planks lining the stalls in the barn. Gaspard was right about one thing: fists weren't very resilient. The skin tore, and the knuckles bruised easily.

Now, his moment had arrived. In his mind's eye, he imagined how it would feel to plunge the dagger into Knape's neck. But nay. Cutting his throat would be too quick, too merciful a death for this devil. Gutting him, ripping him open from his ribs to his groin would be a more fitting death. The man would watch his own innards spill out into the dirt as he died, slowly, in agony.

With the dagger raised high over his head, he and Knape's eyes locked. Now, 'twas fear he saw. He was quite sure of it.

It was enough.

Mathieu hurled the knife at the huge post framing the portico, where it stuck and vibrated in the eerie silence. As he started to his feet, he was surprised to feel Knape's fingers around his wrist, even with one arm twisted and broken beneath him. The Captain's face was covered with blood, and so swollen already, he was almost unrecognizable. Still, he struggled to speak.

"End this, ostler. I plead mercy." he garbled. "Ye have won."

Mathieu shook his head, his eyes raking over the ruined man beneath him. "You don't deserve to die, you heathen. You deserve to live—live out your days in an interminable hell of your own making."

Before he stumbled away, Mathieu paused, swaying. He turned and spat on his challenger, blinking in shock when he saw 'twas not spit, but blood he spewed. He saw Eva running toward him, in slow motion, as in a dream. But he found he couldn't take another step. The ground beneath him was moving. His hearing faded away until silence consumed him. His knees screamed pain when they hit the ground, just before his world went dark.

Somewhere, through the deafening silence, he could swear he heard trumpets.

Epilogue

E va knew the ordeal would be painful, but she'd never imagined just how excruciating 'twould in reality be. She swore, with every wave that took hold of her body, she would split in two. Her body was soaked in sweat, rivulets running into her eyes to mingle with the tears. The midwife told her to scream, as loud as she could. To let the pain out. 'Twould make it easier.

Only one thing could make this easier. To have Mathieu by her side.

He wasn't there, and she was forced to endure this on her own. Only the midwife and two of the Duchess' handmaidens, who took turns holding her hand and murmuring soothing words. But 'twas only a distraction from the anguish that filled her body, her mind, her soul. The physical pain wasn't nearly the worst of the it.

'Twas the wondering. Would the child she bore this night be like her, twisted and deformed? Mayhap worse? In some ways, 'twas better Mathieu was not here to witness the horror when the babe finally slid free from her body and revealed itself. She could not bear to see revulsion in his eyes.

She'd been told men weren't allowed in the birthing chamber anyway.

He paced up and down the long hall before the Duchess' solar, where they'd taken Eva when her pains had grown intense. Keegan and Gaspard paced with him, like penitent monks, heads down, hands clasped behind their backs. Silent, except for an occasional groan when a particularly anguished scream echoed from the chamber.

Had it been days? Or only hours? Or a lifetime?

Then, silence. For a very long time, it seemed. Darkness had given way to dawn, pale fingers of light creeping through the narrow window at the end of the hall when the three men froze to the sound of a creaking door. They spun around to see Lady Isabella standing there, her apron splattered with blood.

His heart rent in two as he searched her face for an answer to a question he was afraid to ask.

His knees nearly buckled when her lips quirked into a small smile.

"Come, Mathieu. Meet your new daughter."

He nearly ran to the door before stopping short. "And Eva? Is she well?"

"Come," the Duchess nodded and waved him into the chamber.

Behind him, he heard the two knights who had become like his brothers hoot and smack each other on the back.

She was propped on many fine pillows, her damp, golden hair splayed across the white linen. Dark shadows slashed half-moons under her eyes. The bundle Eva held in her arms was very still.

Mathieu knelt beside the bed and reached up to brush a tear off his beloved's cheek. "She lives?" he asked, his voice thick.

"Aye, she lives."

"Are you well?"

Her mossy green eyes flashed up at him and one eyebrow arched. "As well as one can who's had a veritable army wage war between one's legs."

Someone behind him giggled, one of the handmaidens. Was it funny? Mathieu was strung too tight to catch his wife's humor, but he forced himself to smile.

"May I hold her?" he asked.

Eva shimmied herself up taller against the pillows and pinned his gaze, her lips pressed flat. "What you want to do first is to *see* her, not hold her. Is that right?"

Flashing a glance at the Duchess, Mathieu noted the smile she was struggling to suppress. Hesitantly, he turned back to his wife and nodded. Was it wrong of him to want to see his child?

"*All* of her. Is that right?" Eva pressed.

Mathieu stared at her, uncertain what to say. It had crossed his mind a time or two when he discovered Eva was with child—he couldn't deny it. What if the child was flawed? He knew he'd love the babe anyway, just as he did its mother.

His love for Eva was all-consuming, blinding him to all of her flaws—and she, like he, had more than a few. He even loved her beautiful, unique twisted ankle, one that gave her curvy hips a sensuous sway when she walked.

He shook his head to try and clear it. How long had he been awake? Eva had gone into labor not one, but two nights ago. Two long nights and one long, day he'd paced and prayed and waited.

Now he could barely hold his eyes open.

Without a word, Mathieu held out his arms and waited. Eva tipped her head to one side, and her eyes softened. With one hand she stroked his cheek. "You're beyond sparring with me, aren't you, my gallant warrior?" she whispered.

Dumbly, he nodded.

Instead of handing him the swaddled babe, however, she sat forward and laid the bundle on her lap. Lifting first one side of the wrapping, then the other, she revealed their child. Their daughter.

One who, in reaction to the sudden chill, promptly began to bellow at the top of her lungs.

Mathieu didn't flinch. His eyes widened as the miracle before him proceeded to scrunch up her face like an apple left too long in the sun. A red apple. The louder she wailed, the redder she became.

He ran his fingers over her petal-soft skin, as pale and perfect as her maman. With trembling hands, he counted them off: five tiny fingers on the left hand, five on the right. Five round, plump toes on one foot, and five on the other—

And two ankles as perfect and straight as arrows. He met Eva's eyes, his own spilling over.

"She is wondrous, my love."

"Well, she is *marked*, you might say." Raising one eyebrow, Eva gently turned the babe over to reveal her round buttocks, white as peeled eggs.

Save for the heart-shaped birthmark on the right cheek.

"Guess your love is so strong, it spills over onto your children," Isabella said, laying one hand on Mathieu's shoulder. "What shall you name her?"

Not waiting for her husband to answer—even though the right to choose a name was his, and his alone—Eva spoke up.

"Why, Meadows, of course. Don't you agree, Mathieu? 'Tis a lovely name. Meadows are where the wildflowers grow."

Mathieu covered his face with both hands and swallowed hard. So much had gone right that could have gone wrong in his life. He could have died the night he tried to save Meadows, yet he did not. He could have died the day he took Knape to the ground in the bailey, yet he did not.

The trumpets he'd heard as he hit the dirt that day were not those of the angels. They were from Philip's party, coming home with La Laing and all the fine colts from Barreau's farm.

He could have been cast out by the Duke for marrying Eva, then for nearly killing his Captain of the Royal Guard. Instead, Mathieu had been promoted to second in command of Philip's cavalry and was named Admiral La Laing's right hand. Soon, although not a knight, Mathieu would be inducted into Philip's Order of the Golden Fleece.

"Her name, husband? Does our daughter's name not please you?" Eva's gentle words jolted him out of his head.

"Meadows." He tasted the name on his tongue, and it felt right. "Aye, my beloved wife. 'Tis a lovely name indeed."

Afterthoughts

So. The tale is finished. But is it, really? Of course not. Eva and Mathieu have just cemented their love for one another, and they are only beginning their lives with their precious new daughter, Meadows. I do hope you have enjoyed sharing their journey thus far.

What of Captain Knape? He did not die by Mathieu's hand. Was he made to pay for his crimes? Who will take over as Captain of the Royal Guard?

What of Gaspard, the handsome French knight? Will he go on to wage war or will he find love?

And what of the other daughters? Alys and Rutger... will their life be filled with children and happiness? And what of poor Beverielle?

What *of* poor Beverielle? The Scottish lass whose future, it appears, will not lead her back to her homeland, to Scotland? It sounds like she will be Eva's replacement in taking Stefano for a husband. It is sad that she will not be permitted to pursue her interest in the big Scottish knight, Ròidh Keegan.

Or will she?

Their stories continue, starting in Book Two of *The Daughters of the Duchess* series.

Many readers love to read time travel novels, such as Outlander or The Time Traveler's Wife. I love them too! But in these stories, we watch as *the characters* travel in time. We are merely observers. My goal in writing historical romance novels is to *literally take **you** back in time*.

Want to be on call for the next trip back to 15th C. Flanders? Sign up for my newsletter and become one of Gemma's Time Travelers, reserving your place in the next scheduled journey back in time.

I will be posting sneak peeks and updates on my website, www.gemmastclaire.com, as well as on Facebook and Twitter/X.

Thank you, valued Time Traveler! Please know this: an author's most treasured inspirations come from their readers. I'd love to hear from you!

Gemma

gemwriter88@gmail.com

About the Author

Gemma St. Claire is in love with medieval history. She's always been mysteriously drawn to Flanders, what is present-day France, Belgium, and the Netherlands, even though she has no family roots in the region. If she ever gets to go back in time, 15th C. Flanders is where she'd want to be.

In this life, Gemma resides in Florida with her very own HEA husband (she's an expert a happily ever after). Her other loves are reading, gardening, and spoiling her grandchildren. Gemma earned her MFA in creative writing from Lesley University in Cambridge, MA, and she now teaches writing at Florida's state college. She also writes award-winning supernatural suspense and women's fiction as "Claire Gem."

Gemma cherishes her readers and loves to hear from them! Sign up for her newsletter at www.gemmastclaire.com.

www.ingramcontent.com/pod-product-compliance
Lightning Source LLC
Chambersburg PA
CBHW030126180626
46812CB00002B/572